NEVER

by

JENNA KIRBY

*Given with love
Jenna x*

Copyright © Jenna Kirby

The right of Jenna Kirby to be identified as author of this work has been asserted by her in accordance with section 77 and 78 of the Copyright, Designs and Patents Act 1988.

All rights reserved. No part of this publication may be reproduced, stored in a retrieval system, or transmitted in any form or by any means, electronic, mechanical, photocopying, recording, or otherwise, without the prior permission of the publishers.

Any person who commits any unauthorized act in relation to this publication may be liable to criminal prosecution and civil claims for damages.

Registration No: 284744592

Books by Jenna Kirby

Love's a Bitch

A Dangerous Mistake

My Name is Angel Love

Dark Dangerous Love

Love Hate Revenge

A Dangerous Love Triangle

Passion & Betrayal

Never Look Back

PROLOGUE

LOS ANGELES

The world believes they know the woman called Madeline Maxwell, but do they really?

I have been abused mentally and physically, sodamized, and made to do unspeakable things to vile, disgusting, powerful men, in the race to get to the top of the manure heap – The Movie Industry.

BUT – I am also an icon of the silver screen, supposedly every hot blooded male's wet dream, and supposedly the most beautiful and desirable woman in the Western Hemisphere, and beyond.

Jeeze, what a joke!

I was born 38 years ago to a manic depressive mother who is now permanently in a mental facility. My father who knows or cares? He has never come into the equation of my amazing, exciting life.

My beloved sister is 5 years younger than me, she is my best friend and loyal confidante, and lives in an apartment connected to my rambling villa.

BUT – my gut is telling me that tonight will be my last night on this Godforsaken Earth, and my heart and gut have never failed me yet, except where the male species is concerned.

Did I mention that I really detest and hate the male species, except for one special amazing man, the father of my beloved daughter Mia.

Unfortunately I married 3 times I thought for the right reasons, but not the right reasons for me. I am in my own words – selfish – self centred – unmanageable, with extremely low self esteem.

In the world's eyes and ears my sister Melody is my beloved child's mother. This was arranged and carried out to stop the baying wolves in the media and frenzied paparazzi from taking over my baby's safe and fragile life, and her mental well being.

In a perfect world our Mia will never know her real mother until she is old enough to fully understand why I made such a difficult decision, with the help of my darling Melody, of course. And so far my gorgeous Henri is totally unaware that he has a beautiful daughter, who is now 2 years old.

BUT – should I cease to exist tonight my sister will have to tell Henri, because it is only fair and right that he should be aware that he has an amazing, beautiful girl-child two years old.

Henri and I met on a weekend while I was making my last mega-movie. I realise that I am not stable and reliable enough to be able to take the stress and strain of movie making anymore. Nobody is stupid enough to touch me with a proverbial barge pole, because of my erratic behaviour, and I don't blame anyone else but myself.

Henri let everyone know that he was happily married with 3 kids, and was not interested in the lewd practices behind the scenes of a major movie. He is a musician of the highest quality, and kept himself to himself.

This of course captured my interest, and I decided he would sleep with me, if it was the last thing I did, and as usual I got my own way.

I was desperate for a much wanted baby, having had by choice because of my career too many abortions and miscarriages. My female equipment was scarred and worn out, so this could be my last chance of a family of my own.

Henri Arnaud was the perfect specimen to be my baby's sperm donor. Tall, dark, handsome, genuinely kind, intelligent, and truly gifted musically. What was not to like? Would you have passed up on this perfection? I don't think so!

So, the old adage that I was on the pill worked a dream, and I trapped Henri with my beauty and sexual experience and know how. A long weekend of continual hot, erotic love-making, wrapped in Henri's strong arms did the trick.

I was definitely pregnant, and Henri none the wiser. And no one else knew but my sister Melody. That was when the plan was hatched to keep our baby safe from the world of insanity – my world of movie making, and megalomaniacs with egos the size of mountains.

Melody and I went to stay at a spiritual retreat in the mountains under assumed names, and were there for the duration of my pregnancy. In my eighth month it was decided for my health and safety to deliver the baby. Mia was born at a good weight and normal in every way, which was an enormous relief. She was the image of me, but her personality all Henri – intelligent, kind, loving, and already with a complete love of music. I am tone deaf, and can't sing a note worthy of listening to.

Well! You can't have everything, as I certainly have other great accomplishments, as my many movies prove.

BUT – I have to put the record straight for Mia. I fell madly in love with her father that long weekend, and I do know he felt the same way about me. It was a meeting of two souls who knew each other from a past life; and Mia was made of this perfect love, as she is perfect.

Mia brings myself and Melody the greatest joy every day and we both cherish and love her. Unfortunately I cannot travel anywhere with her by myself, as Melody is assumed to be her mother, which saddens me beyond belief. So we have to be very strict with our plan, as no one can suspect I am her mother. Kidnapping would also be another huge problem for us in the future, which would be unbearable for my small family to cope with. Mia would always be a target.

The life I have led is slowly and inevitably killing me, with drugs, alcohol, and promiscuity. I wouldn't want my darling Mia to go down the same road.

I have been extremely stupid and irresponsible, but it has all been my own fault, and cannot blame anyone else for my sheer determination to climb the ladder to stardom.

Has it all been worthwhile?

You bet your sweet life, it definitely has been.

But, do I think it will be here tomorrow?

If I wake up to look up at a clear blue sky, and feel the hot sun on my face, and see my baby's sweet smile. It will be a bonus from God, that I really don't deserve.

<u>NEWS FLASH</u>

<u>WORLD NEWS ASSOCIATES</u>

MADDIE MAXWELL IS DEAD!!

Found naked in her bed by her housekeeper early this morning!

So far the LAPD are indicating that it was an accident. Too many barbiturates taken with alcohol.

Come on guys! Maddie knew far too much about the under belly of society, and wasn't known for keeping her beautiful mouth shut.

She was well known for her rotating bed sheets, with Politicians, Presidents, Kings, and totally mad musicians, and more.

Come on girls, we were jealous of this sexy woman's capacity to fall in and out of love daily.

But it seems strange that the two security men supposed to keep Maddie and her home safe from over zealous fans seem to be missing, and can't be found by the LAPD.

Doesn't that make a mockery of the accident scenario put out by said LAPD?

Good luck with that! We sincerely hope that her little black book is found.

There will be many red faces in Hollywood, and beyond.

RIP Maddie Maxwell we loved you with all your frailty and faults. You were one of us, girlfriend.

<u>20 YEARS LATER</u> **PART ONE**
<u>HOUSTON TEXAS</u> **ANTON**

<u>CHAPTER ONE</u>

"Please Papa – P-lease. Let me go with you this weekend." Lisette was determined to wear her father down. She always got her own way, because she was her father's favourite child. "You know you love it when I go with you."

"Sweetheart give me a break. It's the Mardi-Gras in New Orleans, and we will be swamped, and I won't be able to keep an eye on you my little trouble-maker. All the testosterone filled young men will be hanging around you like bees to a honey-pot."

He put down the paper he was trying to read knowing his girl would not give up easily. "Also, I am getting a lift from one of the guys who has been visiting his parents in Dallas, and not taking my usual seat on the red-eye tonight. You Lisette Arnaud are not capable of sitting quietly for seven hours with only Mike and myself for company."

"Oh Papa, don't be so ridiculous. You know I'm not interested in stupid guys." Her gorgeous face lit up with the killer smile that usually made her father give in to her often ridiculous demands. "Perhaps I'm gay and don't realise it?" She saw her father look up at the ceiling and shake his head.

"Well! I could be, and you know that once the evening jazz starts, or a Jam Session, I am totally into the music, and not interested in the audience, male or female."

Henri took a deep calming breath, and looked to his very patient, very loving wife Josephine. But she also shook her head, she wasn't so susceptible to their daughter's demands. Out of their four children, Lisette was the most obstinate and difficult. Henri and Lisette were a total match for each other, stubborn, but so loving and kind to a fault. Josephine never raised her voice, but was a strict French woman, who would rather converse in their mother tongue – French. Her youngest daughter was the only one in the family who absolutely refused to listen to her in that language. Always stating that she was an American through and through, and wasn't going to change for anyone, not even a French mother.

"It's an absolute NO! Lisette, and I won't change my mind. So please behave, and be quiet. Perhaps next weekend if that makes you feel any better." As far as Henri was concerned the subject was closed. But knowing his baby girl with the big, brown soulful eyes, she wasn't about to give up so easily, she never did.

He picked up the newspaper again trying to read the sports page, but he really needed his spectacles, his eyesight wasn't so perfect these days. "Sweetheart, would you get my reading glasses for me, I think I left them in my office, earlier."

Lisette blew out an impatient sigh knowing he was just trying to change the subject before it turned into a full blown argument, which often happened between the two of them. She was the last sibling living at home. Her sisters Paris and Mitzi were both married and had moved away from Houston, Lisette didn't shed any tears for either of them, they were both stuck-up cows! Her favourite person in the whole world was Christian her older brother. Who was married unhappily to the most evil bitch alive, and was living in Washington DC. He was a Federal Agent working in the White House guarding the President and his family.

So Lisette got the full attention of her wonderful Papa, who she usually adored, but not today. She was desperate to go to work with him in New Orleans. He owned an extremely busy and popular jazz club, and always went there every weekend to play homage to great jazz musicians, past and present.

Lisette's whole world revolved around her music, and her father's amazing talent. He played every instrument, extremely well.

Henri Arnaud was a totally phenomenonal musician.

Lisette stood statue still at her Papa's desk. The drawer that was always locked was open, she couldn't resist studying the mysterious contents. Her Papa *never* ever told anyone what was in that secret drawer, so of course she couldn't resist looking.

The entire content was a large brown envelope, and it was sealed but that didn't quench her inquisitive nature.

There was a name on the envelope – Mia Madeline Maxwell, whoever that was? Really carefully she opened the envelope and began to read the contents.

This is the last will and testament of Madeline Maxwell. All my worldly goods, money, and property I leave to my beloved sister Melody Maxwell, and in the event of her death it all reverts back to my daughter Mia Madeline Maxwell.

Except for ten million dollars in a trust fund for my beautiful child Mia to be given to her on her 25th birthday. Signed Madeline Maxwell – dated.

Lisette wasn't going to read anymore, because it was nothing to do with her, but why did her Papa have such a will?

Then she saw a birth certificate with Madeline Maxwell stated as the mother, and for fuck's sake Henri Arnaud as the father. Quickly she scanned the entire document in total shock. The child had her birthday, the ninth of June, and would be her age now as it was dated twenty two years ago.

But that couldn't be right, because she had a Birth Certificate with Josephine stated as her mother, and Henri her father.

Lisette's heart began to pound, and she felt as if she would pass out with fear of the unknown. What on earth was happening to her?

There was also a letter which she took out of the envelope and began to read it, but felt guilty in doing so, because once again it had Mia's name on it in beautiful, tidy script.

To my darling Mia, I can only pray that your beloved father has already told you about me, and the circumstances of your birth, and why I made difficult decisions about you.

Please believe me when I say from my heart and soul that Henri and I truly loved each other, even though we were together only for a brief weekend. And you were the result of that wonderful weekend an amazing result. I so wanted the world to know that you were my beautiful daughter, but it was impossible, even Henri did not know at the start of your life.

As I am writing this letter to you I am the Movie World's sex icon, and probably the most well known woman in the Western Hemisphere, and beyond. But that is all coming to an end. I am absolutely exhausted and tired of being the false sexual being that I had become, and was truly never comfortable with.

Melody my beloved sister and I decided she would become your mother to keep you safe and out of continual danger from the evil, powerful world I live in. The three of us lived together in my rambling home in Beverley Hills, so it wasn't a problem at home, but outside that safety I was your Aunt, until you were old enough to make your own decision what to do.

Please – please, do not blame your father Henri, this was my decision alone. At this time you are two years old, and he still doesn't know that you exist. My sweet baby I am writing this to you because I fear for my life, because I know far too many bedroom secrets on very powerful men.

Do not think badly of me. I did what I had to do in a stinking world of men with huge egos. My mother, your grandmother was extremely sick and her care cost a fortune. I also had to take care of Melody, who is not the brightest star in the universe. But I am still the proudest mother to have had a beautiful intelligent child like you.

I desperately hope that you can forgive me if I have caused you even a moment of unhappiness or sadness with this letter. Please think of me with love in your heart, because

Kirby, Never Look Back

it means I am no longer here. But wherever I am know that I love you with all my heart and soul, forever and always.

Your dearest Mom,
Maddie. xx

CHAPTER TWO

Lisette stood in the doorway of the spacious solarium where her parents were trying to have a quiet time together before he had to leave for New Orleans.

Silently she studied the two people she had always thought of as her loving Papa and Mama, but now didn't know who they were, but more importantly who was she in this unfolding puzzle.

Lisette Jo Arnaud?

Mia Madeline Maxwell?

Anybody? Anyone? Someone?

Whose child? The Arnaud's or Maxwell's?

Henri looked up from his paper and put it down slowly by his chair, because his girl was standing absolutely motionless with no colour in her beautiful face. Then he saw the large brown envelope in her hand. His heart dropped to his boots and he felt sick to his stomach knowing she would never forgive him for what he had done. His wife Josephine had warned him against keeping this important information from their difficult daughter.

At the best of times she was a volatile volcano always waiting to erupt, and this was going to be the worst eruption ever. Henri took a deep calming breath and indicated Lisette to come and sit down next to him. But she shook her head refusing.

He could see that her eyes were brimming with tears, and she was biting her bottom lip to stop it from trembling. "Sweetheart, I'm so sorry, really sorry. Honestly, I never found the right time to tell you, that your mother and I adopted you when you were two years old."

Adamantly, she shook her blonde head. "But that isn't true is it Papa?" Her voice was dangerously quiet, as she pointed her finger at Josephine, "because she isn't my mother, but you are my real father, aren't you?"

Henri waited for the volcano to blow, as he knew it would, because she was Madeline's child through and through.

"Haven't I always asked you over and over why I am so different from everyone else in this Godforsaken family?" She wiped her nose on her hand, and sniffed loudly.

"Blonde hair – you are all dark. Brown eyes – you all have brilliant blue. I am so tiny – you are all tall and slim, except for Mama. You are all so stinking perfect, me not so. I have always been a square peg trying to fit in a round hole, and failing miserably. Why Papa? Why didn't you tell me the truth, that I don't belong to this family, my only connection is you, Papa."

She threw the fat envelope at him. "Now! Now tell me the truth, *please*!!"

Henri stood up and took hold of his daughter's arm and took her back into his office to explain as best he could. He did not want to upset Josephine anymore than she already was. This scenario was all his fault, and was so unfair on her. This conversation with his extremely emotional daughter was going to be the most difficult in his entire life. He knew his girl only too well, she would never understand why he had kept his guilt from her for twenty years.

Heavily he sat down on the leather couch feeling every one of his sixty years. He was fit and healthy for his years, didn't smoke, rarely drank, and until that glitch twenty two years ago had never thought of cheating on his amazing wife and kids. And that would follow him to his grave, but he would never regret the love he felt for his beautiful daughter sitting next to him right now. Lisette was their last child at home.

Thirty years ago as a newly wed couple Josephine and Henri had left the French Quarter of New Orleans. His maternal grandmother had died suddenly and left him an extremely large Victorian house on the outskirts of Houston. New Orleans was fast becoming unsuitable for bringing up a family that Henri and Josephine wanted badly. So they moved and never regretted it. Their three other children were now all married with kids of their own. But Christian was considering leaving the Federal Agency, and returning home with his wife Karen and tiny daughter Amy.

That decision was a huge relief, as the Agency could be considered as a dangerous workplace.

"Sweetheart, please let me try to explain what happened that weekend twenty two years ago. Please, don't blame anyone else but me. Your birth mother, her sister, or your mother Josephine are not to blame. If you are going to hate anyone," he had tears in his blue eyes, because that was an untenable thought, "make it me alone, my darling."

She looked at him, as if she didn't know the most important person in her privileged life anymore. She shouted, "I want the truth Papa, and only the truth." She was so angry she couldn't sit still, so stood up to confront her father. "No more bullshit. No more secrets. Who am I? Why am I here? Why aren't I with my mother's family?" But then she sat back down with her darling Papa, because he looked so sad and lonely, and she had always loved and adored him all her life.

But now who was he? And more importantly, who the hell was she? The last twenty two years of her life seemed to be a sham, and where did that leave her?

A total misfit in a family that she no longer belonged to.

Henri began to explain. "I was a forty year old man with three young kids. I had a loving, beautiful wife, and the best Jazz Club on Bourbon Street, New Orleans. I was very successful, and financially secure, and never hesitated when a man came into the club and offered me and my fellow musicians a gig in the latest Madeline Maxwell movie.

"As one, we all said an emphatic Yes! It was going to be an extremely well paid adventure. Nobody could see a downside. A week in Los Angeles doing what we loved to do, playing our music. It seemed to be a win – win situation for all of us."

Henri blew out a deep breath, shaking his head, still not really believing what he had done on the last weekend of that amazing week. What a bloody naive fool he had been. He had been played, but in truth had loved every single erotic moment, with the amazing woman he had loved, and to be truthful still loved to this day. But believed he was an honourable man, and had left Madeline's bed and come home to his family and devastated wife. Even though it had been a Godawful wrench, he had never regretted that decision not for a second.

He had confessed what he had done to Josephine, because he didn't believe in secrets in a healthy marriage. In time she had forgiven him, and for that alone he loved his wife unconditionally, and had never strayed again, and never would.

"I was so utterly, ridiculously stupid. My male ego was stroked by the most beautiful woman in the world, who wanted to have an affair with me, and of course I succumbed. I will never forgive myself for that glitch in my well-ordered life."

He took Lisette's pixie face in his big capable hands and kissed her forehead. "But, baby girl you are the result of that weekend, so I can never regret what I did. You are the image of your mother, who was my heart for that long weekend. And God forgive me as I loved her, I now love you.

"And, God's truth I never knew that Madeline was pregnant from that weekend, because she told me she was covered by the pill, and never let me know she had a child called Mia. In fact the whole world didn't know, because everyone believed that her sister Melody was your mother. For some unknown reasoning you were kept a secret."

Lisette interrupted his story. "My mother explained in her letter to me that she was terrified that I would be kidnapped, or even worse." Her big brown eyes were wet with tears, and she squeezed her father's hand. "But what I don't understand is why, why didn't you tell me who I really am? Didn't I deserve to know who my real mother was? How could you be such a coward Papa? None of this was my fault. You and Madeline Maxwell were my parents, as I grew up why didn't you tell me?"

Her expressive face changed with abject horror. "Christian, and my sisters must have known that I wasn't born into this family, and not one person ever told me." Then her eyes lowered into slits. "Now I know why Paris and Mitzi never made any effort to like me. But my Christian always loved me, and made a fuss of me. He is such a kind, loving person, not like his horrible sisters."

All this was making Henri feel even worse if it was possible. "They knew we had adopted you, and your mother and I made them promise to never mention you were adopted, because it would upset you, and to our astonishment they all kept their promise."

He had to admit that for twenty years he had walked on eggshells dreading the truth coming out. But it never had until today, and knew it was too late for his daughter. She would never forgive him, and couldn't blame her, or excuse him.

"When did you actually find out that my real mother had me, and how did the secret come out of my birth?"

Henri closed his eyes trying to ward off the headache that was forming behind his eyes. He rarely drank, but a large aged scotch would go down exceptionally well right now. He had to tell her the truth, because too many secrets and lies had been kept and spoken for too long.

"Twenty years ago a woman we didn't know stood at the front door of this house with a screaming red faced baby in her arms. It was your Aunt Melody, and you were the baby. We of course asked her to come inside, and she told us something that I just couldn't take on board, or believe."

Henri shook his head still feeling the emotion of that fateful day, of Madeline dying, and meeting his golden haired daughter for the first time. "You have to understand what a shock it was for your mother and myself. At first we thought it was a huge mistake, but then your Aunt produced your birth certificate with me as your father, and the date coincided with me being in L.A. with Madeline at the time. To say we were in shock would be a complete understatement, and then I had to admit to my loving, faithful wife what I had done in L.A. I had seriously played away, and had always said that was something I would never do, ever."

Henri still couldn't believe after all these years that his ever loving, patient, calm wife actually forgave him. It had taken a long time before he was out of the proverbial dog house, and was trusted again as a husband, and back in a normal relationship with his wife. He would forever be on his best behaviour in their marriage, and truly loved his family. He had been taught a lesson he would never forget.

Lisette couldn't keep quiet any longer, she couldn't believe what was unfolding. "What did you do then Papa? Did mama throw you out, and what happened to my Aunt who was innocent in all this drama?"

"Your Aunt Melody truly loved you, as if you were her own daughter. She was heartbroken, it had taken so much courage for her to bring you to us, and leave you behind. And that was exactly what she did. She gave us your documentation, all your habits, food, sleeping, everything she could think of to help you settle down with us."

Tears formed in Henri's clear blue eyes, as he remembered how upset Melody had been. He knew she would always love and miss her sister's baby. But she had faithfully promised Madeline before she died that she would deliver Mia to her biological father.

"That lovely lady walked away and 'NEVER LOOKED BACK', because that was the only way she could leave her beloved baby behind."

But Lisette couldn't understand why her Aunt had never been mentioned in all this time. "But I don't understand what happened to my family that they aren't around anymore, it doesn't make sense to me."

Henri looked into his daughter's big brown eyes that were full of disbelief and hurt. She deserved answers to be able to understand what had happened to her family in the last twenty years. However hard it was she needed to know.

"Your mother Madeline died twenty years ago. Nobody seems to have worked out if it was an overdose or murder. I'm sorry sweetheart, but that is the truth, and I can't sugar-coat it. Then her mother, your grandmother died in a hospital soon after Madeline's death, and there doesn't seem to be any other relatives. We sent photos and school reports of you as you grew up, and we knew she received them, but never acknowledged that she had. As far as we know she is still living in your mother's villa in Beverley Hills, because that was her last known address." He indicated the brown envelope, "it's in there with all the records from your mother."

Henri realised all this information must be overload for his darling girl. "Sweetheart, if you want to go and find your Aunt I will take you as soon as I can get away. It really isn't a problem. I just want you to be happy. I have loved you with all my heart from the day your Aunt left you with us, and always will. As does your mother Josephine, who has looked after you for the past twenty years, as if she had carried you in her womb for nine months."

Lisette wasn't listening to her father. Her hands were over her mouth to stop the sobs from escaping. She was still hearing that her dearest mother had died alone from an overdose, which was bad enough. But had she been murdered and died in pain, inflicted by some unknown assailant? And why hadn't the law managed to find out what had happened to the most beautiful woman living?

It was truly a travesty of American law, and the police department of Los Angeles. Surely it couldn't be right, and why hadn't someone managed to find out the truth by now? And why hadn't her Aunt tried harder to find the answers? Now, that couldn't be right either. It was a question and answer she was determined to find out, herself, or die trying.

She stood up, and glared at her father as if she hated him with every bone in her small body, and she absolutely did for keeping all this information from her for twenty years.

Hate vibrated from her in waves.

"Do not *ever* call me Lisette again, for sure I have hated that name forever. My name is Mia Madeline Maxwell. I will never speak to you again as long as I have breath in my body. I will never go anywhere with you or that ghastly French woman you call wife, or, my supposedly spoilt cows of sisters, because I never really liked them. And now I know why." She smiled through her angry tears. "But, Christian, I will always love with all my heart, because he is truly my brother in my heart. As for the rest of this family I am done, and never want to see any of you again."

Kirby, Never Look Back

Slamming out of the door she ran past the woman she had known for twenty years, or thought she had. Josephine was standing outside the office, hands over her mouth, white as a sheet, because she had heard every word. But she never tried to stop Henri's daughter, knowing nothing would change her mind, and her husband would need her strength and unconditional love for the bleak months to come, because he absolutely adored that difficult, obstinate child, he had given life to with Madeline Maxwell.

Mia went straight to her bedroom still holding onto her large brown envelope, locking the door behind her. She began to gather her personal items to stuff into her backpack to take on her long, possibly dangerous journey to find her Aunt in L.A.

She totally ignored her father banging on her bedroom door, and his emotional pleas to open the door, and please let him in, and not to shut him out of her life, because he loved her *so* much.

Mia sobbed while she packed clean underwear, a few clothes, her bank book, driving licence, and social security card. She had never been a female to wear fripperies and up to date clothes, so her backpack wouldn't be too heavy. Make up wasn't on her to do list, just mascara and lipstick, and she often chopped off her short, curly blonde hair. So only the basic toiletries were her essentials, and that included

Tampax, so a full box was included, just in case of an emergency.

So she was good to leave in a few minutes, but waited until it was silent outside. She so didn't want another altercation with her very persuasive, charismatic father. The man could talk the birds out of the trees.

But not this particular bird, she had the iron will of her mother, and was just as difficult with rules and regulations. She hated them with a vengeance. Mia was a free spirit of the first order.

Poking her head outside her bedroom door she scanned the hallway making sure it was empty, she was going to leave out the back door so that nobody would try and stop her. She really loved this old, creaky Victorian house, that was a large rambling family home. But she wasn't family anymore, it was all a dream, a lie, a secret, because she had never really belonged to this family – The Arnaud's. She was a Maxwell, and now was going to prove it.

However hard that was, or difficult. She patted her real birth certificate, and her mother's letter proving that she was Madeline Maxwell's daughter. And again, however hard or difficult it became, she would try and find out what happened to her mother that awful night she died.

Drugs or murder – or both?

CHAPTER THREE

Mia drove her bright yellow VW Beetle into the parking slot behind Franco's Trattoria on Main Street. She worked there with her best friend Viola as waitresses to earn enough money to carry on at college. Both were studying Business Management, Viola seriously with accountancy, Mia with the Arts, not so seriously.

Of course Henri hated his precious girl waiting tables, as he never kept her short of money, but Mia's best friend was a black girl from the wrong side of Main Street. The difference was huge even though they lived only half an hour from each other. Mia's home was extremely comfortable and safe. While Viola's was the complete opposite with four younger siblings to cope with, and a very unstable mother on drugs, and a father who was more often drunk than sober.

Consequently, Viola often went home with Mia to stay over when they worked together at night. They both loved working at Franco's, because the owner's Franco and his wife were wonderful with the youngsters who worked there. It was hard work, but Franco had a honky-tonk piano in the restaurant that Mia loved to play of a weekend, if she wasn't with her Papa in New Orleans.

And that alone had the tips rolling in, which the two girls split down the middle.

Mia and Viola walked in the back door arm in arm laughing together, but Mia knew that they wouldn't be laughing when she told her friend and Franco what she was going to do today – leave for L.A. later. More so Viola, because they were usually inseparable. Neither bothered with boyfriends, because they believed they were more trouble than they were worth, and in fact took the Mickey out of the guys who came into the restaurant trying to get a date with the two girls.

Mia pulled her friend into the office and sat her down to be able to show her all the documentation about her real mother, and that she wasn't Lisette but Mia Madeline Maxwell.

Frowning Viola looked up from the paperwork. "You are kidding me, sister? Is this for real? And why didn't your Papa tell you, or your Mama?" She kept studying the letter and birth certificate with a puzzled frown. She was as gobsmacked as Mia had been. "What ya goin' t'do, Liss? Go find ya' real Ma, or any relatives of hers? You must be worth a frickin' fortune." Her beautiful face lit up with a grin from ear to ear. "I'll sure carry ya' bags for ya' hon'."

But then she began to realise that the friendship and laughter, and closeness they'd had together for a long time could be over. This was a huge game change in Mia's life.

Although she was beyond being pleased for her friend's good fortune, but where did all this leave her?

Mia could see just how upset Vi was becoming, but not as upset as she had been when her father had told her. She put her arms around her friend and gave her a big hug. "I'm *so* sorry, but I have to go and find my Aunt in L.A. My mother Madeline Maxwell died at least twenty years ago, and I need to know why, and how? It still seems to be a mystery what happened the night she died."

She sat back down next to Vi, she was gutted for her, because she had a crap life with her awful family. Now she wouldn't be there for her, and her Papa thought the world of Vi, because she was always so kind, and caring to his own recalcitrant daughter.

"Look Vi when I get myself organised in L.A. you can come visit. I'll pay for you, as the daughter of Madeline I must have money owing to me somewhere. So please don't be miserable, and don't forget that my parents think the world of you, and I'm sure would want you to go and stay with them." Her voice caught when she added, "I'm not coming back. I can't forgive my parents for keeping this from me. This is all too huge for me to take on board, and I can't trust them anymore," she whispered, "I'm totally gutted Vi."

"When are you leaving, babe? How much time have we got left?" The beautiful black girl blew out a long breath still not believing what was happening to their normal world. She didn't remember when or how Madeline Maxwell had died, but everyone knew about Madeline Maxwell, and just how beautiful she had been. But now when she really looked at Liss she was a replica of her famous mother – tiny, blonde, and stunningly beautiful.

"Sorry girlfriend, but I'm actually on my way. Could you please come with me to George Bush Airport after I tell Franco? I want you to have my car as a gift. I've already changed the ownership to you, and the insurance. So don't argue, because it's all legal." She shook her head knowing her friend would argue. "I'm *not* arguing. I don't want you riding that fuckin' bicycle to work and college every day. It – is – not – safe. And I won't be here to guard your back. So you will take it, and love it as much as I do."

Viola raised her hands in supplication. "OK! OK! I would love to own Millie." She returned the hug to her bestest friend. "I love ya' Lisette Arnaud, who is now Mia Madeline Maxwell, and who the fuck cares? I have always been so jealous of that stupid yellow car. And you can bet on ya' sweet white ass, that I will drive you to the airport in my gorgeous, cute, yellow car. And if you don't let me visit you in L.A., don't think for a second that I won't come and find you, and that's a promise, not just a threat, sweetheart."

Mia grinned, she was overjoyed that Vi was happy about the car, because her gorgeous black friend deserved a break, not much came her way, with the awful family she was saddled with. And she fervently hoped that Vi would go to *her* parents and stay with them, because Papa would need someone to look after, when his precious daughter wasn't causing mischief, and running him into circles.

The friends went into the restaurant to tell Franco that they wouldn't be working that night. They knew that Franco and his wife would cope as always. There were plenty of college students ready to take their place, even though Friday was their busiest night.

But, nobody played the piano like Lisette Arnaud, and never would.

Mia Madeline Maxwell was walking away from a very privileged life. She was loved by her friends and family and always had been. She did not have a clue what she was walking towards.

Would it be her downfall?

Or would it be the making of the woman she could be?

CHAPTER FOUR

Mia came out of LAX Airport squinting in the hot sun, it was Spring and the weather was perfect. She went straight to the designated area for the Airport Taxis. Earlier she had sweet talked to get herself into the upper-class lounge so she could shower and change her grungy clothes. She had slept at George Bush Airport last night, because the first flight to Los Angeles had left at six a.m. this morning.

Immediately she felt the energy of L.A. It was younger, and a much dryer heat than where she had lived for twenty years. Houston could be stuffy and snobby on a grand scale. It was who you were, or who you knew, and very scathing if you weren't rich, and didn't have well heeled past relations. Mia hated all that crap, and skin deep controversy. For her it was shallow and deeply dishonest, as if everything was on show. You got what you got, and definitely didn't dig below the surface. She was sure that people in L.A. spoke their thoughts, felt free to have an opinion, and that was what Mia was made of, which felt free and easy to her.

In that old Victorian house she had been brought up in, it was all about the past. Living in the glory of the past, and she now realised she hadn't been part of that glorious past. But she was going to enjoy the future, if it damn-well killed her.

She got into the taxi starting to feel really excited she was going to meet her Aunt Melody at last. For the occasion she was wearing a tiny flowery dress, a denim jacket, white socks, and platform white and gold trainers. She looked a very cute sixteen with short blonde curly hair, and only a touch of mascara and lipstick. She had been in too much of a hurry to straighten her hair to its usual spiky mess. Her very expensive designer sunglasses were of course an indulgent present from a very loving Papa, because she had bugged and coerced until the poor man had given in, probably too easily.

What Lisette had asked for Lisette always got.

Mia was beginning to realise what a spoilt little bitch she had been. But in truth it was her Papa's fault because he always gave in to her every whim, and whine, and temper explosion. So if she was a spoilt little brat, it was all his fault, because he should have paddled her backside and grounded her until she apologised for her bad attitude.

Her Papa would always be the man she most admired, looked up to, and loved with all her heart. But, right now she couldn't trust him, couldn't be near him, until she cleared her muddled mind about her real mother and Aunt. Honestly, she wondered if she could ever really forgive him for staying silent for twenty years, and sincerely doubted it.

Her big loving heart was shattered, and she wasn't sure it could be put together again, or even plastered over.

But then excitement gripped her again, because she was going to meet her Aunt, and hopefully get a lot of answers on the last twenty years of her life.

She stood outside the home she presumed had been her mother's sanctuary before she died, and prayed that her Aunt still lived there.

The taxi had driven past amazing beaches and properties lining the Pacific Ocean. Mia's eyes were as big as saucers as she looked at the extreme wealth of this area of California. Houston couldn't hold a candle to this place. The weather – beaches – wealth, properties, and atmosphere, it all reaked of serious money.

Now at last she was here, standing outside a rambling cottage that overlooked the ocean in Santa Monica.

It was behind tall electronic gates, so she took a deep breath and pressed the intercom on one of the ornate pillars.

"Can I help you please?" said a hollow voice with a strong Spanish accent.

"Thank you, I have come to see Melody Maxwell, I am her niece Mia Maxwell." She had to stand on her toes to be able to talk into the intercom.

"Si, I understand. I will open the gate for you."

As the gates swung open a tall, well built man was standing waiting for her. "Mia, my God, what a wonderful surprise." He came forward and put his arms around her, which wasn't welcome for Mia, she wasn't the hugging strangers type of female. Also, he was very tall, and she was so tiny, which made her feel even more uncomfortable.

"I would have known you anywhere, Mia. You are the image of your Mother, and your Aunt. It is so lovely to meet you after all these years."

Mia gave him one of her withering looks, "I'm sorry, but who are you? I've come to meet my Aunt Melody, as I've never actually seen her before."

"Come into the house out of the sun, and let's get introduced. I am Melody's husband, Roberto Diaz."

His explanation caught Mia unawares, he was her Uncle by marriage, she was gobsmacked, what else didn't she know about her Mother's sister? As they walked up the driveway Mia quickly looked around, it was an immaculate garden of colourful flowers, bushes, and exotic palms. There was an amazing fountain in the middle of the spacious lawn. She could see that the property and grounds were loved, cherished, and secure from the clamour of the outside world.

Immediately Mia loved it. It felt like home to her, and she wished with all her heart that her beautiful Mother was still living here. But she also realised that this would all be hers when her Aunt died in years to come. And she knew that she could live here happily with her Mother's memory lingering on.

Inside the one story building it was as immaculate as the grounds. A large open fireplace was centred in the spacious lounge area, with comfortable looking couches and armchairs, overlooking a small swimming pool surrounded by exotic bushes and small palms. Roberto showed her around the stainless steel kitchen, with all the modern equipment a good cook would need. Mia would never be in that category, as coffee and toast were her only accomplishments, and usually the toast was a burnt offering.

It was evident that Roberto was proud of his home, so Mia duly followed him on his tour. "We have two main bedrooms here in this area, and two extra bedrooms in the adjoining annexe, all with their own bathrooms. It's a shame our twins are visiting with my sister and her family right now, because they would love to meet you."

Mia stopped in her tracks with shock. She had more family to meet. TWINS? Her Papa never mentioned that her Aunt was married with twins. Where was her Aunt, and the twins?

"Please, can we stop with the tour. Where is my Aunt, and what are the twins, boys or girls, or both?" She was bursting with questions, and didn't know where to start.

Kirby, Never Look Back

Where did he meet her Aunt? How long were they married? How old were the twins? Did he think that her mother Madeline had been happy here? And most important had her mother truly loved her, even though she had been a secret from the world?

Surely Papa would have mentioned all this about her Aunt, if he had known. His guilt was piling up a mile high. Now she knew she could never forgive him for keeping her family to himself.

"Let's go and sit in the kitchen with a cold drink, there is something I have to tell you, and it won't be easy." He fetched a jug of iced tea from the fridge and sat down next to Mia at a small table in the corner. Taking a broken breath he said in a trembling voice, "my darling Mel died suddenly four weeks ago." He carried on quickly, as if he needed to get it out before he broke down. "She was so brave, had been fighting cancer since the twins were born ten years ago. We believed she had beaten the evil curse, but eight weeks ago it came back with a vengeance, and she just didn't have the strength left to fight anymore. W-we buried her two weeks ago next to her sister Madeline in a secret tomb, only I know where it is, and two other people of course."

A lone tear travelled down his cheek, and he wiped it away with the back of his hand. He had cried far too much in the last month, and he was exhausted. That was why his girls were staying with his sister, because he wasn't coping with them, two identical ten year olds were full of energy and mischief, and they were the image of his beloved Mel.

Mia couldn't believe she had come all this way too late by four weeks, and now she would never know her beautiful Mother or her Aunt. Putting her hand over Roberto's she squeezed with love and empathy. Her own life was going down the road to hell, but what must this brave man be going through? Her kind heart ached for him.

"I am *so* sorry, you must be in so much pain and grief. I should never have come at such a dreadful time, and your poor children without their Mama, and she was still so young."

Roberto gripped her hand tightly, his eyes filling with tears. "No! No! Please stay I beg you. Mel would be so angry with me if I didn't make you feel welcome." He smiled through his tears, and blew his nose on a tissue. "She was the kindest, caring, most loving person anyone could meet. Loved her kids and me without ever thinking of herself, only about others." He looked at Mia and smiled. "She always thought of you as her own daughter, but never once wanted to be a nuisance to your new family. Said it wasn't fair on you or them. Henri was your biological father and it was only right that you were with him, but I know how much it played on her mind. The photos and everything that Henri sent to her she kept and treasured them. They were kept in a special drawer in our bedroom, and she would often go sit in that room, and take them out and pour over them.

"Without a doubt she always loved you as her own child in her heart, as she did her girls."

Mia was becoming overwhelmed with everything Roberto was telling her, but was still soaking it all up like a sponge.

"Thank you for telling me that, it means the world to me. Could you please tell me how you met my Aunt, and if you knew my mother? That would be the icing on the cake in my life, right now."

"To be honest Mia, I have so much to tell you, and I would love you to stay at least a couple of days. There is a spare bedroom in the annexe, we won't be here on our own as we have a live-in housekeeper, who is very quiet and very efficient. It would be wonderful for me to be able to talk about my Mel and the kids, and our fantastic life together, and how you have always been in the background."

Mia couldn't believe her luck. To be able to hear about her family first hand was absolutely amazing. "Thank you so much, I would love to stay with you until Monday, if that's OK? But first can I put my stuff in my room, and take these bloody shoes off? I hate wearing shoes – any shoes."

"That is weird, just like your Mom, and your Aunt. Neither of them liked wearing anything on their feet, indoors or outdoors. You really don't know just how much you are like both of them. And it's scary, because our girls, Melia and Myrna, always take their shoes off as soon as they get home."

Roberto used the phone in the kitchen. "Maria could you please get lunch now? Mia is staying for a few days, and we are both starving. Thank you so much." He put the phone back and smiled at Mia, "let's go and sit out on the veranda, and let Maria get on with her work. She would never complain, but the kitchen is her domain." He winked at Mia and whispered, "she terrifies me, but is great with the kids, so I can't argue with that now, can I?"

The next morning at breakfast the day ahead started with memories of the past twenty years. There was often heartache but also laughter, because Roberto had had a wonderful marriage with his beloved Melody, and he wanted Mia to know all about her Aunt, and of course her mother, of which he didn't know much, only what Melody had told him. He was well aware that his wife couldn't say much, because her sister was shrouded in mystery, and secrets.

"I remember so well, a chubby, absolutely gorgeous toddler. At that time of course I thought you were your Aunt's baby, as did the world."

"Oh my God, I didn't realise you had seen me living here." Mia was all ears for information that early in her life.

"My Company had just received the contract for the maintenance of this property. One of Madeline's Security team came next door where we were working and asked me if we would take on their property. Of course I jumped at the chance, because I owned the Company, and we had just started out. I was thirty years old, and very ambitious. The first time I saw my Mel I literally fell in love, even though I thought she was married, because she had this over energetic two year old. I never actually saw Madeline Maxwell, she never came out into the grounds, I think she was quite shy of strangers. But I always managed to talk to Mel, and play with you. She let slip she was a single mom, and for five years I waited and waited. That was after you seemed to disappear off the face of the earth, and I could see that Melody was inconsolable, and heartbroken, especially with Madeline's death as well on her plate."

Mia felt so sorry for her Aunt, she had so much to cope with in her young life, but it seemed as if Roberto was there to help. She was sure he had been, because he was a decent, caring human being, with a great deal of love to give.

"Anyhow, I managed to talk your Aunt into marriage, which was the best thing I've ever done. For five years we tried for a baby, Mel told me that you were with your legal father, and that Madeline was your mother, but nobody could know that, because your life wouldn't be worth living. The world press and anyone wanting to earn a quick buck would be on your case. I have never told a living soul, truly."

Mia couldn't thank him enough for that. She'd had a fantastic childhood with a family who loved her. "You have the twins, so you must have managed to get pregnant after all."

He shook his head adamantly. "No! Mel decided that we couldn't wait any longer as she wasn't getting any younger, and neither was I. So we bit the bullet and went for IVF treatment, and couldn't believe our luck when she got pregnant straight away. And, as you can see by the many photographs around the house that they are gorgeous, mischievous, and so loved."

But Mia wanted to know anything and everything about her mother, so she asked Roberto if he knew anything that would help her really understand why her Aunt had become her mother for two years.

"You have to realise that Madeline wanted everyone to know that you were her beloved child. But, twenty years ago there were many high profile babies and children being kidnapped for millions, and she just couldn't take that chance." Roberto smiled at Mia's frown that said she wasn't so sure of that. "My Mel told me over and over that her sister was absolutely despondent that she couldn't show you off as her beautiful daughter, which was a dreadful shame."

Mia couldn't believe that she felt so relaxed with this wonderful man, he was such a quiet, kind man who had loved his family unconditionally. Then his next words made her realise that her father had been telling the truth about her mother.

"You know that Madeline loved your father even though they were only together that long weekend." He smiled at a long ago memory. "But then I fell in love with Mel the moment I saw her. So I really believe that it is possible to love at first sight."

Mia could see and hear that Roberto was heartbroken over his darling wife leaving him at such a young age. She could only wish that she would love someone enough if it happened to her in the future. In truth she believed it wasn't going to happen, because she was asexual, and had never fancied any male she came into contact with. But also knew she wasn't gay, because she didn't fancy any female either, not ever, and never would.

Roberto was feeling too emotional to carry on retelling all these memories, and decided to change the subject. But he couldn't help but state the obvious. "As God is my witness, my girls are almost clones of you, and Mel, and Madeline. They even have those chocolate brown eyes, and blonde curly hair. It is really spooky, I feel like an outsider in my own family, as I am dark and Hispanic, with brilliant blue eyes from my American mother."

Mia couldn't stop her brown eyes filling with tears for all that he had lost, and her loss as well. "I am honoured to be part of this family, and thrilled that I look like my Mother and Aunt, and your children." She sniffed dramatically. "We must be all *so* beautiful then, aren't we?"

He put his arms around her and kissed the top of her head, she was almost a foot shorter than he was. "I can't argue with that. What a truly lucky man I am to have such a beautiful family."

Now he dreaded this next conversation, but knew in his heart that Mia would be kind in her answer.

"Look sweetheart, we have to discuss this property, because it belongs to you now with Mel gone. I have seen Madeline's will, and it reverts back to you on Mel's death." He put his large rough hand over her small delicate one. "Please! Can I have some time for my girls to get used to their mother not being here? I am not asking for myself, but she adored her kids, as they did her. It's going to be so hard to uproot them, they have friends here, and attend the local school."

Mia watched the tears well up in those blue eyes again, and knew he was only fighting for his kids' welfare. She made a decision she would never regret for the rest of her life. Yes, she was obstinate, difficult, and never took crap from anyone, but had the biggest heart, as her mother had, and had passed it on to her child.

"I wouldn't dream of asking you to leave. This home is yours unless you re-marry, or die of old age." When he went to argue Mia stopped him immediately. "You are my only family, my only connection to my Mom and Aunt, and I don't need to live here. I have to go out there and find out what happened to my mother Madeline. Nobody seems to know what really happened, and I intend to find out."

"Thank you *so* much, you cannot imagine what that means to me and the girls. Again, you are so like your Aunt and your Mother, because I know that is what they would have done."

She looked down at her breakfast realising she hadn't touched it, so quickly gulped down the juice, and turned her nose up at cold coffee, but did break off a piece of croissant and slathered it with butter and strawberry jam. All of a sudden feeling hungry, evidently being a good Samaritan made you hungry and thirsty, and she was definitely both.

"The only thing I ask Roberto is that you maintain the home and grounds as they are now, absolutely immaculate. And you cover the cost on anything that's needed. I don't want any rent etc, I just need to know that my mother's home is loved and well kept. But, I think we have to make it legal in some way, which is way out of my league, and I really don't want to worry about a property at my age. I have to go out there and live an adventure, and intend to enjoy every moment." She grinned that sunshine grin that only Mia could, because she was going to be fast and furious, and couldn't wait to start.

"Mel and I have a lawyer in L.A. who is excellent and very thorough, we trust him absolutely. I have to go into my Company tomorrow early, unfortunately I have to crack the whip as I haven't been around for over a month, and my crews are only human, they play while I'm not watching them."

He shook his head and grimaced, because that situation did make him angry, he was always so good to his men, and sometimes they did take advantage of his good nature. "Tomorrow I will drive you there, and let Marcus sort out any problems. From his office you can more or less get anywhere in L.A. Sorry I can't stay with you but I am so behind in my work, and our customers get antsy and I lose contracts. But please, come back and visit, because your room will always be there, and the twins will be dying to meet you. Promise me sweetheart, that if you have any problems at all, especially about your mother's death, you will let me know, and I will try and help."

He wrote down his cell number, and made her promise faithfully that she would keep in touch with him wherever she was.

And she would! And she did!

Mia Madeline Maxwell grew up to be a woman over that weekend with Roberto, and about time.

She would now take control of her life, and find out what she was really made of – or not!

Have new adventures, but would danger stalk her before her life could settle down and be normal?

You can bet your sweet life on it.

CHAPTER FIVE

Roberto pulled up at a very understated building close to the Airport, and got out of his large black flat-bed vehicle to help Mia get down from the passenger seat, because she was too tiny to manage it herself.

Immediately a tall, extremely good looking man came out of the glass doors to give Roberto a man hug, and smile at Mia. Her safe female world was tilted on its axis, and her rarely used hormones ran for cover, and hid.

Mia had always assumed that she was asexual, possibly gay, had never been particularly interested in a member of the male species. But now knew all that had been smoke and mirrors. When he smiled and took her hand, it felt as though her heart had lost the plot, and couldn't remember to beat to a regular rhythm in her almost flat chest.

Mia fell totally in love, or was it lust, or both? But would she know the difference, never having been in either situation?

God had never favoured her with large breasts, and that had never bothered her previously, but at that moment she desperately wished she had a figure like her mother, so he would notice that she was all woman, to be admired and loved.

"Marcus my friend, this is Mia a precious family member, and is in need of your legal expertise. Do you have a moment to spare in your extremely busy day? I apologise, but I have to leave straight away as my Company needs a kick up the backside. Can you look after Mia for me, my good friend? And, she will need to get a cab when she leaves, if you wouldn't mind."

Marcus was still holding her hand as if he never wanted to let go. "I have just a small amount of time before our free clinic starts." He smiled at Mia, twin dimples appeared either side of his very kissable mouth. "Leave this beautiful young lady with me, and I will make sure she gets safely to where she needs to go later."

Also he couldn't believe that his lower body had stirred in interest when he had taken this gorgeous female's hand, and couldn't recall the last time that had happened. He grinned when his boys came into his mind. They had been laughing idiotically while they measured their so called winkies to see who had the biggest one, which his youngest son held the record, just like his well-endowed father. And that said, his winky was definitely on the move, and becoming a problem, so he let go of her hand.

Roberto gave Mia a tight hug and kissed her forehead. "Come back to us soon sweetheart, we will so love to see you again." He shook his head and sniffed loudly. "Can't believe my Mel's best girl is here at last."

Mia felt exactly the same about her new family. "I promise to be back as soon as I can, you will never get rid of me now I know where you live. Give my love to the twins, and I can't wait to meet them." She returned the hug and then let Roberto get back into his monster truck. She followed the unknown male quantity that had stirred her female hormones, and baby making paraphernalia, into a cool, pleasurable office.

He motioned her to sit in a comfortable armchair, as he went around his desk opposite her. "You must be our Mel's lost daughter from twenty years ago. There is no mistaken identity, you are the absolute image of her. She was amazingly beautiful, as are you." Suddenly he looked so sad. "It was a terrible shock to us all when she died so quickly, even though we knew she had suffered with cancer for so long." He shook his head. "Poor Rob, I have never seen a man so devastated, and just about hanging in there, I couldn't admire him anymore than I do."

Mia couldn't take her eyes off him, she had never seen such a beautiful looking man. He put her in mind of the late Rock Hudson, her favourite Movie Star, but please God he wasn't gay, because she was so attracted to him. To say he was immaculately dressed, with a crisp white cotton shirt the sleeves rolled up, and silk black trousers with a thin designer belt, and no tie. Crisp black curly hair was showing out of his open shirt.

This man was a drool worthy package.

But her heart shrivelled with disappointment, because she looked a total wreck. What was wrong with her that she couldn't be more feminine and lovable. With her torn to death jeans, a minute just about covering her miniscule boobs, pink top. Her antique Harley leather jacket, and high heeled boots, didn't go well in his air-conditioned office.

But still, she couldn't believe that he was looking at her as if she was a woman he wanted to get to know better. Perhaps even want to go to bed with, and not for sleeping.

Nah! Mia fuckin' Maxwell? He was probably thinking that he couldn't believe that anyone could dress that badly and not be arrested by the fashion police. She was definitely having a brain fart. Stupid Mia, what was she rambling on about? She was a ridiculous virgin who didn't know diddly squat about love and sex.

She got her brain back in gear and took out the brown envelope from her backpack and gave it to Marcus. "Please read it all before we can decide what I should do." She quickly looked around the large office nervously. "And, I don't want anyone else knowing what is in that envelope."

Marcus understood perfectly. "Of course that is your privilege, and if you become my client, everything will be confidential between us. But I can see that you are very uneasy about the contents of this envelope, so I need to explain to you what I am all about, and my partners, because I need you to trust me implicitly in the future." He looked straight into her big velvet brown eyes, and knew without a shadow of a doubt they would have a future together.

"I have three partners, between us we run offices in Dallas, Houston, L.A., and Fort Worth. All bon-a-fide lawyers. We met at Harvard University for Law, and passed with honours, my degree is in criminal psychology, but at the moment I prefer to help others who cannot afford to help themselves, hence the clinic here once a month. I actually live outside Fort Worth in a small town called Perseverance with my family. Luckily our Company owns a Cessna Cilitation Mustang plane, which saves me a great deal of time from Forth Worth to here. All the partners are actual pilots, so it's a well used asset. My lucky day was when I met the other three gregarious guys at Harvard, and we did our degrees together, and are now partners."

A young black guy poked his head around the connecting door of the adjoining office. "Sorry to interrupt boss, but can I start the clinic? The line is getting longer to see you, and a bit antsy." He smiled at Mia, and was definitely interested.

"Thanks Ben, that would be great. I think I'm going to be held up here for quite a while. Any problems refer them back to me."

"Will do boss, hopefully no real prob's this morning." He gave a winning smile to Mia, but she was too busy keeping her eyes on Marcus. When he had mentioned his family living in Fort Worth, she had been totally side-swiped, and to seal the disappointment she now noticed he was wearing a very dominant gold wedding ring. The way her life was going down the proverbial drain right now, it was no wonder the only male she was interested in was already taken, and no doubt with kids. And, why not, he was gorgeous, articulate, probably rich, and to die for.

Why would that epitome of manhood still be single?

"And, I expect you are wondering how I know your Aunt and Rob, and how we became firm friends."

This part of his story Mia was truly interested in, anything she could learn about her mother's family was gold to her heart.

"I met Mel and Rob when we were all trying to raise funds for the local Battered Women and Babies shelter. I felt as if it was a truly worthy cause, as did your Aunt. Also there were many families who were struggling to put food on the table for their kids, mainly Hispanic, Mexican, and black families, which the three of us absolutely abhorred. So, we decided to pool our reserves and actually run the shelter, and provide food and necessities for struggling families."

He smiled at Mia, as he could see she was totally engrossed in any information on her new family. "I am an exceedingly busy lawyer and family man, and don't have much available spare time, so thankfully your Aunt took on the heavy workload for us all. But now, we are going to have to organise someone to take over that workload, hopefully Rob will be able to do more, and I will have to pay someone to help him. Your Aunt was one in a million, and I can vouch for the fact that she will be sorely missed, and we all loved her. She was a sweet, loveable woman, and I really don't know how Rob is coping at all, now she is no longer with us." He looked really sad, "don't think Mel was a pushover, that lady had a backbone of steel when needed, which I'm pretty sure you inherited with your DNA."

Mia nodded her head, she certainly couldn't argue with that prognosis. "I just wish I could be like her and help others. I've come to the horrible conclusion this weekend, that I'm a spoilt, selfish, self-centred brat. But hopefully I can change now I know about my family. My papa in Houston has spoilt me rotten, probably because he had this huge secret he kept from me." She indicated the envelope, "please read, and make up your own mind. It is a huge secret, and scary."

Marcus had a puzzled frown on his face, as he put on his reading glasses, and took out all the papers from the envelope. He couldn't understand what could be such a huge secret if Mia was Mel's child.

Occasionally he looked up at Mia, as if he couldn't believe what he was reading. She was pacing up and down as if it was impossible for her to sit still. This was so incredibly important to her, that he believed what was in front of him.

Who she was!

What could they do about it!

After what seemed an eternity Marcus took off his glasses and said "Shit!" under his breath, and just stared at her in total amazement. "This is unbelievable, absolutely incredible! This I'm afraid will cause a tsunami in World News."

He blew out a held back breath, he still couldn't believe what he had just read, but he just knew it was the truth, and nothing but the truth, so help them God. "How on earth has this been kept secret for twenty years? But now when I really look at you, you are the spit image of your beautiful mother, and poor Mel suffered so much heartache with her sister's lies and secrets."

He rubbed a hand over his morning beard that was already beginning to show, even though he had shaved early. He got up from his seat and paused before he went to open the front door. "Would you mind if our P.I. Gerry Swane came in on this? Believe me he already knows so much about twenty years ago. I know he looks thoroughly disreputable, but I promise that you won't be sorry for his input on your problem."

She nodded her head in acquiescence, but with reluctance if he was the disgusting tramp she had noticed outside earlier. He'd had a beer can in his hand, and was sucking on a small cheroot as if his life depended on it. Didn't look as if he'd had a shave or shower since God knew when, and a change of clothes even longer.

He shuffled into the office, with a big grin for Marcus. "Watch'a want pretty boy, 'cos I am just about functioning this morning." He winked with a smirk. "Heavy duty last night with that stripper from that dive on Station Street."

"We really don't need to know that, Gerry." Marcus indicated Mia, as if Gerry hadn't noticed her, but Gerry never missed a solitary thing.

"Sorry ma-am, didn't mean any offence." His voice was a gravel pit, because of the strong cheroot he smoked. "Now, what can I do for this pretty lady?" When he spoke he almost coughed up a lung.

Marcus indicated to Mia if it was OK to show Gerry the contents of the envelope. Hesitantly she nodded her head, not really sure if this decrepit individual would be any help in finding out what happened to her precious mother.

Quickly he scanned the papers after sitting down in the only other chair in the room. Mia visibly screwed up her face, the ghastly man stank to high heaven. She wasn't used to any man smelling so disgusting, and being so close to her, She watched him stop reading, then rub his forehead as if he had a headache, which was probably a hangover from being drunk last night.

Suddenly he seemed to be perfectly normal, as swear words flew out of his mouth. "Fuck – fuck – fuck me! I fuckin' knew it! I knew that baby was Madeline's child. It was such a strong rumour that she'd had a baby. But everyone thought the President was the father, and didn't dare put a voice to the rumour, because people were going missing, right, left and centre." He looked straight at Mia. "Where the fuck have you been for twenty years? Nobody could find you, and believe me we looked just about everywhere that was a possibility."

Mia found her voice, even though she was still not sure about this revolting man. "In Houston with my biological father, and half sisters, and half brother, but a few days ago I found that envelope in my papa's desk, and realised who I am. My father had lied to me for twenty years, so I left Houston and came here to find out what really happened to my real mother."

"Please sweetheart, *please* go home, and forget what you came to do. I cannot say that more urgently, it – is – too – dangerous, to raise your pretty little head above the parapet." He gestured to Marcus. "Tell her Marcus, what will happen to her if she pursues this horrendous secret."

But Marcus wasn't going to explain, it was down to Gerry. "You were there in the front line all that time ago, I was just a kid."

Can I have a smoke? Pretty please, Marcus." He was coughing his lungs up, because he needed nicotine badly. It was obvious to Mia that he was upset and angry at what he had read. This was all giving her a weird feeling in her gut, and her gut was rarely wrong.

"Absolutely not in this office, you can surely wait until we are finished, and for crissake take a shower you stink, my friend." Marcus physically shuddered, he was always immaculate in his clothes and hygiene.

"Fuck you, Marcus Medina. The perfect male with a stick up his ass. You know how much I hate walking around looking like this, and smelling like horse manure. But I am in deep undercover for the DEA, trying to track down you know who, and I'm sure I don't have to tell you who that is. The big drug boss that we have been trying to nail for years, but for some unknown reason still manages to evade capture."

"Excuse me gentlemen, remember me, with the huge problem here?" Mia raised her voice to make the men take notice of her. She was getting royally pissed off with both of them. They were getting nowhere with their obvious animosity towards each other.

"Listen to me carefully, sweetheart. I am not going to repeat myself, because walls have ears, and this conversation stays in this room." He glared at Mia. "If you want the three of us to go missing?" When she visibly moved backwards in her chair, he repeated himself. "And I have no doubt that we will, but Marcus already knows all this, because we have discussed it before, right Marcus?"

Marcus was looking decidedly worried for Mia, not for Gerry or himself, they were grown men and hopefully could look after themselves, but she was so tiny and naive.

"I need you to seriously promise me Mia, that you will listen to what Gerry has to say, and do as he advises you." He scooted round in his chair and held her hand, she was starting to look sick with worry. She in turn gripped his hand tightly and just nodded her head, and whispered, "I promise I will."

"Twenty years ago I was the lead detective in LAPD, and the fallout from Madeline's death was huge. We honestly tried to find out what had really happened, as it didn't sit right in any of our guts that she had accidently overdosed. But every which way we turned we were stonewalled, not by just anyone, but from the top, the President himself. We were all threatened and our families, that if we didn't stop looking and interviewing people we believed were some way involved, we would all end up in a back alley somewhere not breathing. Madeline's two security men who never left her side, and she truly trusted them, were never seen again. Then came the rumour that you were the President's child, and you seemed to vanish off the face of the planet." His raspy, gruff voice faltered, and he gave out the most horrendous cough, which rattled his chest.

Mia seemed to crumble into the armchair and began to sob as if her heart was breaking. She had come so far to be stopped in her tracks. Where did she go from here?

"So you can see, sweetheart, that you can never, ever, tell anyone who you really are, who your real mother is. Let everyone think that our dear Mel is your mother, and you have come home at last." He watched Mia crumble, but didn't stop. "Please let Madeline rest in peace. She knew that you were her beloved child, and so did Mel, and so do you, now. Marcus and I will always keep your secret, if *you* don't, you won't live to tell the full story." He then gave another horrendous coughing fit.

Marcus took her in his arms to consol her, rubbing her back and rocking her in his arms. He could see and hear she was in total meltdown, and couldn't blame her, because this was all about her precious mother. This he could totally understand, because he had a fantastic, precious mother, who he adored.

He looked over Mia's shoulder and Gerry was staring at him as if he had lost the plot. He mouthed, "What are you doing? She is a client? Yes! A very beautiful client, but it is not on, Marcus."

Marcus ignored him, but knew he had to let her go, because he definitely had feelings for this courageous young woman. But he was older than her, probably ten years older. He was pretty certain she was an innocent, because she couldn't look him straight in the eye, but got all flustered and hot if she did. She was also prickly and hot tempered, and if he managed to get involved with her, she would have him running up his own ass trying to keep up with her.

Would she be worth all that trouble?

You bet your sweet life she would!

All this was hindsight, because however much he wanted her, it was never going to happen, not in a million years, or even in their future.

He pulled away and gave her a pristine white handkerchief. Immediately, she stopped the tears, blew her leaking nose, and straightened her spine. That's when Marcus knew that she was made of sterner stuff than he had first thought.

Mia closed her big brown eyes and took a deep calming breath. "I am *so* sorry, I am not usually so emotional, but I gave up my family in Houston to come to L.A. to find out what really happened to my mother. Instead, I find that my Aunt who I have never met, died four weeks ago. I now have a wonderful uncle and twin cousins." She gave a loud sniff and wiped her runny nose again. "And now that – that man," she pointed to Gerry, "tells me that my mom was probably murdered, and I could have the same fate if I try to find out why, or how."

Again Marcus sat next to her on the arm of her chair, he hated to see her so upset. But not Gerry, he was a worn out ex-cop with a hardened heart against the criminal world and beyond. Marcus was worried what Gerry was going to say next, and he wasn't wrong.

"Look Mia, I am only trying to save you a great deal of grief. Your past isn't for the faint heart and weary. Your Mom was a woman who fucked too many high octane men, and was getting into more trouble than she could handle. She drank too much. She was addicted to heavy drugs, and because of that began to gossip about what was said between the sheets in her over-used bed. She was living on the edge, and it all came to a nasty end, that Godforsaken night."

Marcus put his arm around Mia trying to give her his strength, and she leant into that male strength. But he could still feel the sobs deep within her slim body. He could also sense the anger building in her, and feared a volcano was about to erupt. She was definitely holding on to a wicked temper.

Gerry ran a dirty hand over his lined, weary face, he knew the only way to stop this naive young woman from disappearing was to be utterly cruel. "Then the rumours were also circulating that you were the President's daughter, which we now know was not true. But rumours and gossip stick, and your aunt wasn't stupid or naive, she evidently took you to your father in secret, and you just seemed to disappear. I strongly believe that you would have ended up dead as well.

"I'm sorry sweetheart, but you really need to mend bridges and go back home to be with your family, before anyone else finds out who you really are." He looked towards Marcus, but no answer was forthcoming. "So far only Roberto, Marcus, and I know, and that is three too many. *Please* – go home, and forget that you were here. Then all of us here can sleep peacefully in our beds, trying not to worry about you." He glared at his friend, knowing something was going on between Mia and Marcus. He had never seen Marcus interested in another woman for years, and that alone terrified the life out of him. Because Marcus had family ties to the underbelly of L.A., and it was the underbelly that the DEA were trying to bring down, with his help.

Slowly, Mia disentangled herself from Marcus, went over to the disgusting, vile man, and with all her strength slapped him around the face, which jerked him back in his chair. Gerry flexed his jaw, because that had really hurt, his face, and his pride. Mia had a mean whack in such a tiny body, and he started to really admire Madeline's daughter, which of course Madeline had never been a pushover, with a violent temper when provoked.

"That's for talking about my Mom like that. You are a disgusting piece of crap, and I realise that you are trying to scare me off, and yes, it worked. But I will still try to find out what happened to her, she deserves that from me, her only child. My Mom was the world's favourite Movie Star, and deserves more respect from the likes of you, even though she has been dead for twenty years."

She turned to Marcus, who was trying not to grin, because the infamous Gerry had been brought down a peg or two. "Thank you Marcus, for helping me, and please draw up the papers for my uncle and the children to stay in my Mom's home, until he marries or dies. I do not need that property, and probably never will."

She put up her hands to stop him when he went to argue with her, because that property was worth millions, and it was legally hers. "My Aunt saved my life twenty years ago, and there is no way I will put her family out on the street. And yes, I do know, that Roberto isn't poverty struck and can afford to move, but the twins have their school and friends in that neighbourhood, and I won't spoil that for them."

She glared at the older man, and said strongly and clearly, "I cannot go back home to my so-called family, because I said terrible things to them, especially my father, who I love dearly. So I am stuck here, without a job, and somewhere to live." There was no way she was going to put herself on her uncle's good will and take advantage.

Anyway, she had grown up this weekend, and needed to start looking out for herself. Today was the beginning of the rest of her life in the real world, without her papa looking out for her.

Immediately Marcus went behind his desk, because he needed to know that she would be safe in an area that could be dangerous. He wrote on the back of a small card and gave it to Mia. "That is my personal cell number, and I know the owner of the Excelsior Hotel on Sunset Boulevard. They are always on the lookout for trustworthy, honest staff." He gave her a derisory look, because the outfit she was wearing would have to go, that hotel was prestigious and so were its staff. "Can you wait tables? Can you tend bar? Or perhaps house keep? Any, or all three?" In truth she had an attitude that could run the entire country, and he so wanted to get to know her better, much better in fact.

Especially deep inside her!

She grinned that wide encompassing smile for the first time in an hour, especially for Marcus. "Yep, I can do all three. My papa didn't bring up a lazy child, just a difficult one. I have always earned the money he generously gave me every week." She held out her hand to Marcus, and thanked him for looking after her so well. Mia knew she would always be able to ask him for help if she was in trouble. Marcus Medina was definitely one of the good guys. As was her new found uncle Roberto.

"As for you Mr Gerry Swane, you can go fuck yourself. And, don't ever let me hear you speak my mom's name, ever again."

He grinned and winked at her, making him appear much younger than she had thought before. "No ma-am! I'm not that stupid." He rubbed his sore jaw again, "for such a cute, tiny female, you sure pack a punch." He opened the door for her, "Can I offer you a lift Mia? Wherever you are going."

She picked up her backpack, and wrinkled her cute little nose. "Fuck off! You stink! I'd rather ride with a skunk than you. I'll get a cab, thank you."

Gerry looked back to Marcus, who was openly laughing. "See I told you, when I'm working deep undercover I can't get a decent woman, can't get laid, even though my balls hurt. They honestly prefer a skunk to me. It just ain't fair. I've gotta give up this way of life, retire to Florida, and become a beach bum." He almost entirely inhaled the whole cheroot as he lit it going out of the door. He was desperate for a nicotine fix. Emotional women did his brain in, as far as he was concerned, women should stay in bed, open their legs, and shut the fuck up.

Still laughing Marcus shook his head, as if his friend would ever retire, he would rather step in front of a loaded gun, because what would he do all day? Gerry had never married, never stayed in a relationship long enough to fall in love. Didn't have any family to speak of, or even remembered, but if you were in trouble, he was a diamond, always there for his friends. And, Marcus knew he was definitely one of those friends. He could guarantee that Gerry would somehow keep an eye out for Mia, because he knew that she would be a magnet for trouble to come.

That was a huge worry for Marcus, that some evil bastard would get hold of her for his own pleasure. He had

Kirby, Never Look Back

fallen in love with a doe-eyed, blonde, tiny, fiery female, who was stubborn, difficult, and didn't take any crap from anyone, which was *so* dangerous in Los Angeles.

But, was absolutely, unbelievably gorgeous!

And, he truly didn't know what to do about it!

CHAPTER SIX

"I am so sorry Ms," he looked at the card she had given him, "Maxwell. But we are fully staffed at the moment." The manager of The Excelsior would love to give this gorgeous young woman a job, but his boss Mr Santi the owner, would get rid of him if he over-staffed.

Walter Lewis liked his job, and his next breath, so he never did anything to aggravate Mr Santi.

"Honestly, I will do anything, because I am desperate. I am living at The Sea Shore Motel, and need full-time work with accommodation. Please, will you get in touch with me if anything turns up?" Mia had tried at other hotels, but college students were all on Spring Break, and had taken up any spare work. Now, she was getting desperate because her money wouldn't last much longer. There was no way that she was going to crawl back to Houston and her other family.

Her steel backbone was starting to get on her nerves, and she wished she was one of those females who could cling to someone, anyone, to take care of her. Mia shuddered at the very thought to be that fragile and pathetic in her life.

"Look Ms Maxwell, I am really busy and need to get on with my work, evenings are always on the run. I promise to get in touch if anything turns up." He pointed out the bar and lounge close to the ornate front glass doors. "Just tell them that I've told you to have a drink and sandwich on us. You've come quite a journey to get to us, and I don't want you going back hungry. Thank you for thinking of us, and for Marcus Medina introducing you, he is very important to us here at The Excelsior."

He reminded her to come back one evening to have a drink with him, which was never going to happen. Mia was absolutely sick of the male species with their ever needy dicks, and endless propositions.

"Thank you Mr Lewis, I will take you up on the offer of a drink and sandwich." She gave him a withering look. "But nothing else thank you." She gritted her teeth and shook his hand, and as usual he held her hand a tad too long. She needed a job, but not a tumble in bed, and certainly didn't fancy him. He had too much lacquer on his rearranged hair, and far too much aftershave, which was decidedly yucky where she was concerned.

The Steinway Baby Grand was sitting all alone and lonely in the corner of the sumptuous lounge, just begging to be played, and Mia was the woman to accommodate that beautiful piece of machinery. She had finished an excellent sandwich and coffee and was leaving after chatting to Joe the bar-keep when she turned and saw it. Her heart leapt in her chest and she couldn't stop herself from walking over to sit on the stool.

Her dearest Papa had once said to her when she begged to have a piano like this, that if she behaved for twenty years he would buy her one.

Well! He knew that was never going to happen! An instrument as fine as this didn't give any change on a hundred grand, even her Papa wasn't that well off.

The lounge was extremely busy with well-heeled patrons, but that didn't bother Mia one iota. When she played she was in a world of her own. A world connected to her father, and she most definitely had his DNA.

She took off her ankle length boots and began to play, immediately the room dropped into a complete silence. Closing her eyes, she could see and hear her dearest Papa playing the blues, so that was what her fingers wanted to play, and didn't stop. It was far too long since she had last used the gift given to her by her amazing Papa.

Then there was a great deal of noise coming out of the entrance to the hotel, and everyone started to talk once again.

"Good evening Mr Santi, sir. Wonderful to see you again." The manager almost fell over his feet to welcome the owner of The Excelsior. He wasn't stupid, because Anton Santi was surrounded by four extremely menacing looking security men, with shoulder holsters, and hard eyes, that took in everything around them, and beyond. Their boss was precious to them, and they were highly paid to protect and keep him safe.

They also preferred to be alive, and not be eliminated.

Anton Santi nodded to the cretin who was the manager of his hotel at the moment. He never made himself available, or was friendly to his staff. They worked, he paid them, and that was it, as far as he was concerned. But suddenly he stopped, almost causing chaos in his retinue. "Who the fuck is playing that piano?"

"I am so sorry Mr Santi, but it's a young woman who came for live in work, and – and I truly never gave her permission to play the piano in the lounge." He was visibly shaking in his shoes. His boss had never stopped before to have a conversation with him, he could lose his job over this. "I will get her removed, sir, immediately. I cannot apologise enough, sir."

"Don't be fuckin' ridiculous. She is amazing, and will be a huge draw for that bar and lounge. Sign her up. Give her whatever she wants, before our competition finds her. Give her a room, and feed her. Sort out her hours, preferably late at night. She can work for tips, not wages. She will earn a fortune from those fuckin' idiots with too much money to waste." With a grimace he gave his manager the once over. "What are you waiting for? Get in there and give her the good news. Next time I come in I will expect to hear her playing, and when I have a spare moment I will introduce myself." He grinned at his four goons. "And I sincerely hope for your sake Mr Lewis, that she looks as good as she plays that piano, because I don't need to waste my precious time on a female who will turn my stomach."

Anton Santi didn't wait for an answer, because time was money, and standing still didn't make money. He began to move as one with his four henchmen towards the private lift that went straight to his penthouse. It was where his illegal activities were organised. He was the head of everything that was illegal in Los Angeles and beyond.

He was an unabashed racketeer, and proud of it.

Drugs – guns – booze, everything moved through his empire, but never women. Santi never touched prostitution, or slave labour, as his father before him had done, but now he was head of the evil empire, and never touched women or children. Paedophiles made him sick, and his Italian blood boil. He would kill every one of the perverted bastards if it was possible, and he was seriously doing his best on that pledge.

To say he enjoyed his fame, was an understatement. Anton Santi was twenty-eight years old, short and stocky. Had the face of a fallen angel, and was exceptionally good looking.

He was tough, very tough. Some people called him a psychotic killer, but never lived long enough to repeat that. His long, black, straight hair fell to his shoulders, and his olive skin looked soft and unlined, on a face that rarely smiled, because being truly lawless without a conscience was seriously exhausting.

And he was nobody's fool! Always immaculately dressed in Armani. Nobody ever saw him untidy or unshaven, in fact was considered to be OCD. Santi was street smart.

But someone was snapping at his heels just waiting for him to make a bad mistake. Of course the Agencies were always after him, but this was an excellent under-cover individual, who never let up. The DEA – FBI, and LAPD, they weren't as clever as Anton Santi. His father had always outwitted them, and so would he. Money talked, and he had good people in high places looking out for him. He had money to burn, and it would never dry up. Money made money, he was making it faster than he could spend it. It was rumoured that Anton Santi had spent his entire life so far, trying to please his now sick father Theo Santi, and make him proud of his nefarious lifestyle.

But many believed, but wouldn't dare vocalise, that Theo Santi was a total madman, and his son was at the top of the manure heap right now.

But for how long would he stay in excellent health?

After a week of playing through midnight Mia came to the conclusion that she wanted to go home. Had to apologise to her dear parents, because she had come to L.A. on a fool's quest.

Her precious mom Madeline needed to rest in peace, and didn't need her reckless daughter raking through the mud of Madeline's chaotic life.

Home to Houston, where she truly belonged, but leaving Marcus Medina behind, knowing she would now never marry and have his children. If she couldn't have Marcus she didn't want anyone.

But she needed to stay another few weeks, because she was earning a fortune in tips, sometimes five hundred dollars a night. The patronage of The Excelsior was only for the rich and famous.

There was a particular guy who came in every evening, with a dazzling array of gorgeous women on his arm. A Television star, or a Movie actress, or a well known Model, and he wasn't short on good looks himself, and was always dressed in casual designer. If he hadn't been too old for her Mia might have been persuaded to be interested in him. And, he always left her a substantial tip, a hundred dollar bill.

But, last night she had almost fallen off her stool, when he stopped to speak to her. "Hi gorgeous girl, you play like an angel, and look like one. I cannot believe that you are so amazingly talented." As he went to amble back to his stunning girlfriend, Mia flashed him one of her brilliant smiles. "Thank you so much, you are exceptionally kind, and generous."

He stopped and turned back to her. "I'm not such a stinking possum, or skunk, am I? Oh! And by the way Marcus sends his love." He grinned back, his shaggy blond hair flopping over his tanned forehead, and deep blue eyes twinkling with humour. He jangled his change in his pocket. "These evenings have been all down to him, the besotted idiot. But then he is a millionaire in his own right, so who was I to argue?"

Quickly, Mia got up to stop him leaving. "How is he? Is he still in L.A.? Is he really paying you to look out for me? Has he got children? Do you think I could ever be someone serious in his life?"

Mia hated to beg, or ask anyone a favour, but she had fallen deeply in love with Marcus the moment she had met him, knowing it was ridiculously futile.

Gerry patted her arm, he did feel so sorry for her. Knowing Marcus as he did, he knew that he would never leave his family for her. He was a man of high principals, and moral standards, because his other family connections left him no choice.

"Sweetheart, please don't waste your time on ifs and buts. He is in Fort Worth with his family now. Yes, he has paid me to look out for you when I'm not working under-cover. Yes, he has two boys who he absolutely dotes on. Whether you will be in his life in the future is entirely up to him." He shook his unruly mop of blond hair, and gave out that awful cough she had heard before. "Remember, this is only my opinion, however much it hurts, and I'm trying to be truthful here. Marcus ain't ever going to leave his family for another woman."

Gerry couldn't help himself, because he really had a soft spot for this incredible young woman, so he put his arms around her when he saw a lone tear drop down her cheek.

He could only wish he was at least twenty years younger, because Marcus wouldn't have stood a chance against him. Against his bachelor principles, he would have married her, wrapped her in cotton wool, kept her in his bed, pregnant. To keep her safe from the wicked world of psychotic killers like Anton Santi.

He held her at arms' length, and whispered, "I'm afraid this is it tonight, babe. I am back deep undercover." He gave her a mischievous wink. "Gotta' go now to keep my lady friend happy tonight, 'cos it might be a while before I get any relief, as they say." He kissed her small hand. "Behave while I'm away, I will get in touch as soon as I can. And, you really can rely on Marcus if you have any problems working here. You know that he is an honourable man, especially to his friends."

Gerry returned to his table in the dark corner to the beautiful woman patiently waiting for him. Not really understanding why he had a really bad feeling about Mia, which was ridiculous because he knew that this hotel had top-notch security. Santi was a very careful owner.

He shrugged the feeling off, as being utterly ridiculous. He needed all his energy and concentration on keeping his date for the entire night, sexually satisfied, and begging for more.

And, he was so the right man for that job!

Sexual satisfaction and begging for more, was definitely in his job description. Personally, he knew he did his best work in bed, but that was for his sexual partners to extol his virtues.

CHAPTER SEVEN

After Gerry had left Mia could have kicked her own backside. Why? Why had she asked if Marcus had any children, of course he had, and most definitely as gorgeous as their father. But, she hadn't had the balls to ask about his wife. She had just been too scared to know who he was married to. Probably a vision of loveliness. A tall fabulous model, with long dark hair, legs to die for, and skinny as a beanpole, and of course big boobs, man made.

So why on God's-earth would he be interested in Mia Madeline Maxwell from good ol' Houston? A blonde midget, a bit on the chunky side, with non-existent breasts. Unfortunately, she loved donuts, burgers and fries, and couldn't see that changing any time soon. So her situation was a no-brainer. She was never going to see Marcus again.

She was sitting with her favourite young waiter, Cameron, in the empty, very sumptuous restaurant. He finished his shift past midnight, and always waited for Mia to finish around two a.m., so they could eat an early breakfast together. The kitchen at The Excelsior was open 24/7, which allowed the late shift to have a meal.

Mia knew that Cameron had the hots for her, but she never encouraged him, and made it plainly obvious that she was only interested in friendship with him. So friendship it was. Often when he cleared up his station he took his guitar and played with Mia, which she loved, and admired him for it. She was a musician's daughter, and loved to have someone accompanying her.

Cameron was a student at the local college for Drama and the Arts. Sometimes he would ask her if he could sleep on the small couch in her room, when he was too tired to walk back to his dorm' accommodation. It was seriously against the rules of the hotel, but Mia never adhered to rules and regulations.

At the back of the sprawling hotel was a one story building that resembled a motel, and that was where all the live in staff were housed. It was clean, no frills, but comfortable, and Mia was extremely happy to have accommodation that was safe and free, in a city like L.A. But was still determined to go back home to Houston in a couple of weeks.

There was nothing here for her in L.A., but heartache and loneliness.

But through the grapevine there was a rumour that was making her very jittery. Mr Lewis the manager had just cornered her in the restaurant and informed her that Mr Santi was expected to actually visit the bar-lounge the next night to listen to her play. It was news that had astounded the rest of the staff, because The Boss never fraternised with his employees. So it was big news that he wanted to meet Mia the piano player extraordinaire.

But Mia just laughed at the rumour, not expecting it to happen anyway, because rumours were rife amongst the staff, and normally untrue, and never affected her cloistered life at the moment.

She didn't get to bed before three a.m. Didn't get up until midday, then often went to the local park with a sandwich and soda to sit in the sun and relax. Just to sit in her own peace and quiet, and shut out the constant noise and chatter of people and their kids playing. She listened to the birds calling out to each other, and the rhythmic water cascading over the nearby fountain. It was Manna to her soul.

In truth this life-style suited Mia. She had never liked getting up early, much to her family's dismay, they all got up with the Lark, she was definitely a Nightingale. A Cuckoo in a strange nest. She had fantastic food whenever she wanted it, and clean, comfortable accommodation. Mr Santi definitely looked after his staff, and nobody bad mouthed him, but that could be because they treasured their jobs, and their lives.

But Mia was truly happy playing that amazing piece of machinery, and would *so* miss it when she left. And leave she would within the next week, because Marcus Medina was never going to be in her bed, and had probably forgotten all about her.

But, she would never forget him, not in a million years. It had taken just one moment to fall in love with him, but would take a life-time to fall out of love, if that were possible. Her gut told her that they had been together in another time, another place, and they would once again be together in the future. Whenever that future happened.

Because she knew his body. Knew his taste. Knew that they had loved each other many times, in many lives. And, would continue to do so forever.

Her Papa had often said that she was different, magical, even psychic. And, her Papa was never wrong as far as she was concerned. Mia always knew when something bad was going to happen to her. But when Marcus had held her hand, and didn't want to let go, she had known immediately he was going to be someone in her life she could rely on, and always love.

It was Sunday night, close to midnight. So far the enigma that was Anton Santi hadn't appeared, and that had been no surprise to Mia. The restaurant was closed, and she was getting close to the end of her shift. She began to play her favourite music, New Orleans blues, which always made her sad, because she was desperate to get back to her beloved Papa.

Suddenly a chair appeared next to her stool. She turned her head to remonstrate with the intruder, but the words stuck in her throat. She looked into the amazing coloured eyes of the most beautiful male she had ever seen, and he was grinning directly at her, obviously waiting for her anger at his intrusion. But she had forgotten to breathe, and stopped playing.

"Please don't stop on my account, beautiful Mia. May I call you Mia?" He took her small hand in his and kissed it with reverence. "If I close my eyes I think I am back in New Orleans in a small jazz club in the back streets, where an amazing musician played exactly like you." He frowned for a second. "I believe he owned the club."

"That was my Papa Henri Arnaud. And yes, he does still own that bar and jazz club. And yes, he is an amazing talented all round musician. And yes, I absolutely adore him, because he is the very best Papa, ever."

"I absolutely agree with you, even though you are his daughter, because genes will always come out. My father and I lived in New Orleans for quite a few years, and he often took me to your father's club, where I began to appreciate excellent music, and excellent beer."

"Excuse me, but I'm not allowed to fraternise with patrons. I could lose my job, and I really love playing this beautiful piano, and love working here. So, please take your chair with you, as I need to get back to work."

"I'm so sorry Mia, I haven't introduced myself. I was so taken aback by your beauty, and your exquisite mastery of the piano, I completely forgot my good manners." Again he smiled, and took her hand and held it gently. "For my sins, I am your boss Anton Santi, so there is no chance of you losing your job, in fact quite the opposite."

Oh shit! Of course he was! She was such a stupid bitch, and more often than not. She had been told he was absolutely gorgeous, and that had been an understatement. He obviously wore very expensive Italian suits, and silk shirts, but never jewellery. And there he was just as Cameron had told her. His eyes were the colour of the ocean, a mixture of blue and green, she had seen those eyes before, but couldn't remember where.

Mia had never met this man before, but somehow he was familiar to her, but she couldn't quite put her finger on it. She had never met any male as exotically gorgeous as Anton Santi, only Marcus, and he looked nothing like this mobster. She had to admit to being sort of excited to be in his company, because he exuded edginess and danger, both qualities she had come to L.A. to find for herself.

God only knew how she was going to be able to settle back down in boring Houston in a few days time.

"No! I'm sorry Mr Santi, I should have realised who you were, even though we've never met before. Trust me to put my size 4 foot in my mouth, before my brain catches up. But, I really do have to get back to work now." She saw Cameron come into the lounge with his guitar under his arm, but he stopped as soon as he saw his boss sitting next to Mia. She shook her head, not wanting him to get into any trouble because of her. Cameron needed this job desperately to be able to complete his studies at college.

Anton noticed the exchange, nothing got past the highly observant man, he called Cameron over. "Not tonight Cameron. I've been reliably informed that you often accompany Ms Maxwell when you finish your shift. I sincerely thank you for staying with her late at night. But, she is dining with me in the restaurant, shortly. So from now on I need you to go back to your own digs to sleep alone, Cameron. Thank you." He smiled with his mouth, but not his eyes, which were coldly fixated on the young man. His head moved slightly to indicate his four security men, who were very alert, sitting at a table behind him. "Do you understand exactly what I am saying?"

Cameron looked decidedly uncomfortable, and didn't hesitate in answering. "Night Mia, see you around, sometime. It was great while it lasted." He gave her a smile and a wink. "Be careful what you wish for my dearest friend." Cameron wasn't stupid, Santi was staking his claim, and the younger guy knew his place in life, and it wasn't to argue with the likes of Santi and his hoodlums. He turned and walked out of Mia's life, because he kinda liked his face as it was, and didn't want it rearranged.

Mia spluttered on an expletive. "Excuse me, Mr Santi, but Cameron is my friend, and we don't sleep together, whatever your informant told you, and you have no right to talk to him like that." Cam might be desperate for work, but she definitely wasn't. He might be her boss at the moment, but no man was going to tell her what she could do, or couldn't. There wasn't a man living who had that sway over her life.

"I'm sorry Mia, but it isn't safe in L.A. for a young, unattached, beautiful woman, as you are, to not have someone looking out for her." Santi looked at her with an appreciative expression. "So I Anton Santi, have decided to be your very exclusive security, and I will not take *no* for an answer. What's mine is mine exclusively. I never share with anyone, and everyone in this city knows that. Now come, we will have a late dinner in my restaurant, and you can tell me why you are in town all alone." Patiently he waited for her to put on her white and gold platform sneakers, and follow him into the ornate restaurant. He thought he had won the argument, but she was seething.

And of course his four extremely large and lethal looking security guys silently followed them. Mia not realising in the days to come she would have to get used to always being watched and scrutinised thoroughly.

But Mia wasn't having any of his crap, and was swearing up a storm under her breath:-

"Fuckin' cheek, who the fuck does he think he is? Just because he owns the fuckin' hotel, he doesn't own me. I'll make him sorry he ever thought he could tell me what to do. I'm not frightened of you Mr Fuckin' Santi."

Her mouth set and her eyes narrowed as she made a decision that she was getting out of Los Angeles ASAP. Preferably tomorrow. Sooner the better. No cheap, slick, mobster was going to take over her life. Her Papa and family were looking better and better every minute, and boring and the past were going to be her new mantra.

CHAPTER EIGHT

Mia followed Mr High and Mighty Santi into the empty restaurant, and was still seething. She intended to ignore him, and make him understand that Mia Maxwell was not easy or amicable to being taken over. Nor would she allow him to tell her what she could or couldn't do.

But over the next three hours everything altered, she completely changed her mind about the so-called mobster. Anton was articulate, knowledgeable, intelligent, and a thorough gentleman. And, was surprised that she really liked him.

They had so much in common. He had asked her where her parents were. She replied that her mother had died when she was two years old, and her papa lived with her stepmother in Houston. Anton empathised with that, as he hadn't seen his mother since he was four years old, and now didn't want to. He had been raised by his beloved Papa on his own.

He was a non-drinker, so was Mia.

He was a non-smoker, drugs or otherwise, so was Mia.

They both adored and revered their fathers.

Personally he was trying to save the planet, ecologically, something Mia had been preaching all her young life.

Their meeting was definitely spooky, and a meant.

But, even with all these things in parallel, especially hero-worshipping their fathers, they were chalk and cheese. Mia couldn't understand why this dangerous man was taking the time to notice her. She was a total train wreck. Santi was elegant, expensively dressed, obviously worldly, and so ridiculously gorgeous. While she was dressed like a manic psychopath, was still naive, and innocent, and honestly couldn't see how that was going to change anytime soon.

But, occasionally his green/blue eyes turned cold and soulless, and that seriously worried her.

She knew that he hated her clothes, and Mia hated anyone criticising her dress sense, because she loved to be different from her peers.

"Mia sweetheart, you are stunningly beautiful, but your choice of clothes and their colour is abysmal." He wrinkled his nose as if they actually smelt bad. That really pissed her off, because she might be flamboyant, but was scrupulously clean, in fact borderline OCD. She showered and changed her underwear and clothes at least three times a day. "You are wearing yellow pants, a bright orange see through blouse, and a ghastly neon pink cardigan. You look as if you have been dressed by a charity shop. I need sunglasses on to be able to look at you." He slapped his hand on the tablecloth, his eyes changing to that cold soulless look. "You make any red-bloodied male want to lick you all over like a Popsicle. I will not allow other bastards to think about you like that.

"You are with us now," he included the four tough looking guys behind them, who nodded in agreement. "And, we need to get you to a designer boutique for a complete make-over and wardrobe. Under my direction and finance of course."

This was a step too far for independent and obstinate Mia Maxwell. "I like the way I dress. I love the way I look. I have always tried hard to be different, and without your interference Mr Santi. Nobody! But nobody has the right to make me a dressed up doll." Mia wanted to stamp her foot in indignation. It was *so* not going to happen to Mia Madeleine Maxwell.

Anton smiled indulgently, he loved it when anyone tried to go against his wishes. If it was a male, he lived to regret it. Any female he could sweet talk her around. And Mia wouldn't stand a chance when he turned his charm on her.

"Please Mia, would you consider visiting my home in Beverley Hills to meet my ailing father, who is extremely sick. In fact is dying, and I want him to believe that you are my beautiful partner, and willing to marry me." He took her hand across the table and gently caressed it. "Would you do that for me, sweetheart? To please a very sick man who wants to see his son, happily married with a family."

Mia thought she saw tears in his expressive eyes. Nah! Not Anton Santi, that wasn't possible. But her big, soft heart couldn't turn him down, especially for his sick father, as it was plainly obvious that he absolutely adored his father who was dying. She would do it for her own father in a heartbeat.

Anyway it was all make believe, so no harm done. And, she could stay in L.A. for a couple of extra days before going home to Houston.

That was the moment when Mia began to realise that Anton Santi wasn't all that he seemed. She really started to like him and wanted to get to know him better. Even though he seemed controlling, and possibly possessive. But, that wasn't going to be her problem.

Santi turned and called over a really big guy. "This is Larry my Chief of Security, and he is going to be looking out for you." He clicked his fingers at Larry. "Give Mia your personal cell number, she needs to be able to contact you day or night. This young lady means a great deal to me, and from now on her safety is your priority." Larry nodded his shaved head and smiled at Mia. His boss was always taken seriously, and Larry never forgot that.

But, this was just too much for Mia to take on board, she was a free spirit, and said loudly "Excuse me, but I always speak for myself. So back off Mr Santi, otherwise the visit is off, and I am not going to change my clothes for any man, and that includes you."

Santi completely ignored her histrionics, and spoke to his Chief of Security. "Larry please pick up Ms Maxwell tomorrow morning, and escort her to Madame Silva's in the main plaza, and make sure she spends a small fortune, on anything she wants, and that I would approve of."

Larry answered in as few words as possible. "Yes sir. No problem sir. It will be my pleasure." He moved back to his table scowling, like the other guys at the table he detested going anywhere near female fripperies, and waiting impatiently while they constantly changed their idiot minds.

The three other testosterone filled guys were grinning like mad. So relieved their boss hadn't picked them, they would rather stick pins in their eyes than trail after that little bimbo 24/7.

Santi wasn't stupid, he knew he still had to convince Mia that she was safe with him, and always would be. He bent closer to speak quietly to her. "Mia sweetheart, I will never hurt you. I have never hurt a woman. I know what you must have heard about me, but I have *never* killed anyone, unless they deserved to be removed from this life. If they hurt babies or children, and were totally immoral, or evil. Paedophiles and slave traders make me sick to my stomach, and need to be eradicated. I am the man for the job, make no mistake."

From the expression on his face Mia could see that he was totally serious, and would without a doubt get rid of anyone who broke his code. She admired him immensely for that code, even though he was the underbelly of L.A.

Then he looked at the pure gold Rolex on his wrist. "I apologise but I have to leave you. I have a very important meeting in the penthouse here. There are always many factions trying to take away, that which my father almost lost his life to attain." He called Larry over. "Walk Ms Maxwell back to her accommodation please Larry, and make sure she is secure. Then come straight back to the penthouse, we are going to need all the muscle we have tonight. All these factions need to understand without a doubt that we mean business."

Mia watched all this going on, and couldn't believe she was involved with this outrageous insanity. What would her beloved Papa think?

He would say it was all her fault, and she was getting into something far over her head without even trying.

And, as usual he would be absolutely correct!

CHAPTER NINE

Mia grinned all the way to the Goodwill Charity Store a couple of blocks from the hotel. She had got one up on Larry and Anton Santi, by leaving her room early as possible. She'd only had a few hours sleep, but was determined to go out on her own to her favourite store. Yes, she needed some different clothes and footwear, but there was no way Mr know-all Santi was paying for them, because she always paid her way, and would not be beholden to any man, however rich or gorgeous he was.

Again she bought the most outrageous clothes and as casual shoes as possible. Whoever had given these things to charity, were her size, which was tiny, and had the same eclectic taste, and of course were probably colour blind, as was Mia.

Then she went to her usual place in the park, after eating breakfast at a chic coffee shop, which of course was a donut supremo. Three specialist donuts and a black coffee loaded with sugar, and Mia could take on the world.

And, that included brawny Larry and his boss. She could only imagine Larry's expression when he found her room empty with the note she had left him.

Sorry couldn't wait for you. Gone to buy some new togs etc. at the Goodwill Store, which I'm sure your boss will love. Won't be back 'til late, so don't wait up for me. You can find me at work later tonight. Sincerely hope Mr Santi isn't too angry, because you missed me. He really shouldn't underestimate little ol' Mia, 'cos she's as slippery as the proverbial greased pole.

Yours very *sincerely, Mia Madeline Maxwell. xx*

"I'm sorry Boss, but she was gone by the time I got there around ten a.m. I have searched everywhere for her, but she has just disappeared, and no one has seen her. She isn't answering her phone." He needed to placate Santi, as he had woken him up after just a few hours sleep, to give him the news of Mia's disappearance. To say Santi was angry was understatement of the year, and he hadn't had his first coffee of the day yet. A demitasse of the strongest coffee available, and swallowed in one hit, to jump start his busy day, at midday. Once Santi was out of bed, he rarely sat down.

But Santi's day hadn't started well, after hours of threatening language through the long night to the four separate factions trying to encroach on his nefarious business. If he had shown a chink of weakness he knew he would be in the epitaph of the daily papers U.S.A.

He had carefully conceded to all four just a crumb of his lucrative empire, and they could not be allowed to know that he was gradually winding down his father's holdings in so many illegal areas and activities.

Anton Santi was slowly and very carefully becoming the owner of profitable hotels, apartments, and empty buildings, which he intended to renovate and make a killing on rentals, and resales. Only his personal accountant and friend for years Sonny Silverman knew what Anton was doing, and Anton trusted him unconditionally, and without reserve. Sonny was the tangible face of every requisition.

If anyone got even a whiff of what Anton was doing it would be a death sentence for him, from every sleaze bag and too-bit illegal hoodlum to try and take over Anton's territory. So to evade any red flags from appearing he had to tread very, very carefully, to be able to keep his father Theo alive, and himself. He knew he was walking a tight-rope of danger, but he hated what he had become, a soulless killer of human depravity, and evil.

His heart and soul couldn't take any more hits, he was at the end of his rope. When he had asked Mia to act as his partner to his father, an idea had quickly formed in his head. She was an absolutely perfect young, innocent woman (and he was sure she *was* innocent) to take on the job of being his wife and having his children. Mia Maxwell was clean and untouched, and his father was an older Italian Don, and would recognise that phenomenon straightaway. His generation married very young to make sure the young Italian girls were pure and innocent. She didn't know it yet, but he always got his own way, and money talked, and he was a multi-millionaire, and some.

"What are you waiting for, Larry? Go find her, and report back to me when you have. We haven't got time over the next couple of days for this problem. We are back around the negotiation table later tonight, and I sincerely hope it will be the finish of these ridiculous demands. I am exhausted with all this talking about something that isn't going to happen. They are all speaking out of their backsides, and not one has the cojones to confront me outright. It's fuckin' pathetic."

Larry wasn't about to argue with Anton in a bad mood. But he liked his job. Liked the lifestyle that Anton gave them, and the money was terrific. Back at the ranch-like house there was an up to date gym, a swimming pool, and a trail that was great for a 10K run. Anton made sure his security were amazingly fit, and up to the job of keeping him safe from his enemies. So, looking out for a difficult woman that his Boss fancied was OK with him. But he was getting a tad worried about what pretty boy Andi was going to do about Anton and Mia getting close, and personal. That could become a very difficult and dangerous situation. But right now he had to locate this idiot woman, who had gone missing just to prove a point.

Honestly, he couldn't remember what the fucking point was!

Whilst Mia had been relaxing in the park she had texted Roberto, to tell him she was going back home in two days time, but she would definitely be coming back to stay in that room he had so kindly given to her. And, that she had *so* loved meeting her new uncle, and couldn't wait to meet the twins.

Then had texted her best friend Viola, and told her she was coming back home ASAP, and was so excited. But she was not to tell her family, as she wanted it to be a surprise, especially for her Papa. She was going to have to beg for his forgiveness, but knowing her beloved Papa he would be overjoyed to see her again, and forgiveness would be a no-brainer.

Then with trepidation she took a deep breath and phoned Marcus, who luckily was unavailable, so she just left a message. "I'm going home, Marcus. I've realised that I have to leave my mother to rest in peace. No good can come of me trying to resurrect what happened to her twenty years ago. I can only love her with all my heart, and sincerely hope she would be proud of the person I have become. It was wonderful to meet you, and I wish you happiness and love with your family." Mia valiantly tried to stem the tears. "Thank you so much for your help, and Gerry's contributions to my work. We will probably never meet again, but I did cherish our once only meeting, and will never forget you." She turned off her phone before she told him exactly what she felt for him – a forever love that would last her life-time.

Dear God, she wanted! Really wanted! But what the hell did she want so badly? She wanted Marcus to hold her close to his big, warm body to know she was a grown woman, but a woman who was untouched and innocent. She wanted to be his woman in every possible way. But knew it was never going to happen. Now, in a couple of days she was leaving him behind, and honestly didn't know how she was going to cope with that.

It was too much to ask her broken heart. But she was a survivor, and life moved on.

CHAPTER TEN

She checked her list one more time, because once she left her room she was never coming back, ever.

Mia had bought a small carry-on bag for the flight, and her favourite backpack was full to the brim.

Her meagre amount of eclectic clothes and shoes.

Her social security ID and credit card in her old name.

Her meagre amount of makeup and toiletries.

5,000 dollars in cash that she had earned.

Two very fancy towels with the hotel logo to always remind her of her time in L.A. Her triumph and despair, and growing up, not a moment too soon.

She carefully locked the door behind her, as she manoeuvred her two items of travel. To mark her leaving she had dressed up for a change, and was wearing an eye-catching off the shoulder brilliant red, brocade cocktail dress, with matching jacket. The black espadrilles, that were really comfy, finished her outfit. Normally she would have gelled her hair to stand up in spikes, but it was longer now, and she had fluffed it up into soft curls around her face.

In truth she felt an utter fraud, dressing up like a debutante without a date. But her regular clothes were in her backpack ready to put on when she left the hotel later tonight.

She was leaving her luggage tucked away in the staff recreation room, where the night manager or Larry wouldn't find it. Nobody knew she was leaving tonight.

Larry had located her in her room when she had returned from the park, he was furious with her because he had wasted hours trying to find her. She had told him to fuck himself and his boss, because she would never be told what to do especially by Mr Anton Santi. That was when she knew she had to leave that night, before Mr Santi took hold of her life, and she would be powerless to get away from him and his security men.

Immediately she had booked a flight out of L.A. early the next morning in her old name, so no one would know where she had gone. She intended to leave before midnight, and go out the back of the hotel, and pick up a taxi to the Airport.

Mia Maxwell would disappear from L.A., and hopefully would be back within the safety of her Houston family before she was missed. And Anton Santi could also go fuck himself, and that couldn't happen to a nicer man – yeah right!

Before she started work Mia sat at the bar, and the Bar Manager gave her the best coffee on the house, as per usual. Of course John had fallen in love with the tiny golden girl, but knew he didn't stand a chance in hell with her, she seemed totally impervious to any man's overtures to her.

But he was keeping an eagle eye on a couple of young studs who were trying to chat up gorgeous Mia, who, bless her, was being very kind and very considerate to the young bucks, even though he knew she wasn't a bit interested in their ridiculous overtures.

They had started to come in over the past week trying to get Mia into a conversation, but she wasn't having anything to do with them, which John was happy about, because it was pretty obvious Mr Santi the boss was interested in her. But nobody, if they wanted to retain their health and looks, crossed Mr Santi.

They had seemed too young to order a drink when they first came in, but he had checked their IDs, and they were both in their mid twenties, so plenty old enough. But John was an experienced bar worker, and was a good judge of character, and these two guys just didn't add up to their given image. So he always kept a vigilant eye on them, especially when they tried to chat up Mia.

She was always stunningly beautiful, but tonight he had never seen a woman so utterly, perfectly beautiful. A young woman who really didn't have a clue what she did to a man's libido, every man who saw her, absolutely wanted to bed her.

In fact he had never seen Mr Santi interested in any woman before, but that had all changed when he had actually sat next to her at the piano. He hadn't taken his eyes off her, and that had definitely been a one off. Rumours were quietly exchanged that he was gay, but no one was stupid enough, or had the iron balls, to even whisper that thought.

"John, I am finishing early tonight, so when I disappear please keep it to yourself." Mia had called John over and whispered to him, making sure no one else heard her plan for escape. It was imperative that Santi and his henchmen didn't find out that she had left early, she needed plenty of time to get lost.

"No problem Mia, whatever you are doing is nothing to do with me." He zipped up his mouth with his hand. She thanked him with a brilliant smile, which made him love her all the more. He had a very sick wife at home, and he would always love her, but he could dream. As any red-bloodied male could about Mia.

He watched her walk over to the piano to start work, she played like an angel, amazing eclectic music. She had arrived only a few weeks ago looking like a petulant punk rocker, with attitude. Now, she had turned into a beautiful butterfly, leaving behind her ugly chrysalis, full of confidence, all grown up, and utterly gorgeous. Honestly, he thought she was made of glass, and could crack and break any time soon.

Fragile was the word, even though she appeared to be tough and difficult. But it was all false bravado, Mia was really a pussy cat without the claws. Over the last few days everything had changed – like her dreams.

But she was always ready to take on the world when she was right, and never believed she could be wrong. It really nagged him that she reminded him of someone, but he just couldn't put his finger on who. It was like a puzzle with the one important piece missing.

Everyone loved Mia, and the patrons of the lounge came back in droves because of her. If she ever decided to walk away the room would die a slow death, and Mr Santi would be furious with the remaining staff, and especially the bar manager John, for not holding onto their irreplaceable star attraction. He desperately needed this job, because Mr Santi had a very generous Medical Insurance package for all his employees. John relied on the package to pay for his wife's eye-watering medical needs.

John told Miles the other barkeep that he was just going into the stockroom, as it was a busy night and they were getting low on the ingredients for their very popular cocktails. "Keep an eye on Mia, and those two posers at the end of the bar. Don't know why but I don't trust them an inch, with our best girl."

"Right John, will do, but I'm really busy, will do my best." He looked over to where the guys were busy eyeing up Mia, and then talking with their heads together. Suddenly they looked up and called him over to order a couple of foreign beers and a Ginger Ale for Mia.

Miles told them that Mia never accepted a drink from anyone, it was against company policy. They replied very politely that she had accepted one from them previously, they loved her music, and she'd been playing for over an hour and must be thirsty. So, what the heck thought Miles, what was the harm in a Ginger Ale, it wasn't as if they were trying to ply her with alcohol? But, when he turned around to get them a couple of cold beers from the refrigerator he didn't see them put a small phial of something into the Ginger Ale.

They casually sauntered over to the piano, and put the Ginger Ale on a coaster in front of Mia. She smiled sweetly at the guys and thanked them for being so considerate and kind. Then got to the end of a regular piece of movie music before downing the glass in one hit. It was cold and sweet, just how she liked it, and she had really been thirsty after eating some Mexican salty snacks John had made for her before she had started work.

John was such a love, always looking out for her if any guy started to get too close and personal with her. He knew she didn't like being chatted up by strangers, and especially being hugged or kissed by anyone in particular.

What she wasn't comfortable with, was the two guys had pulled a table closer to her and sat down, and that was too close and personal. She looked up to signal John, but he wasn't behind the bar counter. Miles was there but was snowed under with orders, and almost running on the spot.

She realised she was being ridiculously stupid, and paranoid as usual.

But was she? Her tongue felt as if it was stuck to the roof of her mouth. Then a slow lassitude began from her bare feet and travelled up her body. Her fingers were still trying to cope with the piece of music, but she couldn't remember what she was actually playing. And her vision was blurred, her eyes failing to be able to concentrate on anything close to her, or beyond.

Then strong arms lifted her from the stool and held her upright. She couldn't have stopped anyone from touching her if she'd had the strength, or the will to try. She felt like the weakest baby, and was steadily becoming weaker, her vision almost gone.

"Let us help you, sweet Mia. We can see you aren't at all well, we will take you to your room so you can lie down and sleep it off." The two young guys supported Mia either side and quickly exited the lounge before anyone could stop them.

It was exceptionally crowded and noisy in the lounge, so nobody took any notice when the three carefully walked out of the room. Even though they were literally holding Mia up, she looked as if she had over imbibed on too much alcohol for her tiny size.

They also had to circumnavigate the reception area which was also extremely busy with only the night manager in attendance. Customers were impatiently asking for their card-keys for their rooms, or waiting to leave and pay their very expensive bills. The Excelsior wasn't a hotel for the average Joe, only the rich and famous stayed there, and revelled in the overwhelming luxury and comfort. The exorbitant cost was totally irrelevant, and really not worthy of another thought.

Carefully, but as quickly as possible, they bundled a comatose Mia into the nearest lift, remembering to hide their identity by keeping their faces averted from any cameras hidden in the area.

A couple of hours ago they had paid for a suite on the fourth floor with cash. The hotel had a policy of no cash, but they had sweet talked the beautiful receptionist to break the rules just for them, with a promise to take her to a very expensive restaurant on her night off. They had of course had to show their IDs, which of course were totally make believe.

After tonight no one, and especially the LAPD would be able to find them and bring them to justice. This wasn't the first time the two brothers from an extremely wealthy family had degraded, demoralised, and tortured a young innocent female, for their own sexual gratification.

Their combined behaviour was sick and abnormal. They were without any normal conscience whatsoever. In truth they could be described as sub-human, because they had no feelings of remorse for anything they did to anyone, especially women. They believed they were God's gift to females, so everything they did was in God's name, and they were completely innocent of any wrong doing.

Mia had repeatedly snubbed their affections, which had brutalised their huge egos, and now she was going to pay the price for not paying any attention to the rising stars of industry.

They'd heard rumours that pond-scum Anton Santi allegedly owned The Excelsior – so what? There wouldn't be any evidence left behind that could possibly put them in the picture. They would get away scot free, as they had before tonight with other hapless whores. If the police got even a whiff of what they were up to their father the Supreme Judge would kick anyone's butt even if they so much as looked at his righteous sons. Nobody got the better of Judge Williams and lived to fight another day in court. So that alone gave his sons the right to roam the darkened streets of downtown L.A., and commit deviant crimes on unwitting sex workers, male or female.

Larry was absolutely fucked off. Why? Why did it always have to be him to look out for Mia Maxwell? And, wouldn't you just know she wasn't where she was supposed to be, playing her damn music.

"Where is she John? I swear I'm going to wring her fuckin' neck when I find her."

Shit! Now he had to lie to Mr Santi's Chief of Security. "Hi Larry. Haven't a clue, she disappeared about an hour ago. I think she was feeling unwell, and went back to her room." John put his hands in the air in supplication. "To be honest I really can't say. You know women, who can keep up with what or why they tend to do something. But I would check on her room first before you run around looking for her. You know she's a master of getting lost if she really wants some space."

"You're right John. Thanks, personally I wouldn't bother with her, she's an absolute minefield of contradiction. But Santi wants her in the penthouse right away, and what Santi wants, Santi gets. Give us a quick beer, mate, to give me the patience to track her down and not lose my temper with the little shit. It's late and I need my bed, but my boss thinks we can all work 24/7 without sleep."

John gave him a beer by the neck, feeling sorry for Larry who always seemed a regular guy for his size and working for Santi. There was no way he was going to find Mia in that empty room. His gut told him that she had left for good over an hour ago, and was probably hiding out at the airport waiting for a flight to take her away from Santi's clutches.

As Larry had just said 'what Santi wanted Santi got'. But Mia was far from stupid. She had realised she had to get as far away as possible from the deeply immoral Anton Santi, before he took her over completely, taking her innocence and purity for himself.

John smiled. Bless her cotton socks. That girl was a one off, and he would always remember her smart mouth, and big loving heart. And was way beyond happy that she had managed to fly away, back to wherever she had come from. Hopefully to a loving family unit, who wanted to take care of her.

"What do you mean, Larry?" Santi shouted down his cell phone. "She can't have left, without anyone seeing her, she isn't that devious, or clever." Santi was apoplectic, not believing that a woman who he had taken notice of, and liked, could leave without telling him. It was a total embarrassment for a man of his calibre and standing in the underbelly community. He turned to the other three who were sprawled out in easy chairs half asleep, but always ready to tackle any problems with their boss. "Get up you lazy bastards and go help Larry, and don't come back unless you bring that – that stupid bitch with you." He was screaming with temper now.

Nobody! But Nobody! Walked away from Anton Santi. Mia Maxwell would pay heavily for leaving him, and making him look a fool in front of his men.

As they all ran out of the penthouse, he shouted after them. "And, I don't want anyone to know what she has done. Do you understand me? All your jobs are on the line for this, and especially Larry's. Bring her back unharmed, so I can personally deal with her. UNDERSTAND?"

As one they all shouted back. "Yes boss! We understand!" And they most certainly did, because they had the best jobs, ever. Anton Santi was a great boss to work for. Everything he touched turned to gold, and he made sure everyone who worked for him benefitted from his outrageous wealth.

But that certainly wasn't helping him right now. That devious little bitch, was not about to get the better of him. He would get her back, but he wouldn't be Mr Nice Guy in future.

CHAPTER ELEVEN

She was in a dark place, no, not dark, absolutely negative black. Her body felt weightless, but she knew if she tried she wouldn't be able to move any part of her body.

She wanted to scream and scream, knowing that's what she should do, but couldn't open her mouth. She realised she didn't have control of her own body, which was far too much for her brain to cope with. Her brain felt like mush, and couldn't put together a simple coherent thought.

Oh my God! She must have had a stroke, and again couldn't remember how old she was. So, she just shut everything down and went back into the blackness of nothing and nowhere. There was no pain, no degradation and no torment in that place of nothing.

It was just black, and peaceful, and she was truly alone, and thankful for it. But where were her enemies? Her tormentors?

"Larry, please be really gentle with her, wrap her in a blanket and carry her up to the penthouse." Santi had never known such anger, or such helplessness. He had promised her that she would never be hurt, and now look at her. Raped, sodamised, and tortured. He had let her down, but he silently vowed to make it up to her, for the rest of his Goddamn life.

Whoever had done this would not live to enjoy many more days on earth, and would pray for death when he found them, and had them exterminated.

He did feel a modicum of sympathy for the young girl who had found Mia, spread-eagled on the bed covered in blood. The girl was now cowering in the corner of the room weeping copiously. She in turn had phoned down to Walter Lewis, who in all his years in hotel work had thankfully never seen such a blood bath before. But, he had kept his head and had gone against company rules to never, under any circumstances, phone straight through to the penthouse. In Walter's view he should have phoned 911 and called an ambulance, but Mr Santi never allowed the police or an ambulance to be called to The Excelsior. For reasons unknown to his staff.

Walter always obeyed the rules of his employment, because he knew Mr Santi was not the type of man to be crossed, or judged. He liked his job, and wanted to keep it for as long as possible. But he wasn't stupid, heads would roll for this appalling scene in front of him. So, he sat with the young house-maid and kept his council, it was safer for both of them, until the inquisition began.

"Andi, go and bring Doctor Perez from the Clinic, straightaway. No excuses, he must leave whatever he is doing and bring a female assistant with him." Santi was speaking quietly and restrained, which showed just how angry he was. *"Now Andi, go!"* He would be much happier when the Trauma Surgeon was looking after Mia, and they found out what the extent of her injuries were.

When they had all burst into suite 411 guns drawn, expecting something serious had happened, because the day manager had actually phoned the penthouse to say they had an emergency on their hands, which had never happened before. Santi couldn't believe what he saw. Mia, sweet Mia, tied to the bed, naked, spread-eagled, and blood everywhere. He had seen many bad situations in his life, but nothing as vile as this. His heart stuttered in his chest, because she looked as if she had left this life. His life completely, and he had been absolutely gutted, and heartbroken.

But Al, who had been a paramedic in a Special Forces Unit before working for Santi, quickly took charge, while the rest of them stopped in their tracks looking absolutely pole axed. "She's still with us Boss, a bit thready, but still with us." Al covered her naked body with a blanket after cutting her limbs loose, and carefully pulling off the tape over her mouth.

He watched Santi physically draw in a long calming breath, as tears filled his eyes, but were quickly blinked away, so no one would notice. "It looks as if she's been drugged, over drugged, she is completely out of it still. I would take a random guess at the date-rape drug Rohypnol. Mia is tiny, I'm pretty sure they've given her too much, if she was on anything else as well, she would be a gonna' by now."

Santi just nodded, whoever had done this would be hunted down and broken beyond repair. "I'm going with Larry and Al to the penthouse, to wait for Doctor Perez. Ray, I need you to go to the Security Suite on the ground floor and find out why this was allowed to happen, with all the cameras in place." He went over to Lewis and the young girl still sobbing. She was lucky, he would have loved the privilege to be able to get emotional, but that was never going to happen in front of an audience.

"Please, listen very carefully to me. Nobody! But nobody! Must not, under any circumstances find out what has happened here today. Not family, or friends, wife or husband. I give my word that you will be looked after extremely generously by me personally. If one word of this accident gets out, especially to the police, or the local media, I personally will see to it that there will be serious consequences." He stood looking down at them, his eyes as cold as ice, and completely lacking humanity. "Do you understand me! Because I will not have Mia's name besmirched in the dirt under someone's boot."

Walter put his arm around the chamber-maid's shoulder, and spoke for both of them. "No one will hear anything from us Mr Santi, you can absolutely rely on that. I will just say the suite had been trashed by the occupants and it will be locked up in the future. What do you want me to do about cleaning up?"

Larry was waiting for Santi, so he could carry poor Mia up to the penthouse. Santi told Larry to go via the private lift, so no one would see what had happened. "I want everything taken out of this room and burnt. Furniture, drapes, bedding, every solitary item is to be eradicated, and then the room completely redecorated. Nothing is to be left as it is, then I will decide if it can be used again. But, please make sure you and the young lady get rid of everything that is covered in Mia's blood."

Walter was talking to Santi's back as he answered him. "Teresa and I will get on with it straightaway sir. We will put all the ruined bedding into the trash bags that are on Teresa's cleaning trolley, and then straight into the dumpsters at the back of the building."

But Walter was talking to himself, as everyone else but Teresa filed out of the room used for the sexual fantasies and gratification of two extremely sick young men, who believed they had got away with raping and torturing an innocent young woman. Because they had got away with it at least twice before, or was it more?

They were the Supreme Judge Williams' two sons, and believed they were innocent until proved guilty, and that was never going to happen. Was it?

CHAPTER TWELVE

"Anton!" The young doctor walked into the penthouse, and embraced his friend, even though he was angry with him. "You my friend cannot just pull me away from my surgery, when you feel like it. I know you own the damn clinic and pay all our wages, but we are ridiculously swamped, our sick patients need us, badly." Doctor Perez had been forcibly brought to the penthouse without being informed why, he'd had to ask his assistant to take over his patient list after lunch.

Stefan was tired and cranky, and also the best trauma surgeon in the area. Anton Santi had coerced and blackmailed him to leave the largest hospital in L.A. Santi had bought and renovated a building in down town for the down trodden migrants, and unemployed no-hopers, as a free clinic. He had wanted and needed the best ex-migrant to run and help those people in dire need, who couldn't afford health insurance, and were sick – very sick.

Doctor Stefan Perez had dreamt of being able to help people who were without hope of ever getting any help. Three years down the line Anton and Stefan had become the best of friends, even though the good doctor knew exactly what Anton did to make money, because the flip side of the coin was that he spread his ill-gotten gains on many projects to help the poor and needy.

"Please Stefan, you know I wouldn't do that lightly, but we have a very nasty situation in one of the bedrooms, which needs your expertise ASAP." He indicated which bedroom, and Al and Anton followed him into the room.

Stefan stifled a groan of despair as he gently lifted away the covering blanket on Mia, because he knew exactly what had happened. In his line of work he often saw rape victims who had been beaten into submission. But this beautiful young girl had been brutalised beyond anything he had ever seen. He turned and looked straight at Anton. "I don't have to ask if you know the bastards who did this, do I?"

Anton clenched his teeth together to stop the tears from filling his eyes, and just shook his head. "I'm sure it was more than one, when we find them, they won't want to live, believe me."

Stefan didn't want to know what punishment his friend would metre out, but it wouldn't be anything less than horrendous. "Al, I need you to quickly go back to the clinic, and pick up the things I need urgently." He had already taken Mia's vitals, and had written a list for Al, who would know exactly what he needed, and was already leaving, running.

His patient was totally out of it, which was a blessing in disguise, because she was truly in a seriously dangerous condition. "You realise she should be in hospital with all the latest equipment to get her through this. Why wasn't an ambulance called straight away when she was found, for Godsake Anton? And who is she?"

"I'm sorry Stefan, but you know if I call in any emergency the police, and every fucking agency will be down on me like a ton of bricks. Whatever happened I just couldn't take that chance, because what happened to Mia took place in one of our suites. I have become very attached to her since she came to work here." When Stefan gave him a puzzled frown at the last statement, he put up both hands in supplication. "I know what you are thinking, but it's true. I think I've fallen in love with a woman for the first time, and to see this shit happen to her is driving me crazy with heartache, and pain.

"What worries me, is that this was done to her to somehow get back at me. But I can't think of anyone who has the balls to do it, especially in my own hotel."

Stefan wasn't really listening, he was laboriously going over Mia's injuries, and noting down everything in his head, and it was truly mind boggling, and extremely sad for such a young woman to have been so brutalised and so disgustingly abused. He was waiting for Al to return with all the medical equipment and medication he needed to get on with helping her.

Just then Al ran back into the room, out of breath, and sweating profusely, he must have broken all records for being so fast to get to the clinic and back. But Stefan had never been so pleased to see anyone, he needed to get his patient on an Antibiotic IV, and a glucose drip.

"I need your help Al, there is too much to do for one person." He turned to Anton hovering in the background. "You should leave as this isn't going to be a party, and I haven't got time to look after you if it gets too much for you to cope with." Stefan knew most men would turn tail and leave, because they hated their women to be touched by another male, but he knew Anton was made of sterner stuff, and he wasn't wrong. "Anything I can do to help? I need to know exactly what those bastards did to her, so I can do what needs to be done, in return."

Stefan was too busy to answer the obvious, and began to run through everything needed to help their patient, with his assistant Al the paramedic, who must have seen much worse in war-torn countries when he had served in Special Forces.

"Would you wash down every part of her body with the antiseptic to stop any infection, there are so many deep bite marks just about everywhere. Her breasts seem to have taken the worst injury, and her left nipple has been almost bitten through, be very careful when you clean there." He drew in a deep breath knowing what he was going to find internally, complete and utter devastation. Unfortunately he wasn't wrong.

"Shit, I'm going to have to put stitches way up in her vagina, they have used some form of an instrument inside her, it's looking extremely bad in that area. And, I have to be really careful, if this woman is ever going to have intercourse ever again." He shot a look at his friend, who was white as a sheet, and was just about hanging in there.

"I'm pretty sure she was a virgin, she didn't like anyone getting too close to her" said Anton, as he sat down and put his head in his hands. Stefan had been right, he wasn't coping with everything that was happening, it was a total nightmare. A nightmare he wanted to wake up from, and realise it hadn't happened.

"While I am stitching her together, Al, would you set up the portable IV, she needs antibiotics pumping through her, and glucose, because it's imperative that we flush out her system. Also you will find a phial of the morning after meds in my bag, please give her an injection, because it's pretty obvious they didn't bother to use condoms in their attack. An unwanted pregnancy is the very last event that Mia needs in the immediate future."

Al hadn't said a word as he just followed Stefan's instructions. But a couple of times he had slanted a quick look at his Boss. He had looked absolutely devastated, and who could blame him, what those scum had put sweet Mia through was beyond his comprehension. To call them animals was to denigrate all animals.

Every time they touched her Mia gave out a quiet groan, as if in her subconscious she knew what was happening to her. But Stefan was sure she was in a deep catatonic state, and couldn't feel pain, but it would come like a tsunami when the Rohypnol left her system in a few hours.

Stefan was certain it was the date-rape drug, he had seen it before at the hospital, and it was merciless. It could cause brain damage if too much had been administered. And they had definitely given Mia far too much, when he had first seen her he thought he had been called in too late, but with Al's help they had so far pulled her through.

"Would you gently turn her over, Al? I'm pretty certain we are going to have the same outcome as the front of her poor body." When he saw the damage inflicted he just said, "Fuck! Her rectum has been violated, but not by a penis. They most certainly have used this poor girl for their sexual deviations, and seriously sick minds."

Anton's breath hitched and he groaned out loud when he couldn't stop himself looking at Mia's naked back. There were red welts criss-crossing her beautiful skin from a belt buckle, and obvious abuse around her buttocks.

Even Stefan and Al both stopped with shock, not believing what the perverts had put Mia through, it was mind numbing. At that precise moment both men hated being a part of the male species.

Al couldn't stop himself voicing what he was thinking. "I am personally going to cut their dicks off with a blunt instrument after I get another pervert to fuck them both to death."

Stefan patted his shoulder in comfort, because he had to agree wholeheartedly. Death would be far too easy for the evil, perverted miscreants.

But that was never going to be a problem, because he knew what Anton was capable of. He hated with a vengeance – Paedophiles, Perverts, and anyone who abused or misused women. This scenario would be sorted and dealt with in the worst possible way for whoever had been stupid enough to foolishly touch and violate a woman that Anton was evidently more than friendly with.

And Stefan was beginning to wonder if the men were actually gay-bashers, and they believed that Mia was gay because she refused their overt sexual come-on. That had totally pissed them off, if they were young and good looking, so perhaps they were just teaching her a lesson never to be forgotten. Oh God! He so hoped he was utterly wrong, but somehow didn't think so.

There was a couple of knocks on the bedroom door, immediately Anton went and opened it, not wanting anyone else to see what was going on there.

"Sorry Boss, but I need to tell you what Ray and I have found out." Anton put his hand up to stop Larry saying anything, and followed him into the lounge to listen to what he had to say.

"Two young guys escorted Mia up to Suite 411, they were extremely careful not to show their faces on camera. Unfortunately, one of the guys on security last night was sick and couldn't work. So his partner did the midnight walk about all over the hallways, and nobody was watching the monitors, that is why these two guys were left alone. But Ray and I have gone back over them, and straight away noticed what had happened, and got an occasional glimpse of the guys with Mia.

"Andi checked reception and against the rules they paid cash earlier that afternoon, so no credit card could be checked." At this point Anton was so apoplectically furious he was ready to sack everyone who was employed at his Goddamn hotel.

"But these clever little bastards overlooked one big mistake, they checked in their vehicle with the valet service.

The valet always keeps a copy of the vehicle tags that he parks away, just for safety."

Anton was now pacing up and down in impatience, because Larry could sometimes be a bit slow when he was trying to explain something important. "So, what do we know now? Who are these low-life? We do know who they are, Larry? Please, tell me that we have found out exactly who did this terrible thing to our Mia. They are dead men, touching my woman with their filthy hands, and – and..." He couldn't put into words what they had done to sweet Mia, who might never get over this diabolical rape and more.

"Yeah Boss, got in touch with our informant in LAPD, you won't believe who these bastards are."

"No I won't Larry, unless you tell me. Fuck it, put me out of my misery, *please.*" Anton was holding it all together by a thread. What Stefan and Al had to do to Mia to stabilise her, had almost put him on his knees, and that had never happened to Anton Santi before.

"They are the Supreme Judge Williams' twin sons, they are not identical, but still twins." Larry closed his eyes and shook his head, still not believing what he had found out. "We can't touch them Boss, if we do there will be the biggest stink ever." Both Ray and Andi totally agreed, their faces showing that Larry was saying the truth, but knowing that Santi would not back down to any threats from the highest law in the state. Whether it be police, the Feds, and especially a judge.

He clicked his fingers at Larry. "I need names, their address, and where we can usually locate them." He gave his three men a look that was piercing, and menacing. "I do not have to explain that all this stays in this room, do I? Those two pieces of shit do not deserve to breathe the same air as we do. If you think differently, please be my guest and go see exactly what they did to that innocent young woman in there." Nobody moved, they wouldn't have dared go near that bedroom, if they treasured their good health, and looks.

"Larry stay with me, Ray and Andi take a walk, but under no circumstances discuss anything with anyone. *Do we understand!?*" Both men nodded emphatically, no one ever disagreed with Santi, if they liked working with him.

"Boot up my private computer, Larry." He was the only other person who knew Santi's personal password. His computer was re-routed around four different countries, it was almost impossible to ever be able to get any information off the hard drive if it ever got into the wrong hands, i.e. the LAPD, or Feds. "Get in touch with The Executioner. Give him all the information we have on these two pieces of shit. I want them dead in an extremely painful way. And, I want them alive to the last possible moment, and why they are being tortured, because of our sweet Mia, who could be damaged beyond repair. Money is of no importance, I will pay any amount to have the job done properly by the best in the business."

Anton was desperate to get back to Stefan and Al, knowing they were doing everything they could to pull his girl back from the brink. "When you have negotiated a price, take the amount in full from the Columbian account."

Larry nodded his understanding of what Santi wanted. "OK Boss, leave it with me. I'll make sure The Executioner knows exactly what he has to do, ASAP." Larry knew that no one had ever seen this man, but anyone who needed a cold, silent, deadly killer, would get in touch with him for the job. He charged an absolute fortune, but was worth every dollar. He had never left behind a solitary piece of evidence to connect anyone to him, or to his customer. He lived in Nevada somewhere in the desert, and moved around on a vintage Harley, rarely taking to the skies, unless to pilot his own plane.

The Executioner was a vigilante of the first order, without a sliver of conscience, and possibly without a soul. The word was he lived alone by choice. Worked alone. Was always alone. Larry didn't envy his lifestyle, not one bit. When he first met Santi he had thought he was the same, but he hadn't known the real Santi then.

Santi was no pushover, but had a big heart for the underdog, and down-trodden. Larry was a recovering drug addict from his Special Forces deployment. Santi had pulled him up by is boot straps, and had the faith in him to give him this fantastic employment.

In a heartbeat Larry would die to protect Anton Santi.

CHAPTER THIRTEEN

"Sophia, would you please stop nagging me, and go cook something delicious for lunch, me and the boys are starving." Marcus berated his mother, because he knew what he was going to be put through for the next half hour. He loved his parent dearly, but was tired and frustrated, because of a blonde, doe-eyed, pixie of a female. For Chrissake he'd only met her once, and had been pole-axed by love he had never previously known, and honestly didn't want to know. He couldn't sleep, couldn't concentrate properly on his workload, which was always too much to contemplate, but now almost impossible to cope with after five years of sexual frustration.

He was right about his beautiful mother who was giving her son a fulminating look, because normally Marcus was the most patient loving father, and son, but the past few weeks had changed into a bad tempered pain in the ass.

"Marcus darling, please tell me what is worrying you?" She hated the thought that he could be sick, or even worse. She couldn't lose her eldest son, he was so precious to her, and of course to his boys, Micah and Milo. The boys absolutely adored their father, and hated it when he was in L.A. And they in turn were the centre of his Universe, he always showed his love for them.

"Really my son, that wedding ring should not be on your finger still. Our dearest Bianca left us over four years ago, it is time to let her go, and get on with your life. There are so many wonderful women out there who would love to be your partner, or more." Marcus rolled his eyes, and let out a deep sigh, because his mother was on her usual lecture, and nothing would shut her up. "You haven't dated one solitary woman since your wife died, it isn't healthy for a man of your age to go without sexual relief for that length of time."

His mother had always been forthright in her views on sex and relationships, but there was no way he was going to discuss Mia Maxwell with her, when nothing was ever going to happen between them in the future.

"And another thing, couldn't you please call me Mama, or Mom, it isn't respectable to call me by my given name. Especially now the boys are starting to call me Sophia, instead of Grandma."

"Jeeze Mom, give me a break. I really don't need a lecture right now. If you hadn't noticed you are only seventeen years older than me, and don't look old enough to be my parent." He looked straight into her brown eyes, and spoke the truth. "You young lady, are exceptionally pretty, have a really good figure, and long dark straight hair, that is always tied into a ponytail. You are also intelligent, a great cook, and me and the boys can't live without you, and wouldn't want to."

He also added as an afterthought. "Perhaps you would like to explain why there isn't a significant other man in *your* life. Our so-called father left us twenty-four years ago, and I don't remember any other man come a courtin' to you. And you have never explained why you weren't even seventeen when I was born."

Marcus held his breath in anticipation, because his mother never, ever spoke about her long ago husband. Marcus had always wanted to know why he had left them. It had been bugging him for years, because perhaps he had misbehaved badly, or his father hadn't loved him, or his mother.

Sophia had always tried to let go of the past, but always knew her deeply sensitive son needed an answer to the hurt and sadness of not having a father figure in his young life like his close friends. She sat down in her favourite armchair to try and answer some questions. She knew her grandchildren were playing in the family room with their Lego, and dinosaurs, their favourite toys. They were so easy to look after, just like their own father had been.

She decided to not sugar coat her explanation, because Marcus deserved the whole truth, good or bad. "Theo was the most handsome young man in our small village just outside of Naples. But he was a bad young man, always in trouble with the local police, and beyond. Unfortunately, he set his sights on a young virgin, me, but I wasn't interested, so he decided to take me one way or another. One evening I was walking back home on my own, I had been visiting my best friend. He grabbed me and raped me in the nearest field, knowing my family would insist he marry me when they found out. I was still sixteen years old, married, pregnant with you, when he decided to leave Italy and emigrate to America. I was heartbroken to leave behind everything that I had ever known. We ended up in Texas, not a dollar between us, and a baby to feed. And, from that day forward he became the man he is today – a mobster, a cruel violent man. Someone everyone feared, and that included me."

Sophia was now silently crying, but Marcus couldn't move, he was totally transfixed with this horror story of his poor mother's early life. He had never expected it to be this bad, or soul destroying. But why then hadn't she left this monster, because he always thought of her as a strong intelligent woman?

"I expect you wonder why I didn't leave him, because that would have been the most sensible thing to do. If ever I so much as hinted that to him, or even tried to do it, I got a beating to change my mind. Also he kept me short of money, except for housekeeping. Of course he expected to have sex with his teenage wife, even though he was screwing every female who was available, or not actually available." Sophia blew her nose, and took a deep breath to be able to carry on. Marcus had tears in his eyes, not believing what this sweet woman was revealing to him, that his father, who he hated anyway, was a rapist, as well as a wife-beater, and a sick son of a bitch all round.

"Then I was pregnant again, with your brother, and from that day forward my dear husband never touched me again. For that I thanked the good Lord for small mercies." She smiled through her tears, trying to garner the courage to say what had to be said to finish the story. "As you know, because you were there, when your brother was four years old, his father picked him up, and left us for good. My baby boy screamed and screamed, as he had never left me before, and really didn't know the parent that was carrying him away from his doting Mama."

Marcus remembered that dreadful day. His baby brother, who he had adored, was screaming and kicking trying to get out of his father's strong arms, but their father completely ignored all their crying and pleading to put him down, and back into his mother's arms. Marcus would never forget the look on his father's face, he was actually smirking at their heartbreak, and utter misery. He was enjoying every solitary moment. He was truly a monster.

From that diabolical day they had never set eyes on his father, or brother, again. Marcus never told his mother that he knew exactly where they were now, because his father was nothing to him, and he didn't acknowledge that he was a human being. His brother was a different matter, because it was obvious that his father must have spun a story of lies about their mother. That she was the worst kind of mother, and the reverse was the absolute truth. One day, he would confront his sibling and tell him the real truth, because his mother so deserved to know her youngest son. But he also knew she wouldn't be happy that her youngest boy had become his father's son in every way.

Marcus got up from his chair and put his arms around his mother to comfort her. She was such a strong woman, to have gone through what she had, and bring him up to be the man of integrity, and honesty, that he was.

He couldn't love her more, as his mother, and a woman who was kind, loving, and always helping others who were in need. She had always been a shining star in his universe, and unfortunately other women didn't come up to her standards in his life.

But his mother wasn't quite finished with the story. She took his hand and looked into the eyes that were the image of her husband's. "What I am telling you now Marcus is the absolute truth on my grandchildren's lives. You are not the result of that rape, I had a miscarriage two months later, thank

God. You were conceived the week I married that low-life, and were born on time, nine months later."

Marcus smiled in relief, it had occurred to him that he had been conceived in violence, which didn't sit well on his conscience. Hopefully he had been conceived in love, but he felt the jury was out on that verdict.

Now it seemed to be a day for complete honesty, his mother had bared her heart and soul to him, so he couldn't do less. "To be honest Mama, I was not in love with Bianca. But loved her because she was the best mother in the world to my amazing boys. She was pretty, always kind, and a loving wife, for a so-called perfect family. But there was no grand passion, which always left me dissatisfied with our sex life. I know she loved me, but I just couldn't return that love a hundred per cent. Did she know? I'm sure she did, but never questioned that I was faithful to her, because I definitely was." He was asking his mother's forgiveness for what he had done, or hadn't done. "I'm sorry, but I married her because everyone expected that I would. She was convenient, and I needed a wife and family to get on with my future and to settle down into married life. You know mama that I've always found the dating game to be irksome and shallow, and still do.

"But now I have to eat those words of stupidity and selfishness, because I met a woman a few weeks ago who changed my way of thinking." Immediately his mother sat up wide awake, not believing what her son was going to reveal, but was so happy at what his face was telling her, he was in love at last.

"Mia is really difficult, opinionated, and has a bad temper, but she is the most perfectly beautiful woman I have ever seen. She would turn my life upside down, and to be honest I really don't need that aggro'. What am I going to do about her? It's a tired, old subject, that I do not need such a prickly woman in my life to make it more complex, or complete." He blew out a held breath, knowing what he wanted to do.

He wanted to fuck her, and fuck her some more.

He wanted to wake up every morning to her beautiful face.

He wanted to give her a baby in her image, probably more.

He just wanted – wanted – wanted – Mia.

"If you love this woman she must have a big, loving heart for all her obvious faults. And I would grow to love her too, and the boys need such a mother to keep them in line as they grow older, and taller."

If his mother could love her, then he knew he was doing the right thing in pursuing Mia. "She is also tiny, mama, outlandishly different, and has a heart of gold, and the capacity to draw people to her. I can't let her go, but wish I could, because she is a truck load of trouble, and always will be, I fear."

"Always follow your heart, Marcus, because it never lets you down. This Mia sounds intriguing, I can't wait to meet her."

He sincerely hoped that Mia would be on her best behaviour when she met his family. Now, he would have to get Gerry Swane to find her, because she had left a sweet message on his cell phone saying she was leaving L.A., and going home. Every time he tried to return the call her phone wasn't taking messages or calls, that was a worry.

Evidently she had gone back to her family in Houston, because he had been told she wasn't working at The Excelsior anymore. That wasn't a problem for him as he had his own travel arrangements to make the journey. But Gerry would have to find her first. He needed an address to find her, to be able to coax her back to L.A. or Perseverance, near Fort Worth where he lived.

Mia was already becoming a complexity in his well-ordered life. Why couldn't he have fallen in love with a nice homely woman closer to home?

Marcus emphatically shook his head to that argument. Been there! Done that! Worn the hair T shirt for far too long! It was time to plunge in, and take a chance on love, and happiness, and loads of exciting sex. *That* he would bet his last dollar on.

CHAPTER FOURTEEN

Oh shit! She must have been hit by a truck, because she couldn't seem to move any part of her body, the pain was overwhelming.

Mia felt as if her eyelids were too heavy to open, but she concentrated with her hazy dysfunctional mind, and slowly managed to prise both open. Next she very carefully lifted her head off the pillow trying to understand where she was.

Was she in a very posh hospital room? Because there was a tube in her arm, and bandages almost covering her entire body.

Oh dear God! She felt like death, and began to cry quietly, as she was too scared to make a sound. Then she looked around the room and could see two strange men asleep in the armchairs in the room. Now, she was really scared. Was she in a nightmare? Would she wake up in her own comfortable bedroom next to her mama's and papa's bedroom?

She wracked her muzzy brain, what the fuck was her name? Where did she live? She really must have had a bad accident to feel as bad as she did, and the pain was building, not receding. She was too frightened to move again in case it would make the pain worse.

For fuck sake where was a doctor when you needed one? All she needed were strong pain meds. Then perhaps she could put the puzzle pieces back in the correct place, and find out who she was. And what had happened to her.

Then a really tough looking guy was leaning over her, and checking the blinking machinery that she was hooked up to, and tapping two bags that were attached to her arm.

"Hi Mia, how are you feeling? Do you know who I am? Do you know where you are?"

She really tried to appear tough, but failed miserably, because of the volume of pain attacking every part of her body. Even her insides felt as if they had been scooped out, and put back in the wrong place. And, her back was on fire, as she tried to get more comfortable in the bed.

"I don't care a fuck who I am, or who you are. If you are my doctor just give me a really strong painkiller, and take this Godawful pain away." Her voice sounded as if she was a heavy smoker, and her throat as if someone had tried to strangle her with their bare hands, and she couldn't swallow worth a spit.

What on earth had happened to her? It was all overload for her battered brain to cope with, so she closed her eyes and slid back into that deep, dark place of nowhere, no place, where pain wasn't waiting to cripple her, but shadowed in the background – waiting.

"Al, please give our girl the morphine that Doctor Perez left for her, if she woke up." Santi was standing by the bed, his good looking face was frowning with worry. Al and Santi had slept in the same room as Mia to keep watch over her. Stefan couldn't do anymore for his patient, so had decided to go back to the clinic for a couple of hours of uninterrupted sleep. He hadn't had a second thought of leaving Al in charge of Mia's welfare. The ex-Special Forces was an exceptional paramedic, as he would have been to be able to work in war-torn countries.

Al checked his watch, it was past midnight so the Rohypnol had entered his patient's blood stream over twenty-four hours ago. It was pretty obvious that Mia wasn't a user of any other drugs, she had previously told Santi that she didn't drink or take drugs.

In truth when they had found her covered in blood he had been sceptical that they could save her, but Doctor Perez was one of the best surgeons he had ever worked with.

It had been an honour and a privilege to work beside him, and to help Mia.

And Santi? Al had never seen him so angry, or so worried, that Mia was going to slip away from them. Honestly, he had always thought Santi was a closet gay, because no one had ever seen him interested in any woman before.

Thank God, no one had ever dared voice that opinion, because that tiny, beautiful blonde, had turned that on its head. Even a blind man could tell that this tough, mean, asshole of a mobster, had fallen hard and fast.

Al could relate with that phenomenon. He had done just that on a leave from the Special Forces. Had got drunk, fallen in love with a gorgeous red head, married her far too quickly, and lived to regret it just weeks later. They were divorced, and it had cost him all his bank balance to get the lying, cheatin' whore off his back. Luckily she was now a long ago dim memory.

Lesson learnt buddy boy, fuck 'em, and leave 'em. And never let them know who you really were. That was his personal anthem now.

Al checked her vitals again, and decided it would be OK to give his patient a strong painkiller as Stefan had given him permission to do, before he left a few hours ago.

Santi looked across the bed at him, and was holding her hand so carefully and gently. "Thank you Al, I won't forget what you've done for our Mia. She means the world to me, and when she is out of the woods, and when we can put all this – this awfulness behind us, you will be well rewarded my friend." Santi bent over and kissed her forehead, then tried to make her pillows more comfortable around her.

"Jeeze", Al said under his breath, this was a side of his Boss Al had never seen before, and he wouldn't dare tell the other guys, because Santi would deal out severe punishment to anyone who talked about him. He was a very secretive man, who never wanted anyone to know he had a really good side. It would give his enemies or his opposition an edge he couldn't afford them to have. His life was always on a knife edge of violence, so he had to keep up the face of a violent man himself, or end up dead in an alleyway.

Al could not comprehend how Santi could possibly live like that, he must have nerves of iron, and balls of steel.

"Mia, can you wake up for me?" Stefan had taken down the IV, and the cannula out of her hand. She had received all the antibiotics she needed to kill any infection, and glucose for the energy to get her out of trauma. He tapped her good hand, she needed to be conscious now to begin the healing process. But in doing so, he would have to tell her what had happened to her.

This was always a part of his work he abhorred. This was a young woman who possibly had never known a man, and had been raped and tortured by at least two animals, and this could alter her attitude towards men for the rest of her life.

Such a beautiful young woman should marry the man of her dreams and have many babies. Stefan prayed to his

God that this would happen to Mia. Hopefully his skill as an excellent surgeon had managed to repair the damage those miscreants had inflicted on his very sick patient.

Once again Mia went through the process of trying to open her eyes, and this time there was a really nice Hispanic man smiling at her, and hopefully he was a doctor. Because the pain was still with her, but not growling at her so loud. "Are you my doctor? Am I in hospital? Have I been hit by a truck? And, who the hell am I?" She had just about managed to whisper all that, and now was exhausted, and wanted to go back to sleep, badly.

But Stefan wasn't going to allow that to happen. He needed Mia awake to find out if she actually knew what had happened to her, or if she knew anything about twenty-four hours ago, before the assault had taken place. She had definitely been given far too big a dose of Rohypnol for her petit size, which had been a serious problem when he had started to work on her.

"Sweetheart, I want you to concentrate and tell me your name, and where you live, and what you think happened to you. I know you must be in a great deal of pain, and I promise to give you enough pain medication to cope with the worst of it. I am Doctor Perez, Stefan Perez, and I am here to look after you, with the help of Al." He indicated the big, burly man she remembered standing over her previously. "Al is an amazing paramedic, and has been with you all through the night, while I caught a few hours sleep at the clinic I work in." He gave her a quick wink of assurance. "I know he looks tough, but is really a sweet guy when he needs to be."

Even though Al smiled at Mia, she squinted at him not believing a word. This was a queer set up, she didn't have a clue what was going on. There were three strange men in the room, and she still didn't know where she was, or who she was. But then she really tried her hardest to concentrate, and felt as if the cogs in her brain clicked into place, even though her mind was still foggy and dysfunctional.

"I am? I am?" She closed her eyes, took a breath and went for it. "Lisette Arnaud. I live in Houston in a big old Victorian house with my parents." Then her bottom lip quivered. "I want my Papa", her voice sounded rusty, but it was childlike in content and volume.

Stefan looked over to Anton whose expression was cold and indifferent, as if he didn't care what this young woman was saying. But Stefan knew his friend better than that, his body language was screaming out how hurt he was that she didn't remember him. He had been right when he had first seen how worried Anton was, it was extremely unusual for him to be so concerned over any female. Against all odds Anton Santi had fallen hard and fast in love for the very first time. And her loss of memory must be killing him, when he had always got his own way with everything he touched, and took for himself.

He quietly spoke to Al and Anton. "Guys, can you give me some time alone with our patient? We need to discuss what happened to her, and what we are going to do when she is capable of being moved." Stefan realised that Mia couldn't stay permanently in the penthouse, it wouldn't be safe or correct for a young woman to live there with Anton.

"Boss, we've found her property in the staff recreation area." Larry was hesitant to tell Santi what he had found, because Mia had packed all her belongings, and it was evident she had been leaving the Hotel when she had been kidnapped by her rapists.

Anton was exhausted and bad tempered, having had just a few hours sleep in the past twenty-four hours, and now his Mia didn't know him, or who she was. Or did she? Was she actually this Lisette from Houston, or Mia Maxwell the woman he cared for?

Anton waved Larry away, he couldn't care less about any property found in the staff quarters, because she had been staff, so her personal stuff would have been there, wouldn't it? "Larry I really don't care. I am dying from lack of food, as is Al. Please get us two big rare steaks and everything that goes with them. A huge pot of strong coffee, as quickly as possible. I am going to shower, shave, and change my disgusting clothes." Then he turned to Al. "Thank you so much for everything you have done for our girl. You were amazing, and most probably saved her life before Stefan got there. Now, you go shower etc, eat your meal, and then return home and take a couple of days chilling out. You have definitely earned it, if you are as tired as I am." Santi could only wish that he could do something as simple as that – just chill out.

The other three guys couldn't believe they had heard correctly, Santi never talked to his security team so informally. This diabolical thing that had happened to that sweet young woman had definitely altered their Boss, they had never thought to see such a change, not in this lifetime.

Was Anton Santi actually a human being with blood in his veins? And perhaps a beating heart? They looked quizzically at each other, and as one murmured, "Nah! Not a prayer in heaven!"

But were definitely worried, because they truly liked their work. Larry did all the scheduling for Santi, so they all had plenty of down time to be able to scratch the itch of sexual frustration, without the fear and responsibility of marriage.

They all had a very comfortable and financially secure way of life, and wouldn't want to lose all the perks they received from a very generous Mobster and Boss. He never asked questions about their personal lives, but always expected them to be on call if the shit hit the fan. To keep his home and himself safe from his enemies, which there were many, ready to take over his seedy empire.

Apart from that they had a top of the range gym, a great swimming pool they could use, unless Santi was there. And a hot tub for relaxation. A track for jogging, and extremely comfortable quarters that were separate from the main house. But had to abide by Santi's rules of no gambling, no women in their rooms, no brawling under any circumstances, because of booze. They were extremely well paid for any inconvenience incurred by Santi's lifestyle.

They had all been picked up off the streets as homeless by Santi. Because of their past lives in war-torn countries, and what they had to endure and carry out in Special Forces – Post Traumatic Stress Disorder was rampant in this elite group of men. All six of Santi's security men had suffered with that phenomenon, lost their families, and their dignity. Santi had offered them work, and saved their sanity and most probably their lives. They all would take a bullet for him in a heartbeat.

But, now a woman had come into their well-ordered lives, and seemingly threatened to change everything. Andi had the most to lose than anyone else. If he lost the man he adored, he would be suicidal, and could do something he would regret for the rest of his life. What that was, he wasn't sure yet.

Anton was the love of his life.

He was beautiful.

A kind, considerate lover.

Basically a good person, under the facade of violence, and gang warfare.

But would this ditsy, difficult, prickly young woman take Anton over to the other side?

Time would only decree the outcome!

CHAPTER FIFTEEN

Mia could not believe what the doctor was telling her. Surely she would remember something so evil, so bad. Stuff like that happened to other women, not Lisette of staid old Houston. Her heart didn't allow her to take on board that such vile, sick young men had kidnapped her, and used her for their perverted sexual gratification. In all her short life she had never hurt another living soul, if she had, she certainly didn't remember doing so. Could only pray she was a kind, loving soul.

"What is the last thing you can remember, Lisette?" Stefan didn't want to push her too hard, so decided to use the name she was comfortable using. And, Anton was standing in the shadows at the back of the bedroom, because he didn't want to aggravate the situation. Even though he was casually leaning against the wall, hands in his pockets and feet crossed, seemingly not involved with what was being said, Stefan knew differently. He was perfectly still, too still for Anton. A man who was always on the move, always in control of every situation, but now at a complete loss as to how to help the woman he loved.

Everything about this Godawful situation was totally out of Anton's control, and he didn't like it one little bit. Those involved would suffer beyond anything they could ever imagine. Surpass what they had put Mia through.

Mia closed her eyes and frowned, as if really trying to put pieces of the puzzle together, and then her big brown eyes popped open, she put her hand over her mouth, as if she didn't want to say something so important. "Oh my God! Oh dear God! It was those two young idiots at the bar. I knew it! I just didn't trust them. They were so smarmy, and too fuckin' nice to me. They must have spiked my Ginger Ale. I thought it tasted too sweet, but I was hot and thirsty." Her eyes filling with tears she looked at Stefan, still not believing what they had done to her.

"Why? Why pick on me? I only said I didn't want to see them out of work. They tried for a week, and wouldn't take no for an answer. The fuckin' bastards. I hope they rot in hell." She began to sob, because he had said that she may never get over the attack. Coupled with the awful pain in every part of her body, it was just too much to cope with.

Anton couldn't stop himself, it was unbearable to watch Mia tearing herself apart, and looking so distraught and unhappy. He moved away from the wall and went to her to take her in his arms and console her as best he could. It was a difficult decision as it was the first time for him. Anton Santi actually holding a woman in his arms, trying to give her comfort and support.

Stefan had never been witness to this scene previously.

Mia looked at him through her tears. "I'm Mia Maxwell aren't I? I left Lisette Arnaud back in Houston weeks ago. What's happening to me Anton? I don't know who I am anymore." She held on to Anton as if her life depended on it, as if he was an anchor she needed to cling to.

Stefan smiled at his friend, knowing he probably was going to be the catalyst to get Mia back on track. And, she would need that anchor in the days and weeks to come for her recovery, if that actually happened at all.

Anton was whispering soothing remarks to their distraught patient. "Sweetheart, we will find the sick perverts who did this to you, and they will absolutely live to regret their actions. Believe me when I say they will never be able to do these terrible atrocities to another young woman. You have my sacred word on that, Mia."

But Stefan needed to break up this sweet cameo, as Mia needed to try and get out of bed and go to the bathroom for a shower. Because she was a strong, healthy young woman, apart from her injuries, and would feel a lot better if she at least felt clean in mind and body from the touch of those sick young bastards.

In fact probably would never feel clean, ever again.

"Mia, I need to get you to the bathroom, would you prefer that a woman helps you, or is it OK if I do it? I really don't mind if you want someone else to help you." He was also asking Anton's permission at the same time, as he was a typical Italian male, who wouldn't like another man helping his woman take a shower.

Mia was wearing a surgery gown to hide her broken body, but that also needed changing now. Stefan always carried a multitude of necessities when he made visits to his sick patients.

Mia had given up on preserving her modesty, evidently everyone had seen her naked when she was unconscious, so a doctor seeing her naked wasn't a problem for her. But she was worried about all the stitches holding her together. She pointed to her personal stuff that must have been brought in when she was asleep. "Please doctor, I would prefer that you helped me, but may I wear my own clothes? And what about all my stitches, won't a shower wash them out?"

"No Mia, I told you they will all dissolve in seven days. Now be a good girl and let Anton help you put your legs over the side of the bed, as you are going to feel really disorientated for a moment."

Both Stefan and Anton held onto her making her way to the bathroom on shaky legs. But Anton stood back when they reached the door, and let Stefan carefully take his patient through, and shut the door behind them.

Anton didn't want to let her go, but common sense told him this was just the beginning of a long road to recovery for Mia. And he intended to be there for her every moment that she would need him. However long that took.

He had sworn that he would make it up to her for the rest of her life for allowing her to be raped and tortured in his hotel. On his watch!

Anton Santi always kept his word – Always!

Gerry Swane sauntered into Marcus's office as usual looking like Robert Redford on an extremely good day. Marcus quickly gazed at the office door as it opened, and smiled at his P.I. He could never fathom out how Gerry could look so bloody immaculate one day, and a dog's dinner another day. The man was a chameleon, but also the best P.I. in the county, probably California.

"How did you get on? Where is she? Do we know why she decided to go back home? When she was here, she was adamant about finding out about her mother's death." Marcus gave Gerry a withering look. "And, please put out that disgusting cheroot you are chewing on." He pointed to the No Smoking signs around the room, but knew Gerry wasn't about to accommodate his demand. Gerry hated rules and regulations, and was perverse enough to ignore them just to irritate everyone around him.

"You're so not going to like my bill for 48 hours of my time, because I honestly have come to a blank wall, a dead end. Believe me that has never happened before. Mia Maxwell seems to be a figment of our imagination, and is a puff of wind that has disappeared from the horizon of our lives."

"For crissake Gerry stop prevaricating and tell me exactly what you found out. She is a beautiful young woman with attitude, and a really strong mind of her own. She can't possibly disappear without a trace, after leaving me a sweet message on my phone saying she was returning home to her parents. She also said she had booked her return ticket early the next morning, and – and she would never forget my kindness in helping her with Roberto and her family here. Does that sound like someone who was going to do a disappearing act from everyone she loved?" Marcus didn't add that he returned that love, absolutely. He could not lose her after just finding her a few weeks ago. Perhaps in hindsight he should have made contact with her instead of asking Gerry to keep an eye on her safety, because it seemed she was missing.

"Honestly Marcus, I've tried everything I could think of. I did manage to get in touch with her family in Houston, trying not to worry them. But did telephone and ask to speak to her, and was told she was in Los Angeles." He sat down heavily in an armchair, and ran his hand agitatedly through his long blond hair. Not finding Mia was driving him insane, because in truth he was really worried about her. She had just disappeared from the hotel where she had a really good job, and was earning a fortune in tips, and seemed happy.

"I'm friendly with John behind the bar where Mia played the piano every night, but his usual gossipy mouth was tightly clamped up. He did indicate that there was an incident a few nights back at the hotel. Santi's henchmen were running around in circles the next lunchtime asking questions of all the staff, and threatening them that if they opened their mouths to anyone they would lose their very lucrative jobs. Then John added that it was weird, because that was the morning after Mia had supposedly left, but her luggage was found in the staff recreational area untouched."

After Gerry had slipped John a hundred dollar note, he whispered under his breath that no one had set eyes on Santi, but there had been a great deal of coming and going to the penthouse by his security.

"Do you think this has something to do with Mia?" Marcus asked, really worried for her safety, trusting Santi went against everything he knew about the gangster. If he or his men had hurt her in any way, Marcus would find a way to hurt his life in the shadows of crime. The Agencies would love to get any information to put Santi in prison for the rest of his misbegotten life. And Marcus knew plenty.

"You've certainly earned your money, Gerry. Is there anything we can do next? I have to find her, she has come to mean everything to me." Then he had to admit to Gerry to telling Sophia about her, which let Gerry know that he was serious about how he felt about the pint-size, beautiful termagant fire cracker.

Gerry gave his friend a puzzled look, he had come to realise that Marcus was taken with Mia. But this acknowledgement was on a whole different level. Marcus was in love, and he was hurting at a level that Gerry had never experienced, and didn't want to – thank you very much.

"I am reliably informed that the penthouse is empty, and Santi has gone to ground on his estate in Beverley Hills. My gut never lets me down, and it's telling me that is where they have secreted Mia. I heard that Santi is taken with her, which beggars belief if the rumours are true. But knowing her she wouldn't have gone without a fight. It's a fuckin' fortress with at least half a dozen seriously armed ex-Special Forces." Gerry shook his head and took a deep drag from his smoke, and almost coughed up a lung. He knew Marcus would expect him to somehow get in there to find out if Mia was actually there. That could be a step too far for even Gerry to consider.

He shook his blond head again, sometimes or often, he wondered why he contemplated this work. *Oh Yes!* It was never the same two days running. It made his heart beat faster than was good for him. And, it paid for his extremely lavish lifestyle.

"Yeah! I'll do it. Give me some time to consider just how I will do it, without getting my backside kicked." He grinned that boyish grin at Marcus, and winked as a bonus. Marcus went over to him and gave him a man hug. He was so relieved that Gerry would do that for Mia and him.

"Yeah! Yeah! A hug's OK, but please no kissing. She's a royal pain in the ass, especially if I get mine kicked. But she is very lovable, even I can see that buddy. This is going to cost you a fuckin' fortune."

Marcus smiled, whatever the cost Mia was definitely worth every dollar. He let out a huge sigh of relief. He'd been worried to death when Gerry started to tell him that Mia was missing, and he couldn't find her.

That wasn't an option he was willing to even consider. Gerry was a lethal magician, and he trusted that he would do everything possible to find his Mia.

"I forgot to ask you whatever happened to your undercover work? Did it pan out, or not?"

"Nah! The asshole I'm after is a clever bastard. But the word on the street is that he is gradually retiring from his illegal, and going legit', and there will be a gang war soon. Let them kill each other. I'm gonna' let the Fed's take over. I'm just wasting my time trying to knock down a brick wall of silence. Like you, the head of the snake has a genius IQ, so that beats my mediocre brain at every turn. Time to know when to give up. And my time is way past its due date."

He sauntered back to the door, walking as if he had all the time in the world. "Get back to you when I know something concrete. Don't worry about our girl. She can definitely look after herself, even Santi won't be able to cope with her. Unless the poor sap has fallen in love with her? But to my knowledge the man is a closet gay."

"Yeah! That's what I heard whispered." Marcus prayed that this was true, because he didn't need that good looking bastard keeping Mia for himself.

That would be the biggest joke on Marcus to lose the woman he loved to the likes of Anton Santi, an unspeakably evil, piece of pond scum.

CHAPTER SIXTEEN

"Well Mia, I think this will be my last visit, unless something unprecedented happens. You have gone against all my previous predictions, and have come out the other side amazingly well."

Stefan had just given his patient a thorough physical, with a female assistant at his side. Santi had absolutely refused Stefan permission to be with Mia alone, demanding that a female nurse be with him if he had to examine her internally.

Mia could not have cared less. She trusted Stefan one hundred per cent, but Anton was paying the cost of her treatment so she wasn't about to argue any time soon. Let him be difficult and possessive, which he was without any effort.

"Your stitches have all dissolved, and I am surprised how well you have healed internally. A couple of weeks ago I would never have believed we would be at this stage in your wellbeing as we are."

But Mia was chewing on the inside of her cheek, not really wanting to ask Stefan the obvious. "Will I – will I be able to have a family, eventually? Or have those sick bastards changed the course of my life forever?" She quickly added when she saw Stefan frown at her question. "Not as if I ever want to get married, or have kids." She shrugged dismissively. "You never know what's down the road for anyone. So thought I should ask." Stefan smiled and just nodded his head, Mia was a healthy young woman, exceptionally so.

She shuddered at the very thought of another man touching her after what those sicko's did to her. Except Marcus Medina of course. And that was never going to happen in this lifetime.

Her mercurial Gemini brain changed course. "Can I? Can I leave this hateful bedroom, now? I so want to sit in the sun. I know I've been out on the veranda every day, but it feels as if I'm a prisoner in here. Anton has been amazing, but I need space to breathe in. Just being able to sit round the pool would be fantastic."

She knew that Anton stuck to a rigid timetable in his life to keep super fit. Every morning he got up around eight a.m., swam a hell of a lot of lengths of the pool, then went straight to the gym with his security to work out until ten a.m. They all had breakfast in the solarium behind the pool. Anton then got ready for the day ahead, as he was always immaculately dressed. Larry and Anton were then ensconced in the office until lunchtime around two p.m., or it could be all day.

Evidently, that rigid routine had only changed when he had wanted to look after Mia's recovery. It was obvious he had been sick with worry about her, and she could definitely love him a little for that consideration, above and beyond.

She was amazed how the huge rambling estate was run on a strict regime. Anton was totally meticulous about his staff and family were safe in their environment, and especially his father Theo, who always had two young men in attendance, a physio and medic. She knew that Anton absolutely adored his father, the ex-gangster, who now was unable to do anything for himself due to a serious illness that started four years previously, and could only get much worse.

Anton had told her all this when they were together every afternoon sitting on her veranda, they had become very close. Slowly she had become very attached to him, because there wasn't anything he wouldn't get her, or spoil her with. Ordering in books she loved, any food she fancied, a new iPhone, and her own credit card to buy new clothes online, which of course hadn't been used, yet.

God Almighty – who wouldn't fall in love with this gorgeous looking man, and she couldn't care less how he earned his millions. It was nothing to do with her, and never would be.

Proudly, he had told her about the huge estate he had bought when he was twenty five years old, from an ancient movie star, who had since died in his dotage. It was on three and a half acres enclosed by cliffs on three sides. Spectacular views over the Pacific Ocean, and San Gabriel mountains. Mia could smell and hear the pounding ocean on a calm, sunny day. There were twenty-seven rooms with thick stucco walls. They were built around a courtyard with a flowing fountain filled with huge Koi carp, mouths always open gaping for food. Flowers grew everywhere – Azaleas, Gardinias, Jasmine, their perfume was amazing. Her suite had spectacular views over the ocean.

Downstairs, vast lounges, a cinema, and guest rooms were situated. A huge rustic bar, and fireplaces were in strategic areas. All the furniture was white, or beige with colourful pillows and throws everywhere.

Some of the essential staff had accommodation at the back of the main house, but could go home when they were off duty. But the security preferred to live in, because of the fractured hours they worked, and preferred all the conveniences on offer.

Anton seemed to have exemplary staff always on call. A young Mexican couple were the chef and housekeeper. And a few mornings a week at exactly eight a.m. a van brought in cleaners and maintenance from Roberto's company, because Anton trusted Roberto and Mel without any hesitation. It wasn't easy to gain Anton's trust, but

Roberto Diaz definitely had, and he would never betray that trust. Anton Santi always paid over the odds, and always on time.

After Anton had explained all this to Mia, she had confessed that she never wanted to leave, because he made her feel safe, comfortable, and truly loved for herself.

Anton had physically given a sigh of relief, he had constantly worried that she would leave him when she had got over her traumatic ordeal. But he also knew that she had grown up, and had realised that she could become a target again, if she left the security of his estate, and his security men.

Only that morning they had discussed that possibility. "Sweetheart, you would break my heart if you left me. But, I want you to understand that my home is not a prison. You are free to leave any time. If you decide to stay, you will never want for anything. Name it, and it will be here. But, I need to explain something important to you that will probably affect what happens between us, eventually." He had taken her small hand in his and was gently stroking his thumb over the back of it, as if he was really nervous.

Mia grinned at the gorgeous man who she was beginning to fall in love with, even though her heart would always belong to Marcus Medina. Well, she was a Gemini and was capable of loving more than one man at a time.

"Anton, nothing you could tell me would change my mind about loving you, unless you've murdered someone today."

Anton smiled back at her, he was so in love with this brave, complicated, kind, human being. They were so totally compatible, or would they be when he confessed to his sexual connotation, and usual preference? He looked straight into those big brown eyes, that were full of concern and worry for what he was going to tell her. As usual she totally got how he felt and if he was worried or angry. She knew he could never be angry with her, often impatient, but never angry.

Anton cleared his throat to stop his voice from wavering, and just went for it. "I am bisexual, but truthfully have always favoured men, sexually in preference." He waited for the backlash, but she never batted an eyelid, not a ripple of derision in her facial expression. So he asked, "Do you want to talk about it?" Shit! He had never felt so scared. This was all new to him, and he didn't like the feeling one bit. Evidently, it hurt like hell to be in love with a woman. Had he made the right choice? You bet he had!

Honestly, he didn't understand female logic, or female emotion. His mother had walked out on him when he was four years old, and his father never brought any girlfriends home to meet him. Anton was a female wilderness, until Mia had walked into his well ordered male life. And she *was* scary, but extremely lovable.

"What's to talk about? Are you gay, or not? Because I always thought I was sort of gay. I never fancied anyone, and believed I was asexual, until I did fall for someone I only met for a few moments, and it hurt bad. I didn't like it at all. All that crap is for the la la romantics, evidently not for me."

Anton felt a sick surge of jealousy, who was this paragon of virtue? But knew she would never reveal who it was, hopefully in the past, and forgotten. He was in the here and now, and fully intended to keep Mia for himself.

"You do understand Mia what I am telling you is a secret. If it ever gets out it will make me seem weak, and could get me killed. Tough, evil men in my line of work do not tolerate the sexual gay orientation."

Mia wasn't stupid, she could completely understand that Anton would have a big problem being gay in his line of work. So would absolutely keep her mouth shut on anything about Anton, and his predilection.

"Since you came into my life I have no intention of being with another male. I want to be with you, only you for the rest of my life, however long or short that is."

When Mia quickly backed away from him in apprehension, because no way was she anywhere near being able to have a relationship with anyone, especially Anton Santi, he explained exactly what he had in mind for them both, trying to ease her over-active mind. "I do not expect you to be ready any time soon to be able to sleep with me, but have I the smallest chance to be that person when you are ready, if ever?" Anton looked so woebegone Mia actually felt sorry for him.

"Anton, I can't even sleep without medication, because my nightmares are so graphic, horrible, and disgusting. If I ever, and it's a big if, manage to put this diabolical time in my life behind me, I would want to be with you. You have saved my life, and my sanity, nobody but nobody could have done more for me."

She got up from her comfortable chair, and kissed him softly on his very kissable lips. He wanted to deepen the kiss, but held back knowing she wasn't ready yet. But one day! Anton was used to having sex whenever he wanted it, this abstinence was killing him. Perhaps he'd been too hasty in knocking back Andi, but Mia wasn't stupid, she was bound to find out if Andi paid a visit to his bedroom. It just wasn't worth the consequence. His own fist would have to do.

"It's Andi isn't it, who is in love with you? He never takes his eyes off you when we are all together. Be careful Anton, please let him down easily, because I think he could cause you a whole heap of trouble." Mia didn't know why she was warning him, but as usual her Papa's words came back to haunt her, that she was a psychic witch.

The next two weeks passed in an organised blur. Al had become her personal bodyguard, which he was quite happy about as it got him out of a great deal of other security work. He was teaching Mia how to play chess, not an easy task, as her Gemini active brain couldn't stay quiet enough to take all his instructions on board, and be constructive. But Al was the epitome of patience, and would not give up – whatever. But she was teaching him Gin, and taking a fortune from him, and he didn't dare complain to his Boss, because his Mia could do no wrong in his besotted eyes.

Al swam with her every morning, and was utterly amazed the first morning when she was like a dolphin in the water. She had laughed at his expression of disbelief, and explained her father had made his four children learn to swim before they could walk, because he feared they would drown in their pool if they fell in with no one to save them. Then they walked through the estate for miles, which she wasn't that happy about, but gave in otherwise he would make her work out in the gym. That was a step too far for lazy Mia, who would rather read trashy romantic novels all day, 24/7.

At lunchtime, while Anton was working, she would find a quiet spot in the gardens, take a blanket and pillows, and eat a simple sandwich. Read in peace, take a nap, as she still wasn't up to speed yet, which gave Al a couple of hours to himself with the other guys. She was a totally spoilt young woman, being the only female amongst so many alpha men. Everyone was always asking her if she was OK, and did she need anything. At first it had been a novelty, but now she needed time to herself, and just peace and quiet to think about her future. Did she have a future outside these safe and secure walls? And where? She couldn't go home yet after what had happened to her, if her Papa found out he would wreak vengeance on the two men who had violated his precious daughter. And possibly get into deep trouble himself.

Evenings were spent with her favourite person, Anton Santi, they were totally comfortable in each other's company, and discussed and tortured every subject under the sun. Mia was very opinionated, and vocal on every subject, and Anton loved to question her on her eclectic views, and mostly agreed with her, except on drugs, booze, anything illegal he dealt with on a daily basis. It was pretty obvious he would defend his way of life, but even that was beginning to be in question since meeting Mia, and her views on his work, and how it affected other people's addictions, and lifestyles.

But one thing Anton was adamant about, that she wore a bracelet that technically connected her to Al, just in case she needed him medically. She was doing extremely well, but her body was still fragile and could break down any time. She had grumbled and used vile language, but Anton would not give in to her histrionics, and so she wore it constantly. It had been Al's idea, and Anton had agreed wholeheartedly, because he felt so relieved that her vitals were being constantly monitored. He had almost lost her, and never wanted to feel that vulnerable ever again.

Today Mia was very apprehensive, because Anton had asked her if she would visit his father. Evidently his father had found out that she was living on the estate and was insisting on meeting her, especially as his son seemed to be besotted with her.

But first Anton had tried to explain just how disabled his father was, because he didn't want Mia to be taken aback over just how sick his beloved father was.

Four years ago Anton had taken his father to every available specialist that could help his deteriorating illness, money had not been a problem, but a diagnosis had proved to be difficult, or up for speculation. His father had been tall, upright, and as strong as an ox, mentally exceptional, and one hundred per cent healthy. But slowly everything was going into reverse, and he was becoming unstable, angry, and unable to function normally, which had broken his son's heart.

Then at last they found a specialist who had given his solid prognosis. Theo had Als-Amyotrophic Sclerosis, with a four year death sentence. It can possibly be passed on genetically. (Theo recalled that his grandfather had been struck down with the same disability, but nobody had known what it was) : Gradually paralysis takes over hands, feet, and all limbs. Nerve cells are destroyed, and eating is impossible. But because Anton could easily afford the latest state of the art technology, his father could speak through a voice synthesiser by facial movement. So at least father and son could have some form of communication, but time wasn't on Theo's side, and he wasn't expected to manage to live through the next month or two.

Anton was beside himself with grief for how his father had been, and how he was now. A great mind living in a total wreck that was still his body. A prison with no get out clause for good behaviour, or parole.

Mia had dressed in a brilliant yellow sundress. Had tried to tame her usual riotous curly hair, and her make-up was minimalistic as per usual. She didn't ever realise just how stunningly beautiful she was, without even trying. She was always her beautiful mother's daughter.

Holding Anton's hand tightly she entered into Theo's quiet, peaceful apartment. She smiled at the young men that were hovering at the door to greet Anton, who always rang through before he visited in case it wasn't convenient for him to be there, because his father needed a great deal of care to keep him breathing, and alive.

But even though Anton had warned her how bad his father looked, she had to take a deep breath trying to keep the expression on her face normal, and not full of empathy for the frail elderly man hooked up to a myriad of tubes in and out of his frail body. Nobody would believe that this frail, emaciated man had once been the mastermind of a seedy underworld of gangsters and crime lords, who ruled everything that made billions of dollars in guns, drugs, and slave labour.

Now he looked like anyone's old, frail, sick, scarily thin grandfather. But there was still a banked fire of hate and murder in his watery blue/green eyes. Anton's eyes.

Immediately Mia went straight to him, taking his heavily veined hand she very gently kissed it, her voice cracked as she spoke to him. "Mr Santi, I am so honoured to meet you, Anton has told me so much about you." She wasn't going to add that Anton was so proud he was his Papa, but not so proud of how he had earned their fortune to be able to live in luxury with so much wealth. Mia believed this was totally obscene. It wasn't her place to voice how she felt about the Santi family's way of life – thuggery.

Theo Santi very slowly looked straight at her, and became very agitated, and couldn't seem to be able to use his voice synthesiser, and the monitors managing his vitals were going off the scale. Anton became extremely worried for his father's obvious agitation, he was literally shaking.

"Papa please, you have to calm down, otherwise your blood pressure will go sky high, and Dennis will have to give you a sedative to quieten you down."

Theo tried to smile at Mia, but it came out as a grimace. He glared at his son daring him to carry out his threat. Theo was still in charge of his waning health. Then a disembodied voice came out of Theo's computer, it was slow and choppy, but clear enough for everyone to understand without question.

"Mia is Maddie Maxwell's baby girl.
I saw her when she was born and kissed her cherub lips.
She is beyond beautiful, her mother's absolute image.
I was in a relationship with Maddie for five years.
I made it possible for her to get into the movies.
I called in favours from people who owed me big time.
She was the love of my life, but I gave her up.
Because of the corrupt world I lived in.
Also I was still married to Anton's mother."

He stopped talking and Dennis gave him a small drink of his medication through a straw, allowing Theo to be able to carry on after a pause. Mia was looking at him through eyes full of tears and disbelief. Was Anton's father going to give her the information she was desperate for about her mother? The very reason she had come to Los Angeles in the first place.

Anton was staggering under what his father was revealing, he had never mentioned any of this to his son previously.

Theo took another sip of medication determined to finish what he had to tell Maddie's daughter.

But, firstly he had to answer the worrying question of Mia's conception. He was certain that Mia must have wondered?

"As much as I would love to be your Papa, that would not be the truth. I was not with Maddie at the time her darling baby was conceived. A baby that she so desperately wanted. Henri Arnaud is definitely your father, and to my knowledge is a truly wonderful man. My Maddie fell in love with him that weekend they were together, and I am sure that he loved her. And, you were conceived in total love, even though it was impossible for them to stay together, because of his family commitments."

Mia physically slumped with relief, and gave out the breath she was holding, because for a moment she had believed she was Anton's half sister. She was starting to have feelings for Anton, how sick would that have been?

"Twenty years ago my darling girl was steadily falling apart, drugs and booze were taking their toll on her health. She was becoming very unstable, and a serious threat to the high powered men in her life and bed. The murmur on the street was that she had to be eliminated and quickly. Bearing in mind that I had contacts in every Agency that mattered, I was approached out of the blue to get rid of the love of my life in a way that would not involve any Agency. I was horrified, and flatly refused, but realised it was going to happen without my help or not, because the contract had come from the top man himself. She was my darling girl, and I could not have hurt her in any way. I also knew that anyone associated with me would not have dared to take on the contract, because it would have been a death sentence from me. So, I am certain it was those bastards in the CIA who did it."

A lone tear was tracking slowly down Theo's face, because it still haunted him to this day. Anton was holding her tightly in his arms to support her, because she had her hands over her mouth trying to stifle her sobs of heart break.

She had come to L.A. to understand what had happened to her beautiful, fragile mother over twenty years ago. But wished she hadn't found out that in all probability the President of America had killed her mother, his lover, to shut her mouth permanently. And to keep himself pure and innocent from harmful gossip.

Poor Madeline! Poor Mia! Poor Theo!

CHAPTER SEVENTEEN

Gerry Swane settled into his comfortable recliner to watch a game on his fifty-four inch television. He couldn't believe it was Saturday night and he didn't have a date with a gorgeous, tall, blonde female, who would always end up in a king-size bed at the end of the evening.

Instead he had done a friend a big favour and agreed to take out his out of town cousin, who was lonely, and didn't have a date for Saturday night. And no fuckin' wonder! Oh yeah! She was tall, gorgeous, and blonde, but that was where any attraction ended for a man who would expect his date to have at least one brain cell in working order.

Bimbo, or Bambi, had plastic tits, plastic ass, plastic lips, that could have done severe damage to his manhood. And just about enough plastic to destruct the planet.

In fact he wasn't too sure if Bambi hadn't been previously a male, before all that plastic. Sorry girlfriend, he wasn't that desperate for a fuck, not tonight.

So, here he was with a cold beer in one hand, and a toke in the other. Wearing an old pair of baggy shorts, and an even older T-shirt. When he relaxed at home he never, ever, brought a date back to his apartment. Shouting his fuckin' head off to his favourite NBA team the L.A. Lakers, who were being slaughtered by a lesser team who shouldn't have a rat's ass hope of winning, but definitely were.

Absolutely pissed off he changed channels to the late, late news, and could not believe what he was seeing. Supreme Judge Williams unbelievably crying on the news. Surely he was hallucinating, or in an altered universe, but he glanced around his lounge, and he was definitely wide awake, and in real time in his own apartment.

"My beautiful innocent twin sons were kidnapped by an evil psychotic totally insane murderer. This happened a week ago. But everyone involved with this horrendous case asked me to keep quiet so they could try and track down the perpetrator without any hindrance from the public. But so far nothing is forthcoming."

He gulped down a drink of water, trying to stop the agonised sobs from leaving his throat. It didn't work.

"My boys were dragged from their beds, tied up, and thrown into their 4X4, and driven out of L.A. into the area of the Santa Monica mountains, where it was extremely difficult to find them. We have not yet found anyone who saw anything that has helped us solve this ghastly mystery. Experienced Army trackers were employed to find my missing sons, and it took a week of 24/7 surveillance of the highest order to find them.

"I will not rest, nor will the Agencies of this state give up until we find the person, or persons, who have carried out this obscene and terrible crime."

He gulped down a heartbreaking sob, not caring anymore.

"My – my sons, were crucified, nailed to separate trees. Hacked to ribbons, and then their genitalia were removed and burnt in front of them. By this time they must have bled to death, which must have been a relief, because they must have screamed and screamed to be able to die from the torture inflicted on them.

"I am begging anyone who has the slightest piece of information on this unspeakable atrocity to please come forward and speak to the LAPD. Believe me you will be richly rewarded if it helps us find this – this psychotic madman."

He was a ruined shell of a man, and swayed when he got up, because he couldn't hold in his grief any longer.

Gerry had sat there totally transfixed on the judge's face. He hated the man with a vengeance, because he had fingers in every monetary pie, and kickbacks from everywhere else. But he doted on those boys, they were his life, and they didn't deserve to die like that.

But Gerry's brain and gut were already trying to understand why? Or had they done something to someone who wouldn't tolerate what they had done?

Immediately one name came to mind – The Executioner. He was capable of such horrendous violence, but never for himself. He was a paid Assassin. The very best in the business, and extremely expensive. Who could afford such a luxury? Anton Santi, that was who! He was a billionaire, and was very vengeful, and never forgot and forgave. Yeah! It was definitely Santi.

Oh fuck! Fuck! Fuck! This had to do with the episode at The Excelsior. Was Mia involved? What had actually happened that night when the hotel was in an uproar? Nobody had heard from her since that night. Was she dead or very much alive?

In his forty years Gerry had never become so attached to a woman as he had gorgeous, difficult Mia. He hadn't allowed himself the privilege of getting to know her more personally, because Marcus was head over heels in love with her. Gerry was far too old for her anyway, but he would still have given his left nut for a shot, but for Marcus.

Now, Santi seemed to have taken over. Tomorrow he would give Santi's estate a visit. Come what may.

He needed to find out for himself what had happened that night to cause Santi to call in the dubious talents of The Executioner. And hopefully find out where Mia was, and if she was OK.

He definitely didn't believe in a merciful God. But just this once God, please let our beautiful, obstinate, and spiky Mia be alive and giving Santi the hell he deserved, he said to himself, but still didn't consider it to be a prayer. Nah! When he died he fully expected to go to hell, wherever that was.

Hopefully full of tall, gorgeous, leggy blondes, who were nymphomaniacs, and please God he wouldn't have to wear a soddin' condom, ever again.

CHAPTER EIGHTEEN

Anton was playing poker with three of his security. He always lost a shit load of dollars, but loved being one of the guys with his everyday problems left in his office, and allowing his mind to get some relief.

Mia had taken to her bed earlier than usual, because she was exhausted after visiting his father, and promised that she was going to visit him every day, which had meant the world to Anton. And, he couldn't love her more, because his very sick father meant the world to him, and knowing he was coming to the end of his pain and hopelessness, and the prison of his body that didn't function anymore. Mia was a ray of sunshine at a thoroughly bleak time in his life.

So playing poker with the guys was relaxing, and a million miles from his enemies that were slowly and very carefully stalking him at every turn.

Mia yawned big time, and settled back down into her thoroughly sumptuous kingsize bed. Theo's explosive information about her beloved mother, was still running around her brain, as she tried to assimilate everything he had told her. She had believed every word he had uttered, because there wouldn't have been any reason for him to lie.

Theo was slowly dying, and was evidently now happy to allow that part of his life out in the open.

Mia was absolutely certain that he had loved her mother, and her mother had loved him. That made Mia so happy for her mother, who, for all her celebrity status, and loving fans, seemed to have led a lonely, secretive, unhappy existence, except for the five years she was Theo's mistress.

She turned up the volume on her flat screen TV and was totally surprised to see an important looking gentleman in tears. In fact almost sobbing with emotion and heartbreak. Behind him was a blown up photo of two young men.

Oh fuck! Oh shit! No way!

Mia went icy cold, began to shake, never, ever in her worst nightmare did she expect to see their psychotic, evil faces again.

Then the older man who evidently was their father was talking, and it sounded as if he was in a long tunnel of torment. His flat monotone voice was saying that his beautiful boys, innocent boys, had been crucified, cut to pieces, and their genitalia had been hacked off and burnt in front of them. Then they had bled to death.

Mia stumbled out of her bed, and fell to the floor, knowing she had to reach the bathroom before she threw up everywhere, or blacked out in remorse and unmitigated despair.

This was her fault. She must have done something wrong, or egged them on, that they had used her in such a horrific, torturous, disgusting, sexual deviate way. But what had she done?

Somehow, she managed to crawl her way to the bathroom, hanging over the toilet bowl and kept throwing up until she couldn't heave anymore. Automatically fingering the button on the bracelet to connect to Al, before she embraced once more that black, silent place. The place only she knew she would be safe from the world of disgusting, hateful human beings, and dark secrets of sexual deviants.

Al felt his phone vibrating in its holder on his waist, quickly scanning it he got up immediately, and nodded to Santi. Santi threw down his cards, and without any explanation followed Al on a run, who was already taking the stairs as fast as humanly possible, with Santi on his heels, both were very fit young men.

"Her vitals are all over the place, totally out of sync. Can't think what's happened to her to cause this breakdown." He explained to his boss as he reached Mia's suite, not bothering to knock, he crashed open the double doors. The television was still blaring and the cause for Mia's collapse was pretty evident on the screen. Santi just said "Fucking

Hell!" when he saw the two sick bastards grinning from a photo their father was holding up to the lens.

Al found her out cold on the bathroom floor. She must have hit her head as she had fallen forward, there was a bad gash bleeding profusely in her hairline, and all over her tank top.

He turned to Santi who was as white as a sheet, and just staring at Mia, frozen where he was standing in the open doorway. "Get my medical bag in her lounge. I keep a spare one there in case of an emergency." This was definitely an emergency. "Boss now please! I need to bring her round, in case she has a head injury and we need to get her to a hospital."

Santi shook himself back to reality, and murmured, "Sorry, right away." In seconds he was back with the small canvas bag that Al had used before.

Swiftly Al put a rolled up towel under Mia's head, and with a dressing gown he found thrown over a chair, he covered her body, because she felt extremely cold, which was not a good sign. Taking a small phial of smelling salts he gently wafted it under her nose, all the time checking her vitals, which at best were sketchy.

Anton knelt beside him trying not to crowd him, knowing Al knew exactly what to do. But Al had to stem the bleeding, because head injuries were notorious for an excess of blood, for even a small cut.

"While I try to stop the bleeding, would you take her hands and gently rub some life into them? She is too cold, and too deeply unconscious for my liking, I need to bring her round ASAP." He held a pristine pad to her injury, and continued to hold the smelling salts to her nose. If she didn't wake up, they would have to call an ambulance, and Santi would not easily agree to that, but he looked absolutely shell shocked. So that was in Al's favour to make the call, if he needed to for Mia's safety.

Suddenly without any warning Mia's eyes flew open, and she sat up coughing from the acrid, disgusting smell from the smelling salts. She looked straight at Anton and threw her arms around his neck, hanging on for dear life. Luckily Al had managed to stem the flow of blood from the cut in her head, with a strong disinfectant solution, which made her swear like a truck driver with the godawful sting it caused.

Al gave a huge sigh of relief, when Mia started to talk in her usual fast dialogue. Her slick brain hadn't been compromised in any way, thank God. But he couldn't believe his eyes when Santi held her face in his hands, and he gently kissed her mouth in a loving, caring way. In all the years he had known Santi he had never seen him be so loving to any woman, or anyone else either.

"Sweetheart what happened to make you so unwell? You worried the life out of Al and myself." He nodded his head at Al, and mouthed, "thank you my friend."

Mia began to cry in earnest, as she leant into the safety of Anton's chest. She still felt uneasy and afraid she would see her tormentors in her suite.

"I – I saw those two disgusting madmen on the television. Their father was saying they had been crucified, and cut to ribbons, then their private bits chopped off, and burnt in front of them." She really began to wail then at the very thought of what someone had done to them, and it could be her fault.

Anton took her in his arms and began to rub her back, and rock her in his arms. They were both still sitting on the cold tiled floor. "Honestly, I really don't know what happened to them, but can find out if I make a call to someone. Whatever I find out, it will *not* be your fault, my darling. You are the innocent party in this dreadful occurrence. Those two insane psychotic sexual deviants only suffered the dire consequences of seriously hurting my woman. Nobody, but nobody! touches anything belonging to me, and gets away with it. Now, everyone in my world knows not to mess with Anton Santi, ever again."

Mia stopped crying, because she didn't like the implication that she belonged to anyone, even Anton. Al had removed himself to the next room, and was watching the news programme on Supreme Judge Williams, who was still shouting brimstone and fire, on how he wouldn't rest until the perpetrators of his sons were caught and tried, and an arrest was imminent. Al snorted, and thought good luck with that scenario, because that was never going to happen if Santi was involved. He was certain that his Boss was definitely involved, but had paid someone to execute the little bastards. So his hands were clean, as usual in often annoying incidences.

Al went back into the bathroom to collect his patient after knocking on the door, in case of any embarrassment. He needed to stitch up that nasty gash in her hairline, but wasn't looking forward to it. Mia would rant and rave, and throw a tantrum. She hated needles, but with a head wound it would have to be stitches proper. Her language would be vile, but he'd heard much worse in Special Forces. She was a tiny termagant with a ferocious temper, but Santi would have to hold her down, and Al was sure he would probably enjoy that position.

But would he then realise exactly what he was taking on? And perhaps decide that Andi was the better option, after all?

Al wouldn't bet his week's wages on the outcome, but he also wasn't stupid, our Mia was one hell of a package. She came in so many layers to unwrap and discover her many talents, and Santi didn't seem to know if he was gay or not.

Jesus Christ what a conundrum to sort out. Good luck Anton Santi, you are *so* going to need it!

In the space of a few weeks Al had become Mia's bestest friend, because he was always with her. Well! He was second best to Viola, who would always be her lifelong best friend. But right now he was called a mother fucker – cock sucking bastard. He had warned her that the stitches would sting a bit. Sting a bit? They fucking hurt like the blazes. Poor Anton had held her down, because she couldn't sit still while Al persecuted her. She had looked at both men while cursing like a trucker, and they were both trying not to grin at her very explicit vile outburst. She was a tiny, explosive, dramatic, gorgeous female.

Now, Anton had gone to his suite of rooms to shower, and change his clothes, because they had been ruined with Mia's blood all over them. They would go straight in the bin, Anton would never wear anything that wasn't perfect. He always ordered designer, plain pristine white, golf T-shirts, and white linen, fitted long sleeve shirts, by the dozen. They were all made especially for him, and no one else. Teamed up with tight black jeans, again designer, or black cashmere trousers, and always a thin designer black belt. He most certainly could have been a top male model.

Anton Santi was always immaculately dressed. His long black hair gelled back from his too beautiful face for a man, and often his hair was clipped back with a gold clasp.

Mia was completely foxed as to how he could possibly want and seemingly love her? She had terrible colour sense, and fashion sense, was truly volatile, and couldn't seem to keep her Gemini mouth shut. Couldn't keep a secret to save her life, which in truth could be dangerous, especially around Santi, and his many enemies.

Al, bless him, who was now her best friend again, had washed the blood out of her hair in the bathroom basin, mindful of her stitches, and had cleaned her all over with a face cloth as she stood completely naked in front of him. Then he dried her with a white fluffy towel. Mia didn't seem to care who saw her in the buff. Of course he knew she had the perfect body, and the cutest tiny feet with pink nail varnish on her toes, feet that never wore shoes. But this child/woman trusted him unconditionally, and he would never betray that trust. But at times like this he really had to keep his libido under strict control. He was now rummaging in her underwear drawer for clean nightwear for her. She always wore a tank top and shorts to bed, especially in the summer.

May had come and gone, so the weather was a perfect eighty degrees, and didn't drop down too much of a night. This L.A. weather definitely suited Mia, and she hated the thought of going back to Houston. Stifling hot in the summer, and miserable in the winter. But that was her home, and she expected to return, any time soon.

Al came back with a clean pair of shorts and top, and stayed with her while she changed, because she was still a bit unsteady on her feet. She didn't care if she was naked in front of Al, because he had seen all there was to see, over and over again. He was a paramedic for crissake, which was the same as a doctor.

One day whilst they were exchanging information about each other he had told her that he had a steady girlfriend, and that they were trying for a baby. If they succeeded they would get married, and he would quit working for Anton, and go to Medical School and train to be a doctor, specialising in Paediatrics. Mia had been so happy for him and his girlfriend, and wished them all the luck in the world. Al was an extremely good person, and deserved to have a fantastic life full of love and happiness in the future.

She loved Al like a brother. She loved Christian her real brother, and missed him desperately, but wouldn't want him to see her naked – yuck!

By the time Anton came back, pristine clean, and totally gorgeous, Mia was back in bed, exhausted and almost asleep.

"Anton, do you want me to stay with Mia tonight? I don't think she should be alone, after hitting her head, and being unconscious for so long."

"Thank you Al, but I will stay with her. I agree she shouldn't be left alone. You've done as much as you could. As usual, beyond your duty. Again, I can't thank you enough. If anything changes I will immediately call you back in. Go home my friend to your very patient girlfriend." They both looked at the patient in question. She was quietly snuffling, and couldn't care less who stayed with her, because she was fast asleep.

Anton shook his head, and grinned at Al. "It's the only time that female is quiet, when she is asleep, but often talks in her sleep, so I am told."

He didn't tell Al that he often went into her bedroom when he retired for the night, just standing and looking at her perfection. Wishing he had the moxy to get into her bed and make love to her. Often she was having a conversation with herself, unaware that she was telling Anton the secrets of her heart.

That was how he knew she had fallen in love with him. And he returned that love without any doubt, whatsoever.

But getting into her pants was another matter, especially after what she had been through with those vile psychotic sexual deviants. It meant he had to proceed slowly.

But he was a very patient man, and it would happen, or he wasn't Anton Santi.

CHAPTER NINETEEN

Anton stripped down to his black silk boxers, then meticulously folded the rest of his clothes into a tidy pile on the bedside chair. Usually he slept naked, but if Mia woke up in the night he didn't want to scare her, or repulse her. If he had to stay the night there was no way he was sleeping on the couch. It would be too uncomfortable, and he hated to have a disturbed night's sleep, except for sex of course.

After what Mia had been through he couldn't take any stupid chances. He was on a serious mission to have fantastic sex with his gorgeous, volatile woman. So slowly, very slowly, was the password to victory, and also to try and be very gentle, and careful not to upset her in any way. In truth he was also very nervous, not having had sex with a female for almost ten years. He could only pray it was like everything you did for the first time, and your memory managed to remember exactly what you were supposed to do, and how to do it.

Why had fucking suddenly become so complicated?

He slid silently next to Mia in the bed, and very carefully pulled her back towards him, trying desperately not to wake her. She grunted and shifted her backside against his dormant sex, which of course decided to respond with the action. Anton used all his concentration to keep it under control, but was actually overjoyed, because he hadn't been certain that he would be able to perform to expectation, and that situation would have been so embarrassing for him and for Mia.

He was also exhausted with all the trauma of Mia collapsing on the bathroom floor, and so much blood, and not being able to bring her round. As he drifted off to sleep he was smiling about the ridiculous female he had fallen for. One minute she was a volcano, swearing like a ribald truck driver, and then a sweet angel, who apologised for being such an evil bitch. She was of course her mother's daughter, who had been known for her volatile temper. Mia was so utterly beautiful, with a body to die for, whether you were gay or heterosexual, and he wasn't sure what he was anymore.

God! She was such a slob, her clothes were strewn with abandon on every available surface. So many eye-watering colours, all mixed up. Mia must have tried on her entire wardrobe earlier today, when she met his father, and his father had been totally smitten with her, because she was Madeline Maxwell's daughter.

He would have to employ a maid to tidy up after her every day, because he couldn't personally live in such a disgusting mess, and so untidy. It wasn't his nature to be untidy at any level. Neatness and cleanliness were rigid rules in his life, as it was in his father's. DNA served him well.

Evil bitch, or sweet angel? This woman he was holding in his arms would never bore him, would always tear him off a strip if she didn't agree with him. But, he knew without a doubt, that once she loved she would never betray that love, never be unfaithful, and love with all her precious heart and soul.

What man could ask for more? Anton felt as if he had come home, at last. And, wanted to spend the rest of his short or long life with this wonderful woman, who had come into his life out of the blue.

Still smiling as he relaxed into a deep sleep, he knew he would never look back into his past, only towards his future, with Mia.

Anton thought someone was trying to strangle him, or do him bodily harm when he slowly came awake. But it was a warm female body that was closely entangled with his. An arm around his neck, a leg over his crotch, and curly blonde hair in the crook of his neck.

Shit! His morning erection was extremely happy, and outstanding. He lay there for a moment just enjoying the smell and erotic sensation of Mia being loving, and evidently comfortable with him in such close proximity. He just took in her stunning beauty, she looked so young, so innocent, and so utterly sexy, and gorgeous.

Big brown eyes popped open, looked straight at him, and she smiled that huge, guileless smile only Mia could do, and make your heart turn over, and love her even more.

"Hi Mr Santi, when did you get into my bed?" She yawned big time, and cuddled up even closer to him. Then mumbled against his chest, "are we going to fuck, or what?"

Anton laughed at her usual way with words, Mia never held back when she had something to say. "No! We are not going to fuck, shag, screw, or have hot monkey sex. We are going to make sweet love together, gently, slowly, and carefully, like two consenting adults that love each other, in case your battered and bruised body hasn't healed properly."

"Anton Santi you are such a spoilsport, and you know that Stefan has given me the all clear to have sex if I am so inclined to do so." To add to the mixture, and change his mind on the electric subject, she decided to play her own game of torture, knowing he was a sexual animal. That's what she had heard when the guys were talking together when Anton wasn't around.

Her small hand felt the soft silky hair across his chest, and she touched each nipple, surprised at how erect they were, like a female's. Then she followed the line of hair down his body, and found his morning erection, which had become very erect all of a sudden, and realised he didn't come up short in that part of his perfectly, perfect, manly body. She kissed his right nipple and then ran her seeking hand all over his hardening penis, and then did the same to his tight scrotum. Humming in her throat, she realised what she had been missing in her innocent, and naive, young life. Fucking a gorgeous male.

Anton moaned and grabbed her questing hand, otherwise their first attempt at sex would be all over before they could enjoy it. And, he realised and noted, exactly what he had been missing for the last ten years. A warm, sweet smelling, female body, that he could love, and satisfy.

"Sweetheart, let's slow down, and take a breather. Otherwise I will come, and spoil everything for you, and me. I really want to make it special for you, and for me as well. Let's get naked, and start over." He looked so young when he grinned at his exuberant lover, and began to strip off her pyjamas, and then his boxers.

For a moment Mia was angry at him for stopping her touching and acquainting herself with his male physique. An unknown quantity to her, never having slept with a man previously. Of course she knew what sexual intercourse was all about, because she had read so many trashy romantic novels. But Anton was in a league of his own, and she was worried that after today she would fall madly in love with him, and he would expect her to behave herself, and then he would be able to control her. That had never featured in Mia's future plans, her independence and obstinacy in any rules and regulations were well known by her parents, and siblings. Mia Maxwell was a one off bolshy female, who treasured her independence, never wanted to get married and have screaming kids taking up her spare time, and making her fat.

"Sweetheart promise me, please. Promise me that if you don't want to carry on, and feel uncomfortable with whatever we are doing, you will stop me immediately. Just say *'no Anton'*, and I can back off. I won't be angry, of course be disappointed, but this is your time, and I want you to be comfortable and happy with our first time together."

Anton was steeling himself for rejection. He knew it would be so difficult to stop, but he would do it for her, only her. He would do his damnedest to please her, but for crissake he was out of practice, and could only pray it was like riding a bike. Actually he had never ridden a bike, so that was a bad omen.

She lay there naked, eyes wide open, just looking at him, waiting for him to start, not sure what she was supposed to do.

He gave her a long lingering kiss on the lips, not hurrying as if he had all the time in the world. That did not suit Mia, so she put her hand around his penis and began to stroke up and down, just a tiny bit too exuberant for Anton's comfort. To stop her wandering hands, he clasped them in one hand and put them above her head, opening her up to his close scrutiny, and making her impatient to just get on with whatever was going to happen.

Her small breasts were absolutely perfect with large strawberry nipples just begging for his attention. He took his time licking and stroking them both, and then taking them into his mouth to suckle deeply. Mia's hips came off the bed, seeking his hard and swollen penis, but Anton was not going to let that happen, it wasn't time for that yet. Slowly he kissed his way down her body to the main attraction, completely ignoring her vile language that explained erotically what she thought of his appendage.

Putting both hands under her hips he drew her closer to his mouth, and licked her vagina, and then pushed his tongue into her opening and sucked on her clitoris, pulling and sucking until her body began to automatically move to his rhythm.

Mia couldn't stop her body from pushing into his mouth, and she felt herself losing control, and a tsunami taking her over into a journey she didn't understand, or want. "Fuck! Fuck you Anton Santi, what are you doing to me?" The world shattered around her, and reality faded, and she couldn't stop herself from power-housing into an orgasm that seemed to go on forever. She was just about to shout angrily at Anton that he was a whore mongering bastard, when he moved up over her body, and entered her in a strong, deep penetration. Shutting her up completely.

"Shut up Mia. Just for once shut that beautiful mouth. That was just the foreplay, now the real loving begins. Lay back, open your legs, and let me show you just how much I love you, and want to satisfy you, and give you pleasure, as I can only do so for as long as humanly possible."

Over the next few hours they made love so many times. Being so fit Anton found he was insatiable, and could keep going with his ever ready penis making him a proud man. And Mia had grown confident and demanding, even taking him into her mouth, and almost sucking him dry. To say Anton was a happy and content male would have been an understatement.

They were now showering together, as both were obsessive about cleanliness, Anton making sure her stitches stayed dry. He was holding Mia up against the tiles, her legs around his waist, and he was as deep as he could get, probably touching her womb. The womb he fully intended would carry his babies. Purposefully, he hadn't worn a condom with her, because he wanted to get her pregnant as soon as possible. His father had demanded it, and he never disobeyed his Papa.

He latched onto her distended nipple and sucked deeply, bringing Mia straight into an explosive orgasm. His woman had become so easily overtly sexual all within a couple of hours. To say Anton was ecstatically happy would again be an understatement.

Carefully he turned off the shower, and still inside her he carried her out of the cubicle, snatched a large white fluffy towel and wrapped it around them. Then walked back into the bedroom and laid down with her on the bed. This last time he hadn't come, as he wanted to sleep still deep inside her, hoping to get her pregnant with his seed deep inside her womb.

She yawned, and started to drift into an exhausted sleep. If she had known how amazing sex was, she would have tried it years ago. God, she was *so* hooked onto foreplay, orgasms, going into the dark side of sexual deviation, and especially making fantastic love with Anton, her amazing lover, and love.

"Mia please don't go to sleep for a moment, I want to ask you something important."

She yawned again, and made sure his outstanding penis didn't leave her. She loved the feel of his hard, swollen sex inside her, it made her feel safe, and loved, and incredibly feminine. With difficulty she tried to keep her eyes open, and her fuzzy brain awake. But she was absolutely knackered, sex was hard work.

"Mia my darling, will you marry me, and have my babies? I love you with all my heart, and want to be with you every day from now on." He looked into her big, soulful brown eyes, and said truthfully, "We haven't used any contraception, so I'm pretty certain we must be pregnant. I wouldn't be happy that my baby wasn't born in wedlock."

The only answer Anton got was a huge sigh, and a snuffled snore. He would have to wait for an answer, but he wasn't going anywhere with his dick taken prisoner deep inside his lover's body.

Marriage and babies would have to be discussed when Mia woke up, because he was determined she wasn't going anywhere without him.

There would be a total blow up of her volatile temper, because marriage and babies were not in Mia's vocabulary. But he now had coercion on his side, because his darling girl loved sex, and he was the man to provide it. He would kill any other man who tried to have sex with her.

Mia Maxwell was his woman, now and always, and no one crossed Anton Santi, and lived.

He was proud of himself today, because he had been patient, caring, and loving, and had managed to exorcise Mia's tormented subconscious memories.

Al had previously told him that when he had stayed in her suite through the night she would constantly cry in her sleep, but didn't remember anything in the morning.

Anton fully intended to stop that circle of pain. If sex was the answer, his apparatus would definitely enjoy the prospect of working overtime.

He had always been a consummate lover. Always giving his partner his undivided attention. Never playing the field when he had a lover. He had been with Andi for two long years, and lately had decided to end it with him, because they had become stale, and often arguing over the most trivial stuff.

Then Mia had come into his life, and everything had changed completely.

Now he wanted marriage, kids, a change in his lifestyle, which meant a complete turnaround in what he did for a living. He had to become legit. No more walking on the dark side, because that amazing woman he had just made love to all night would not allow it.

And she was right on all counts. And, Andi could be a problem, because he was a jealous, possessive lover. Was already giving Mia a hard time, because they hadn't made love since she had come into Anton's life, and taken it over.

He would have to have words with Andi, and sort out the situation once and forever. That was a conversation he wasn't looking forward to. But it had to be done.

CHAPTER TWENTY

They had soft, warm, fuzzy, morning sex, before Anton had to leave to start his day. A very busy day, because one of his trucks carrying embargoed goods out of Mexico had been stopped at the border. A high-end official was paid a fortune to turn the other way when Anton's trucks went through the border. Yesterday that hadn't gone so well, so Anton was looking into what had gone so radically wrong, and try to put it back on track. They were in trouble if they couldn't find out what was happening. If the greedy bastard was making a statement that he wanted more money, he was a dead man walking.

Anton made Mia even more comfortable in the already sumptuous bed. Kissed her lingeringly on her sweet lips, and ordered her to stay in bed for another couple of hours of rest. Straightaway, she had snuggled down and gone to sleep, before he had picked up his clothes and left her bedroom.

It was pretty evident to Anton that his woman could sleep at the drop of a hat. She made love with endless energy, on full power, and then fall asleep in a second.

He made contact with Al on his phone, and told him to let Mia sleep for a couple of hours. Then take a breakfast tray up to her suite, because she would be starving for sustenance by then. And make her eat on the veranda, so she got some fresh air. She was such a lazy so and so, and would always try and get out of any exercise. He couldn't tell Al that she'd had more than her share of exercise last night.

Often without Mia knowing, he watched her arguing with Al when he made her walk for miles around the estate. She looked so cute and gorgeous in Doc Martin boots, ripped up jeans, and a rude T. shirt. Al, bless him, completely ignored her swearing about his bodily functions. Sometimes when they returned she was slung over his shoulder in a fireman's lift, if she had refused to walk another step. Then the volcano temper had lifted off into the ether.

All the maintenance staff around the estate called out to Al to stop manhandling her. She was a magnet to be loved by everyone, because she was kind and considerate to everyone alike, whatever their job. She was in fact a truly loving woman, but look out if you upset her. She was a crazy straight talking virago.

One person – two personalities – always truthful.

Every day she astonished him a little bit more. Often child like, laughing at the stupid jokes the guys told her. Then all grown up, asking after the workers' families, and they all loved and respected her. Anton could only dream of such love and respect from the people around him. But with Mia's influence he was going to damn well try, and fit in more with the legitimate side of the community, and give up being on the dark side. Over the past few months he had slowly and carefully begun to wind down his many contacts in the underworld. Nobody knew this except Larry, who he trusted beyond any other.

A huge commitment, but he could do it in time.

Jesus Christ! He was totally in love with this complex female, and was in too deep for his own good. If she ever left him he would be devastated. She was a ray of sunshine in his lonely life. For all the chaos in his life, and surrounded constantly by people, he was a lonely man, until she exploded into his orbit, and carried him away with her love.

He was certain he would always love her, wanted to marry her, and have kids with her. Even when he was too old to get it up without help, he would love her. Being married to Mia, he was pretty certain that was never going to happen, because she would find a way to coax his equipment to stand to attention, or else.

He had left her bedroom laughing, something he now did more often since meeting Mia, his love. She had opened those big, beautiful brown eyes, and muttered, "I *so* love your upstanding and outstanding organ of absolute pleasure, Mr Anton Santi. And the rest of you ain't bad either. See ya later, lover boy."

And he muttered to himself, "and I love you more than you can possibly know, my darling girl. I will definitely see you later, without any doubt whatsoever."

Mia hadn't noticed it yet, but he had left a small jewellery box by the side of her bed. And that gesture would give him kudos in her commitment to him, and the huge favour he was going to ask her, later that day.

Gerry Swane was really trying to cool his temper, and Gucci loafers, but was royally pissed. The muscle bound gorilla called Derek who was guarding the electronic gates of Santi's estate was not in a hurry to invite him in. It had been over an hour since he had asked who he was, and what his business was with Mr Santi. He also had a Kalashniko assault weapon slung over his massive shoulder, and was at least six foot-five, and about as wide. Gerry wasn't an idiot, he wasn't going to argue with that beast, because he treasured his face too much, and the rest of his body.

He had told him that he wanted to visit with Mia Maxwell, if she was in residence. And, that he worked for Marcus Medina, who was Mia's lawyer. He also stated that Marcus hadn't heard from her in eight weeks, and was concerned for her safety and welfare.

Evidently that had done the trick, because Derek had then told him that someone was on their way to escort him to the house, as soon as possible.

Gerry parked his classic Triumph Roadster in the shade, as the old girl needed to be treasured, and cared for in her dotage. The car was Gerry's pride and joy, and he revered every nut and bolt in her makeup. He had bankrupted himself when he had bought her at an English Classic Car auction ten years ago, for the princely sum of twenty-eight thousand dollars, and had never once regretted the money he had spent on her. She was an elegant maroon, with pristine cream interior.

Was she a bird puller? You can bet your sweet ass she was, and some.

The huge gates swung open at last, and Gerry was gobsmacked to see Santi in person waiting for him. He had never seen him up close before, and he was unbelievably good looking, too good looking for a mobster, who was deeply immoral, downright evil, and earned his millions on the weaknesses of vulnerable addicts, misery and hardship.

But Gerry had to admit jealousy at the way he held himself, upright and powerful, even though he wasn't tall, but very trim and healthy looking. And, his clothes were outrageously expensive, and handmade. The fucking man was beyond immaculate. But, there was a slight effeminate side to him, that suggested the rumours were true that he was gay.

Santi held out his hand to Gerry in welcome. "How can we help you, Mr Swane? Derek says that you want to visit with our Mia, is that correct? I can assure you that she is well and happy, and very content. But if Marcus wishes to make sure, I will take you to her, as her lawyer he has every right to know that we are all looking after my darling girl."

Gerry was almost rendered speechless with Santi's good manners, and calling Mia his darling girl? What the fuck was going on here? Was he in an alternative universe? He would never believe that the Mia he knew, the tiny bad tempered firebrand, was anyone's darling girl. And especially Anton Santi's special girl.

Really? Wasn't the mobster gay, or not? What the fuckin' hell was going on?

"Thank you Mr Santi, I did get to know Mia when she was playing the piano in your hotel. I won't take up much of her time, but Marcus asked if I would look in on her, as she hasn't been in touch for at least eight weeks." He followed Santi up the long driveway, and noticed that everywhere was immaculate, beautifully landscaped with a multitude of exquisite flowering trees and bushes, a profusion of colour everywhere. Santi had a wonderful, peaceful estate, to be able to hide away and relax from his everyday life in the underbelly of L.A.

But all this luxury and wealth worried and puzzled Gerry regarding Mia. This wasn't her scene at all. Why was she living here with Santi? And were they in an actual relationship?

When they reached the large, rambling house, Santi stopped in front of the marble steps, and shook Gerry's hand again, evidently he wasn't going any further with him. "I'm going to leave you in the very capable hands of Al, our live-in Paramedic. When you have finished your visit with my Mia, he will collect you and see you safely out, Mr Swane." Santi took a breath, and grimaced, as if not wanting to add anything further.

"Please, be very careful with our girl, she had a terrible trauma about eight weeks ago. It is her story to tell, not mine. But knowing her she cannot keep anything to herself. Please, be kind and caring towards her, she is getting better every day, but I fear it will be a long time, if ever, that she gets over it."

His deep blue/green eyes became glacially cold, and entirely ruthless. Those eyes gave him away. He wasn't friendly, or human. Life was a game to him. A cat and mouse game, and he couldn't be trusted to be honest, or truthful.

That's when Gerry realised he had to get Mia out of Santi's clutches, before it was too late. But how? When the security was so tight, with so many lethal men patrolling everywhere with fire power.

"I'm sure you must have seen the late news on television last night about Supreme Judge Williams' innocent twins. I would like to believe that they richly deserved the ending of their precious lives in such a horrendous manner." Santi grinned, and looked even more beautiful, but evil in content. "I'm pretty sure you get my drift, Mr Swane. Never, but never, take my good humour and good manners for granted. I wish you a lovely visit with my Mia, and please stay for lunch with her. Unfortunately, I have a pressing conference with a colleague, who has let me down badly, such a ridiculous thing to do." He sighed heavily, as if the world weighed heavily on his shoulders, and he *really* didn't like teaching people a lesson.

"Ah! Here is Al to take you to Mia's suite. I will say goodbye, and please thank Marcus for worrying about Mia. But, there was no need as you will see for yourself." This time he smiled genuinely, and Gerry could see that he truly loved Mia. "She is still difficult, obstinate, and bad tempered. But everyone who works here loves her, and that includes me. And please to take into account that our Mia lost her Aunt Mel in awful circumstances when she arrived here. Our friend

Roberto must have been devastated, as was Mia. Also my father Theo has managed to put Madeline Maxwell to rest for which Mia was duly very thankful, which pleased *me*."

Santi turned on his heel, and left. That's when Gerry realised that he'd hardly spoken a word, because Santi hadn't stopped talking about Mia, and that was a huge concern and worry for Gerry.

Santi was an enigma, he exuded power and energy, and charisma. A totally focused male, who got what he wanted, always. There was no doubt he coveted Mia. But was he sleeping with her?

If he had then Gerry was too late. It was plainly obvious that he believed that Mia belonged to him. Marcus would be devastated, because he had fallen in love with her the moment they had met.

Knowing Mia she would tell him what was going on. The ditsy female couldn't keep anything to herself. He would ask her straight out if she wanted to leave with him, and would somehow make it happen.

Shit! He felt naked, because he'd had to leave his 9mm Glock pistol with Derek, who had been insistent on keeping it for him. So he was absolutely defenceless now. But, he remembered at their first meeting Mia had mentioned that her brother was a Federal Agent.

Now, that was something Gerry could work with, because he often did work for the FBI. They owed him a sackful of favours.

Favours, he could call in when he needed them, and this could be one of those times. He couldn't help but grin. The thought of a dozen Feds glaring at Derek through those fancy gates made him chuckle.

CHAPTER TWENTY-ONE

He found her asleep on the veranda off her bedroom. Al had left him at the door, and then had silently disappeared. Everyone seemed to work silently in the huge, amazingly gorgeous home of Anton Santi. Gerry had to admit the man had fabulous taste, combined with his perfect good looks, and perfect trim body, Gerry wanted to be gay, and fuck the absolute perfect non-human being.

No! Just a random fucking thought, with no substance whatsoever. Being absolutely heterosexual was just about all he could cope with – today!

Jesus Christ! He stood looking down at Mia and was star struck. She was *so* her mother's daughter. Always gorgeous, unbelievably stunningly beautiful, without a shred of make-up, and blonde hair a mass of unruly curls. And his not gay dick wanted to stand to attention and be noted, but Gerry mentally willed it back to normal, and adjusted his Levi's to accommodate it comfortably. For crissake she still had her pyjamas on, a tiny vest, and even tinier shorts, and a perfect strawberry nipple had escaped from the vest, and needed to be stroked and licked. And he was definitely up for it.

She opened those soulful brown eyes, screamed, jumped up, and threw her arms around his neck, and kissed him all over his face. Jeeze! There was no way he was going to stop her, at least for a while. Gerry could dream even at his advanced age, at just over forty. Old enough to be her father, damn it.

"Whoa, give me a break sweetheart, I am only human, and you are a beautiful woman. Reckless, talented, and very naughty, and unfortunately far too young for dear old Gerry."

She let him go, and put her hands on her hips, a frown marring her unlined forehead. "Gerry Swane, you son of a bitch, what the hell are you doing here? You are just about the very last person I would expect to be visiting Anton Santi's personal space."

"Firstly, could you please put your very pert breast away? I cannot concentrate, my brain has gone south and I can't seem to get it under control worth a spit, sweetheart."

She completely ignored his blatant request, because so many people had seen her naked body lately she didn't bother to cover up anymore. And she didn't dare tell him how pleased she was to see this tough, rough man, but worried because Anton would not be happy that the P.I. had invaded his personal home, especially to visit her, his woman.

After last night she was definitely his woman, and now it was far too late to change anything, because against the odds she had fallen in love with the gangster. She had seen the other side of Anton, which was the complete reverse of the man that the world thought they knew. He could be kind, patient, so loving, when he really loved someone, and he loved his ailing father, and now her.

Gerry sat down and poured himself a coffee that was still hot in a thermos. Buttered and put jelly on a croissant, and then put perfectly picked fruit in a dish, and ate it all with relish. He hadn't realised he was so hungry. Then of course he was gagging for a smoke, but knew Mia would tear him off a strip for hurting his health. For fuck-sake, his health was already compromised badly, so why bother to hold back now? He let go of his disgusting cough just to aggravate her, but she never commented, which was extremely unusual for the Mia he knew.

"While you are feeding your face I will have a quick shower and get decent." She touched the stitches in her head, reminding herself that they mustn't get wet, otherwise Al would very patiently and very quietly tell her off, again. As she went into the bedroom she heard Gerry light up one of those disgusting small cigars he always smoked. She grinned, because he'd waited until he thought she wouldn't find out, and as usual he sounded as if he was trying to cough up a lung. He would be lucky if security didn't come racing through the door. Anton was fanatical that no one smoked anywhere in his home.

Good luck with that one Gerry Swane!

As Mia walked past her bed she noticed a small jewellery box on the bedside table. Anton must have put it there when he left for work.

Oh shit! Shit! Shit! It must be a ring! She never wanted to get married, and have a brood of kids. For crissake, she'd only had sex with him, which didn't constitute putting a ring through her nose. And Anton was used to getting his own way, wouldn't take kindly to having a ring returned to him, and someone saying, 'NO THANKS'. She wasn't stupid, this could be a very tricky and dangerous present for her, if she returned it to him.

Holding the tiny box she ran back to Gerry, because he would know what to do. He was leaning over the iron filigree railing smoking his stinky cheroot, with obvious enjoyment.

She held it in front of her as if it was a poisonous snake. "You gotta help me, Gerry. If it's what I think it is, I am in deep fuckin' trouble." She gave it to him, because she didn't have the guts to open it, but was just a little bit curious, just how big it was, and had it cost a fortune?

"Give me a break, Mia, I definitely don't want to marry the bastard. You slept with him, now take on the consequences, big time."

But she couldn't open the box, it was too much to cope with. She thrust it into Gerry's hand, not giving him the chance to back out of helping her.

"You sure you want to do this? Once you accept a present of this significance from Santi, he will not let you get away." He grinned that cheeky grin that made him look so much younger, and with tongue in cheek he commented, "If you and that egomaniac ever have kids, they will be too fucking beautiful to be normal, and will be the envy of every psychotic nutcase everywhere, that have been allowed out of rehab, or a mental facility. Your combined gorgeousness, and DNA, will shake the planet off its axis, and we will all die, because of you two having had unprotected sex."

"Gerry Swane, you are a wicked bastard. Now, please do me a favour and open the bloody box."

Still grinning he couldn't not open the box, as he was as curious as Mia as to what type of ring Santi would choose for his reluctant fiancée. As slowly as possible he opened the box, just to annoy her even more. Then burst out laughing and coughing at the same time. "It ain't a ring, sweetheart, so you can calm down. He ain't proposing. I thought that would be strange for Santi, because he would have wanted to give it to you himself."

Mia snatched the box from him, and looked at the content, then burst into tears of absolute joy. It was the exquisite tiny cross that her Papa had given her when she turned twenty-one. She absolutely treasured that cross, and was utterly desolate when she thought she had lost it on that dreadful night at the hotel.

Gerry was at a loss for words, he never thought that he would ever see Mia crying. And, she had stated that she didn't want to ever get married, and have a brood of kids.

What the fuck was going on here? Females and their up and down emotions did his head in. Both heads, he added to himself.

Mia sniffed and wiped her runny nose with her hand. "Sorry, I need to explain what happened to me over six weeks ago, then you will understand exactly what this cross means to me. I thought I had lost it forever, but Anton must have found it, and had it repaired. He has such a kind and caring side to him that nobody understands. But over the past weeks that I have lived here, he has been nothing but loving, and patient, and generous to me.

"If it wasn't for Anton, Al, and Doctor Perez, I would not be alive today. And, that is the absolute truth. Al and Stefan patched me up like a broken doll. Anton kept me sane and focused, when all I wanted to do was give up and die of shame, because my dignity had been taken away, and I wasn't whole anymore."

"I know what happened is connected to those two cretins who died in an atrocious heinous act. How were you and Anton involved? And I know that The Executioner walks a fine line between insanity and evil. I am sure Santi paid millions to teach those two brothers a murderous lesson." He looked straight at her with his deep blue eyes asking for the truth, and only the truth.

"I am deeply sorry for what happened to them, but I need you to understand what happened to me." When Gerry went to move closer to her, she stopped him immediately, because she wouldn't cope if he touched her in empathy and concern. "I can only remember taking a glass of Ginger Ale from the brothers, and everything else I tell you comes from Doctor Perez explaining to me about the horrendous injuries I had suffered at their disgusting hands. I woke up the next morning after the effect of Rohypnol had left my system, my body was battered and bruised, covered in blood, cut to ribbons and internally massacred. Hang on to your breakfast, it is not a story for the faint-hearted, and weak stomached.

"And throughout all this trauma Anton has been my rock, and steadfast love, without him I don't believe I would have survived."

Gerry hadn't moved an inch once she began in a monotone voice, as if reciting a shopping list. He had his elbows on the table, his blond head in his hands, eyes closed, and silent tears leaking through his fingers. And no one had ever seen Gerry Swane cry, *never*. He couldn't look at Mia, because he was utterly ashamed to be of the male species, and could not take on board how two privileged young men could commit such sexual deviate torture on a young, innocent female, as Mia.

Now! He wanted them alive, so that he could cause such horrendous pain, and torture to them all over again. God bless The Executioner, for ending their evil sick lives so painfully slowly, as to make them scream out it would be a relief to die.

The balcony went silent, and Gerry sat back up, and saw that Mia had tears falling down her beautiful face, and he knew she was having a hard time holding everything together. Without hesitating, he took her in his arms and rocked her gently, trying to give her his strength and love, because it was evident she needed both from him, big time.

"Thank you Mia, that was brave telling me what happened, and now I understand why you feel beholden to Santi. He was there for you from the beginning, and stayed right through to the end, and now tells you that he loves you. I understand. I really do. Because you think you return that love. It's your way of thanking him for everything he has done for you, keeping you in luxury in his fabulous home, and obviously spoiling you rotten."

He held her away from him, and wiped away her tears with a napkin. "Please sweetheart. Please, leave with me today. You can stay at my apartment on the beach, and can sleep in my bed." He grinned at the look of horror on her face at the thought of his bed. "And I will sleep in the lounge, while you can take my bed. Honestly, Marcus would castrate me, if he thought I was coming on to you at my age. It was his idea that I came here today, because no one had heard from you for over eight weeks." He didn't add that for the first time in his fractured life, he wanted to look after Mia, as a father would his only daughter. It was weird, he had never loved anyone, as he did this grown up child. A loving parent with a hurting child, who was fragile, and needy.

Those big brown eyes lit up when he mentioned Marcus. "Did he really? Was he really worried about me? And, how is his family? Great I hope, as I would like to believe that he is really happy."

She would always love Marcus with all her heart, but now she did love Anton, especially after last night. Anton was easy to love, but Marcus much more complicated, far too complicated for her in the future and at the moment.

"I don't think you realise that I can leave any time I want to. Anton has told me that even though he would be devastated, he just wants me to feel safe and happy." She needed for Gerry to understand what she was feeling right now. "I'm not the selfish, obstinate, prima donna I was when I left Houston. Living in L.A. has changed me beyond anything I ever thought it would."

"Sweetheart, I understand that you are scared and nervous, but please don't shut yourself away from everyone. You are your mother's daughter, far too beautiful to be in the shade of life. I need you to get out and enjoy yourself. You are young, intelligent, and gorgeous. Enjoy the world while you are still able to.

"If you are telling me that you are happy with Santi, without any coercion from that mobster, then I can't help you. But you have to understand that I will have to keep in contact with you in case you ever need me." He fished out a card from his jacket. "That is my personal cell phone number, and don't let anyone else have it. I don't want Santi knowing anything about me. Contrary to what you believe, he is a murderous bastard, and can't be trusted." He remembered something he wanted to ask her. "Did you ever hear anything about your birth mother, Madeline Maxwell?" And couldn't believe what he heard next.

"Oh God! Yes I did! I completely forgot the reason I came to L.A. was to find out about my mother." She told him almost word for word what Anton's father had managed to tell her.

Gerry leapt from his chair, and took her surprised face in his hands, and gave her a wallop of a kiss on the lips, overjoyed at what she had told him. "I knew! I fuckin' knew! Theo Santi had had a relationship with Maddie, wanted to marry her, but was still married to Anton's mother. I fuckin' knew that he had been asked to get rid of her for the President, who was going to be compromised by Maddie, and his brother, and every other fucker who was shagging her." He was pacing up and down, couldn't slow down, because he had worked all this out twenty years ago, and nobody would listen to him. Thank God, because it would have caused a tsunami in American politics. When his team in LAPD got too close for someone's comfort, they were completely shut down, and dispersed to other police departments.

Now, Gerry was on a run. "It was the CIA, wasn't it? They murdered her to shut her mouth up, and your Aunt Melody took you to your father. He *was* your real father, to take care of you. Because everyone thought you were the President's daughter, but that was not true. If you had been you would have gone missing, without a doubt."

"I love my papa Henri, and couldn't be happier that he believed my Aunt Melody, and has taken care of me for the past twenty years."

She went to her bedside cabinet and took out a white envelope with an address on it, and gave it to Gerry. "Please Gerry would you post this to my Papa for me? I don't want to upset Anton that I am writing to my family in Houston, telling them what has happened, and why I can't go home yet. But I will eventually go back home when I feel more normal, and can cope with leaving this safe place." She hated to admit to anyone how she really felt. "In truth Gerry, I am paralysed with fear that someone will get hold of me again, and kidnap me, and torture me, because it was so easy to do the first time."

Gerry completely understood what Mia was going through, if he could put her mind at rest, he would. But nobody could guarantee that wouldn't happen again. In fact she was much safer here on Santi's estate, because he would never let anything happen to her on his watch. "Does Santi ever leave this estate himself?" Gerry knew there were plenty of Agents who would give their left ball for a shot at the drug lord. He would be a feather in anyone's cap, big time.

"Yes, he does. A couple of nights a week he stays over at The Excelsior in his penthouse. I think he conducts all his illegitimate business from there. Al always stays with me when Anton is away. Anton never leaves me on my own, because he knows how nervous I am since that awful night."

Gerry took the envelope from her, and was surprised when she asked if he would read it, because she didn't want to worry her family unnecessarily. Also her Papa might storm Anton's estate and demand she went home with him. Mia wasn't well enough yet to take on any stress or anger from even her family.

"Are you sure you want me to read your private and personal thoughts, because I'm not the most sympathetic and caring person in the world?"

"I trust your judgement Gerry Swane. You are a much better person than you admit to being. I've grown to love you as a friend, and I know you care for me, however difficult, obstinate, and downright pigheaded I am. In fact I think you kinda' love me in your couldn't care less attitude in your lonely bachelor kingdom."

"OK! OK! Give me a break. I'll read your fuckin' letter out loud if you like?" He opened the envelope and was surprised at the neat, articulate writing. Not something he would have thought about Mia, the consummate untidy, lazy, tiny virago.

My dearest Papa,
"Please forgive me for the dreadful things I said to you when I left. I love you and Mama with all my heart. I have now found out what happened to my

birth mother, and have decided to leave her in peace now, as she deserves to be left in peace.

Unfortunately, I was attacked at the hotel I was working in, but have since recovered completely. The gentleman who owned the hotel was very kind to me, and took me home to his estate, which is amazingly beautiful, and I am very happy and content here, and very spoilt.

"Before that happened I did manage to find where my Aunt Melody lived, but I was devastated to find that she had died of cancer four weeks previously. But Papa, she had been married for fifteen years to Roberto Diaz, who was the kindest, loving husband anyone would be happy with. They also have twin girls, ten years old, and can you believe it, they are the image of me (poor girls!). So I now have a new family, and am so happy about that.

"I'm sure you will be happy to know that I have really grown up since living here, and miss you all desperately.

"I have a lawyer now called Marcus Medina, who has given my mother's estate to Roberto and the twins, because honestly Papa, I didn't want it, and Roberto's family didn't really want to move. It was my special gift to them from my mother.

"My new friend, Gerry Swane, is posting this letter to you, and he is also taking care of me. As you know, I can be obstinate, difficult, and bad tempered, and Gerry puts me straight, lucky for him he is far too old for me, and has become sort of a father figure to me. But of course, no one could ever take your place in my heart, and life.

"Please, give my love to Viola, and I hope she has kept you company while I am away. I will be coming home soon Papa, and hope to bring Anton with me, but he never leaves L.A., because he is a very successful businessman. I think I have come to love him Papa, as he has been so patient and loving towards me.

"You see, I really have grown up!

"Please give my love to all the family, and especially Mama, who I treated so badly, when she has been the best mother any child could have.

"Love you always and forever, and forever more.

"Your precious daughter, Mia. xxxxxx

"P.S. Sorry I haven't phoned you, but I couldn't bear to hear your voice, and not be with you. Still love you so much, you are the bestest Papa in the whole world. xxxxxx Mia."

* * * *

Gerry meticulously folded the letter, put it back in its envelope, and looked at the name it was addressed to. Then he cleared his throat of all the emotion lodged there. "If I was Henri Arnaud I would think I was the luckiest bastard on earth to have such a beautiful, loving daughter as you Mia. Against all the odds you make me wish I had married years ago, and had kids, believe me that would have been a huge mistake, 'cos I'm a selfish, self centred, arrogant shit, and that's just for starters.

"You be happy my darling girl, and pretty please, put my phone number on speed dial. I have a really bad feeling about you and Anton. I need you to promise me that if anything bad happens, you will call me, and I will come immediately."

"I promise faithfully that I will." She answered, smiling that beatific smile that always lit up her expressive face. She was on the road to recovery with the gorgeous man she loved, what could possibly go wrong?

CHAPTER TWENTY-TWO

She clung tightly to the bathroom vanity, with Anton covering her while he pumped frantically into her. They had just made love in the shower, but Anton was insatiable, and while they were still wet from the shower he had crowded her against the vanity and entered her from behind. A particular position that usually had Mia screaming with a strong orgasm, something she always encouraged, Anton was pleased to help her with any orgasm she encouraged, and had come to love more each day.

He had one hand massaging her nipples, again another turn on, and the other hand down between her legs tweaking her clitoris. "Harder Anton, for fuck sake harder, I'm not a fragile fairy, just a greedy female who gets off on hard, and frantic fucking."

She looked up into the mirror and could see that Anton was on the edge of coming. His eyes were closed, and his teeth bared in an erotic grimace. She knew he would wait for her to climax first, then when her inner muscles would clamp around his hard and swollen sex, only then would he lose control, and fill her with his hot essence. Her wonderful lover was forever patient, caring, and loving par excellence. But this time she took control by pushing back against his hard muscled belly, allowing him to go deeper than ever before. He cursed loudly and couldn't stop from ejaculating into her. Mia followed him immediately, grinning, because she had made him lose control of their lovemaking, something Anton would not be happy about.

Mia was one very happy sexual being. Extremely content that she pleased Anton every day and night, and more. And she knew that he loved her, and would do anything to please her. But tomorrow she was going to be a miserable grumpy bitch, and that would not please him one little bit. But he would live. But not as content and happy as per usual, and his virulent dick might have a day off, which wouldn't hurt it, probably give it a reviving day off to make more sperm to try in vain to get her pregnant.

Fat chance of that happening, gorgeous boy 'with virulent dick'.

Every afternoon when he was at home he would find her wherever she was, and laughing they would run up the stairs to their bedroom to make clandestine love. After locking the door they would strip off their clothes on the way to the bed, and fall onto it in an untidy mess of arms and legs still laughing with excitement, and anticipation of bawdy sex.

Mia would lay back with her arms above her head, and legs wide open in invitation, even though Anton never needed any help in that department. He would slowly kiss down her perfect body, after sucking both breasts taking his time to thoroughly love each one in turn. Then he would kiss and lick her sex, making sure she was wet enough to be comfortable when he entered her deeply and fiercely, which Mia was always ready for. She usually liked her sex just a bit on the rough side. And Anton could always oblige her with that, but still be alert if she found some positions not quite so comfortable, then he wouldn't attempt that position again.

After making love all afternoon they both would be really hungry and go down for dinner. Everyone they came into contact with would avert their eyes, because Anton and Mia literally glowed with post-coital satisfaction and love. Everyone to a man, was totally jealous, and some more jealous than others.

Mia slowly opened her eyes, yawned big time, and rolled over to start the day with loving the most gorgeous male on the planet, but came up cold and empty. Her lover wasn't where he was supposed to be, which had never happened before.

Anton always said that morning sex was the best sex ever, now he was permanently with Mia. So where the fuck was he? Evidently, the novelty must have worn off, quicker than Mia had ever expected. Men really couldn't be trusted.

Then she was yanked out of her comfortable bed by strong arms, and by the litany of expletives flowing out of her mouth, Mia was not a happy woman, and extremely pissed at being woken up far too quickly, and being man-handled as well.

"Come on sleepy head, get in the shower, and don't be so grumpy, and disagreeable. It's your birthday, and I want to spoil you rotten today, because I love you, and feel the need to let everyone know that I love beautiful Mia Maxwell, and that she is my woman."

Anton was dressed for the day, as immaculate as ever, having got up over an hour earlier than usual to surprise Mia. She hadn't mentioned her birthday, but had told him the date when they had met, and Anton had remembered, because she had made such an impression on him. He had known that first night they were meant to be together, and had worked hard to make it possible.

And he hadn't been wrong, even though dreadful heartache had brought them together in the end.

Now, he slapped her bare backside, as she ran into the bathroom, blaspheming again. She poked her blonde head around the door, grinning. "Dontcha' wanna' get naked and wet with the birthday girl, Mr Santi?"

"Hurry up Miss Nymphomaniac. If I come into that shower, and excuse the pun, it will be hours before we get downstairs again, and my surprise could get ruined." Anton knew that would get her moving quicker. She loved surprises, but hated jewellery, so it was very difficult to buy her a present to spoil her. The present he had ordered for her birthday he knew she would be over the moon to receive.

It had been delivered in the night by special courier, so that Mia hadn't seen it before. He had gone down earlier to make sure everything was perfect, because this was going to be a very special day for both of them.

Anton had planned it to be so, and nothing was going to spoil his well laid plan.

Not a solitary thing! Especially not Mia Maxwell, who was *so* loveable, but so difficult!

"Oh my God! You are kidding me! Anton Santi you have taken the piano from the hotel, and moved it here for me. Thank you *so* much, I have missed playing desperately, but didn't want you to think that I needed you to do something about it." Mia had already been blown away by what Anton had managed to do to the solarium overnight.

Every surface had been covered by amazing red roses. There was a sumptuous breakfast buffet laid out for all the staff that worked on the estate, who could safely leave their work for an hour. And, now the best piano in the world was actually taking centre stage in the large, air controlled casual room. A Steinway Baby Grand, for her to play whenever she wanted to.

And, boy did she want to, right now. Anton was grinning like a man who had done something right in his life, at last. He watched Mia cut the wide silver ribbon that had been put around the precious piano, and was overwhelmed when she went to him and threw her arms around him, with tears in those big brown eyes. His Mia never cried, and to him he had hit the jackpot with those held back tears of happiness.

But this was only the beginning!

Kissing her very lingeringly on her luscious lips, he then managed to untangle her away from him, as he could feel the room becoming restless, everyone wondering what on earth was going to happen next.

"Sweetheart, this isn't the hotel piano. This one is yours to keep, and cherish, and play for the rest of your very talented life. Wherever you are, if not here, I will have it shipped to you, with my love, always."

"Anton! It's worth a fortune, I can't accept it. It's far too much for my birthday." But she looked at the beautiful machine, and so wanted to sit down and start playing, but didn't dare, because then she wouldn't be able to give it up.

Anton put his arms around her knowing she would be so excited to play his gift. "But it comes with a big question from me, and with all the love in my heart for you." He sat down on the piano stool with her, and took out a small box from his pocket, and gave it to her. He couldn't believe how nervous he was, because he could never be sure of what Mia would do or say next. Nobody would ever be able to read her, because she was so complex, and out of the normal realms of a mere female. That was why he had grown to love her.

But Mia was ahead of her lover and even before she opened the box, she answered him, with eyes glistening with tears again. "Yes, my darling Anton, you are my best friend, my wonderful lover, and I love you with all my heart, and I will marry you. And yes, I will have your babies, if possible." Laughing at the staff all clapping loudly, she opened the box, and gasped. In it nestled the most beautiful, and hugely expensive, wide silver band, encrusted with the most perfectly formed tiny diamonds.

Anton could not have bought anything more perfect. It wasn't showy. The diamonds weren't ostentatious. The ring was simple, but utterly beautiful. She kissed him sweetly to seal the deal. "May I keep it for our wedding day, as I would like to wear it as my wedding ring. It's just perfect. You have wonderful taste, and I truly love it."

She was amazed to see that Anton had become very emotional when she had received his gift with words of love, and also that he had seemed nervous that she could possibly turn him down.

What she hadn't told him was that Theo had already asked her to marry his beloved son, and have his beautiful babies, a couple of days ago, so she had been prepared for Anton's proposal. She had promised Theo that she would think about it. He had replied that he hadn't much longer on earth, and he would love to see his son settle down, and have a family of his own, and that he knew his son loved her deeply, as did Theo.

That alone had made up her mind. Theo had truly loved her mother, and would have married her, had he been free to do so. Now, Anton truly loved her, and she believed that she returned that love, and could be happy with Anton, especially if he gave up all the illegitimate business he dealt in.

He had promised that he was already dealing with the situation, and she believed him, sort of.

She began to play her beloved piano, as her Papa had taught her. Good ol' New Orleans Jazz, which stopped everyone eating, and talking. Anton sitting at her side, was completely enraptured by the unbelievable talent of his future wife.

His Papa Theo had told him what to buy Mia for her birthday, which had been a brilliant idea. Then Theo had been sure that she would agree to marry him. Anton hadn't been so sure, but had plucked up the courage and had gone for it.

Knowing Mia she could have laughed in his face, and run for the hills in her bare feet. But his father was usually right.

Anton was a multi-millionaire, because he still talked his deals over with Theo, whose sound opinion he always valued. His father was the only person he truly trusted in their world of high octane, illegitimate goods for addicts, gamblers, and unsavoury characters, who often dealt in murder, and evil.

The underbelly of Los Angeles!

CHAPTER TWENTY-THREE

"Al, would you please move? You are standing in my light, as it is I am reading too much, and my bloody eyes ache." Mia was not in a good mood, her lover had been away for two whole days on some sort of business, which meant illegitimate business, and she was missing his gorgeous body next to her in bed. Well, she missed his extremely virulent dick, always ever ready, as was she, they were the perfect match. Him and her, always up for it. Anton would laugh at that pun.

Al hated Mia when she was prickly and bad tempered, because she usually took it out on him, her constant companion. "Sorry your highness, but there is an FBI Agent demanding to see his sister, waiting at the security gate. Could that be you, princess?"

Mia screeched loudly, shot to her bare feet, and started to run across the grass towards the entrance of the estate. Al had never seen her move so fast, hadn't thought she had it in her to run at full speed.

A tall, well built, black haired buzz cut, dark suited male, who was extremely good looking, caught Mia in his strong arms, and whirled her around, laughing at her enthusiastic welcome.

"Christian Arnaud, you bastard." She covered his face in sisterly kisses. "Why didn't you let me know you were coming? You know I hate surprises. But this time I will forgive you, because I love you *soo* much." She gave him a puzzled look, as he set her down on her bare feet. "How the f---- f, did you know I was here?" She didn't dare swear in front of Christian, because he would paddle her backside. He never used bad language, rarely drank, sometimes smoked, when under stress, and would never leave his total bitch of a wife, because he loved Amy his daughter, far too much, and knew his ghastly wife would take her from him in absolute spite.

"Gerry Swane managed to get in touch with me through his contacts in the Agency. He was really worried for your safety, Lissy. Should *we* be worried, baby girl? And before you interrogate me about Papa, he doesn't know I am here, or even where you are living." He looked at Derek, who hadn't taken his piercing eyes from Christian, but Christian wasn't spooked one bit. He was on the team that was the President's security, so beefy Derek wasn't a problem to tackle.

Mia went to get into her brother's black 4X4, with tinted windows, bullet proof Mercedes, but Christian had to help her up, she was so tiny. Without taking a breath he just lifted her in his arms, and plonked her in the front seat. He put his hand up to the idiot with the Kalashnikov assault rifle over his shoulder, wondering if he actually knew how to fire the ridiculous piece of crap.

"And no, I will not disarm myself, as an FBI Agent I cannot give over my firearm to anyone. And I am going to drive my vehicle through those gates, right now. If you have a problem with that, I can summon a team of Special FBI Agents, all armed to the teeth, to be here very quickly to back me up. They will go through this estate with a fine tooth comb, which they have been waiting to do for a very long time. I am sure your boss Santi will be extremely unhappy about that situation – Derek!"

Christian took off his suit jacket, undid his tie, and rolled up the sleeves of his pristine white shirt, and settled into a comfortable armchair in Mia's lounge. Knowing once his sister began talking it was going to be a long afternoon. She had a lot of explaining to do, and he desperately wanted to understand his wayward sibling.

"What's going on here, Lissy? Why? Why are you getting up close and personal with Anton Santi? You surely know that Santi is at the top of our list to be brought down for his transgressions. For crissake Lissy, he is a common mobster, without a normal human conscience."

Mia went to her brother and put her arms around him, and then looked straight into his ice blue eyes, which were a family trait. "He has changed. I know you won't believe me, but he isn't the gangster that everyone thinks he is. Ever since I met him, he has been kind, patient, and loving, and nothing is too much trouble, regarding anything I want or need. Please Christian, I love him, and he loves me, and I don't care what anyone else thinks, because we are getting married next week. Whatever you say to me I will *not* change my mind. His father, Theo, is dying, and wants to see his son married, with a family, and I want to be that woman, desperately." Mia waited for the explosion, but it didn't happen, which in some way was a disappointment, because she had always loved to wind up her too good, too uptight, too military, older brother.

Christian gave a long sigh of indulgence for a baby sister who always pushed his uptight buttons.

"Baby girl, why do you always have to push the boundaries? You know Papa will be here the moment he hears what you are going to do. Our father worries about you all the time, and will not allow you to marry this hoodlum. This will be the biggest mistake of your young life, and Papa would rather end up in prison than let you destroy the rest of your pampered and spoilt life. Please! Please Lissy, for once do as I ask and come home with me now, today. I have a couple of days leave from the White House, so can see you home safely to be with our family. Even for you this is a ridiculous situation, and has gone as far as it can go. Unless of course Santi is keeping you a prisoner on this estate?"

Mia gave her beloved Christian a huge smile of love, a love which she had always felt for him, because he had always been the best brother any girl could have wanted. "Honestly, I can leave here any time I want. But, I truly want to stay. I didn't want to explain what happened to me a couple of months ago, but now I will, so you can understand what Anton has done for me, and why our love has grown into something special. But, you have to promise me that you will never tell another person what happened, and especially Papa."

With dread in his heart Christian promised, but after she had told him everything, he truly wished he hadn't known, because he would never forget her voice, or her face, as she recounted the horror of her evil, diabolical experience. And how Anton had kept her alive with the help of Al, and Doctor Perez. For that reason alone, Christian Arnaud would never come after Santi, or his henchmen.

Mia's suite was silent as she finished telling Christian everything that happened that fateful night, and how long she took to get over it, if she ever really did. He was holding her in his arms, crying with her, for her, because he hadn't been able to keep her safe when she needed him. A big brother, who had always looked out for her when she was younger, but now lived in Washington D.C. A Federal Agent who had become detached from his warm, loving family, because he had married a bitch of a wife, who didn't love him, and he didn't love her. But he stayed married because of his sweet, beautiful daughter Amy. He couldn't envisage living without his child, who was the centre of his universe, and kept him going in a loveless, cold, sexless marriage. But he hadn't told Lissy yet, that he was leaving the Agency, and returning home to his family in Houston. He had been offered an important job in the Houston Police Department, and on impulse had accepted it, much to the chagrin of his irate wife, which had been the turning point in his acceptance. Karen loved Washington, and was going to hate Houston, and his extremely close family.

So that was a bonus not to be overlooked.

"Santi had the Judge's twins murdered, didn't he?" Christian couldn't believe what Lissy had just told him, and now that horrific scene of the crucifixion had been explained. Everyone at the Agency had been scratching their balls, trying to find out who had contracted this abhorrent murder. They realised who had done it, but who had paid for it? Who could afford The Executioner? Santi, that's who!

"Yes! He paid for it. No! He didn't know what was going to happen to them. Anton couldn't let them live after what they did to me. And, I sort of had to agree, they were worse than animals, and didn't seem to worry what they had put me through. As if it was nothing, to rape and torture an innocent female, to the level that they could have killed me. Evidently, they had done it at least four times previously, and got away with it. Where were the FBI when I needed you?"

"I'm sorry darlin', but the law is the law. We can't help if nobody tells us, and Anton Santi took the law into his own hands. His way of life can't be involved with the law, so he would have had to pay millions to get pay back for your pain and almost loss of life. And between you and me, I really can't blame him, if he loves you as much as I do." He would have killed them for touching his sister.

As usual Mia changed to another track, she hated to be miserable, and keep harping on what happened in the past. "You are coming to my wedding next week? Please bring Amy, but leave that bitch of a wife behind. Her sour face will curdle the drinks, and our happy day."

"I'm so sorry darlin', but I'm travelling with the President as his security. He is visiting Europe, it's very important, and he needs a lot of his security with him, which includes me. I truly can't get out of this, as I am his Chief of Security."

Mia gave him her worse scowl, as none of her family would be there now, but she couldn't be angry with her Christian for too long. "It's OK, 'cos Anton is coming with me to Houston to meet our family, as soon as he can get away.

He is going to pay for a lavish party to celebrate our marriage and get to know all the people I love, which includes you, big brother."

"I will be there Lissy without fail. I have one more month left in Washington. I am leaving the Agency to live back in Houston with Mama and Papa. Karen, Amy, and myself are going to rent the apartment upstairs in our family home. I don't want my girl spending her young life in that cesspit Washington. And I can't trust Karen to look after Amy without hurting her, as she drinks too much now. Hopefully Mama will take Amy over, and give her the love she needs, and craves. I can't be there all the time to watch what Karen is doing, it's a huge worry for me."

"Please divorce that dreadful woman before she really hurts Amy. I know that she threatens to take Amy and leave you, but surely you can take her to court to stop her. Anyway, Mama and Papa will make sure that she doesn't hurt Amy when you have to work. Friggin' hell, I *so* hate that woman. I could never hurt Anton like that. If we ever have kids, he will be a fantastic father." She grinned and winked at Christian. "If not, I will beat the crap outta' him. So he'd better be afraid! Very afraid, of little old me from Houston."

Christian just shook his head. She was off on another track, and he'd never met Santi, but was beginning to feel sorry for the poor bastard for falling in love with his recalcitrant, obstinate sister. The gangster was evidently mentally deficient, or was cleaning up his act, and Mia was telling the truth for a change.

He had known Lissy from the time she had come to live with his family. He had fallen in love with her immediately. Had fought her battles for her, and laughed at her ridiculous antics. But her truth wasn't the same as everyone else's, so he always took everything she said with a pinch of salt.

He prayed that Santi was trying to go straight for her, but wasn't going to hold his breath, because Theo and Anton Santi had their dirty fingers in every illegal contract coming into California, and out again.

If Santi was trying to go legal it could be a big problem, because there were plenty of other groups who would try and bring him down, permanently.

And Lissy could be caught in the crossfire. If that happened Christian would never rest until he hunted the perpetrators down, and killed them.

CHAPTER TWENTY-FOUR

They both lay panting, a little breathless, a lot boneless, and totally in love, after having the best fuck ever. Morning sex couldn't be beaten, and for Mia and Anton slowly waking up to be with each other, couldn't be surpassed. But then the erotic spell was broken when he slapped her bare backside, and whispered in her ear. "Get up lazy bones, we are getting married in one hour's time, and you'd better not be late, or else I might marry someone else."

She hated to be rushed in the morning. Early morning was not Mia's best time of the day, except for fucking Anton. "It's your fault, you shouldn't have organised a breakfast marriage ceremony. Who the fuck gets married at ten o'clock in the fucking morning? It's hardly light, even the birds haven't started singing yet, it's too bloody early." She started to snuggle back down into the extremely comfortable bed, hoping for another round of great sex with her soon-to-be-husband.

But the impatient soon-to-be-husband wasn't having any of her tantrum. He hauled her out of the bed and pushed her all the way to the bathroom. Kissed her firmly on her luscious lips, and shut the door behind her. "See you in the solarium at 10 sharp, dressed for a wedding, looking drop dead gorgeous. So we can show our kids how beautiful their mother was when she married their father."

The only reply was something heavy thrown at the door, which must have shattered on impact.

Anton was grinning as he went to his own suite to shower and get dressed. God, how he loved that woman, and couldn't wait to marry her. She was never boring, always volatile, but always sorry afterwards, and make up sex was amazing. He was impatient to start a family, but Mia didn't seem to be in any hurry. He knew that for however long he lived he would always love her, would never stray, because she had warned him she would cut off his dick with a rusty knife if he had an affair, or a mistress. And she didn't appear to be joking.

Anton Santi was not stupid. His woman was smart, extremely beautiful, and would defend him and their kids with her last breath. Any problem that came her way, she always tackled it head on, and solved it.

What sane man would cheat on such an amazing woman? Not Antony Theo Santi! He was no man's fool!

Anton, Marcus, Gerry, Al, Doctor Perez and wife, Roberto and twins, and Theo, with his two medics, were all standing, talking, and laughing together waiting for the bride's big entrance. Theo of course had been wheeled into the solarium in his technical contraption, and Anton was hovering close by in case he didn't cope with so many people, but he seemed to be doing OK, and communicating through his electronic synthesizer. This was the day that Theo had been praying for ever since Maddie's daughter had come into Anton's well ordered life, and he had fallen irrevocably in love with her, and she him.

But today his work was done, his beloved son was getting married, so this life as he had suffered it was over. Theo was ready to meet his maker, and atone for the evil and dreadful sins he had perpetrated in his lifetime of crime. He didn't expect to be forgiven, but could only hope that God did have a forgiving nature, as the priests always preached. If not, he would die in the fires of hell knowing he deserved everything that he would suffer.

He looked across at his other son, and could see how much his older son hated him. He didn't blame him, because he had treated him and his mother abominably. For that alone he deserved the wrath of hell, but he had done it in good consciousness, knowing he wasn't capable of loving one woman. So had left before his family had got too entrenched with being a reliable unit, and loving each other.

The joke was on him though, he had never divorced his wife, and still loved her after all this time, and the journey he had travelled without her at his side. He would have liked to see her today at their son's wedding, but had known that was never going to happen.

And, could not blame her for that decision, but it still made him feel sad, and very lonely. She had been the very best thing that had happened to him, and he would take his last breath, thinking of her, and still loving her. Should he have stayed with her, of course, but he had been young, ambitious, and a total bastard.

Mia twirled in front of the long bevelled mirror, and laughed, because now she really looked like her mother, and it made her so happy. She wished that her mother could have seen her today marrying the man she loved with all her heart. A mother should have the right to see her child marry for love, and feel her happiness and joy.

Anton had promised, that as soon as possible he would take her home to see her family in Houston, and they would marry again in the happy, clappy church locally, so that all her family would see just how happy and content she was with her new husband. Because she was! Against all the odds, Mia Maxwell had grown up, and had fallen in love with Anton Santi, and actually married him.

Standing still she looked herself over, and was really pleased she had made such an effort. Al had taken her to a 1960's vintage boutique, and she had found everything she had needed for her big day. An off the shoulder chiffon dress in creamy pink, with a tight basque top that pushed up her boobs to emphasise them, and cinched her tiny waist. Then the flowing skirt swished down to her bare feet, with creamy pink varnish on her toes to match her dress, and a shiny new silver toe ring for extra effect. A circle of silk flowers was fitted into her blonde curly hair, now much longer than usual.

But the object she was most proud of was Theo's present to her, its value couldn't be put into dollars. It was a small bible given to him by his Italian grandmother when he lived in Naples, Italy, as a boy. It was a gift he had revered and kept safe all his adult life. Also it had come with a Rosary, which Theo had also given her, and Mia had told him she would keep it safe for him as long as she lived, and that she was honoured to accept both items, and loved him for the gifts he had given her. Her only jewellery was the cross her father had bought her, and of course the wedding ring that Anton had given her previously, which she was now wearing.

Roberto knocked on her door, and asked if she was ready, because Anton was becoming very nervous that she might change her mind. There was no chance of that, she thought, as she opened the door.

Roberto visibly stepped back with tears in his eyes. "Mia Madeleine Maxwell you look beyond beautiful, and *so* much like my wonderful Mel." He tried to smile but it didn't work. "She would have so loved to be with you today as a substitute for your beloved Mama." He held out his arm to her. "Come my darling, let's go down and wow everyone, and especially Anton, who is so worried you would change your mind."

Mia stood at the door to the solarium where just a few people were waiting for her to appear, and she knew there wasn't anyone there who shouldn't be. Mia appreciated that, as her own family couldn't be there, and as usual Anton was being very considerate towards her, so he had kept the invitations to the minimum.

Anton looked up from talking to his father, and his gorgeous face lit up when he saw the vision at the door. Without breaking his stride he was at her side in seconds, took her in his arms and kissed her with all the love in his heart, showing everyone that his heart and soul were in this marriage.

Everyone in the spacious room laughed and clapped loudly, after gasping at how beautiful the bride-to-be looked. Anton took her hand and walked her slowly to Father Michael, grinning at the Priest, who was waiting under a bower of amazing flowers, also smiling hugely at the beautiful couple.

Mia managed to quickly scan the solarium, and was knocked out at how beautifully it was decorated for the wedding. There must have been a team of decorators working all night, because when she went to bed last night nothing had changed. Trust Anton to organise everything, because she hadn't lifted a finger to help, as usual, as the spoilt brat she was.

With tears in her eyes, and she only had eyes for her gorgeous Anton, because she knew just how much he loved her. "Thank you so much for today. For spoiling me rotten, and for making me so very happy, soon-to-be-husband, Anton Santi. The very best lover in the whole world."

He took the hand wearing his ring, and kissed it reverently. "No, thank you my darling girl. I have never been *so* very happy. You look absolutely exquisite, and I couldn't love you anymore than I do, and you make me the best lover in the world, because I love you *so* much."

Father Michael coughed loudly to remind them that he would like to get on with the service, as he needed a large drink, and a large plate of the goodies on display at the buffet table brimming with amazing food, absolutely good enough to eat.

Anton and Mia hardly heard the legalities spoken by Father Michael, until he asked them to say a few words of commitment to each other, to end the wedding service.

Anton went first and surprised everyone with his words of love to his new wife.

"I will love you until my last breath on earth.

I promise to always be faithful to that love.
I will never stray in heart, mind, or soul.
If we argue I will always apologise, because you never will.
When we have children I promise to do my share.
And, when you throw something at me, I promise to duck."

Everyone laughed at the last promise, and laughed even louder when Mia whacked him on the arm for telling everyone about her horrible temper. But Anton just grinned and kissed her soundly. Nothing was going to upset him on this momentous day in his life.

Then Mia took a deep breath because she was really nervous, she hadn't prepared a speech beforehand.

"My heart overflows with love for you Anton.
I will truly always be faithful to you, and love you.
I would never tarnish that love with lies or secrets.
I will try my hardest to be the very best wife I can be.
And will truly try to keep my bad temper under control, even when you are being a jackass, and controlling.
I will try desperately to be all sweetness and loving."

Again everyone laughed, as they all knew how volatile and difficult Mia could be, and couldn't see that changing, ever.

Then, the legalities were over, everyone was gasping for a drink, and even Anton and Mia had a glass of the very best champagne that money could buy to join in the toast that Marcus gave, which surprised Mia.

"Please raise your glasses to a truly happy, beautiful couple. My younger brother Anton, and his new, extremely beautiful wife, Mia. May you both be full of love for each other, always hold each other tight when life gets tough, and be there for each other against the rest of the world." He raised his glass and smiled at Anton and Mia. "Everyone drink to their health, to Mr and Mrs Santi, my lovely in-laws."

Mia was gobsmacked and couldn't believe what Marcus had just said, and was rendered speechless. When she looked around the room, she realised she was the only one who hadn't known they were brothers. How had she not known, because everything was slotting into place now?

Roberto taking her to Marcus to be her lawyer. Marcus telling her to go to work at Anton's hotel, so that he could look out for her. Look how that had turned out. Anton insisting she came to live on his estate. Mia had a gut feeling she had been set up from day one, but for what reason?

Carefully she put her champagne flute down and went straight over to Marcus, trying to keep hold of her temper. "And, where is your lovely wife today, Marcus? Surely she would have wanted to see her brother-in-law married?" He was talking to Gerry Swane who looked as dashing as usual, but with a beer bottle in his hand. "Congrats sweetheart, wonderful service, wonderful commitments, made me want to get married myself." Gerry winked with a grin, there was no way he was ever getting a ring through his nose.

"Shut-up Gerry! I am fuckin' furious with you. Why didn't you ever let me know they were brothers?" Gerry backed up and left Marcus and Mia to sort it out, he wasn't that stupid, but did reply. "Sweetheart you never asked me, and it was never a secret."

Mia glared at Marcus, and realised that was where she had seen those coloured eyes, blue/green the same as Anton's. "My wife died four years ago giving birth to our youngest son Milo. She was the sweetest woman, called Bianca, and left a huge void in all our lives." But he could have added I never really loved her, as I loved you from the first moment we met.

"So when we met you didn't have a wife, but everyone kept telling me you had a family, so I kept away from you." And *she* could have added that she didn't allow herself to love him, as she wanted to.

"I do have a family. My two amazing boys, and my mother lives with us on our ranch near Fort Worth. I just don't have a wife, and don't ever intend to change that situation. I'm sorry if you feel you were misinformed, but I now need to go speak to Theo, my so-called father, before I have to leave to go back to work, it will be a busy day at my office."

At his next words Mia's heart almost shattered. "Always remember that I am always here for you, whatever happens in the future. And will wait for you for however long it takes. I fear you have wandered into dangerous territory, as much as my brother loves you, he moves in dangerous company, and won't always be there to keep you safe. Remember to keep in touch with Gerry Swane. He will always let me know what is happening, and if you are in danger."

Just then Anton came up behind Mia and put his arm around her, and smiled indulgently at both of them. "I hope you are not chatting up my new wife, 'cos I will get ridiculously jealous, brother." He gave Marcus a legal looking piece of paper. "As Mia's lawyer, would you register our Marriage Certificate online when you get back to your office? And sometime this week would you drive Mia to my friend and accountant Sonny Silverman with that certificate, so that he can explain exactly what she will be entitled to if anything happens to me? Would you ask Gerry Swane to follow you, and I don't want anyone else to know what we are doing. My legal properties are my own business. I'm beginning to feel that I have an enemy in my own camp, so I must be more cautious who I trust. You, Gerry, and Mia, are my constant, but everyone else is suspect." When Marcus nodded and gave him a man hug, Anton physically relaxed. He trusted his brother without question. But had to be careful with Mia, because she couldn't keep a secret. That was why Marcus and Anton had decided to keep their relationship from her, until it was absolutely necessary.

Everyone at the wedding knew they were brothers, but outside this room it had never been discussed. Mia couldn't believe it, because although they were both gorgeous looking males, they didn't look alike at all. Even their personalities were poles apart, except for those distinctive eyes. The colour of a perfect ocean. And she definitely didn't want to know what Anton was worth, and didn't want to touch it. All she wanted was Anton, healthy and alive, and loving her.

But now Marcus had come on the scene, and how did she feel about that? Her racing mind, and heart, was in turmoil. She absolutely loved Anton, but how did she feel about Marcus, who wasn't attached to anyone? But the brothers were talking again about their father, and Anton was explaining what Theo had told him about their mother.

"I'm so sorry Marcus that I didn't understand about our father and mother. He had never told me the truth until the last couple of days. I didn't know that he had taken me away from you and my mother when I was four years old. He had always told me that our mother left us, but that was not true, was it?"

Again Marcus shook his head, and said an emphatic *no*. "It was awful, you were screaming for your Mama, kicking and trying to get out of Theo's arms, but he was a bull of a man, and I was frightened of him, as was our mother. We didn't get over the trauma for years. But now our mother is happy, and lives with me and my boys. They absolutely adore her, and she is their teacher at our local school. Sophia Medina is loved in the community, and lately has been dating a local sheriff, which makes me happy. She is only forty-seven years old, and still as attractive as she ever was. Unfortunately if the affair comes to anything serious I could lose my babysitter, cook, and laundry woman." He shrugged as if he didn't mind at all, just wanted his mother to be happy.

"She didn't want to come to my wedding, did she? And, I wouldn't blame her." But Anton would love to see his mother again. He couldn't remember anything about her, but he knew she would sing him to sleep if he had a bad dream. And she had felt soft and comfortable when he cried if he hurt himself, which had been lost permanently.

Marcus gave his brother another hug, and kissed Mia's cheek, because it was time to leave for a busy day ahead. He needed to leave because he was jealous of his brother's marriage, but also content for him. They were brothers who loved the same woman, and Anton had won the beautiful woman, who looked like an angel today.

But he was a steadfast, patient man, and God forgive him, his gut was telling him there was danger ahead for Mia and Anton. And he would always be there for her when the shit hit the fan.

But right now he had to go and say his farewell to Theo. He couldn't call him father after the pain he had caused his mother. But he could put the past where it belonged, in the past. He could see that Theo was on the brink of death.

The death mask was already in place!

CHAPTER TWENTY-FIVE

Mia was happy and content. It had been a wonderful day, which she had spent with Roberto and the twins. Melia and Myrna were an absolute joy, and Mia knew that her Aunt Mel would have been so proud of her girls. They had impeccable manners, and talked to everyone, and especially their cousin, Mia.

In the afternoon they swam in the pool, with Roberto, Anton, and Mia, everyone had sighed with relief when they changed into swimming gear, and dived headlong into the pool. Marcus and Gerry had left to go to work, and Al was keeping a close watch on everyone as Anton's security had been given the day off. But Larry and Derek were manning the estate front gate to make sure no one managed to slip in unnoticed, that didn't belong to the wedding party.

Theo and his medical staff had left as soon as the ceremony was over, as their patient was physically and mentally worn out. But Mia made sure that the two young guys took plenty of food back with them to Theo's apartment. She didn't want them to miss out on the amazing breakfast buffet that Anton's chef and his wife had organised. It had been a magnificent feast.

Now, it was late evening and the married couple were back in bed, relaxing, and showing each other just how much they loved each other. Anton collapsed on top of his wife, gasping for breath, after having the most explosive orgasm he'd ever had. It had completely wiped him out.

"Jesus Christ woman, you are going to be the death of me," he managed to gasp out, as he gulped in air to his starved lungs. "It's absolutely true, that married sex is the best ever. And being married to a raving sex maniac is definitely a huge plus. Mrs Santi, I love you, love you, love you, and love you even more than I ever thought possible to love anyone."

Mia was flopped out on her back with her arms around the man she loved with all her heart. "Gee Mr Santi, I do believe you love me, and only me. And God knows I truly love you. But let's get back to business, and get that piece of sex equipment up and ready to go again."

Anton groaned, he was a dead man if he had to perform to his wife's needs, day and night. "Sweetheart, a man's equipment does need a rest, we can't just keep it up non-stop. Could you please give me a moment to take a breath, and get going again?"

Mia grinned, that's when Anton knew he had a problem, because she always got her own way. "You just lay back and relax, darling, and I'll do all the work." She scooted down the bed, and took his soft penis in her hand, and began to caress it as if it was hers to love and nurture. Mia knew that no other woman would ever feel Anton inside her. Would never feel his love, because he was all hers for the rest of her life.

It made her feel as if she owned the world, because her Anton was in it with her, loving her, keeping her safe, always with him at her side.

Anton put his hands behind his head, and just whispered, "Mercy!" And closed his eyes to be able to enjoy what this woman of his was going to do to him. Complete and utter joy, and total pleasure.

One hand softly caressed his testicles, and she felt them tighten up to his body, while her other hand began to run up and down his slowly hardening penis. She touched the very tip with her tongue, and he nearly jumped off the bed. She grinned because she already knew how sensitive the opening at the top was, now he was really swelling and becoming hard again. Taking him fully into her mouth she began the rhythm of giving him as much pleasure as only she knew how to.

Anton clung to the carved headboard and just went with the sucking of her mouth, and took the exquisite torture and pleasure that Mia could give him. He exploded into a long, satisfying orgasm, that left him weak and soft, and so full of love for this woman who had just become his life partner.

He wanted to just go to sleep and bonelessly relax, but he had to give back what he had just received, as Mia was always so generous with her love for him. He pulled her up above him, and he went down on her to give her the pleasure she had just given him. He took his time, didn't rush a moment, and didn't stop until she was screaming his name, even then he carried on, and entered her with a dick so hard he was in pain for relief once more.

At last they were thoroughly sated, and were just dropping off to sleep when his cell phone rang. He rolled over swearing, and answered in one word. "*What?*"

Mia was already asleep, and was too tired to even wake up to the noise, and didn't even hear Anton pull his clothes on. He leant over her, and whispered, "I have to go to my father, there is a problem. Go back to sleep, I don't know when I will be back. Promise me that you will stay here, and not leave the suite. I will send Al to you when I know what has happened." He shook her awake, and she grumbled in her sleep, but opened her eyes. "Listen to me, sweetheart. Stay here until you hear from me. Promise me that you will, and not go looking for me."

Mia sighed, then swore profoundly, and yawned. "I promise! Now can I go back to sleep?" Her eyes closed and she was asleep, not really understanding what on earth Anton was talking about.

But when she woke up late the next morning Anton wasn't asleep next to her, and Al was asleep in the large comfortable armchair, snoring his head off, as usual.

Mia lifted her head off the pillow and grumbled. "Well, fuck me! What happened to my wedding night? It must have been bloody fantastic, 'cos the groom has run off and left his bride the first night."

She began to laugh, because she could see the funny side, but then thought where the hell was Anton? Trying to remember what he had said to her when she couldn't keep her eyes open. Something about not leaving the suite until he came back, and that he would send Al to her.

Well! Al was here, but where was Anton?

CHAPTER TWENTY-SIX

Mia stood in the open doorway of the solarium, the cavernous room where only yesterday she had married her Anton. It had been a gloriously happy day with only close friends of Anton attending. But now a dark gloom had invaded the usually sunny, open area, because only men in dark suits and sad faces were sitting at the long table that overlooked the luxurious pool.

Mia's stomach did a nauseous roll over, because she feared what had happened. Marcus and Gerry were talking animatedly to Anton, whose face had a grey tinge to it, and he looked really sad. Doctor Perez was talking to Father Michael, who seemed to be enjoying a tumbler full of rare scotch. And, there was a small elderly man, who looked like an accountant, Mia thought it could be Sonny Silverman who she was supposed to see some time this week.

Then she realised that everyone at that table were family or close friends of Anton, and there weren't any staff or security about, which was unheard of. Al had escorted her downstairs when Anton had phoned him, and asked that Mia join him in the solarium. She had been swearing like a truck driver, because she hated being stuck in her room. It was her first day as a married woman, and had wanted to flaunt it. Had dressed in her prettiest white eyelet brocade sun dress, with white tennis shoes, and had arranged her curly hair up into a top knot, and was feeling really grown up and beautiful for her very new husband.

She turned to talk to Al, but he had silently disappeared, evidently Anton must have told him to, once he brought her downstairs. Then Marcus looked up and saw her standing nervously in the doorway, and he spoke to Anton, who immediately got up, and came over to bring her to the table to meet everyone.

He sat down with Mia on his lap, after kissing her lovingly, and giving her a comforting hug. She smiled shyly at everyone, which wasn't her usual demeanour, but they were all sombrely dressed, and nobody was smiling back. "You know everyone here, my darling, except Sonny, who is my very good friend, and accountant." Everyone said their hello's, and then did manage a smile for her.

She noticed that there were platters of sandwiches, pots of coffee, and very expensive bottles of scotch, and bourbon covering the table top. What on earth was going on? A horrible thought came into her head, but she wouldn't take it on board.

"I'm so sorry that I didn't come back last night, but my father Theo died just a few minutes after I got to his apartment." Anton rubbed her back as he knew she had come to love Theo, and would be terribly upset at the news that he had died.

He watched as she dissolved into tears, her big brown eyes were literally overflowing immediately. Her hands came up to cover her face, and she was trying to stop the sobs from leaving her throat, but was failing miserably. Anton turned her into his chest, and held her tightly, trying to comfort her, he wished he could have done the same, but it didn't seem a manly, or adult thing to do.

He whispered in her ear that Theo was out of pain now, and had suffered five miserable years with his declining health, so please do not be sad for him.

Mia physically managed to pull herself together after listening to Anton. Everyone in the room was moved emotionally at Mia's obvious love for Theo. Especially Marcus, it was taking all of his control not to go to Mia and comfort her, because that was Anton's privilege now, but for how long?

Mia looked around at all the men, and began to realise why they were all there together, and all dressed for a funeral. She turned back to Anton with a puzzled frown. "Is the funeral today, and why are you burying Theo so quickly? I don't understand. It usually takes at least a week to organise a proper funeral."

"I'm *so* sorry, my darling. Theo was interred in the family mausoleum early this morning." He watched her bottom lip begin to tremble again, so quickly explained the reason for the unusual speed of the burial. And he knew her volatile temper was about to explode, because she hadn't been invited. The only woman here, and she had been left behind intentionally. It was as if she was a stranger, and of no account, when family was involved.

"Mia darlin', listen to me, because you really have to understand what my father was involved with. He had many, many enemies, if they knew he had died, and where his body was interred, would without a doubt make it disappear. Everyone in this room knows where my father rests, and I know I can trust each and every one of them." Everyone sitting round the table nodded seriously, because they knew what Anton had gone through last night organising Theo's secret burial.

"Stefan completed the death certificate. Marcus and Gerry organised the burial within the law. Gerry pulled in favours with the owners of The Hollywood Forever Cemetery to allow us access to our mausoleum. Father Michael conducted the burial service at the cemetery." Mia could see that Anton was becoming very emotional as he was going through what had happened earlier, and how difficult it had been to secretly bury his beloved father Theo, with only a few people in attendance. She was becoming to realise what a wonderfully caring man she had married. A son who loved his father without a bad word to say about him, whatever he had done in his life.

If her Papa Henri had died last night she would have been inconsolable, and wouldn't have been able to function for weeks or months to come. She also noticed that Marcus was watching his brother with concern, as if wanting to comfort him, but decided against it because she was sitting on Anton's lap. In fact had been half out of his seat when Gerry yanked him back down with a few choice words in his ear. Mia thought that was really strange. Was Marcus going to comfort Anton, or her?

Mia kissed Anton's stubbled face. She had never seen him so dishevelled, without a shower, shave, and immaculately pristine clothes on his fine muscled physique. She cuddled up to him closer, and put her arms around him, because her husband needed someone to hold him, and she was always going to be that someone. He kissed her forehead, and spoke quietly to her. "We can never visit Theo's last resting place, my darling, because no one can know he is there. I have arranged for fresh flowers to be placed on the plot for years to come. Marcus will make sure that the contract is fulfilled, as no one knows that he is Theo's eldest son. By law we had to put my father's full name that was on his birth certificate, and death certificate, on the door plaque."

Carefully and gently he got up and placed Mia on his seat, and she dutifully sat quietly waiting for what Anton was going to do next. She had never been to a funeral, or a wake before, and this was both, and of course very unusual.

Anton stood with a glass of aged scotch in his hand. "Friends and family, please be upstanding and drink a toast to my beloved father, and best friend, Enrico Theodore Santiago. May he rest in forever peace and love. Your son Anton sends you off with the deepest regret, and with my forever deepest love, Theo. May God be the all forgiving and loving God that the church always preaches, because you are *so* going to need that love and forgiveness." He raised his glass and drank it in one hit. "To my beloved father."

And everyone agreed with Anton!

"God bless Theo!" But under their breath they all added "The Bastard!"

CHAPTER TWENTY-SEVEN

It was two days after Theo's wake, and Anton and Mia were showering together before he had to spend the day in his office. They had already had the best ever morning sex, and now Anton was crowding her up against the tiled wall, pulling her legs around his waist, and pushing his hardening penis into her warm, wet, opening.

"Jesus Christ Mia, I seriously cannot get enough of you." His strong arms were braced against the wall, as the water pounded against his back, which made him push deeper into his wife's always welcoming body. The harder and deeper he managed to fuck her, the happier and more content his sexy wife became. She had become insatiable, even more so since marrying him. If this carried on much longer Anton could die an extremely happy man, and he certainly wasn't complaining. His over-worked dick wasn't complaining either. Surely his virulent seed must have managed to get Mia pregnant by now, but she didn't appear to be any different as the weeks went by. He was certain that if she was carrying his baby, the whole world would know immediately. Mia could not possibly keep such a game change a secret from anyone.

His gorgeous woman was motor-mouth personified, while he kept everything close to his chest, as taught by his father to do, because evil was all around them, and danger written in his DNA.

He kissed her deeply, using his tongue to mimic what his hard, swollen, dick was doing to her. She began to tighten her inner muscles around him, causing friction to tighten his balls, and exquisite pleasure to radiate up his back and around his heart, which felt as if it would burst with his love for this incredibly giving woman. They both came looking into each other's eyes, and gasping out just how much they loved each other.

Too much! Far too much! It was dangerous to love another person with the intensity they both felt. It made them deaf, dumb, and blind to what was happening in the outside world, and inside the walls of Anton's private estate.

"Coffee, Danish, and orange juice, OK for you sweetheart?" As usual Anton was organising their breakfast on the veranda in their now combined suite. They had given up sharing their breakfast time with the rest of the household and staff, since Anton had moved into Mia's bed.

He'd altered a small area of the lounge into a mini-kitchen to suit them both. A state of the art Italian coffee machine had been delivered, and an expensive compact refrigerator had appeared. They both agreed that they needed privacy in the mornings when they managed to stop ravishing each other. It was always difficult to stop the ravishing, because it was their favourite time to fuck, and fuck some more.

Early every morning a platter of delicious pastries were brought up from the kitchen, with a large bowl of seasonal fruit. For some unknown reason Mia couldn't stop hungering for exotic fruit, which Anton was beginning to wonder if that was a sign of pregnancy. But he didn't dare query Mia, because she would bite his head off, for daring to say such a thing. Mia Maxwell Santi pregnant? Absolutely no way! Mia was absolutely scared spitless that she was going to be a mother. She was far too young! Too incapable of pushing a large baby out of her small vagina. It was far too painful to even consider. And she was totally happy and content being in love with her gorgeous new hubby, just the two of them.

Anton came and sat down after bringing Mia's breakfast to her. He didn't seem to realise that he was spoiling her rotten, as did everyone else who worked for him, every day. "Mia, I really need you to listen to me carefully, as it is extremely important that no one else in this house knows what I am going to say to you." He shook his head with impatience, because Mia had just rolled her eyes heavenward, and dramatically sighed, as if she had heard it all before – boring!

He took a deep breath and continued, because this was of the utmost importance, especially for his wife. "In a couple of hours Al is going to collect you, then come down to my office, and tell me that you want to go shopping, so that Larry and Andi won't think that is unusual. He is actually going to take you to Marcus, who is driving you to Sonny Silverman, my friend, who came to our wedding." He looked at Mia to make sure she was understanding what he was saying, and was relieved that she smiled back at him. Mia got easily bored when a serious conversation was happening, especially to her.

"Sonny is now your financial adviser, and of course Marcus is your lawyer. Between them they will explain my new will regarding you, which Marcus is looking after for you. Gerry Swane will follow you and Marcus, in case anyone else has got wind of where you are going, and he is always armed and ready for any action. Only Marcus, Sonny, and Gerry are in the loop of this situation."

They were already dressed for the day ahead. Anton as usual his immaculate self in fine black trousers, a crisp white cotton shirt, and the softest black Italian loafers, and always black socks. Mia had for a change put on a long floaty colourful gypsy skirt, with a miniscule white T-shirt, and was adding a tiny white jean jacket, and enough bangles to deafen anyone when she moved her arm, which she did a lot.

Mia laughed when Anton leaned over, and put his hand down the front of her daringly low top, and manoeuvred her breast out of its confinement and began to suck her nipple into his mouth. He then groaned with sexual frustration, "you haven't got a bra on again, sweetheart. You know that every male in your vicinity will have a hard-on, because your breasts will be noticeably active when you walk around. And, I really hate other men lusting after my very beautiful wife." In fact Anton was extremely jealous of any man ogling his property, his wife. It made him feel murderous.

Mia wriggled onto his lap, which was already showing evidence of a hardening erection. She laughed at his obvious discomfort. "Oh dear! I ain't wearing panties either, so that is going to cause a definite hard problem, donch'a think Mr Santi?"

"Oh shit!" Anton said under his breath. They were definitely going to be late, as she straddled him, her skirt around her waist, and she guided him to paradise, once again.

When they passed a drugstore and Mia asked Al to stop, because she needed to buy some personal items, Al wasn't happy when she wouldn't let him come in with her. She couldn't tell him she was going to purchase a pregnancy test, because she was now pretty certain she had been caught, and was pregnant. So she told Al she was buying Tampax and a vibrator for when Anton stayed away for a night. Mia knew that he would be too embarrassed to be with her. She left their vehicle grinning because he had gone as red as a beetroot, and mumbled he would wait for her outside, knowing his boss would be furious if he found out she had gone in alone to a store. For crissake he was her personal bodyguard and shouldn't let her out of his sight, but Mia was her own person, and definitely not frightened of her besotted husband.

Mia wandered round the store picking up items she had never been able to afford before, but now she was married to Anton her whole world had opened up to being wealthy, even though she would never take advantage of his wealth. Her Papa had taught her wisely, to never take advantage of privileges other people didn't have, and to always look after others before herself.

Last night poor Anton had nervously asked her why with all their lovemaking, with no restrictions, she hadn't become pregnant? Because she wasn't certain if she was pregnant, she told him that it was possible she couldn't conceive, ever.

Mia explained as best she could that she never had a proper period every month. She didn't know when it would happen, and it was only for a couple of hours, and absolutely of no consequence. Vehemently he had told her that he would take her to the top specialist to sort the problem out. Anton had been so upset for her, and she knew he was looking forward to a family together, but wouldn't let her know, because he didn't want her to think that was why he had married her in the first place.

Mia already knew that to be true, Anton would never be that shallow. He would be content and happy to be the loving couple they had already become, on their own.

She quickly disavowed him of rushing around to sort out her so-called problem. Her Papa had taken her to every available specialist on that subject, and everyone had scratched their heads, and couldn't find anything wrong with her. They all had said she was still ovulating a few eggs, so with luck would eventually make a baby, if her partner had sperm that were strong and excellent swimmers, and didn't give up easily.

Well! Of course the very virulent and highly sexed Anton had grinned and said that he was the man for the job, and would make it happen. However long it took.

So watch this space! He was probably correct!

Mia was surprised when Al drew up outside Marcus's office, because Anton had told her that she was going to his accountant Sonny Silverman. But Al explained that the plan had changed, as Marcus thought it would be safer for the meeting to be held at his office. As Mia got out of the 4X4 she saw Gerry Swane sitting outside smoking a disgusting cheroot as per usual. Immediately Marcus came out of the door, and ushered her inside, as Al drove off, evidently he wasn't privy to what was happening at the meeting. Mia began to feel a trifle uneasy, it all seemed to be too serious for her to take on board, and she hated secrecy in her life. This was Anton's affair not hers.

Sonny was going through a stack of papers, but immediately got up, and kissed Mia on both cheeks. "No wonder Anton absolutely adores you Mrs Santi, you look so beautiful today, but then with your genes could you possibly look any different?"

Mia really liked this old gentleman. "Are you flirting with me, Mr Silverman? And please call me Mia, as I am not used to being married yet, and can I call you Sonny, please?"

It was weird but then everyone seemed to relax. There seemed to be a great deal of testosterone in the room, with three powerful men, Marcus, Gerry, and Sonny, waiting to explain what it meant to marry her Anton. And Mia couldn't care less what Anton was worth, and what the hell it meant to her everyday life, and marriage.

Marcus gave her a warm hug, and kissed her lightly on her lips, which made Mia's heart beat faster, which annoyed her intently. Didn't she love Anton with that same stupid heart? How could she still love Marcus, when she had married his brother only days ago?

But now as she studied Marcus close up, he was so like Anton. They were two very gorgeous males, and had the same mannerisms. She couldn't understand why she hadn't noticed the similarities before. And they both favoured Theo, because even though he had been so very sick, he had still been a charismatic, handsome man. When he had been younger he must have been a gorgeous package of a virulent, testosterone man, of great power. She now understood why he had left his wife and son when he did, because the world had been his oyster, and he would have needed to test his ability to journey down that road ahead, and move on.

But of course that did not excuse what he had eventually become, and the life he had made Anton traverse. But that was all going to change now he had fallen in love with her, and married that love without any hesitation. And she certainly loved him.

Gerry grinned and gave her a lascivious wink. "Hi, gorgeous married woman, how goes married life?" He couldn't get used to the idea that Madeline Maxwell's beautiful child, a very difficult, but loving child, had actually married that fuckin' gangster. What could she have possibly seen in Anton Santi to have tied the proverbial knot with him?

Mia went over to him and gave him a very close hug, and whispered in his ear. "He is the best fuck in town, donch'a know." Gerry burst out laughing, then tried to cough up a lung. As per usual, Mia always got her own back.

By now Sonny was getting impatient, as he wasn't as young as the rest of the group, and decided to bring the meeting to order. "Mia I am going to explain as simply as possible what Anton your husband has asked me to provide you with if anything should happen to him, and you are left on your own. Marcus will explain it in more detail when I have left to go home."

Mia sat up straight in her chair, and put her hand up to stop Sonny from explaining. "Look everyone here, I am not at all interested in what Anton has, or what he is worth. I did not marry him for his wealth, I married Anton because I love him, and he loves me. I know he lives with danger all around him, but has promised within a month to stop all his illegal money making. I have plenty of money coming from my birth mother, and I know that Anton is not penniless. I would rather he gives all those illegal earnings to the poor and needy, because I will *not* touch it, and I truly mean that." She smiled at everyone, and then apologised for such a long speech.

Sonny shuffled the papers in front of him, with a very serious look on his face. "I am really sorry Mia, but I do not have anything to do with Anton's illegal earnings. I only deal with his personal and private legal money, made from his acquisitions over quite a few years of buying up hotels, apartments, and corporate buildings, within a company of his own making, under an assumed name. His will splits all this down the middle between his wife, Mia Maxwell Santi, and his birth mother, Sophia Medina." Marcus looked absolutely stunned at the mention of his mother Sophia, he had never expected that bombshell in a million years.

Sonny carried on regardless of everyone's shock. "I am afraid Mia, this will is written in stone, and can't be broken. Both you ladies will be multi-millionaires should anything happen to Anton Santi. Naturally, we all wish Anton a long and happy marriage to you Mia. I have never married, and consequently have no children of my own. Anton, I have always treated him as my son, and love him dearly." He shuffled the papers in front of him emotionally. "I'm going to leave you now, and pass you over to Marcus who will explain all the legalities of Anton's wishes. Who I might add was in sound mind and heart, when he made this new will, which Marcus as his legal representative will countersign my signature."

He nodded to everyone in the room, and left before the conversation could get louder and more explosive. He wasn't stupid, only older and wiser than everyone else in the room, because he was well aware that Mia was going to hit the ceiling, and would want Marcus to have her half of Anton's money. And Marcus would absolutely refuse, so it was going to be a long, arduous afternoon.

Far too long and arduous for an elderly Jewish gentleman, who needed a refreshing nap after a long lunch with a large scotch as a chaser.

CHAPTER TWENTY-EIGHT

She was so ashamed, couldn't believe that she had hit Marcus so hard, when he was only trying to help, and calm her down. She was a total bitch. A spoilt brat, because her Papa had always spoilt her, then Anton, and now Marcus.

But it was all down to her, and had to stop, right now. Her emotions were all over the place, and to sob all over Marcus was *so* embarrassing. She was a married woman and needed to start acting like one, not an out of control child, as she had been today.

Mia had begun to argue with Marcus, when he categorically refused to split Anton's will between his mother and himself. She did not want Anton's wealth, and she categorically refused to accept it, in any form. She argued that she only wanted Anton, because she loved him *so* much, and would not accept his personal wealth, and wouldn't accept that he would die before her, because she didn't want to live without him.

It was obvious that Marcus would not, and could not accept that situation. And, it was legally impossible as Anton had already signed the will, and Marcus had counter-signed it.

Out of the corner of her eye she had seen Gerry put his hands up in surrender, and move closer to the door, because he knew what was going to happen next. Volatile

Mia was going to get very volatile with someone, and he wasn't going to be that someone, not again.

Then Marcus came round his desk, and went to Mia to calm her down. She stood up and began to pummel his body anywhere she could get to him, with stinging blows, all the time screaming out that he was her lawyer, and should do what she told him. In fact threatening to sack him, if he didn't change the will.

She couldn't understand why she was so out of control. Would never have wanted to hurt Marcus, because she loved him for crissake. She knew he was a good lawyer, and couldn't do what she was asking of him.

Marcus put up with a lethal battering and then ran out of patience, and physically overpowered the tiny termagant, who was still screaming out indecent obscenities whilst being restrained, which didn't go down well with Mia.

But suddenly she ran out of steam, and fell against Marcus's warm hard chest. She began sobbing as if her heart was breaking. He put his arms around her, and began to rub his hands over her back in an effort to give her his support and love. Their bodies connected completely, and she was shocked to feel that he had a semi-erection. Oh my God! She didn't want to notice, but felt her own traitorous body respond to that hardness. She wanted to rub herself all over him like a purring cat. What the fuck was wrong with her, she loved

Anton, didn't she? She was married to him, he made her happy, and she would not betray him in deed, or mind. Marcus had realised that all this drama was because Mia was terrified that Anton's lifestyle left him open to violence against him. He mixed with some very evil people, who would enjoy killing him, and her if they could get to her through her husband.

That also terrified Marcus, he constantly worried that his brother would end up dead, far too young, and now Mia was on that list since marrying Anton. His brother was so selfish in marrying this gorgeous young woman, because he could have signed her death certificate in doing so.

The sobs gradually began to subside to sighs and tears, and Mia took a step back, looking up into Marcus's blue/green eyes, and they both felt a sizzle of electricity arc between them, and just stared at each other as if transfixed. He broke the moment by gently kissing her forehead, hugging her tightly, and then stepping away from temptation as he phoned Al to come pick up Anton's wife.

Gerry blew out a held breath of stress. He didn't know how this altercation was going to work out, and was so relieved nobody had committed murder. Mia in full flow tantrum was scary. He felt sorry for Anton Santi, because he was obviously besotted with his young beautiful wife, and she would definitely take advantage of that adoration.

But Gerry had kept alive by his gut feelings, and his gut was telling him something was going down within Santi's domain. Gerry believed that Santi was in dire danger. The word on the street was that someone close to Santi was making a takeover bid while he was constantly bedding down with his new wife, and wasn't watching his enemies.

Gerry had decided because of Marcus, and Mia, that he would pay a visit to Santi, and try to warn him to be alert to the people working close to him. He wasn't keen on Santi, in fact didn't like the bastard one iota, but for Mia he would try and get through to her new husband to warn him.

When Mia got ready to leave he asked her for her phone, he was surprised when she gave it to him, but she was still upset, and just wanted to go home. "I'm going to put my phone as an emergency number on yours. All you have to do is press that button on the right-side there." He showed her what to do, it was so easy. "It will trigger my phone to ring, and I will leave whatever I am doing. It also shows me where you are." When she looked at him as if it was all too technical for her, he began to wonder what he was doing. "Look Mia, trust me. If that emergency number rings I will find you. So please, please do not use it to test me. I will be fuckin' furious if I'm in the middle of great sex, and I have to leave, because great sex is pretty hard to find at my advanced age."

She didn't understand why he was explaining all this load of crap, because she was never going to call Gerry Swane if she was in trouble. There were so many security men around her, how was she possibly going to get into trouble? It was a ridiculous idea!

She got into Al's 4X4 still hiccoughing tiny sobs. He looked at her wondering what on earth had happened to upset her, but didn't dare ask in case she bit back at him. Al had realised early on that he had to be careful when making idle conversation with the Boss's wife.

So they rode all the way home in stressful silence. Mia sniffing and tearful, and Al trying his hardest to not care, but he actually did. Like everyone who knew Mia, he loved her as a friend, and a confidante, and didn't like to see her upset. He also knew Anton would be furious with Marcus and Gerry for whatever had happened at Marcus's office today.

When they got back to the estate he would have to tell Anton how upset Mia was. Otherwise he might get the blame, and nobody wanted to be on the bad side of Anton Santi, and expect to live.

Anton shot up the stairs worried that Mia was evidently very upset, and had been crying. It wasn't in Mia's nature to cry, or to be upset, he couldn't think what had happened at Marcus's today. He realised too late that he should have gone with her.

Probably, Sonny, Marcus, and Gerry had been too much for her to cope with, and he knew she wasn't feeling one hundred per cent. Hopefully for a very good reason?

He found her laying across the bed crying her eyes out, and sobbing at the same time. Anton thought it must have been a catastrophe for Mia to act like that. Yeah, she could get angry, and extremely difficult, and obstinate, but never hysterically upset, and desolate, as she was now.

Bodily he picked her up, and sat down in a comfy armchair with her on his lap, taking her in his arms he tried to stem the tears pouring down her still beautiful, but wet face.

She cuddled up close to his warm body, and began to slowly quieten down, but a miserable sob still left her chest, and she said in a broken voice, "I was so mean to Marcus who was only trying to help me. I hurt my hand and arm because I hit him so hard. Oh God! What must he think of me, that I'm a total bitch, who's a spoilt brat, and can't control her emotions?"

Anton tried to stifle a relieved laugh, he had thought something catastrophic had caused all this drama. But Mia wasn't laughing, as she carried on. "And, it was all your fault Anton bloody Santi, leaving me all that – that crap in your will. And, nobody can change that fuckin' will, including me." She gave a loud sniff of anger, and poked him in his muscled chest. "I do *not* want any of your so-called wealth, because you are going to out-live me, because I won't live without you, because I love y-you far too much to be in this world alone." A large fat tear rolled down her cheek, and she sniffed very unladylikely again.

Anton smiled and kissed away that tear, and then kissed her lips sweetly, with all his heartfelt love for this incredible woman, that he now called wife. But Mia wasn't finished yet, she needed a definite promise from him. "And Marcus kept saying you are always in danger, and move around in dangerous company, and you shouldn't be so trusting. And – and then Gerry agreed with him, and that I was in danger because I married you. I am so frightened Anton, that you are going to get seriously hurt, or even worse."

Anton realised it was time to come to a serious decision to allay her obvious fears. He had discussed it with Marcus, and they had decided to keep it to themselves until it came to fruition. But he would not have Mia living in fear every day they stayed in Los Angeles. "Sweetheart if it is OK with you I have asked Marcus to look for a hideaway for us close by where he lives outside Fort Worth in Perseverance. Just a small ranch, with a few animals, and breeding horses, which I have become very interested in working such a retreat. I can also become close to my mother again, and

Marcus's boys who are just four and six years old. We have a readymade family to get to know and love."

Nervously, he watched Mia's expression as he set out what he wanted to do. "Of course I need about a month to close down everything here, because this part of my life will be left completely behind. No regrets! Nothing illegal! No looking after my back, just loving my gorgeous wife, and hopefully our own kids."

Mia changed immediately, and began kissing him all over his handsome face. She was deliriously happy, but then took a breath. "We *can* go to Houston first to get married in our local church, and have a great big noisy party after? And you can meet my Papa Henri, and my Mama Josephine, and my best friend Viola, who has taken over my bedroom, so Papa wouldn't miss me too much."

When Mia was on a verbal onslaught Anton just about managed to understand what she was saying, because she spoke so quickly. "We are definitely going to meet your parents, and marry in God's house, because we are going to be married forever and a day, and be ecstatically, wonderfully happy."

He waited for the blow up with his next words. "Now, are you going to use that pregnancy test you bought today, and find out if it's positive or negative?"

Actually Mia couldn't help but laugh, because she couldn't keep a damn thing secret from her husband. "How did you find out? It was Al wasn't it? I didn't put him off, with the Tampax, and vibrator, did I? I'm never going to tell him a secret ever again."

"He has a very savvy fiancée, and they are trying to get pregnant. When you wouldn't let him go into the drugstore with you, he cottoned on to what was happening. And, he also knew that I am desperate for a family of my own."

She got up and went to her bag and took out the slim white box. When Anton went to follow her into the bathroom, she stopped and gave him one of her drop dead looks. "If you think you are going to watch me pee on a stick, think again Anton Santi."

He put his hands up in surrender. "But, I don't trust you to tell me the truth, my darling girl."

"Oh, you will know. If I scream loudly, it means it's negative. If there is deadly silence, it means I am pregnant, and beyond terrified of the consequences. And you are going to spend the next eight months pandering to my every whim, mentally, physically, and sexually. And, I ain't joking, mister."

Anton paced, and paced some more. It was at least fifteen minutes since Mia had closed the bathroom door on him. There was complete silence in that bathroom after she had flushed the toilet.

Then he heard her cussing violently, and then complete silence again, and he knew what he had known for a couple of weeks, but had never dared believe it.

Anton Santi was going to be a dad, he was overjoyed beyond normal words. But Mia Maxwell Santi was going to be a nightmare for months to come. Simply because she was terrified of the birth. If he could have the baby for her he would do so in a nano-second.

But, he could be there for her 24/7. It would be worth the aggro' to hold his son in his arms for the very first time. And, he knew that Mia was going to be a fantastic mother, whatever she said about herself. She was a giving, loving, caring woman, who would be a mama bear with a cub to care for, and keep safe in a treacherous world.

He opened the door to the bathroom to begin the rest of his life, content and very happy, with the woman he adored even more now, she was pregnant with his child.

CHAPTER TWENTY-NINE

Marcus and Gerry were sitting together the next morning drinking coffee, and mulling over what had happened in the office yesterday.

"Jesus Christ! You know that your brother is not one of my favourite people, but I've got to admit to feeling sorry for the poor bastard, having to cope with our Mia on a daily basis. She is the main reason I've never wanted a ring through my nose. Yeah, sure it must be great to have great sex whenever you feel the itch, but then I'm pretty certain that pleasure soon wears off in marriage." He took a swig of really strong coffee, and looked exceptionally pleased with himself at still being unrestrained by a wife at forty.

But Marcus was feeling the exact opposite. He was so envious of his brother, and would give his left ball to be married to Mia. He was totally screwed. He couldn't get her out of his head for five minutes at a time, and he was walking around with a hard-on from hell wanting to feel that amazing body intimately. Just loving her, spoiling her, and make-up sex when she lost her temper with him. She was a firecracker of a tiny, stunningly beautiful, but loving female. And he was hurting not to be able to hold her permanently. When she had felt his erection against her belly he knew she felt the same way as he did. Her eyes had widened in shock, and she had licked her lips in anticipation of what was going to happen next, absolutely nothing.

Mia was the perfect woman, or the perfect storm.

Marcus knew what he had to do now. Never see her again, because he would betray his feelings before long. He had never loved anyone as he loved her from the moment he had looked into those big, soulful, brown eyes. Of course he loved his kids, and had loved Bianca. He had married her for crissake, so he must have felt something for her, but it had gradually died when they made love, but only because he instigated it, and normal conversation had only been about the family. Nothing stimulating, or humorous, that had all died with the loveless fucking.

He realised that Gerry was talking to him, and he was dreaming about having dirty amazing sex with Mia. "I'm sorry Marcus, but I'm going deep undercover in the next few days. The DEA and FBI are gaining evidence on the underworld in L.A. I have to try and put it all together for them to come in guns blazing. Sorry buddy, but you know Anton will be at the top of that hit list. I cannot let him know what is going down, and neither can you. Something really big is happening. Huge amounts of money are being transferred from the Cayman Islands, Columbia, and Aruba. We believe that Anton is being sidelined and taken over." He shook his blond head, drew on his cheroot, and swore explicitly at the work ahead for him.

Now Marcus was listening to every word, because Gerry never prevaricated, or usually told secrets about his work, so he must be truly worried.

"What can we do in this situation? You are worrying me. More for Mia than my stupid brother."

"You are going to do nothing, because we haven't had this conversation. But this morning I am going to Anton's estate, and will try to warn him that he has enemies within his workforce. I will also try to get Mia to leave with me, but don't hold your breath on that outcome. You know how fuckin' obstinate she is, and she does love Anton, I'm pretty certain of that." He took a deep draw on his smoke, and coughed horribly again. "That's if I can get past that gorilla on the electric gate. I sure ain't giving up my weapon this time, I do not trust one fucker working for Santi." He coughed up again. "Can I borrow your 4X4 Mercedes, 'cos my Roadster is too easy to notice. And no! You absolutely cannot go with me. I can't look after two of us, if the shit hits the fan."

Marcus shook his head in reply. "I'm sorry, but I can't go anyway. I have to go back to my ranch, because the boys are playing up my mother, who isn't coping with their combined bad manners. I've been away longer than usual. What with the wedding, and organising Anton's will, it's been well over a week. I'm afraid my kids have taken advantage of their father being away too long."

He threw a set of keys at Gerry. "Take the Jeep flat-back in case of trouble. I don't need my Mercedes getting shot up, it's my favourite vehicle. And, *please* keep me in the loop."

Gerry grinned good-naturedly. "Thanks Marcus my friend. You worry about your precious Mercedes, while I'll worry about my ass getting severely kicked, or shot at. If anything bad happens I will definitely let you know."

The two men slapped each other on the back in friendship. Marcus went back to finish the paperwork on his desk. Gerry went out the door whistling Dixie, and decided he would go straight to Santi's, hopefully the newlyweds would have managed to get out of bed by the time he got there.

They were still in bed laughing and whispering when they should have been up at least two hours ago. But they had talked well into the night, Anton was beyond normal excitement about the baby, and was trying out names for his boy. He was adamant that his virulent sperm could only produce a male child. So Leo, Gianni and Marco, were in consideration, and of course Theodore was favourite.

Mia argued that her family only produced girl babies, so her eggs were definitely female, and wanted Madeline, Melody, or Mary-Anne.

Last night after the trauma of the explosive day for Mia, and now being pregnant, Anton was treating her like a precious princess. He had declared they were not going to have sex for at least twenty-four hours, to give each other a break from the stress and utter satisfaction of fucking like proverbial on Viagra rabbits. And, Mia actually had agreed because she was exhausted.

They both agreed they couldn't sleep naked, because it would have been too much to expect them from wanting full blown sex together. So Anton was wearing a pristine white T-shirt, and white silk boxers. And Mia her usual tiny tank top, and miniscule shorts in two eclectic colours, which definitely clashed, but she never noticed colours that didn't work together.

They were whispering and laughing, because he had stated that walls had ears, even though the entire house was swept for bugs continually. They were laughing because Anton had said that if the baby came out a girl, he was sending it back. Mia had fallen about laughing, and said, "You have to be fucking joking. If I have managed to push a baby out of the small opening in my body, it ain't fucking going back for nobody, and especially you, Anton Santi. So suck it up, mate."

She kissed him so lovingly on the lips, changing her mind about no sex for twenty-four hours. She was completely addicted to his hard, very inventive, and spectacular equipment of mind-blowing pleasure. But she hadn't finished about the instructions on child birth. "And, I'm warning you now Anton, that I will be asleep in eight month's time, 'cos I don't do pain under any circumstances. As the father of your daughter you are going to have to do all the work for me."

Anton couldn't help but laugh at his adamant wife. The so beautiful mother of his future children. He bent down and kissed her still flat belly, feeling so much love for this incredibly strong woman he had luckily married, and who was now pregnant with his baby. He was just going to agree to anything she wanted when the baby was born, when their bedroom door crashed open with violence, and the words died on his lips that he would be so very honoured to help her through the birth of their first child.

And was so impatient to get through the coming months to be the family he'd always wanted with Mia at his side.

CHAPTER THIRTY

Mia believed that they were being targeted by an enemy, so was too frightened to move. Anton knew exactly what was happening, and for the past five years had wondered who would try and take over his territory. Who would have the nerve? And the guts to try and cut off the head of Santi's Empire.

To say he was shocked and in total disbelief, and total dismay, would be a severe understatement. But, he would not show his fear, and his heartbreak at what he knew was about to happen, because his utmost priority was to keep Mia safe.

Taking her beautiful face in his hands he kissed her sweetly, and gently, then spoke very quietly to her. "Remember, whatever happens today I will always love you. Keep my son safe for me. Now, I want you to stay exactly as you are, and keep really quiet. Don't move, and now press the button on your bracelet, and get Al here ASAP." Mia understood, and nodded her head fearfully.

Anton very slowly and carefully got out of bed, his hands above him to show he wasn't holding a weapon. The two men who had invaded his privacy already knew that he never brought a weapon into his home. They of course both had their own weapons trained on him, because they didn't trust their own instincts regarding their so-called boss.

Anton shook his head in dismay at one of the traitors, "Andi! How could you? Didn't I treat you well enough? A Porsche. An Apartment. Designer clothes, and the most expensive Rolex that money could buy. What did I do wrong, that you could possibly do this to me?"

Andi was in tears when he answered. "You left me. I loved you, and pandered to your every sexual demand." He pointed at Mia. "Then that scheming bitch came along, and you gave your love to her. Without a moment's thought as to how I was feeling. I loved you Anton with all my heart, and thought you loved me the same."

Anton shook his head at Andi's ridiculous love declaration. "Yeah! At the beginning I did believe that I felt something for you, but that soon died a death of make believe. You! Are selfish, self-centred, greedy, and totally shallow. You only love yourself, and our relationship was already at the end of its time when I met Mia, and fell head over heels in love with her."

Then he looked at Larry, he knew this was his doing. Anton had always kept him in line, because he knew he was ambitious, and ruthless, and wanted to be the Chief Honcho, and had waited patiently for Anton to take his eye off the game. "Well! It didn't take you long Larry, did it? You know this situation is ridiculous, because Mia and I are leaving as soon as possible. We are going to live in the country and hopefully raise a family out of the limelight."

As he was speaking Mia got out of bed very carefully, and went and stood behind her husband. She put her arms around him, and laid her cheek on his back, hoping to give him some comfort with all the drama in the room. She was scared shitless, and was so proud of Anton in trying to stay calm in such dire circumstances.

Anton clasped Mia's hands in his, thankful that he could hold her, possibly for the last time. "There isn't any point in making this situation any worse than it already is. Take over all the contracts. Take all the money. I am not interested in any of the millions that are due to me. Mia and I are going to live a much simpler lifestyle. I am done with my father's empire of drugs, weapons, and gambling, I just haven't got the stomach or the heart for it anymore. I will not beg for *my* life, but I will beg for Mia's. She is the innocent in all this, and does not deserve to be hurt in any way." Mia was gagging to get her say in what was happening, but didn't dare get in Anton's way. This was far too serious to interfere with, so she kept behind Anton and literally held her breath.

She couldn't believe that Larry and Andi could turn against Anton, because he had always treated the people who worked for him so generously. In truth she thought Andi was capable, because he had made it *so* obvious that he hated her, especially when they had married.

"Sorry Anton, but you are too late. For the past few days I have been emptying all your secret accounts, and changing the contracts into my name. All your computers have been destroyed. Andi and I are moving to Mexico City where we will resume our work, and complete the takeover of your father's empire, and yours of course."

He waved his firearm at Anton. "Please ask your wife to step away from you, *now*, unless you want her to get hurt."

Anton pulled Mia's arms from around him, and pushed her away. The look on her face almost brought him to his knees, but he still managed to push her far enough away from him. He had tears in his eyes when he quickly said, "I love you, my darling." Then Mia heard a strangled pop from the silencer, and the love of her life fell dead at her feet, with a clean shot to his forehead.

All Larry said was, "You think I am going to fuckin' look over my shoulder for the rest of my Goddamn life in case you decide to kill me, Anton fuckin' Santi?"

Mia didn't have the chance to take a breath, or scream out the pain of what they had done to Anton, when it felt as if her chest had exploded.

The power of the pain was all consuming, it knocked her off her feet, and she realised she was dying before the world disappeared and blackness descended. She didn't have time to even think that she would meet Anton on the otherside, wherever that was?

"Well done Andi, didn't think you had the balls to kill her. I would have done it, if you hadn't. She knew where we are going, so we had to eliminate her, however bad it is killing a woman." Evidently, Larry still felt he had some decency left, not wanting to have to kill Mia.

They went out of the door laughing to begin a new life in Mexico. All the rest of Santi's men had already left after they realised what Larry was going to do. They had all been paid off very handsomely, so didn't mourn Santi for a moment. In their line of work they never stayed permanently with one boss. Whoever paid top dollar got their undivided attention, and affiliation, and gun power.

Andi grinned at Larry. "I detested that bitch, and couldn't wait to get rid of her. Believe me, killing her was a pleasure. I never thought that my Anton had gone straight, because he truly loved me. It was all her doing. She bewitched him with her beauty and overt sexuality. She was a whore, and he fell for it. Neither of them are a loss to me. I am with you now Larry, and we are going to be rich and famous together. And, I will never give any of my wealth to the wretched, stinking poor. Fuck that, this is all about you, and me Larry, and the millions we are going to make, and spend, spend, spend!"

"Mexico here we come!" They both said at the same time, leaving the estate empty of people, and the electric gates wide open.

PART TWO
MARCUS

CHAPTER THIRTY-ONE

Al reached the open gates, as Gerry and Marcus pulled up in the Mercedes 4X4. He got out of his state of the art Jeep to talk to Gerry. Nobody wanted to get into some unknown action until they decided to exchange information on what was happening inside Anton's estate.

But no security on the gate meant there was big trouble ahead, so they needed to be careful, and coordinated. And, put their weapons ready for use. Usually there were far too many mean guys carrying firearms to ignore at your peril.

Al was on a few days holiday, he hadn't had any time off since he had become Mia's personal bodyguard. But her security buzzer had gone off, and he had immediately driven to the house, because that was his job, to keep Santi's wife safe, day or night.

Gerry was just about to leave to confront Santi, when the emergency signal went off on his phone. He had run back to Marcus to tell him, and Marcus left with him immediately. Both men had a really bad feeling that something was going down at the house, and they would probably be too late to help Santi, or even worse, Mia.

"Marcus and I will follow you to the house, Al. Everywhere has been abandoned, my gut is telling me it could be carnage inside. Keep your gun handy. There are a lot of mean bastards working for Santi, we don't know if there are any inside the house." Gerry blew out a held breath of anxiety. He never wanted to be a hero, but for Mia he would do his damnedest to find out if she was still OK. Right now, it was not looking good.

Al shook his hand, and then looked at Marcus with a sombre expression. This was Marcus's brother, and he could already be dead. "OK! I'll take the lead when we get to the house, as I know the layout better than anyone. And, shoot to kill, because the bastards that work for Santi, are killing machines and won't miss their target, if you hesitate."

The three men stood silently in the bedroom, it was a heartbreaking sight. Anton lay as he had fallen, eyes blankly open, with a bullet hole clean in his forehead. A bullet that must still be lodged in his brain, but would have caused total destruction before stopping in its trajectory.

Al could see immediately that Anton was dead, so he quickly moved to Mia, who seemed to have been flung backwards with the impact of a bullet hitting her chest. She was covered in blood chest high.

He pulled out a clean dressing from his medical bag, which he had grabbed before leaving his home. In truth he had first thought that Mia had been fatally wounded, but now felt a glimmer of hope. She had a faint heart beat, and needed medical attention immediately. "Gerry hold this dressing tight over the wound. We have a chance here that we can save her." He very gently moved her to look at her back. "Thank God, the bullet has exited, but she is bleeding out, and probably bleeding internally." Mia gave the tiniest moan when Al set her back down, and he quietly said to her that she was going to be OK. Even though he realised she couldn't hear him, but he felt better saying it. But he looked up at Gerry, with tears in his eyes, and shook his head, because he honestly believed they had got there too late for Anton, and now Mia.

Then they both turned to look behind them as they heard a strange noise. It was Marcus sitting on the floor with Anton in his arms, rocking his brother with tears tracking down his face, with an expression of sheer grief gripping him. They both turned away giving Marcus his few precious moments with his younger brother that he would never have again.

Al pulled out his cell phone, while Gerry kept his hand firmly on Mia's dressing, and the bullet wound. He so wished he could break down in tears, Anton's death had always been inevitable with the way he earned his dirty money. But, Mia did not deserve what had gone down here today.

Probably she had witnessed her husband being gunned down in front of her in cold blood. Then whoever had done it had silenced her with an intended heart shot to kill her, but with Al now on the spot there was the smallest chance he might save her.

"Doctor Perez? Yes, it's Al from Anton's security. We have a big problem. Anton is already dead, but Mia is hanging on by a thread. The bullet has exited, but I think it might have hit her lung, spleen, and kidney. She must have moved just as the bullet hit her. Yes, I am trying to stabilise her, but she is bleeding out. Can you meet us at the Cranbourne Hospice, she is going to need an operation ASAP. I know you and your partner Doctor Sanchez do carry out major medical procedures there. We need somewhere safe for Mia to be operated on. And we need to register her as Mia Madeline Maxwell. No one must know she is married to Anton Santi. If the people who did this find out she could live, they will make sure she doesn't." He listened to what Stefan was saying then nodded his head. "Right, I understand. Marcus and I will get her there immediately."

Gerry understood completely what he had to do now. "Do you know who did this? Was anything different lately? Anything suspicious? Out of place? I presume it was in house, as there is no one left on duty, not one person, but you Al." Al was too busy to answer Gerry.

"Marcus could you please cover Anton? And, help me get Mia to Stefan's hospice. We have to be exceedingly gentle and work as one. Gerry is going to stay here and call in the M.E., and L.A.P.D. We do not want anyone knowing that Mia is his wife, and was here when it happened." He looked straight at Gerry to answer him. "Since the wedding there has been a lot of rumours and innuendoes running around. Larry and Andi have become thick as thieves, which makes me think this was their doing. It would be extremely easy for Larry to make a bid at running the whole system. Anton has been totally besotted with his new bride, which has angered a very jealous ex-lover Andi. Anton took his eye off the game, and has paid the price with his life."

Al was seriously worried about his patient's condition, she was getting colder by the minute, and told Marcus to get a blanket to keep her warm. Between them they managed to manoeuvre her into Al's arms, with Marcus trying to stem the blood still oozing from the wound. He felt as if he was losing her, and had never had her. She wasn't his to lose. She had been Anton's, and he was jealous of that love.

Gerry felt like a fuckin' whore at a church tea party, totally out of place, without anyone to fuck with. Sniffing loudly, he managed to keep his emotions under control. "Look after our girl, you guys. Please, don't let her die because she had the misfortune to fall in love with that piece of shit. Sorry Marcus! And marry him, and could end up dead because of one stupid mistake."

Marcus didn't take offence, because Gerry always talked straight on any situation. That was why he worked with the P.I. constantly. "Thanks Gerry. We need a death certificate in the name of Antonio Theo Santiago. We also need for Anton to be put in the morgue under John Doe. I don't want anyone knowing that my brother is dead until he is laid to rest with my father. Everyone can be bought. Whatever it costs, pay them." He went to follow Al out of the room with Mia in his arms. "I know you can do it, Gerry. Do it for Mia if not for Anton. The FBI will take this place apart as soon as they find out. I want Anton to be missing, and Mia completely out of the picture."

Marcus stopped at the door, taking one last look at Anton, knowing he would never see him again. He had lost a father he hated, and a brother he loved all in a week. "Are we OK with all this, Gerry? It's a lot to ask of you, and you know a huge bonus will be waiting for you, when it's sorted. And, Al of course." He hurried to catch up with Al, who would need help to get Mia carefully into the Mercedes.

"I'm not doing this for the money, Marcus my friend. I am doing it for you, because I know you loved your brother.

And, I'm doing it for our Mia, because you love her as much as Anton did. The FBI will tear this place apart brick by brick. I'm sure the computers have been smashed to smithereens, because I would have done that first. They will find two specimens of blood, but nothing to compare it with, as neither Santi or Mia have ever given them a blood sample. So they will be looking for two people who have mysteriously disappeared after being seriously hurt, or dead."

After Gerry stopped prevaricating with himself, he began the meticulous job of eradicating all the many finger prints left by everyone. The blood wasn't his problem, because you could never completely get rid of blood stains.

Next job, get his mate the L.A. Medical Examiner to come in and verify what had happened, and they needed a death certificate to be able to lay Anton to rest with his father. Also he needed one of his cohorts in the police force to back up the M.E.'s findings. It was going to cost a fortune to keep this out of the Media's attention. Ten thousand dollars each, was a sure bet. But inflation was rising every day, so it could cost a lot more. That wasn't Gerry's problem, it was Marcus's.

He went into the bathroom to find some bleach to start getting rid of any evidence that the FBI didn't need to help with their enquiries. In time they would work it out, but by then Mia hopefully would have left Los Angeles, and disappeared. And Anton would be interred in the family mausoleum out of harm's way.

And Gerry could get some well earned rest, after a very long, very dirty session, or two, with an extremely experienced first class hooker, or two. He certainly wasn't fussy, nor was his dick, who could always rise to the occasion, however much it cost.

And he couldn't let a bonus go to waste. Now could he?

CHAPTER THIRTY-TWO

Marcus paced, and kept pacing, he couldn't sit still, because he was gripped by grief and worry. He was outside the small theatre where the two surgeons were fighting to save the life of the woman he loved. It had been five hours since Al had carefully but quickly carried Mia into the Hospice that Stefan and Tomaz worked in together in down town L.A.

Marcus knew exactly what was accomplished daily here, because Anton's money had built it, and maintained it. He paid for the staff, and the drugs that helped to cure the cancer patients that couldn't afford to pay towards their own treatment.

It cost millions every year to upkeep, but Anton never queried how much, just kept an open tab with Stefan and Tomaz for what was needed. It was small but immaculate, with the State of the Art equipment. There were only two wards, always full of patients, and one small theatre for operations when needed. An ICU, that was run by an eagle-eyed, very experienced Nursing Sister. Stefan ran his external clinic there for immigrants, and extremely poor Americans, who would never be able to afford the crippling cost of Health Insurance.

Only Marcus, Tomaz, and Stefan knew where the money came from, because Marcus was the go between for

Anton. As Anton's Power of Attorney, Marcus would now take over the reins of Anton's many and diverse philanthropical good deeds. No one was aware of the wonderfully giving side of Anton, only his brother Marcus, who vowed to keep up his good work.

Marcus was heartbroken at losing Anton, his baby brother, but losing Mia as well, he couldn't contemplate, couldn't wrap his head around that diabolical thought. At one time in the Mercedes they thought they had lost her, but somehow Al managed to hold on to her, and had run with her into the arms of Stefan. The two surgeons had whisked her into the theatre, and Al and Marcus had been left outside the swinging doors almost in breakdown mode. Both feeling totally helpless, and inadequate.

Then Al had left to go back to the house to help Gerry sort out the mechanics of removing Anton out of sight, and the law into the mystery of what had happened.

Marcus's cell phone vibrated in his pocket. Immediately he walked towards the door leading to the garden, not wanting to break the silence in the area of the Hospice that was for terminally ill patients. "Gerry! What's happening? Yeah, I'll be there as soon as I can, but hopefully you and Al are coping OK?"

Gerry had been running around like his ass was on fire, and using expletives he didn't know he even knew. "Sorry

Marcus, but it's cost a lot more than even I thought. Evidently backhanders are at the top of the list for easy money. Also the mortuary manager is absolutely adamant that Anton has to be moved tonight, because they are often subject to checks. I've sorted that out, and Father Michael is free, as Al and I can be at the Mausoleum when it's closed. Nobody will ever know that Anton is buried with his father. And, the L.A.P.D. are here going through everything, but there is nothing left to find. Al and I completely cleared Mia's things out of the house."

Gerry had a fit of coughing before he could carry on. Marcus shook his head in disgust. Those bloody cheroots were going to be the death of his friend, and he never listened to anyone when they kept warning him that cancer was a disease nobody deserved or wanted. But it was like talking to a brick wall. Gerry always came back that his life consisted of sex, booze, and smokes, and if he died of those three he would be fuckin' happy.

"Before you go, Marcus. Those bastards absolutely annihilated Anton's office with steel baseball bats. And, I think Andi shot up Mia's beautiful piano until it wasn't recognisable. He hated her with a vengeance, and took it out on the present that her husband gave her with his love. Sorry Marcus, how is our girl doing? We've been so busy here we haven't had time to think about her, and I know you would have let us know if it was bad news."

"Honestly, I don't know. I thought someone would have told me what was happening, but since Al left hours ago, there has been nothing. I'm worried sick about her. I can't lose her, Gerry. Not after losing Anton, it's not fair. They are both my family, and somehow I've got to let my mother know that her youngest son is dead." Marcus was dreading that conversation, but knew it had to be done, sooner rather than later.

"As soon as I'm done here, I'll pick up some clean clothes for you at the office, and toiletries. You must be a mess from what happened here, and can't bury your brother less than immaculate. You know how meticulous he was in his clothes and grooming. It's only fitting we all make an effort for him on his last night on earth. Hopefully by the time we pick you up, you will have good news about Mia. Keep positive buddy, that girl is bloody obstinate, and incredibly strong. She will come out of this, swearing and vowing vengeance against whoever killed her beloved Anton, and don't forget she is the only witness of what actually happened.

"If we all get through this Mia cannot stay in L.A., neither can she go back to Houston, because everyone who is interested in her future welfare knows that is where she lived previously." He coughed up again to get his breath back. "Just a thought in passing Marcus. Anyhow, let's get her back on her feet before we decide what to do." He was just going to cut off when he remembered what Al had told him.

"By the way, Al is going to secure the house, which I forgot to organise. Evidently, Anton has set him up in his own Security Company, because Al gave his notice to leave to get married, and wanted to start a family. So, Anton is going to be his first contract. Al is going to organise Roberto to maintain the clean-up of the house and grounds. Al is going to secure the electronic gates, and keep the grounds secure until further notice." Gerry didn't want Marcus to think he was over-riding his authority, but also knew that his friend had more important things to worry about. Mia!

"I can't thank you enough, Gerry. I can't think straight right now. Just do what you think is correct. And, I would appreciate the clean clothes etc. I'll be waiting for you when you turn up. I can't leave Mia here on her own while she is in surgery. Hopefully she will be in ICU by that time. And thanks again, couldn't have coped without you. See you later."

"No problem", Gerry replied. "Always here for you, and Mia. But, expect a humungous bill for my services when this is all over."

Marcus rang off with the words, "What's new in my world, Gerry Swane?" But he knew he couldn't leave talking to his mother and kids any longer. He quickly drank the coffee that a volunteer had bought him, with a sandwich he had to force down, because he needed to stay on his feet to be with Mia, at some level she would need him.

He prayed to a God that seemed to have given up on his family. He prayed that Mia would turn to him now Anton was no more, but was sure that his presence would always be felt. He had been a big man, with a big heart.

Certainly a racketeer, because of Theo's influence. But also a very generous philanthropist. Gorgeous looking. Immaculately dressed. Hated by a lot. Loved by a few. But, he had married the beautiful woman that Marcus loved, and for that Marcus could never forgive him.

But, he had still been one of the few that loved him, and always would.

"Hi Sophia. Mom!" Marcus was on video, so he could see his mother while he explained what had happened to Anton, and Mia his wife. A phone call wouldn't have felt comfortable for Marcus. The subject matter was too sad and too serious for a disembodied phone call, and he didn't want to break down in front of his mother and kids.

"Marcus, what has happened, you look terrible? You need a shave, and your clothes are in a state. But, shall I get the boys? So you can talk to them, the little monkeys are playing me up constantly. I must be getting old, as I don't seem to have the patience lately to be able to cope with their mischief."

"Mom, you don't look a day older than in your thirties, always gorgeous, and impeccably dressed. I'm beginning to think I'm the parent, and you are the child." Sophia was a beautiful woman, and always so neat and tidy, that was where Anton got his perfect genes from, and he unfortunately took after Theo. "Please Mom, don't call in the boys yet, I need to talk to you on your own, because it's serious."

Sophia looked at her eldest son and could see he was having a hard time controlling his emotion, which wasn't like him. Marcus had never been particularly emotional, usually he took every problem that appeared, and worked out how to solve it as easily as possible. That was why he was an excellent lawyer, and always busy.

"Please Marcus, just tell me, and I will decide how serious it is. Then we can decide what to do about it." Her teacher mode was coming into play. Every day she sorted out tantrums, arguments, and kids fibbing to get her attention. And her two grand-kids were just as bad, even though she loved them far too much, as she did her son she lived with.

"Anton died this morning!" His voice broke as he said the fatal words. His mother clasped both hands over her mouth, and gasped out a stomach churning sob. She hadn't seen her boy for over twenty four years, but he was still her baby, and she had loved and missed him for all those years. Marcus had kept in touch with him once Anton lived in L.A., and always kept her up to speed on what he was doing. Sophia would not see him or keep in touch all the time he was living with Theo. She hated her husband for what he represented, and for taking her baby son away from her, for whatever his evil, twisted mind had made him do it.

Marcus watched his mother wipe her eyes, and blow her nose, then sit up as straight as possible. He knew her, and this was a blow too far to cope with, because she would never see her flesh and blood ever again. Her youngest, the child she had lost at four years old, and had never got over that diabolical day, when Theo had literally pulled him out of her loving arms.

"D-did he have an accident? A car accident? Where is he now? C-can I go and see him? Wherever he is? I need to see my beautiful boy, for the last time. Please Marcus! Please!"

Marcus wanted to cry a river of tears, but had to keep himself together for his mother's sake. She had suffered twenty four years of agony and now this. "Mama, I am so sorry, but two of the men working for him shot him, and then shot Mia. Anton died instantly, but surgeons are still working on Mia trying to save her life, and it's not looking good. I'm sorry Mama, but Anton is being put to rest at the cemetery later tonight. We can't allow anyone to know where he is, because so many people have a grudge against him, and we don't know what they will do if they find out where he is buried."

Sophia put her hands over her mouth again to stifle the sobs, and she was battling with the need to curl up on the floor in a foetal position, and just give up. But she had two very healthy boys to look after, hopefully their father would be home soon to take over.

"Look Mama, I have to go as I want to be close to Mia when she comes out of surgery. I can't come home yet until I know she is going to pull through. I've decided to leave L.A. for good now that Anton isn't here, and work permanently in Fort Worth. It will be better for the boys, as they are getting older and need me more. Also, if it's OK with you I will have to bring Mia back with me. It's too dangerous to leave her in L.A., and she can't go back to Houston, because she is a witness to the shooting, and the perpetrators know she came from Houston originally. But, they don't know that I am Anton's brother, and live in Fort Worth."

Sophia didn't want to remind him of his love for Anton's wife, but could see bringing her to his home was going to create a huge problem. "Are you sure Marcus? You have a conflict of interest with Anton's wife, is that going to be a problem for you, and her? But, this is your home, and you must do what you believe is right for everyone. I love you, and will go along with your decision. And, that decision has to include your boys, as well as yourself. It's a big responsibility you are going to take on, but you know that I will help in any way I can." She stopped for a moment to ask a question she really needed to know the answer to.

"My beautiful son *is* going to be laid to rest within the Catholic teachings and creed? I need to know that is going to happen. After the life he chose to lead, his soul must be saved. I won't have anything less."

"Father Michael will perform the service at the Mausoleum. I wouldn't have anything less, Mama." He hated to leave his mother after giving her such awful news, but he was desperate to find out what was happening in the theatre.

"Give my love to the boys. I will talk to them as soon as everything settles down, and I can come home. Love you Mom. And please don't worry about me, you know I will cope with whatever happens. I am tougher than I look, and my family mean everything to me. I can't thank you enough for looking after my boys for me. Sorry, but I have to go, because my assistant from the office has just brought me clean clothes, and shaving gear." He rubbed the stubble on his face, and grimaced. "Anton would be so angry with me if I turned up at his interment, less than immaculate, and perfectly groomed."

His mother touched the screen as if wanting to touch him with all the love she felt for her incredible son. "Let me know what happens. I will try not to worry, but every mother worries for her children, however old they are. But I don't have to worry anymore that Theo now has any influence over our beautiful son. He always wanted Anton completely to himself. Unfortunately, he is closer to Anton now than he was before they both died. I really can't win on that frustrating situation, can I?"

"Love you Mom, always have, always will. You are the best Mom, and Grandma, ever."

Marcus clicked off with a gut wrenching sigh. The next few hours were going to be Goddamn awful. And he needed a shower, shave, and a large, very strong drink to be able to get through it.

CHAPTER THIRTY-THREE

Stefan and Tomaz stood in the garden leaning against the building, both smoking, with a mug of strong coffee in their caring hands. Both still in their surgery scrubs. Both covered in Mia's blood. When they finished their cigarettes, and reviving coffee they would both shower, and take a well earned rest.

It had been a gruelling eight hour surgery. Twice they thought they were going to lose her, but twice they had managed to pull her through. She was now being taken care of diligently by Sister Amelia in ICU. Who would not allow anyone near her patient unless she gave them permission.

That permission had been given very hesitantly to Marcus, who had begged almost on his knees to be allowed to sit by Mia's bed, and very gently hold the hand that was free of an invasive IV, or other equipment keeping Mia alive.

When the entourage had exited the Theatre Marcus had been waiting outside, desperate to know how bad the entire situation had been. When Stefan explained the eight hour surgery they thought he was going to be their next patient. Stress, anxiety, pain, and love, had been written all over the poor man's face.

They had explained that the bullet had ruptured her liver. Her spleen had to be removed completely. Had nicked a lung, and shattered two ribs, and also had caused collateral damage before exiting her body. When Stefan had told him that by sheer luck or obstinacy the baby seemed to be hanging in there, Marcus had been side lined, and didn't know that Mia was pregnant. Then sadness, and disappointment, and even a few tears were there in his guarded expression.

It was pretty obvious to Stefan that Marcus was shocked and extremely jealous that Mia was pregnant by his brother. But he tried to hide the obvious by saying how overjoyed he was that a part of his brother could possibly survive the trauma of the attack.

They had left Marcus waiting to visit Mia in ICU, under the eagle-eye of Sister Amelia. Stefan and Tomaz were going to take turns in the shower, and then were going to have a quick rest in the Doctors Lounge, which had a cot, and a couch to nap on. Both knowing there wasn't going to be much rest for either of them, because the Hospice was always full to overflowing with sick, needy patients, and Mia would need a great deal of attention over the next forty-eight hours. If she managed to survive for that amount of time.

Marcus kissed Mia's clammy forehead. She didn't move or register his presence, because she was heavily sedated. Amelia had told him that her patient wouldn't even flicker an eyelid until sometime tomorrow, and if she did she would be in a tsunami of pain. So, best if he left now, and got some rest, because Mia would need him there, when she managed to come back to the world of reality and seering pain.

Marcus would not have the comfort or pleasure of sleep, because he had to bury his brother within the hour. He had showered and shaved in the Doctors Lounge. In respect for his immaculate brother he was wearing a pristine button down white dress shirt, and a navy blue work suit, and navy tie.

Gerry had poked his head around the door a moment ago, indicating that they were waiting for him to drive to the cemetery. He had quickly disappeared when Amelia had run towards the ICU door, as if to attack him for daring to even show his good looking face in her domain.

Gerry Swane was a total coward where hospitals, and fearsome females working in them were on the warpath. Nobody could ever say that Gerry was a stupid male, where females in charge were concerned. Even though he would quickly get out of breath, he would run as if the devil was up his backside, to evade a warrior female, if they were not warming his bed.

Marcus, Gerry, Al, Roberto, and Father Michael were all seated in a booth together at a local, busy pub near the cemetery. Anton was safely resting in the Mausoleum with his father. Father Michael had done Anton proud with his sincere words of praise for the giving human being that had been Antonio Theo Santiago. For that Eulogy Marcus would forever hold Father Michael in the highest esteem. There were only a few privileged people who really knew the other side of his loving brother, and they were all seated in that booth right now.

Marcus fully intended to use most of the money left by Anton to keep up his philanthropic work. He knew that neither his mother, nor Mia would want to touch the huge amount of money left by his brother.

Marcus was wealthy in his own right, and would always look after both women in the future. He was pretty certain his very attractive mother would marry the Sheriff she was seriously dating. And he fully intended to eventually marry the love of his life, Mia. The baby was a setback, and totally unexpected. But Marcus was man enough to love his brother's child, as if it was his own. He would never let his brother's flesh and blood feel unwanted in any way or form. It was also Mia's child, so he would never resent it, and bring it into his family, as if it was his own child.

Marcus rarely drank, but lifted his glass of rare bourbon to toast his beloved brother. "To Anton my brother, who has left this mortal coil. He was complex, two sides to the coin. A Racketeer, who had a heart of gold, and truly loved his wife, Mia, with all of that heart. I will always love you Anton, and will always miss you, my beloved brother. Rest in peace, and may God forgive the other side of the coin."

Everyone agreed with Marcus, and raised their glasses in a silent salute. Even Gerry was beginning to warm to the man he had mistakenly disliked, but he hadn't known what Anton had given to others less fortunate than himself.

After they had all eaten a very good meal, and were getting a bit mellow on their favourite tipple, especially Marcus who would dearly love to get roaring drunk, but was wise enough to stay coldly sober. He had to get the facts straight about what had happened today, because everyone around that table needed to have the same story if questioned by LAPD, or the DEA, even the FBI. And Gerry was pivotal to any enquiry, as he had worked for both Agencies trying to bring Anton to justice. But Anton had always managed to be one step ahead.

"Father Michael if you wish to leave before we all decide what our knowledge of today's events have been. We will understand as we may have to tweak the truth to stop any rumours about my brother, and how we were all involved with him."

Father Michael lifted his glass in a salute to everyone around the table. "I cannot lie, but I can move around the truth somewhat. I loved brother Anton, and will not listen to a bad word against him. So fire away, as I need to get my story straight as well, with the help of God, of course."

Everyone laughed, because the good Father was an exuberant story teller, and you never knew if he was ever telling the truth, or just embellishing it.

"OK! No one knows where Anton is. He has just disappeared, and left his estate free of any staff. We do not mention to anyone that Mia was ever there, or married Anton. Gerry tells me he has cleared the house of Mia's possessions, completely." He nodded to Gerry, who said he had cleared her suite, and everything she owned was tucked away in the private lock-up where he kept his beloved Harley. And, he had totally eradicated her presence from the estate.

"Thanks Gerry, that was a huge commitment for you to carry out." He looked at Al, who was taking up a great deal of space, because he was such a big, tall presence. "Al! Even though you were part of the security at the estate, you were having a couple of days off due to you. You were not there when Anton disappeared, but you believe that Larry, and Andi were the instigators of whatever happened. And, you've mentioned that Anton has set you up in your own security company. Had you been in touch with any of the other security guys to work for you?"

Al nodded his head. "Yes I have. But only four who I would trust with my life. And I will make sure that they have no recollection of what happened. You have my word on that." He looked straight at Marcus. "I did not enter the house with you and Gerry and take Mia to hospital. I do not remember her ever being there, either. You also have my solemn word on that. I loved her like my kid sister, and would never want to cause her any harm. If Larry and Andi find out she is still alive, they could possibly get to her, and finish what they started."

Marcus turned to Roberto to confirm what he had to do now, but Roberto got in first. "Nobody will know from me about Mia. She is my Mel's niece, and I will uphold anything you tell me to do. Otherwise my darling will wreak Armageddon on me from the Spirit World."

Again everyone laughed, but did totally agree. "Thank you Roberto. Would you please still maintain Anton's property, it has always been kept immaculate, and I want to keep it the same. Just send your account as usual to Sonny and he will pay it."

He turned back to Al. "I expect you to keep the grounds secure, and the electronic gates with a presence of security. I am going to put the estate up for sale, as soon as the police, or whoever finishes their enquiries, I am keeping out of any enquiries, as nobody knows I am Anton's brother. So Gerry is going to be our spokesperson in the future." He looked back at Gerry, who held his full glass up to Marcus, and nodded in agreement. Because, this was going to cost Marcus a fuckin' fortune.

"I am going to be working in the background, with Sonny, and Gerry as front men. I will be looking after Anton's prolific portfolio for my mother Sophia, and his wife Mia."

His gaze travelled around the good people around the table who had also loved his beloved brother. "I am leaving L.A. for good. I cannot in good faith stay now Anton is no more. I am giving my office down town to Gerry to use as his own, with my assistant Ben to look after the clinic I set up. I own the property so Gerry will be overjoyed to not have to pay rent, but will have to maintain it. I fully expect you Gerry to look after Ben. He is studying Law and Business Management, so will be a great asset to you."

Gerry was just about to take a gulp of his vintage bourbon, and he almost choked with astonishment, and couldn't believe his fuckin' luck. He was actually going to have a ready-made office to work from. That was going to give him so much extra street cred', and so much more warm pussy. He couldn't believe it.

Marcus winked at him, because he knew what was going through Gerry's oversexed mind. Sex, and more sex. Bring it on baby! And he would definitely survive to tell the tale! And, would definitely look after Ben.

"I'm sorry to have made such a long speech, but Mia's welfare is my top priority, and I do not want people who never knew the other side of my brother, tearing him apart. When Mia is well enough I am taking her to my home, where my mother will look after her, who is a very loving, caring woman. Mia cannot stay in L.A., and cannot go back to Houston, as her enemies know that is where she originates from. So, until she is back to full health, she can stay at my ranch. After, she will be free to live anywhere she wants, as long as she stays out of the limelight. The vicious men who killed Anton will surely try to get rid of her. And, that is *never* going to happen on my watch."

They wholeheartedly agreed, and began to pick up their jackets, but left their sleeves rolled up, and their ties undone around their necks. They had all made an effort for Anton, and Marcus, as they respected the brothers, who gave so much to the community, and to migrants from Mexico, and Puerto Rica.

"Roberto could you give me a lift back to the hospital, as I need to go over what has to be done at the house? And I expect you would like to see Mia if it's OK with the Gestapo Sister in charge?"

They all went their different ways, now knowing what was expected of them in the difficult days ahead. But so relieved that Anton was safe, and his wife even safer in ICU, where no one could find her.

CHAPTER THIRTY-FOUR

Marcus waited impatiently outside ICU, while Roberto said goodbye to his niece by marriage. Roberto never expected to see Mia again, because Marcus was intent on whisking her away to his ranch as soon as she was well enough to travel. Roberto couldn't fault that reasoning. Everything that had happened early that morning indicated that she was in serious danger from the men who had murdered Anton, her husband. He kissed her forehead so very carefully, because she looked like a colourless doll that had been in a terrifying accident, with so many pieces of sterile equipment entering and exiting her tiny, fragile body.

He tried in vain to hold back the tears for this brave, but still beautiful young woman, but they silently crept down his face. "Please get well my darling girl. We all love you my fierce little warrior. I know you are going to be in diabolical pain when you wake up. But you are a tough cookie, and can get through it, with the help of our good friend Marcus. He loves you desperately, and will do everything at his disposal to get you back to full health. Always remember that your family here love you, and always will, and please come to visit us when you can."

He gave one last look at his wife's lovely niece, and then briskly went to join Marcus, who looked worried to death.

Immediately Marcus went through the door that Roberto had come through. He needed to make sure that Mia was still alive, and might be awake, but Sister Amelia stopped him from going any further. "She hasn't moved an inch. She will not wake up anytime soon." She crossed her beefy arms over her very ample bosom, and gave Marcus the evil-eye. "Now, enough with the visitors. *Please*, go home and get some rest, wherever that is. I am here all night, sleeping on the cot in the corner. I have your cell number, if she moves even a little finger I *will* let you know immediately. You will not be any good for our patient if you are stressed, and worn out. She is going on a very long road to recovery, and that hasn't begun yet." When he went to argue she stood her ground, and indicated the door he had come through. "Now! Mr Medina please!"

Marcus knew he was never going to get past her, but he looked over her shoulder, and his darling girl hadn't moved a muscle since he had left earlier. He scrubbed a hand over his tired face, turned and went back to Roberto, to ask for a lift to his own office where he could bed down for some rest, if that was possible.

Roberto of course insisted he come home with him, as he would be more comfortable in his spare bedroom. But Marcus needed absolute peace, and needed to be on his own to allow the grief of his brother's death, and the terror of Mia's injuries to be let out of his system.

He had always been an emotional Italian man, but today had overwhelmed him, and he had held it back far too long. It had to come out, and he needed to be alone when it broke out of him, engulfed him, and then set him free to help Mia get better.

He hadn't slept for one moment, so decided to get up at dawn to get set for the busy day ahead. Luckily Ben wasn't at college so Marcus called him in, and they meticulously boxed up all his current workload, and his computer, and put them carefully into his 4X4 Mercedes. He was going to ask Gerry to drive to Fort Worth to deliver it to his office there.

Marcus had never taken on much work in L.A., only Anton's legal acquisitions, and Roberto's legal problems, and of course a few favours for special acquaintances. His main work was in Fort Worth, and his partnerships with his three friends were in Dallas, Houston, and San Antonio. So it wasn't a big deal for him to leave Los Angeles. He had opened the clinic there just one week in four to help anyone who couldn't afford a bonafide lawyer to take on their grudges. Also Anton had moved to L.A., and Marcus wanted to be closer to his then estranged sibling.

By ten a.m. the office was pristine and ready for Gerry to take it over, and Marcus was restless to get back to the Hospice. Nobody had got in touch with him, so he wasn't particularly worried that Mia was back in the land of the living, yet.

Then Ben decided that he would keep Gerry company as it was at least twenty hours driving. Marcus implored them to break it up into ten hours over two days, and then leave his Mercedes at his office in Fort Worth. They were to fly back, but not in First Class, as he was paying the bill, and he knew that Gerry would take any advantage he could. Marcus gave Gerry one of his black credit cards, and told Ben to keep an eye on his travel companion. Ben was a very responsible young black guy, but Gerry definitely couldn't be trusted with a credit card that had no limit. It was too much temptation for Gerry to behave himself, and Marcus was worried that he would encourage Ben to wander off the straight and narrow as well.

Ben was going to become a top notch lawyer, and was intent on helping the poor in society. He needed to have a pristine background whilst continuing his studies, so Marcus was taking a chance in allowing him to accompany Gerry. But at the end of a diabolical week that Marcus was going through, he just shook his head and waved them off. He had too much to worry about at the Hospice, which he desperately needed to get back to, right now.

He had completely cleared all his clothes, and toiletries out of his office's rest area, putting them into a couple of hold-alls, and threw them into his Flat-back Jeep. He expected to take a room in a local motel close to the Hospice until he could move Mia to where he lived on the outskirts of Fort Worth. In fact he really wanted to bunk down in the Hospice, but didn't think eagle-eyed Amelia would allow that, but he could always get round most females. He had the Santiago DNA.

But was she actually a female? The Jury was out on that verdict. Amelia seemed to have had a charisma by-pass.

Marcus went to go through the doors of ICU, but eagle-eyed Amelia stood barring his way. She even put a restraining hand on his chest to make sure he didn't manage to go any further. "Sorry Marcus, but our patient already has a visitor, and you know that Doctor Perez has strict rules for ICU patients. Only one visitor for a short period."

Marcus's stomach dropped like a stone in sheer panic. What bloody visitor? Nobody knew she was there except close friends, and they weren't allowed to visit yet. How had anyone found out? Could it be one of the Agencies, or God forbid, an enemy? It was a dangerous situation, and he had to rectify it straight away.

"It's OK!" Amelia could see he was really worried. "He gave us evidence to prove how close he is to Mia. It's Henri Arnaud, her father, so we had to let him see his daughter. I know we have to be extremely careful, and not let anyone know that she is here, and we have all kept to those rules. But, he showed me his passport and driving licence, so I couldn't stop him, could I?"

Marcus let out a shaky breath of sheer relief. For a moment he had thought that Mia had been found by one of Anton's enemies, and there would be plenty of them lining up to eliminate Anton's new wife. "No! It's great that her father is here. Is there any hope or signs that she could wake up soon? What is the usual recovery in such a complex operation?"

"Sorry Marcus, there is no right time for recovery. It could be in an hour, or tomorrow. But for now her father has to wait outside, as Doctor Perez is going to change her dressings, and check over all of his hard work, which will take quite a while, as our Doctor is very conscientious, and thorough with all his post-operative patients. I will send out Mister Arnaud so you can explain exactly what happened to his gorgeous daughter."

Kirby, Never Look Back

Gee thanks, thought Marcus. That was one explosive conversation he didn't need. To explain to a much loved father how his precious daughter had got mixed up with Anton Santi. And, he would have to be truthful and own up to being the catalyst that brought those two together. Not a happy thought, with the outcome yesterday.

Henri came through the doors hand outstretched to Marcus in a friendly greeting. Straightaway Marcus liked this tall, upright, handsome man with very dark brown hair, and startling clear blue eyes. If Mia hadn't been a clone of her amazing mother, she would still have been truly beautiful with her father's genes. As Madeline and Henri's child, there wasn't any doubt that Mia would be stunningly beautiful.

"The Sister told me that you are Marcus, the brother of Anton Santi, my girl's husband. I am truly sorry for your loss, but can't thank you enough for bringing my badly injured child to this wonderful Hospice." He shook Marcus's hand very strongly. "I can never repay you for obviously saving her life. We have been so very worried over the past few months, not knowing what was happening to her, and she was as usual very sparse with her communication to us. All she was saying was that she was absolutely fine and not to worry. But Lisette-Jo has always been far too quick to get into trouble, especially as a teenager. Her poor mother and I have found it impossible to keep up with her outrageous demands. We have three other children, and not one has caused us a modicum of worry." He shook his head smiling. "Lisette put all three in her shadow, as she went about her life at full throttle, and we all had to run to keep up with her."

Marcus could only wish that he had had a father like Henri, who had loved her passionately whatever problem she brought home with her. And, he could understand that, because he loved her with the same passion, and didn't know her like her father did. "Sir, I haven't eaten properly since yesterday morning. There is a diner a short walk away, would you care to join me? I can fill you in with as many details that I actually know. Sister Amelia doesn't think that Mia is going to wake up anytime soon. So now could be the only spare moments we have before she needs our attention, and love."

Henri totally agreed, as once his precious girl woke up he had no intention of leaving her until they both left for Houston. And, this time he would get his own way. As far as he was concerned, Los Angeles was too dangerous, and too power hungry for men such as Santi to take advantage of an innocent girl like his daughter, and almost get her killed.

This adventure was going to stop right now. He really wasn't interested in what Santi's brother Marcus was going to explain to him. His Lisette was going back to Houston as soon as she was well enough to travel, full stop.

"By the way, Henri, how did you find out that your daughter had been shot? And my brother was dead? Only a few close friends knew what had happened." Henri being here was a problem he hadn't expected. Marcus had envisioned he would be the only person visiting with Mia. He was royally pissed off, but wouldn't let Mia's father know that.

"Gerry Swane contacted me, and I managed to get a quick flight out of Dallas. I had heard from him previously, so I didn't doubt he wasn't telling me the truth." They were walking out of the building together, and Henri stopped to make a point. "Was it true that your brother was a gangster, a racketeer?"

Marcus hesitated for a moment, he hated anyone calling Anton that. "That was one side of him, but he was a complex man, and a long story to explain."

"Why? Why would my beautiful girl marry such a monster?"

Keep hold of your temper, and try to make him understand, Marcus said under his breath, "Anton loved her with all his heart and soul, and wouldn't hurt her for the world. And Mia, bless her, loved him the same. They were a perfect couple, and *so* happy together. They had decided to move closer to my family in the country, and lead a quieter life, with a gang of kids."

Henri turned to him with tears in his clear blue eyes. "With his lifestyle that was never going to happen, was it?"

"No sir, it was just a dream, but a beautiful dream for both of them."

They carried on walking, and Marcus cursed Gerry for getting in touch with Henri. He had wanted to be there when Mia woke up, however long that took. So his face would be the first one she would recognise. Now, he would have to wait outside while Henri took centre stage. Marcus knew he was being outrageously jealous, and a total shit. But, he had stood back and watched his brother marry the woman that Marcus truly loved. They probably would have lived a long and happy life together, and would never have known how he had felt.

All he had to do now was convince Henri to go back to Houston, because he had to understand that Mia couldn't live there. She had to live with him on his ranch as his wife, carrying Anton's baby, if it was the last fucking thing he did.

He vowed that, on his kids' lives, and he *never* bargained with his kids' lives, ever.

CHAPTER THIRTY-FIVE

Marcus and Henri were sitting in a booth at the back of the diner, apart from other customers. It was late for breakfast and too early for lunch, so the large room was sparse of people. Marcus didn't want anyone listening in on what he had to explain to Mia's father.

From now on until well into the future, Marcus would always be extremely careful of his immediate surroundings. Walls had ears, and Mia's safety was his main concern. Anton was out of reach of his sworn enemies, and for that Marcus thanked the Gods. He loved his brother, and couldn't have borne the agony that somewhere in the future someone would be able to get to him, tortured and maimed him, just because of who he was.

At least his death had been so quick he would have barely known what had happened. But it looked as if he had pushed Mia away from him, trying to save her life. Anton had truly loved his wife, and for that Marcus was so very grateful. His brother only had a short time with Mia, but everyone could see they were both besotted with each other. Laughing and happy, and must have been ecstatic that they were going to be parents.

Marcus prayed that the baby managed to cling on to life, because then his mother would always have a piece of her son to make a fuss over, and love.

"May I call you Henri, please sir? I feel through Mia that I know you."

"Of course, I would prefer that. To be called 'sir' sounds as if I am ancient, doesn't it?" They had both just eaten burgers and fries, and drank two cups of coffee. Now, Marcus was beginning to feel human again, as he couldn't remember the last time he had eaten a hot meal. Henri hadn't fared much better as he had dropped everything and driven hours to get on a plane.

"I'm sorry Marcus, but I cannot understand what my rebellious daughter was thinking when she married your brother. For God's sake he was a gangster, and I'm sure must have had other people murdered, or hurt badly. And dealt in drugs, guns, and whatever made his fortune. In my book there is no excuse for that kind of life. He deserved to die, but my girl did not deserve to almost die with him."

"I completely agree with you, but my brother was groomed by my father, who I hated. Theo wanted a mini Theo to take over his immoral empire. And, Anton only ever wanted to make his father proud of him. To cut a long story short, my father snatched Anton from my mother and myself when he was four. My wonderful mother never got over it, because she has never seen her youngest child since, and now has to mourn him. I at least got to know him over the last couple of years, and can grieve for him properly. Believe me Henri, there was another side to Anton. He was a truly philanthropical helper of people in need. And, I am going to carry on all his projects of helping the underdog whatever colour or background they come from.

"Mia saw this side of my brother, and she loved him heart and soul. And, he was *so* in love with her, it was wonderful to see them both so happy, and so truly in love with each other. I was actually in the process of finding them a property close to where I live near Fort Worth. Anton wanted to get close to his mother, and my children, and live a quiet life in the country." Marcus stopped for a moment as he battled from getting too emotional. He had been so excited for his mother that she was at last going to see her sons together, and of course her new daughter-in-law.

Henri took the opportunity to ask a question. "Where is your wife Marcus, you haven't mentioned her so far?"

"My wife died over four years ago. Bianca had just given birth to our second son, Milo, when we had come home and were talking in the kitchen, she died instantly with a pulmonary embolism. She just fell on the floor in front of me, and was gone forever."

"Oh dear God! I am so very sorry, that must have been a trauma beyond coping with. I am truly sorry I asked. And now your brother, it's awful for you, and your poor mother."

"My mom is pretty strong, and my boys have been a life saver for her. Especially with what my father put her through all those years ago. Theo was a dark, evil man, and I never forgave him for taking Anton away from us. But I always loved Anton, and always will."

Marcus was dreading telling her father that she couldn't go back to Houston, because he knew that was what Henri expected. He'd had enough of his daughter living in L.A. and almost dying because of the Santi family. Henri expected arguments, and tantrums from Mia on the subject, but this time was going to put his large foot down with severity.

"I know you are going to hate me for this Henri, but Mia can't stay in L.A., neither can she live in Houston with your family. She is the only witness to Anton's murder, and can tell us who actually carried out the brutal act. No one knows except close friends that she is still alive. Everyone who knows is committed to silence on Anton's death, and Mia's injuries. If the killers find out she survived, they will have to silence her permanently. They know she originates from Houston, so could go back there. They do not know I am Anton's brother and live on the outskirts of Fort Worth." When

Henri went to argue his case, Marcus had to be firm about Mia's welfare, and his commitment.

"I am sorry Henri, but since Mia is Anton's wife you cannot make a judgement on her future. I am a lawyer, and a very good one. She is worth a fortune now, and we cannot allow her to be used by anyone for gain. I am totally aware that your family would not do that, but she is going to be very fragile for quite some time. As her lawyer, I must make decisions for her welfare. As soon as Doctor Perez says she can be moved I am taking her home in an Air Ambulance with a doctor present to look after her. I am setting up a room for her to be looked after by a care-therapist in my own home. My mother will also be there to help in any way she can. No one will know who she is, and what has happened to her. I will not allow Mia to be in any danger from now on. I promise you on my life, that I will take care of your precious daughter." Marcus covered Henri's hand with his. "And, I promise that when she recovers and realises that she always has to be careful what she says or does in the future, only then she can live wherever she wants to."

Henri enclosed Marcus's hand with both of his, knowing this man was somebody you could trust with your life, and a beloved daughter. Everything he had said made complete sense in a dire situation, and Henri had to comply whether he wanted to or not.

"When did you fall in love with my obstinate, difficult, outspoken, but loving daughter?"

Marcus smiled at the father, who also adored that difficult, but absolutely gorgeous woman. "The moment I met her, Henri. But unfortunately my brother won her with his amazing good looks, and sheer determination. For that I can never forgive him, but I will never give up hope that one day she will love me, as she loved him."

"Good luck with that Marcus. She is my precious child, but has always been a handful, and doesn't seem to have changed much." He got up to leave, as there didn't seem anything else to discuss. He was desperate to find out if his girl was going to wake up, and argue with everyone who was taking care of her.

"By the way Henri, you and your family are welcome anytime to stay at my ranch to be with Mia. We have plenty of space, and would love to see you all. And, I know that Mia would also love that."

"Thank you Marcus, that is a very kind offer. I know her mother Josephine can't wait to see her, and her brother Christian, who has left the FBI, and is working as the Chief of Police in Houston just recently.

"We are a very close, loving family, and all miss the baby of our family, desperately. Now, I really must go back to the Hospice, and hopefully she is awake, and wondering where her doting Papa is."

He would be deliriously happy if she would just wake up and be his naughty, demanding Lisette, or Mia, whatever she wanted to call herself. As long as she survived the next critical forty-eight hours, and woke up to give him a loving hug. He would never ask God for another miracle when he went to church the very next time.

Sister Amelia was waiting for them at the entrance to ICU, and in a whisper told Henri that his daughter was awake, but was about to be put back to sleep within the next few minutes. After checking her dressings and making sure the equipment was working properly Doctor Perez had spoken to his patient making sure she knew who she was, and where she was.

Mia had been in too much pain to answer coherently, but it was obvious to Stefan that she did know exactly what had happened to her, and was asking for her Papa.

"Please hurry Mr Arnaud and let your daughter know you are here. She will rest better knowing you are close, before she lapses into a drug induced unconsciousness."

Henri didn't have to be told twice, and left Marcus on the other side of that damn door again, rushing to his daughter's side before she went back to sleep.

Oh God! The pain was too much for her tiny fragile body. All Mia wanted was to slide back into the dark deep space that didn't have or want that crushing explosion of pain that filled her entire being. It was excruciatingly hot. It clawed at her, taking her every breath, and making it as if it was a very sharp knife hacking at her, and making her plead for the peace and quiet of death. Just as Anton had died in silence and peace, as his last breath left his body. And he died with her name on his lips. His last gift to her as he left her alone and bereft on earth.

As best he could, Henri tried to put his arms so very carefully around his precious child, with tears pouring down his handsome face. "Sweetheart, Papa is here, and loves you so very much. Please go to sleep now, so that your body can heal. We all want to see you strong and healthy again. Your mother Josephine wanted to come, but is not a hundred per cent well at the moment, and Christian is beside himself with worry for you." Softly he kissed all over her face, he never wanted to stop making a fuss of her.

Mia struggled to focus on her Papa, and tried to stay above the weariness and lethargy that was attacking her whole body. Darkness, peace, and silence called to her, but she fought it to be able to say a few words to her father. She had to know something that Doctor Perez wouldn't tell her, but Papa would tell her the truth, however bad or good it was.

Only then could she sleep the sleep of the dead for as long as it took to join Anton, wherever he was. She was determined to do that!

She just about managed a raspy whisper into her Papa's ear. "Am I dying Papa? I won't mind if you tell me the truth, please. My Anton died in front of me, and I loved him *so* much, Papa. I want to be with him, he promised he would wait for me. Please tell Gerry that – that it was - ." She took a painful shallow breath, and then just about continued. "T-tell Gerry it was L-Larry and – and Andi that shot m-my Anton." Mia managed to gulp in a tiny breath and her chest actually rattled with the effort.

For a tortured second Henri thought she had died, because some of the connecting equipment began to eerily bleep and ring out. Then all hell happened around her bed, and Henri was rushed out of the room. At least four people had come bursting in, including the two doctors, and another nurse with Amelia.

Marcus was still waiting, worried to death outside when Henri came rushing out as white as a sheet, and shaking all over his big body. He put his head in his hands and sobbed. "My baby girl! I think she has gone. I'm sure she is dead. Oh my God! This can't be happening to me. My family will never get over her loss, so young. So very beautiful, and so very young. Our darling Lisette! We all loved her so, so much! Too much!"

Marcus put his arm around the distraught father and moved him to sit down on a plastic chair. He knew exactly what Henri was going through, because *his* brother was dead, and he couldn't lose the woman *he* loved. She was too vital, too obstinate, too strong, to die by the hand of a greedy, no-good, power driven, evil bastard like Larry. A man who Anton had trusted with the security of his life, and Mia. And, that piece of shit had sold Anton down the line for his millions. Knowing Anton as he had, his brother would have given those millions without a second thought to save Mia's life, and his. Money had never been Anton's motivation. It was Theo's. Always had been. But his son had followed in his father's evil footsteps, just to make his father proud of him, and that had certainly worked for Enrico Theodore Santiago, but not for Antonio Theo Santiago.

Henri lifted his tear streaked face, and spoke to Marcus. "She managed to speak to me before it all happened. She said it was Larry and Andi who killed your brother." He wiped his eyes and nose with a napkin, then carried on. "Then she said she wanted to be with her Anton, as he said he would wait for her, wherever he was."

They both noticed all had gone really quiet in Mia's room, and both held their breath waiting, as the two doctors walked out of the ICU talking animatedly, and smiling with relief.

Stefan stopped to speak to the obviously upset men. "Sorry gentlemen, just a small glitch, for a very noisy panic. Mia's blood pressure almost hit rock bottom, which set off the unit connected to her heart rate, and everything took off to warn us." He went to Henri and clapped him on his shoulder, because he understood how frightening ICU was for a family member. "She is fast asleep now, out of pain, and comfortable. Hopefully she won't raise her head for quite some time. The more she sleeps the quicker she will hopefully recover." He looked at both men with a frown. "Now, I need you both to leave and do something outside this unit. Mia is going to need a great deal of patience and help very soon. She has a long way to go before she will be back to some semblance of normality. Two very worried men hovering over her is not going to work in my experience." He again looked at both alpha males with a question hovering in the air.

"I understand what you are saying doctor, and am sure you are right." He shot a glance at Marcus who was not going to give an inch. "I'm afraid I have a problem at home, with my close family, regards my granddaughter. My wife and I have to look after her, because her mother is inclined to be hard on her, and my son Christian is constantly worried about his daughter. My wife isn't too well at the moment, so I really need to get back to Houston to keep the peace. I know that Marcus will be here for my girl, and I trust him to keepme up to speed on her condition.

"I can't thank you enough for what you have done for my daughter. You have literally saved her life, and for that I will never forget your hard work. And Marcus is taking her home when she can travel. Marcus has also told me that Anton's money has built this Hospice, and pays for its upkeep. So my heart goes out to him, wherever he is. He was a son-in-law I never met so I cannot judge his life, but my daughter truly loved him, and that is good enough for me. We will always remember him with loving thoughts for the rest of our lives."

"Thank you Henri," Marcus replied. "Anton would have appreciated that, without a single doubt. Can I give you a lift to the airport? It will give me something to do, and take my mind off what has happened here. And, I also need to talk to *my* family, and get my mother to start organising a special room for our patient, who I know can be very prickly. But I am not worried because my fantastic mother will cope magnificently with anything thrown at her." He laughed, "And I mean that, literally."

The two men walked off laughing, both knowing that Mia was capable of just about anything. They had forged a friendship through her that would never be tested or broken, while they both lived.

And, Marcus had to somehow get in touch with Gerry to inform him of what Mia had told her father. That Larry and Andi, a pair of evil bastards, had killed Anton, and thought they had killed Mia.

They had to have a serious discussion on what to do next. Go after them? Or, make sure they never found out what happened to Mia, and where she was going to live in the future?

Marcus was *not* going to live permanently always armed against danger. But would do anything asked of him to keep Mia safe. Whatever that meant. Whatever that took!

CHAPTER THIRTY-SIX

Marcus was standing outside the Hospice again, but this time talking quietly to Gerry. He needed Gerry's expert opinion on what to do about Larry and Andi. Gerry as usual had been gagging for a smoke, so Marcus had to comply and meet him in the small, peaceful garden. Otherwise Gerry wouldn't be able to stand still long enough to have a civil conversation on a very serious question.

"What do *you* think we should do about those two maniacs Gerry? Get out a contract on them, or go after them ourselves? I can't stand back and do nothing, now I know they murdered Anton in cold blood. My Italian heritage will not let me take this lying down. But, my mother cannot know what I am going to do. She will never forgive me, acting as my father would have done."

Gerry took a strong drag on his cheroot, and shook his head, not believing that Marcus could possibly believe he could take on those vicious bastards, and make them pay for Anton's death. Marcus was an extremely good lawyer, and had a genius IQ, but was hopeless at being tough, and lethal. He was a pussy-cat against the type of men that Larry and Andi were. Die-hard criminals, greedy, bent on anyone's destruction that got in their way.

"Your mama is right in every sense of the word, and you should listen to her. Anton lived and worked on the wrong side of the law, and luckily got away with it, and I am testimony to that fact. Someone was always going to want to take it all away from him, and that is exactly what happened that morning. Unfortunately Mia was in the way, and she could have died too, but hopefully she is going to pull through, eventually.

"Now listen to me, Marcus, because I am going to try and stop you doing something really dangerous, and stupid. You are *not* going to do anything, because you have your family, and now Mia to take care of. I am going to let them think they have got away with killing Anton and Mia. But, I would never let that happen, not to your brother, or our Mia. I'm going to lie low and silent for a couple of months, until they are not looking over their shoulders for someone to avenge their deaths. Leave it to me to work on a plan to rid the world of those fuckin' evil bastards. I will hit them when they least expect it, and they will never know what happened, or who it was that brought them down."

After that long speech he had a coughing fit, and had to get his breath back before he could continue, which annoyed Marcus intensely, who was super fit, and worried about his friend's unhealthy lifestyle.

"We know they have set up an illegal compound just outside Mexico City, and I have a great deal of contacts in that area. We also know that all of Anton's shady millions have ended up there, so let them settle in, and grow complacent. Only then will we be able to get them, because their security will be strong, but also will have relaxed by then. Leave it to me, Marcus. I won't let Anton down, or Mia, or you. You have my sacred word on that."

Marcus was just going to shake Gerry's hand on that, and promise a huge bonus when it happened, when all hell let loose inside the building. Both Marcus and Gerry looked at each other with fear in their eyes, because Mia was the only patient in the Intensive Care Unit. They both said 'shit', and ran towards the unit where highly professional people were working as one to try and stabilise their extremely sick, possibly dying patient.

She was totally lost. Definitely had never been there before. What on earth was she doing standing in a meadow full of amazing coloured wild flowers? Bees hummed as they moved from flower to flower. Brightly coloured butterflies flitted amongst the undergrowth. And the plethora of so many different birds filled the air with their fluttering wings, and their songs, a natural beautiful sound.

A warm, tropical breeze ruffled her blonde curly hair, and she could hear an angelic anthem floating towards her from a long distance away. Mia looked above her, and could only see a vast cornflower blue sky, with not a whisper of a cloud to mar its perfection. She looked down at her feet which were bare, and she was wearing her elegant toe-ring that Anton had bought her, and her pink nail polish was perfect. She was wearing her favourite sun dress, the rich, white eyelet one that was Anton's favourite also.

Then she looked into the horizon and could see a figure walking purposefully towards her, and knew it was her love, her Anton, coming to be with her. She put a hand over her heart to stop it beating so loud, because she now realised she was in heaven, where she wanted to be.

To be with her love. Her heart and soul. And, never wanted to return to that empty and soulless place without her husband with her.

When he reached her, he held out his arms and enfolded her in a warm, loving embrace. He looked so young, so at peace, but so full of life, and pure love, just for her, always her. She noticed he was dressed in a white tunic, and white loose trousers, something he would never have worn on earth. This was Anton as she had never seen him before. A patient, unhurried, and stress free Anton. And, he was looking at her as if he couldn't bear not to look at her beautiful face forever more.

"My darling girl, what has happened? I only just got the message that you were here, and that I had to see you. This meeting wasn't on my agenda, but here I am, and *so* pleased to be here. I never thought I would ever hold you again." He was touching her hair, her face, as if he could never let her go, in a life-time.

Their lips touched and the kiss seemed to go on forever, but he stepped back as if it was a rule that only he knew they were breaking.

"I don't know what happened Anton. I was in hospital, and was very sick, and then suddenly was standing in this glorious field. Please, don't send me back. I can't live there without you. I want to be here with you. Wherever this is? I want to be with you, only you, and not with my family and friends in Houston, or Los Angeles." But she knew by the expression on his beloved face that she was never going to get her own way. Not this time, because Anton did not make the rules and regulations to suit himself as he had on earth. But after all she was his wife, surely that should mean something to whoever was in charge in this Paradise.

"My darling girl, it is not your time to be here. Of course I would love you to stay, but we live in peace and harmony here, and I cannot ask for any favours of any kind. I am in a state of prayer and meditation, until my Guardian believes I am able to stand on my own feet, and move on to higher work. I have to learn to forgive myself for the truly awful life I lived previously. I was giving millions away, but for the wrong reason. My self esteem and ego were being boosted and blown up out of all control. It made me feel on top of the world, but it didn't resonate on my soul. It is only because of you coming into that life, and changing me so radically, that I have been given a second chance to redeem myself. I have a great deal of hard work in front of me to show everyone here that my soul has goodness and love to give others, within it. And, that is all because of you, my darling." Swiftly he kissed her again, and then quickly stepped back away from temptation.

Mia wouldn't cry in front of him, and wanted to scream out that this wasn't fair for either of them. But she knew this wasn't the time or place to be demanding, or selfish. This was Anton's time and place, and it was pretty obvious he had left her behind, and she wasn't allowed to follow him.

"Never forget that I will always love you, whether we are together, or not. Now, you have to go back, and let Marcus look after you. He loves you, and wants to keep you safe, and happy. Trust him, Mia. He loves you as I loved you, and for the rest of his life will always put you first in that life. And, let our friend Gerry seek out the men who took my life, and almost took yours. Don't let Marcus take his revenge, as it will only taint his soul, which I would not want to happen. Be happy my darling, and know that I loved you with everything that I was, and always would be."

Then they both heard a bell ringing, and Anton took her hands in his, and he kissed them both. "That is my signal to return, as our time is up, and I have to resume my studies." She tried to hold onto him, but he was already turning away to leave. She knew she had lost, and he couldn't stay with her, and she would have to live the rest of her lonely life, without the man she would always love, and remember.

Then Anton turned back, as if he had forgotten something. "Just make sure you take care of our beautiful girls, and tell them about their Papa, who loved them with all his heart and soul, and always will."

Mia took a shuddering weak breath, because someone was hammering on her chest, and the pain was too much, and beyond excruciating. When she got her strength back, and her next breath, she was going to tear off the fucking bastard's head, and feed it to a dog.

Stefan and Tomaz both let out a huge sigh of relief and stress. They had both been working on her for at least a half hour, and hadn't had any hope of bringing her back. In fact had just looked at each other, and were going to call it a day, as it just wasn't working, when Mia let out a very small puff of air, and her eyelids actually flickered.

A cry of joy went around the intense room full of caring workers, and made it out to the two men who were actually holding their breath in anticipation of absolutely catastrophic news.

Gerry clapped Marcus on the shoulder, and sniffed back the emotion that was hovering, ready to let out. Marcus couldn't hide his emotion, took a tissue out of a container, wiped his eyes and blew his nose. That had been the longest thirty minutes in his entire life. He had really believed Mia wasn't going to make it, but as usual she had defied the odds, and had put up a finger to the devil.

"That female is going to be the death of us, Marcus. Are you sure you really want to take her on? My advice is to walk away while you can, my friend." And, Gerry really meant every word. She was going to be a whole lot of trouble. Trouble Gerry would never want to be saddled with, not in this lifetime, or the next.

Marcus pulled himself together, and sighed heavily. "Well! I could say I am doing this for Anton, but that would be an incongruous lie." He was desperate to be with Mia, loved every part of her difficult, obstinate, but loving personality. It was nothing to do with Anton. From the first moment Marcus had met her, it was love at first sight. A love so strong he would have done anything to be with her. Of course he hadn't wanted his brother to die, but honestly he would have taken any advantage he could get.

Now, let the battle begin. It was going to be a battle of opposite personalities. First, he would have to slowly eradicate Anton's love and for spoiling her rotten. Then, he would have to show her that he loved her beyond reason, and he could love that baby as if it was his own flesh and blood. Marcus knew it was going to be an uphill battle, but he was up to whatever Mia threw at him.

His mother Sophia was his back-up plan. She would help him wear Mia down, with her patience, and motherly love. Something Mia seemed to have been missing all her young life.

And they were going to have a new baby to cope with. Marcus was excited at that turn of events. He loved kids, and the more the merrier, but wasn't sure that Mia felt the same.

Well! If the baby actually survived, and they had become a couple, he would look after the baby himself. Anton's baby was going to be a bonus that Marcus would definitely love and nurture. But he was pretty certain that Mia would learn to love her own child, and be a fantastic mother.

Fingers crossed Marcus went into ICU to begin the rest of his wonderful life with the woman he loved beyond all others. Now, he just had to convince her, and that could be one hell of a problem. But, he wasn't a man to give up, that was written in his Italian DNA.

To love! To love! To love even more!

CHAPTER THIRTY-SEVEN

The next week was a total nightmare for Marcus, because Mia was in and out of consciousness, and lucidity. It was confirmed that somehow she had been afflicted with a serious infection of the chest and lungs. Stefan and Tomaz battled to keep her alive and stable for the entire week. And, Marcus was wrung out with stress and worry that she would leave this life on earth, and join Anton. Leaving him behind, lonely and bereft, and heartbroken.

He was giddy with living part at the Hospice, and part at the motel, and trying to keep in touch with his family, who missed him as much as he missed them. It was like being on a roundabout that was going nowhere in particular. He had promised his extremely patient mother that he would be home as soon as Mia was well enough to travel with him, and she had understood.

Luckily his three partners in their law firm were keeping his office in Fort Worth ticking over, for which he couldn't ever thank them enough, as they were always up to their ears in work in their own offices.

Then after battling Mia's rattling chest, coughing, and up and down temperature, and fearing she would never get through another night to see the dawn; Marcus entered the ICU one morning to find Mia sitting up in bed talking to

Amelia. When she saw him she put out her hand that was free of any medical paraphernalia and beckoned him over. He knew she had an IV for antibiotics in the other hand. A heart monitor attached to the serious machine monitoring every solitary thing keeping her alive. And, a tiny clock fixed to her chest, giving out a steady flow of morphine that tried to register her pain, which Marcus knew was pretty bad so far.

Her voice was weak and raspy when she spoke to her visitor. "Marcus, what are you doing here? Where is Anton, my absent husband?" She pursed her lips. "I don't expect he can leave the estate, as usual. But, it does look as though I've had a bad accident, and nobody has told me what happened to me. Did I have a really bad car accident, Marcus?" She leant her head back on the pillow, because she had run out of breath, even though she had oxygen taped straight into her nose.

Marcus looked at Amelia asking silently if he should try to explain what had happened, he didn't want to set Mia back in her recovery. This morning was the very first time she was lucid since the shooting, and he really hated telling her about Anton. He still couldn't believe that he would never see his brother again. Putting it into words would upset him, but he realised he had to do it. It wasn't Amelia's or Stefan's job to inform Mia what she had lost, her new husband, her lover, her future with him. But, at the moment their baby was hanging in there, only God knew how, because of the trauma Mia's body had suffered. Unspeakable trauma. But, Mia was strong, spiky and resilient. It was obvious the baby must take after its mother, and wouldn't give up on life without a goddamn fight.

Marcus quickly glanced at Amelia who nodded her head in acquiescence for him to tell their patient what had really happened. Mia had to know that Anton was never coming back to be with her.

"Oh my God! We must have had an awful car accident and poor Anton is here really badly hurt, and can't come to visit me." She blinked her eyes trying valiantly not to cry, because she had never been a cry baby, even as a child.

Marcus pulled a chair over to her bed, and sat down heavily, dreading what he had to do to the woman he loved, but couldn't let her know. "Mia sweetheart! You and Anton were involved in a terrible incident. Anton didn't survive. I am so sorry my darling, but he died instantly, and you almost lost your life. Stefan and Tomaz have worked tirelessly for the past week trying to keep you stable and alive."

"Don't Marcus! Don't be ridiculous! I was with Anton last night. He - he told me he would always love me. He k-kissed me, a beautiful kiss full of love. And – and when he had to leave me he said to look after our beautiful girls, and to tell them that their Papa loved them, and always would." She put her hand over her mouth, and began to cry in earnest. "Oh my God! Oh my God! He was in Heaven, and I must have died, but he sent me back. No! No! No! I don't want to be here without Anton. I love him too much to be here, it's not fair. They should have let me die. Why? Why, didn't they let me die?"

Marcus took her carefully in his arms, and held her while she sobbed, a heartbreaking sound that almost brought him to his knees. He didn't dare shed any tears, because he wouldn't be able to stop. He felt Amelia come close to him, and she whispered into his ear that Mia needed to rest, and not get any more bad news. He watched her inject a liquid into Mia's IV, and felt her immediately begin to relax in his arms.

As he laid her back down, she looked up at him sleepily. "What did Anton mean about our girls, and that I had to look after them? I didn't understand."

"You are pregnant, sweetheart. Anton must know more than we do. Now, go to sleep, and we will talk about it when you wake up." He was dreading that conversation, because he was pretty certain that Mia hadn't wanted children. And, he couldn't allow her to get rid of Anton's baby. It was a part of his brother he desperately needed to keep Anton alive in the future.

She yawned tiredly, and then gave him a watery smile. "A baby girl? I can't believe it. I am *so* happy. But poor Anton, he so believed it was a boy, and was so proud of himself." She gazed up at the ceiling. "I am sorry my darling." Mia touched her flat belly. "I will keep her safe for you, and she will have your name. I love you Anton, my darling husband, and always will."

Marcus watched her relax into a deep sleep, and knew he was going to be a hard sell, after Anton, and now Anton's baby on the way. But, Marcus was known for his patience, and his lawyer gift of the gab, and he loved this tiny, fragile, gorgeous, pregnant woman more than he had ever loved anyone. His boys were a different type of love. They were a part of him, a part of his lineage. He would give his life for them in a second without any doubt on his part.

But Mia was his future, with Anton's child as a bonus, a wonderful, wonderful bonus. He loved her with every breath he took, every heartbeat, every moment in a day. She had become an obsession he'd had to cope with when she had married Anton. Of course he hadn't wanted him to die, but he had!

Now, they were both free, and he would walk carefully, but persistently into her everyday life. He didn't care how long it took, but it would happen, because he would make it happen.

Kirby, Never Look Back

He loved Mia! Always would! They were a meant!

CHAPTER THIRTY-EIGHT

"Gentlemen, I'm sorry to have to call you here so early this morning, but I need to get back to the Hospice ASAP." Marcus had called a meeting of the four people he needed to talk to urgently. And, they did not have a clue why any one of them was there. But patiently waiting for a very serious looking Marcus to give them a heads up on what they were there for this early.

Marcus was a quiet, patient man, but they all knew that if he was upset, or crossed, he changed like a chameleon, and the Santi gene came to the fore. Then they would need to run for cover.

"Firstly I am retiring from my law firm, so that I can look after my family, and that includes Mia, and Anton's baby." He waited for everyone to get their heads around that bombshell. They were all gobsmacked, but polite enough to keep their opinions to themselves. "I am going to take a much bigger interest in my ranch, which has been run by my manager Pablo and his wife Ria, and also my mother Sophia. But that isn't what I want to talk about right now." He was sitting at his desk, which now belonged to Gerry, but got up to perch his backside on the desk, so making it easier to talk to the other four in the office.

Kirby, Never Look Back

"With the help of Sonny Silverman I am setting up a company to carry on Anton's legal acquisitions in property. Mia and Sophia have inherited his very healthy and very wealthy pieces of extremely sought after buildings; hotels, apartments, malls and office buildings. Everyone in this room helped me when we lost Anton, and I could *not* have got him away to safety, nor Mia, without your help. I know that my brother would want me to thank you in the way that Sonny and I have envisaged."

Roberto was the first to speak, but really for everyone else as well. "Marcus we did it for Mia, and your good self, as well as your brother. I for one do not need anything but a handshake, and a genuine thank you." He looked around at everyone, and they all nodded in agreement, except Gerry of course, who always looked after number one, but was waiting to hear what Marcus was going to explain. The two brothers were well known for their generosity, and Gerry was intrigued as to what was happening to all of Anton's multi-millions.

"Sonny and I are finalising the accounts of Anton's assets, and are preparing to form a company called Santiago Property Development. Mia, Sophia, and myself as Company Directiors. But we need boots on the ground, as I am not coming back to L.A. unless there are exceptional circumstances. Hopefully you four will be those boots for us. I am asking a great deal of you, but you will be paid exorbitantly high retainers to run the company for me." He looked at the four sitting in front of him, and they were all silently taking in what he was saying, but not quite believing their combined good luck. And not quite believing that they had the experience to do as he asked. Except of course Gerry, who was always up to earning an exorbitant amount of money, whatever.

"Al, we need you to take over security on all the properties, and work out how many employees you need to do so, bearing in mind there are managers in place, but you will be in charge. Roberto, you will be in charge of all maintenance with the employees you already have. Ben, you are on your final exams to be a fully fledged lawyer, and will be my backup on anything legal." He looked at Gerry and grinned, as he could see Gerry was puzzled at what he could actually do in the scheme of things. But, everyone liked Gerry. He was everyone's friend, and that was his strength.

"Gerry is going to be my second in command. Any problems whatsoever, and that includes anyone who doesn't want to pay their rent, or dues, even if it's a large company, Gerry will have to sort them out. That will be his problem, not mine. So, if you have a problem, don't get in touch with me, everyone's problems are Gerry's. Is that OK with you Gerry? You will have to be in constant liaison with Sonny and his team."

Gerry was smoking his usual cheroot, so he gave a wheezy cough, and grinned back at Marcus, still not believing what was happening here. It was like having a fuckin' dream that you didn't wake up from.

"Oh, and by the way Gerry, the other office here Ben is going to be using. And, that way he can also keep an eye on you, making sure you actually do some work in between the booze, smoking, and hot women. Is that OK with you?" Gerry winked at Ben, knowing he was going to be able to run rings round the young black guy. "Not a problem, boss. You don't have to worry about me. I'll work my ass off, and my nuts to help everyone." And Gerry meant it, he had been knocked sideways by Anton's death, and Mia's almost death. He admired Marcus's integrity, and for looking after Mia, and the unexpected baby. That alone meant a great deal to Gerry, he loved Mia like a younger sister, and also knew that Marcus loved her, and wanted her as his wife.

Marcus stood up and went round to shake their hands. He wasn't surprised they were going to be on board with him. "Are we all agreed on my proposal this morning?" As one they all said a resounding 'Yes'.

"In the coming days we will all meet at Sonny's office to go through exactly everyone's duties. In future I will be at the end of a video call 24/7. Any problems, and I mean any problems Gerry can't fix, you talk to me, and I will try to fix it.

Also, Sonny will need to know what you consider your time is worth for this Company. Do *not* sell yourselves short, as it's going to be hard work for a while, before routine will settle down, and we all get used to working together. Again, I have to thank everyone for helping me look after Anton and Mia, and trying to keep them safe from the paparazzi, and the media. Al, I can never thank you enough, you went beyond your duty. Mia would not be here if it wasn't for your quick action, and expertise. Thank you so very much."

Al gave Marcus a hearty handshake. "How is she, Marcus? I don't visit at the Hospice, as I know you want to keep it quiet that she is there. And, I did know about the baby."

Marcus blew out a worried breath. "She is getting there, but very slowly. How that baby is still hanging in, is a bloody miracle. It's still too early for a scan, so it's fingers crossed. Mia isn't talking to me, because I can't let her go home to Houston. She doesn't realise what danger she is still in. That is why I have to get back to the Hospice, because Stefan is preparing her for the journey to Fort Worth today. He is going to give her something to sedate her, otherwise we would never get her on the Air Ambulance for the journey with a doctor in attendance."

Al laughed, he knew Mia only too well. "Good luck with that, Marcus. I would not want to be in your shoes when she wakes up. You need to keep your distance until she calms down. She might be tiny, but she is like a tornado when she takes off on one."

Marcus shrugged his wide shoulders. "What's new? I am always in the line of fire. Hopefully my mother will be able to cope with her? If not, we will all be in trouble, but hopefully I'm man enough to get through another crisis concerning Mia the formidable."

Marcus turned to Gerry who was talking to Ben. "See me outside Gerry, we need to discuss something important, that isn't anything to do with this morning's meeting."

Gerry moved to go outside immediately, knowing what Marcus was talking about. He had ruminated about the problem of dealing with Larry and Andi. He had come to realise he wouldn't be able to easily get into Mexico and then out again after killing them. Sure, he had contacts over the border, but Larry and Andi would have security crawling up their asses. There was only one solution, it wasn't one that Gerry relished, but he couldn't see any other solution. The Executioner was the only madman that could get in and out of Mexico without being caught. Gerry did not want to see or get used to living in a Mexico jail. It was a no brainer, but he was going to have a hard time convincing Marcus. He was one of the good guys, and using such a psychotic maniac would go against his morals, and scruples.

Just as Marcus was leaving he remembered something else. "Anton's estate is going up for sale, and the proceeds to go to the Hospice, and other charities that Anton subscribed to. Roberto, could you organise the sale for me, as I know you have been maintaining its pristine condition? Get in touch with Sonny, he has all the details. Thank you everyone for your time. We will meet at Sonny's in about a month's time, and thank you for keeping my brother's work alive, with this new Company."

He looked at Gerry as they both walked out of the door. "OK, tell me the bad news. I can tell by your face I'm not going to like what you are going to say. Any more bad news, and I will want to give up and go live on a Pacific island all on my own. Christ! Mia ignoring me, my mother nagging me to go home, because my boys are becoming little monsters, and, my legal secretary Debbie in Forth Worth, is threatening to quit if I don't get back there immediately." He shook his head in despair. "P-lease somebody shoot me, and put me out of my misery. Forget I said that Gerry, it was not in good taste after losing Anton that way. What's wrong? I presume this is about the bastards who murdered Anton, because that was why I needed to talk with you, alone."

Gerry lit up another cheroot, had a good cough and just went for it. "Sorry Marcus, but it has to be The Executioner. I can't think of anyone else who can do it, and get back free. And, Larry must be banking on that outcome, that he is safe inside Mexico."

"Oh fuck" was all Marcus could say, and he rarely swore. He hadn't seen this coming, and didn't want to agree with Gerry. But knew it was inevitable. He couldn't allow his brother's murder to go unpunished, but The Executioner was a psychotic madman. What did that make him if he agreed to the contract?

Just as bad? Or, a loving brother doing his very best for a younger brother, who hadn't deserved to die so young. Especially when he had at last found happiness with his new wife, and unborn baby. Marcus realised it was a conundrum he would now have to live with for the rest of his goddamn life.

"Get in touch with him! Tell him he can have whatever millions are left of Anton's money, and the bastards who killed him. It will be a hefty pay day for his sickening work.

"May God have mercy on my soul, and Anton's for being the sons of Enrico Theodore Santiago. Wherever our father is, may he never be forgiven for his eternal sins, and for grooming my brother into a life of crime, and ultimately his early death."

CHAPTER THIRTY-NINE

"Marcus, this has to stop right now." His mother was not a confrontational woman, but he could see that she'd had enough. But, then hadn't everyone in his home had enough? "If you don't sort out the problem you won't have anyone working in this house. The physio has left. The young girl from the village left today in tears. Ria has threatened to go on strike, and her husband agrees with his wife. And, I am about ready to pack my bag and go live with Ward Haslett, hopefully he won't mind. This was a happy, loving home, that was filled with people who cared for each other. That all changed a week ago when you brought Anton's wife to live here. You know I never speak ill of anyone, but that – that ill-tempered virago, is just too much to bear." Sophia stopped to take in a much needed breath. "Can you believe, that when Ria took her a tray with her breakfast on, she actually threw it at her? That was when I decided enough was enough."

Marcus ran his long fingers through his short black hair, and groaned with fatigue. He was late home because he had just closed his office in Fort Worth for good, having paid off Debbie his legal secretary with a golden handshake that would allow her to retire in comfort. Then had taken her to dinner at a very exclusive restaurant as a special thank you. Over the past five years they had become good friends, and great colleagues. She was a single mother with two grown up kids, had always turned up for work on time, and never took advantage of Marcus's good nature. Over the past month since Anton's death, she had held his office together, and gradually turned over all his workload to his partners in Dallas, Houston, and San Antonia. For that alone he could never thank her enough, but the over generous pension he had given her would go a long way to ease his conscience, if nothing else.

But now he had to sort out this problem at home. His mother never complained, everyone loved Sophia. He adored his mother, as did his boys. He was not going to allow Mia Santi to alter the schematics of his household. Sophia was the Matriarch. She ran the home, with kindness and love, but also with a firm, caring hand. Mia could not be allowed to upset that loving harmony. Marcus was well aware that she always wanted her own way, and let everyone know when she didn't get it. Henri her father had all but ruined her, and Anton had perpetuated it.

Well! It all stopped this evening. Marcus had had enough of the sulking, and the bad temper, and not being spoken to for weeks now. Mia *had* to stay there, and couldn't go home, which she still didn't seem to understand why.

His mother had told him that Mia hadn't eaten enough to keep a bird alive, and she was worried about the baby. She had tried to get her to see a doctor, and an obstetrician, but she adamantly refused, saying she wasn't pregnant, which was totally untrue. She hadn't showered for a week, or washed her hair, which Marcus knew wasn't the OCD Mia that he knew. He realised she was in total meltdown from losing Anton so cruelly and mind blowing. Being so sick herself, and just about managing to survive, and staying alive. On top of that, she couldn't be with her family, and was living with strangers, who wanted to love her, but didn't know how to get through to her.

"It's OK Mom." He put his briefcase that was overloaded with paperwork onto the long table in the entry hall, and hugged his mother close. "I'm just going to have a shower," he ran his hand over his dark stubble, "and a shave. Change my work clothes, and get comfortable. I've already had dinner, so will go straight to Mia's rooms." He always wore a dark, light-weight, silk suit to work, coupled with a pristine white cotton, button down, shirt. At home he wore shorts and a T-shirt, because it was exceptionally hot in Texas all summer. Luckily he loved the heat, but Mia wasn't used to such intense heat, and would suffer. He took a quick glance at the staircase with a frown, because his boys usually ran down from their bedrooms when they heard his voice. It was unusually quiet tonight, without the dogs coming to greet him as well.

"The boys are staying with friends for the weekend, and the dogs are sleeping in one of the stables." She nodded at a holdall at her feet. "I'm going to stay with Ward for a couple of nights, if that's OK with you? I thought it would be best if you had the house to yourself for a couple of days to try and sort out your ongoing problem. Ria and her daughter are in the kitchen, so you don't have to starve, as well as get kicked in the balls for your sins." She laughed at the look of pleading on his gorgeous face, and kissed his cheek. She absolutely adored her son, and felt *so* sorry for him to have to cope with that out of control female. A woman she knew he still loved, even though she had married his brother, and was carrying his baby.

That was the strength of her eldest son. He lived his life with principles, and honesty, and when he loved, he truly loved forever. She had loved like that. She had loved Theodore with all her heart and soul. Had hated him for taking Anton from her, and for grooming him to become his shadow in the dark side of life.

But, she had still loved him until the day he died, and always would until she was put into the cold earth! Marcus wasn't aware of her feelings for his father, because he hated him with an Italian vengeance.

She was just a woman, with a woman's heart. Loving a man who had given her two beautiful sons. And for that reason alone she would always love him. She had loved him at first sight when she was sixteen, but Theo had stalked her and raped her, so she had to marry him because she was pregnant. He had been a proud, upright, gorgeous looking young man, and naive innocent Sophia from the outskirts of Naples had been easy meat. She had followed him to Texas and even after he had left her taking Anton with him, she had always loved him.

She had told herself over and over that she was being ridiculously stupid, but real life was like that, you rarely chose who you fell in love with for the rest of your life.

But now Theo was dead, cold in his grave. And she could move on with a new love, and hopefully be free and happy at last.

Marcus slipped silently into the suite that Mia was living in, and locked the door behind him. He did not want anyone interfering with what he had to do or say. She was laying on top of the big bed, a tiny, bedraggled woman, not the Mia he loved, and wanted for his wife, from the moment he had set eyes on her, and he had become besotted with her.

She didn't move, but just lay there with her eyes fixed on the large flat screen television, that was on but completely silent. Marcus knew that she was definitely aware he was in the room, but had no intention of acknowledging the fact.

He was not going to take anymore of her crap. Marcus was tired, short on temper, and was horny as get-go. So tonight was going to be a defining time for the rest of his life. His Mom, kids, and staff on his ranch deserved better from him. He now had the time to take care of everyone, and that included the difficult little bitch, that was intent on winding him up way beyond his usual patient, and loving persona.

He went over to the television and turned it off. As he moved towards the bed Mia turned her back on him, determined to totally ignore him. But, he got hold of her by her shoulders and turned her towards him, and held back a gasp of dismay. She looked terrible. Her beautiful face had no colour, and those big brown eyes were sunken, and held no life in them, but were so very, very sad. As he held her he could feel that she was almost weightless, and so terribly thin. Her once glorious blonde, curly hair was straggly and lank, and this meticulously clean woman smelt pretty disgusting.

"Christ sweetheart, what are you trying to do to yourself? I know that you have had a terrible month since Anton died, but killing yourself isn't the answer, and he wouldn't want you to be like this. My brother loved you *so* much. Please, if you loved him, don't do this. Everyone in this house wants only the best for you. To help you get better, and back on your feet again. I am here for you now, and will be here 24/7 starting tomorrow." Marcus was taken completely by surprise when a seemingly sleeping tiger suddenly woke up, defended herself, and turned on him, eyes blazing.

She was all spitting anger and bristling temper. "Don't you dare touch me, Marcus fuckin' Medina. I am not your fuckin' sweetheart either. I want my life back. I want my Anton back. I don't want to be pregnant. I don't want to live in your home. I want to go back to hospital, because I don't feel well enough to be here." She narrowed her eyes at him, and gave him a look of sheer hatred. Then decided to really go for him, her tormentor, her jailer. Her – her whatever! Everything wrong in her life was his fault. She absolutely hated him.

She prodded him with her finger, then pushed him away from her, and he quickly moved back against the headboard of the bed. Mia in full flow of anger was a scary proposition even for a man of Marcus's stature. He remembered her slapping Gerry, and how Gerry had reeled back in pain.

"I cannot eat because everything makes me sick, because of this damn baby. I can hardly walk unaided, because of the godawful pain I am still feeling. I cannot shower, because I haven't got the energy to stand under the water on my own, or wash my stinking mess of hair. I cannot sleep, because every time I close my eyes I see my Anton with a hole in his forehead, and falling dead at my feet. And, then the diabolical pain when they shot me, and the explosive fire in my chest." Her voice began to falter, and she found it harder to breathe, but she tried to carry on explaining her pain, and trauma.

"And then – then I was dead, and my darlin' Anton was holding me and saying I couldn't stay with him, but had to return home." Tears were now pouring down her pale, stricken face. "I want to go home. I want to be with my Papa and Mama. I need their love, and my own familiar room, my own personal things. I don't know anyone here. And I hate that they don't like me, or want me here." She threw herself into Marcus's arms, and gave out heaving sobs, her entire body shaking. Then managed to repeat. "I want to go home. P-lease let me go home, I am begging you. I want to die and be with my darling Anton."

Marcus rocked her in his arms, and just let her cry out the storm. He was quietly crying himself. Crying for the loss of his brother. Crying for the pain and the despair of the woman he loved. Crying because he couldn't allow her to go home until the two murderers had been eliminated. Crying because his brother had recklessly married the woman that Marcus loved, knowing that his lifestyle was conducive to violence at any given time.

Now, he really felt disgusted with himself. He had been vile to her, and all the time she hadn't been well enough to look after herself. Couldn't shower, or eat anything. Mia had always been outspoken to the point of rudeness, asking for help wouldn't have sat well with her. That was all going to change now, because he was personally going to look after her, and get her back on her pretty feet.

She gradually quietened down with exhaustion, and he realised she had gone to sleep still hiccoughing tiny sobs. But at least it felt good that she trusted him to keep her safe from her nightmare of losing Anton to those evil bastards.

Carefully he moved down the bed with her in his arms, and somehow managed to get more comfortable. He got rid of his tennis shoes, and pulled the light-weight comforter over both of them. All the fans and the air conditioning were blowing freezing cold air over them. Turning off the bedside lamps he cuddled her close to his big body, she felt like a tiny fragile bird that didn't have enough substance to stay alive. He could only wish that they were a couple together going to have great make-up sex, but knowing that could never happen in the future.

But, he could dream, couldn't he?

He would try and explain everything in the morning. But for now his love was resting in his arms, and he was happy and content, but a very foolish man. Marcus also knew she was going to be an absolute bitch to convince that she couldn't go home to be with her family. They would also be in danger, if Larry and Andi found out she was still alive, and was their only witness to Anton's murder.

He settled down to a long night of just cat-napping, there was no way he would allow himself the luxury of a deep relaxing sleep. He needed to stay alert in case Mia suffered her usual nightmare of watching Anton being murdered.

If he was being truthful he wanted to watch Mia sleeping. And, hoping this was the start of them sleeping together, every night.

Marcus stopped his personal cell phone from vibrating on his side of the bed. Mia was still fast asleep, and he didn't want to wake her, she needed as much rest as he could give her. Only four people had this number, Sophia, Sonny, Gerry, and Anton. So he knew it must be an urgent call this late in the night.

Very carefully, and very gently he disentangled Mia from his protective arms. He held his breath when she yawned heavily, and wriggled onto her stomach, groaning because she had been disturbed.

Silently he picked up his phone, and moved onto the balcony closing the sliding glass doors behind him, but still keeping a wary eye on the exhausted woman in bed.

"Gerry, what's up? I am trying to get some sleep here. This had better be on a need to know basis, right now."

"Sorry Marcus, but I thought you would want to know what I have found out. Hopefully I haven't wasted my time, energy, and your dollar?"

"OK! Where are you? What have you found out? Are you in your office? And, dare I ask, who is keeping you company in your bed? Blonde, brunette, or red head?"

"Thank you so much, Boss! Right now I am working for you, and Mia. I am deep undercover in Mexico, mixing with alcoholics, druggies, and stinking homeless. Trying to find out where our adversaries are hiding out. The word on the street is they are working from an abandoned warehouse on the outskirts of Juarez in the Borough Cuauhtémoc. That is my next port of call. It appears they are buying up unregulated vaccines for out of control viruses to sell to rogue governments. Evidently, it is a cold storage facility, and they are making money hand over fist."

Marcus wasn't surprised at this piece of news. Larry was a shrewd bastard who wouldn't lose a moment's sleep if millions died because of him. That was where Anton had differed. He never would have considered touching anything that would cause such desolation and misery to ordinary citizens, who were innocent of any crime. Taking drugs, or selling arms, to him were a personal choice. But a man-made virus was suicidal, without anyone having the choice to die, or not.

"Why the hell are you there, Gerry? Haven't you been in contact with our mutual psychotic maniac? If so, why isn't he there sorting out our problem? I really don't like the idea that you always put yourself into the middle of danger."

Gerry just shook his head in exasperation. Marcus really didn't have a clue. The very last thing Gerry wanted was to see the inside of a Mexican prison, and viewing the outside world from behind bars. And, those were the exact words The Executioner had mumbled to Gerry when he had explained the contract.

"My expensive contact in The Federales walked me across the Border, past the Border Control. When the owner of a very dilapidated, clapped out Dodge, wasn't looking I borrowed his so-called car. Hopefully it will manage to get me back close to the Border, which is only nine miles away. Our mutual maniac stated that he wouldn't take the contract unless he knew exactly where the luckless participants were to be found. Only then would he consider to complete his part of the contract, as per arranged." Gerry gave out a disgusting cough, as he drew on his cheroot.

"He also stipulated that he only wanted to be in Mexico for one night to complete said contract, as he dislikes this country intensely, because he doesn't trust anyone living here. Also, he was extremely pleased about the pay off. But, should he fail to extract the passwords for their computers, he would expect you to pay him regardless." Gerry thought that was scarily humorous. Who for fuck's sake would hold out on that psychotic maniac? Only another murdering psychotic idiot, namely Larry.

Marcus could see that Mia was becoming restless, he needed to get back to her immediately. "OK Gerry, your work is done, get back over that border, and home safely. Agree to our contact's stipulations to the letter. Anything that has to be paid is my problem, and you know I never go back on my word. Can't thank you enough. As usual, you always go above and beyond your own safety. I really have to go now, as I am taking care of Mia, and she isn't good right now. Not sure if I should fly to L.A., and bring Stefan here to take a look at her. Hopefully that won't be necessary, as we have a great doctor locally, if she will see him."

He looked back at Mia, and she seemed to have settled back to sleep. He rubbed the back of his neck trying to ease a headache that was building.

Gerry laughed. "And you thought I was living dangerously. Good luck with trying to talk Mia into something she doesn't want to do. I love that obstinate, bad tempered female, but look after her, not a chance in hell. I'd rather be chasing the bad guys in and out of Mexico. At least they would leave my balls intact."

"Thanks Gerry! Let me know when the deed is done, and those bastards have paid the ultimate price." He disconnected, and went back to Mia's bed to hold her throughout the night, and keep her safe from bad dreams.

CHAPTER FORTY

Mia snuggled down into the warm, comfortable bed. She loved feeling Anton's arms around her, he always made her feel safe and loved. Morning sex was the best sex ever, because it was slow, lazy, and totally loving.

She ran her hand over his bare chest, and then followed the line of fine hair down his body, but encountered the waistband of his boxers. Anton never wore anything in bed, and neither did she. But she was still wearing her PJ's, perhaps they had been exhausted last night, and too tired to completely undress each other. Lowering her hand she began to stroke his morning erection, and purred with excitement, because he was exceptionally hard, and seemed much bigger than usual.

Anton had never been that long, or that swollen, but she wasn't going to complain, because he was a wonderful, and always considerate lover. She had touched, kissed, licked every solitary part of Anton's beautiful, perfect body. But, this body was different in a subtle way, bigger stronger, just as beautiful, but not Anton – never Anton.

"If you don't stop right now, I'm afraid I might not be able to control myself." A very sleepy male voice said quietly in her ear. "As much as I am enjoying every moment, I would rather wait to make love with you when you know who is actually your very willing partner in bed."

Oh God! Mia was mortified and took her hand quickly from his very obvious morning erection. She was beetroot red when she looked up into Marcus's smiling, but strained face. He was desperately trying to coax his penis back into its usual soft, indifferent attitude of not being used for five long years. Marcus feared she had awakened a sleeping tiger, which would now need to be utilised and fed, and enjoy a normal sexual life of its own. After losing his wife he had never bothered with sexual relief. In fact Bianca wasn't a particularly sexual being, so Marcus had learnt to tamp down his own sexual needs, and put all his energy into his work, and ranch, and kids.

Tears formed in Mia's eyes. She was totally bereft, because for a few precious moments Anton had been alive, and she could feel his loving presence in her bed. "I am so – sorry. I was dreaming about Anton, and must have woken up thinking he was here with me. I would never have done that to you if I realised what I was doing."

Marcus moved away from her, and pulled the comforter over his embarrassing situation. "No harm done, Mia. You didn't know that I slept with you last night. I didn't want you to be alone after all those tears and upheaval."

Marcus could only fantasise that one day in the future she would wake up and do exactly that to him.

He could dream couldn't he? But he also understood that it was early days for Mia yet on losing her husband. Anton had been madly in love with her, and she him. Now, he had to pick up the pieces, and try and get her back to good health, and that began today, with no arguments from a lazy woman with big brown soulful eyes, who was far too thin. He wasn't stupid, he had a very difficult job in front of him, but for his brother he would get Mia back to normal, and on her feet. She would fight him all the way, but he was determined to ignore her obstinacy, and bad temper, because he loved her, and wanted Anton's baby to have the very best start in life. Marcus was a stayer, and patient, and good tempered, and he was going to need all three to wear Mia down, and keep her safe from harm.

Marcus got out of bed and put his T-shirt and shorts back on, and then sat down in an armchair, because he had to set out the rules of the next four weeks in his home. Finding the right way to tell her was going to be difficult, but before he could say anything Mia got in first. "I'm going home. I *want* to go home, and I don't care what you say, I *am* going. You cannot keep me prisoner here against my will. My Papa will come and pick me up, when I phone him. Please Marcus. I know you have been very gracious because of Anton, and I thank you sincerely. But enough is enough. I have to be independent, and I can't be that here." Slowly like an old woman she made an attempt to get out of bed, but couldn't make it on her own.

Swiftly Marcus was at her side and helped her limp to the other armchair, and then sit down carefully. Her conversation was null and void, she was as weak as a kitten, and totally helpless. He knelt by her bare feet, looking at her with concern and love on his face. "Mia sweetheart, you are not well enough to go anywhere, and until Larry and Andi have been located and dealt with, I can't even ask your family to visit here. You have seen what those murdering bastards are capable of, and we don't want anything to happen to your parents, or you, do we?"

She answered with tears in her eyes, and shook her head in acquiescence. Mia knew that Marcus was talking sense, but hated not being her independent self.

"While you were asleep I got in touch with Stefan, and he agreed that you need at least another four weeks in recovery, right here. He also agreed that I get in touch with John McCrae our local GP. He will send him your medical records, so that he can best help you to recovery. Stefan doesn't believe you need to go back to hospital, and it will be much better for you in a family home. Also John's wife works at the Fort Worth General Hospital, and is the head of the Obstetrics there, her name is Sally Collins. I know both of them, and they are willing to take you on as their patient." Marcus was happy with that situation. They were good friends of his family, and both excellent doctors.

Mia was sitting there, big eyes fixed on his face, but looking at him as if he was talking a load of crap. She was dying to get a word in, but Marcus was determined she was going to listen for a change.

"Starting from today I am your care assistant. I will be with you every minute of your day. Believe me when I say no one else wants the job, and I cannot blame them. And, I won't tolerate bad behaviour, bad attitude, bad temper, and you not wanting to take care of yourself. If I could have Anton's baby for you, I would. But I will be there for you at every appointment, and every scan. This baby *will* be born, and I will help you through it whatever happens. I know you are scared, but Sally is the best doctor to help you, and get you through the next six months or so."

Mia hadn't blinked an eyelid, but she was listening to every word intently. Marcus didn't realise just how difficult and obstinate she was going to be. His well ordered life was about to implode, and she was going to make sure it imploded about as bad as it could be.

Kirby, Never Look Back

"I am now going to help you into the bathroom so you can clean your teeth, and use the facilities. While you are doing that I am going to order breakfast." When she shook her head against any food, as she was already feeling nauseous, he completely ignored her. "I promise I will order breakfast you will be able to keep down. My late wife Bianca had awful morning sickness with both pregnancies, so I am all clued up with what you can eat, or can't."

He picked her up in his arms, which she didn't like, so screeched into his ear, but he completely ignored her, and set her down on the small chair in the bathroom. "I'll be back to help you into the shower, and wash your hair. I do not care how much you screech or show off, you are pretty disgusting, and need a shower badly."

Grinning, Marcus left her in the bathroom with the worst expletives she could utter out of that sweet mouth. He was really enjoying himself, and seeing her naked and vulnerable was a complete turn on. He had looked into those expressive eyes, and had seen she was scared, scared spitless. So she was showing him the face she showed to the world. At heart she was a pussy cat, but with claws. She was still a small girl who didn't want to grow up, vulnerable, needy, and unloved. Marcus could give her everything she needed and more. He had been correct when he had said she had awakened a sleeping tiger. His dick was almost standing to attention, ready and waiting for action. And, he had believed mistakenly that it had died a death when he had seen Bianca fall at his feet dead, on the day Milo had been born.

He had phoned through to the kitchen, and asked Ria to make up a breakfast tray for Mia. But vehemently she had told him she would not deliver it to that insane female. Marcus told her to ask her daughter Elena to bring up the tray and leave it on the small table outside the bedroom door, as he was in the bedroom with their guest. He understood how everyone at the ranch was wary of Mia, because she had been her usual difficult and bad tempered self. But that was about to change now that he was home permanently.

Life as Mia Madeleine Maxwell knew it was changing its course once again, whether she agreed or not. He had a formidable task ahead of him, but God help him, he loved that tiny termagant, and always would. She was a one-off, as difficult as Anton had been, and Marcus truly appreciated that. Now, he had four weeks to get Mia to trust him, rely on him, but more importantly to love him, as he loved her. He also knew he would be pushed to his limit with her demands and violent outbursts, but was actually looking forward to every exciting moment of the next few weeks.

Then all bets were off on a relationship between Mia and himself. Everything depended on Gerry and the contract with The Executioner. Once the murdering bastards were dealt with permanently, only then could Mia safely go back to Houston, which Marcus didn't want to happen. He had lost her to Anton, and wasn't prepared to lose her to Houston, and her family.

Marcus knew he was man enough for all of this shit. He was doing it firstly for his brother, and his baby. For that reason alone failure was not an option. Secondly, he was of course doing it for himself, and he had never – ever – failed at anything he put his genius I.Q. to.

He walked straight into the bathroom without knocking, because that would have been a waste of energy. From now on he would see her naked to help her shower and shampoo her glorious hair. Modesty wasn't going to be a problem for either of them in their future relationship.

It would be a normal state of affairs. For that thought alone Marcus was a truly happy man.

CHAPTER FORTY-ONE

She was sitting dejectedly on the closed lid of the toilet seemingly waiting so very patiently for her tormentor. Mia looked up at the tall imposing man who she still loved, but could not fathom out why. There was something seriously wrong with a female who loved two brothers at the same time. Her maternal grandmother had been put in a mental institution, perhaps she took after her. She must have her DNA, so that must be the answer to all her problems.

Madeleine Maxwell's daughter was a complete nutcase, at least that answered how she always fucked up anything good in her life.

Mia bared her clean teeth at Marcus. "See, I've cleaned my teeth all properly." She put up both hands to him. "Been to the toilet, didn't throw up, 'cos I ain't had anything to eat, yet. And, washed my hands, Boss. Or should I call you Bossy?" She gave him a withering look, and slumped back down to dejection.

Marcus shook his head, smiling. "Sorry sweetheart, but it's me, or nobody. You are going to hate me even more over the next few weeks. Believe me when I say, I will not take any of your crap, now or down the line. I truly have better things to do with my time. But, for my brother and his baby I

Kirby, Never Look Back

will look after you to the best of my ability. Now, let's get those disgusting PJ's off you, and get started."

She looked up at him again with tears welling up. "Please Marcus don't do this for Anton, but for me and the baby. I know I am selfish, and difficult when pushed or told to walk the line. And, I hate rules and regulations." She blinked rapidly to stop the unwanted tears from falling. "But please, please be patient with me, because I really will try to be on my best behaviour, and really try to do everything you ask me to do. Not for my darling Anton, but for myself and his baby. Who deserves to have the best mommy I can be." She couldn't stop the held back tears from falling then, and she really hated crying at any time.

Marcus hunkered down in front of her, and took her in his arms to comfort her. He knew she hated to cry in front of anyone, so this was a big deal for her. "Sweetheart this is going to be a team effort. Everyone here wants to help you, and whatever it takes I will be here for you. Sometimes I will have to walk away from you, because I am pretty certain you will test my patience to perdition, and that will only happen because I will want to strangle you. So it's best I leave the situation."

He gently pulled her to her feet. "Now let's get you under the shower, so I need to help you undress. I cannot leave you under there on your own. Would you prefer that I leave my boxers on, I really don't mind either way?"

She gave him that beautiful open smile he remembered so well. That wide all encompassing smile that drew you into its orbit, but he knew there was always an agenda behind that brilliant smile, and he was the agenda. Her mother had bewitched a million men with that same smile, and look how that had ended. This vulnerable, beaten up woman was Madeline's daughter, and also had a backbone of steel, and would rise up again like Venus. She was very unsteady on her feet, as if she was drunk. "Don't be ridiculous! Anton hated wearing anything in the bedroom, so did I. It would have been a waste of time to keep getting dressed. We made love at least three times in the day, and usually twice in the night. So clothes were out of the question for both of us. I think I've seen it all before, unless you're embarrassed? Are you?"

Marcus almost swallowed his tongue, only Mia would think it OK to reveal her sex life to him. Christ, he wished he could get it up five times in twenty-four hours. That would be any man's dream. He also wished he knew what Anton had been taking to be able to keep up that phenomenon, again and again. It was a wonder his penis hadn't dropped off from over-use. The seriously lucky bastard. Closing his eyes, Marcus took a deep breath, and put up a prayer to the Gods to stop his hard-on from manifesting while they showered together.

Why? Oh why? Did she have to casually mention five times when he hadn't had it for five long, frustrating years? It was no wonder Anton had been *so* extremely happy married to Mia, but it was a wonder he could crawl out of bed with exhaustion.

Fixing his eyes steadfastly on her grinning face, he managed to quickly get rid of her wretched nightwear. She kept herself steady by holding on to his wide shoulders, and just left him to do all the work. But to his disgust he did notice that she was a natural blonde, as he had suspected. He also couldn't help notice that she was scarily thin, and even though she had large brown nipples, her breasts were almost non-existent.

He held onto her while with his other hand he divested himself of his own clothes, but for decency's sake kept on his boxers. Completely naked wasn't an option for Marcus. He worried he wouldn't be able to hold back his sexual fantasy, of being deep inside Mia since the first moment he had met her. He didn't like himself for that fantasy, especially as she had been his beloved brother's wife. His hard-on had woken up with a vengeance when he had seen that amazingly beautiful face for the first time, and of course had held her close to his body.

But, how could he possibly touch every part of her body without any reaction? Well! He was about to find out in spades. Taking a deep calming breath he turned on the shower, and stepped inside the spacious shower area, with Mia in his arms.

Fortuitously Mia was residing in one of their guest bedrooms, and his blessed mother had refreshed a basket of expensive soaps, shampoos, and moisturisers. So Marcus had religiously soaped every inch of Mia's perfectly sculptured body. He had to admit to lingering over her slightly rounded belly, and wishing it was his precious baby still developing safely there, but would never have voiced that to a grieving wife. Mia didn't need to know how Marcus felt about her. She had enough to cope with, with Anton's murder, and her own close encounter with death. She was still so weak and sick, especially having to cope with a pregnancy she really didn't want, or need.

She had really awful scars that Marcus didn't comment on, as she would probably freak out if she managed to see them, as he could. Where the bullet had entered her chest it had left a small looking crater, which Marcus was sure would eventually heal over. But there was a nasty red wound that ran around the left hand side of her body where her spleen had been removed, and a kidney.

Kirby, Never Look Back

It made Marcus feel sick that this tiny, beautiful woman had suffered so much because of his selfish brother. Of course he had loved her totally, but in doing so had caused her life threatening trauma, pain, and almost her far too early death, and his unborn child.

He could see she was at the end of her energy, and patience, so he quickly shampooed her hair and rinsed it off. She hadn't opened her eyes once since he had started to shower her. He had literally held her up against the tiled wall of the cubical. Turning off the water, he leant out and snagged a large, soft bath towel, and wrapped her in it. She was starting to shake with fatigue, and he wasn't doing much better. He had never had to shower another person before, and it was tiring. Of course he had bathed the boys when they were younger, but that had been a father's pleasure, and perk for having kids.

And luckily she hadn't noticed his hard-on, which he had desperately tried to keep under control. But Mia had opened her eyes, as he gently rubbed her down to dry her, and totally disavowed that embarrassment, as she looked down at his crotch. "Do you need some help with that er – problem? I'm just a bit tired at the moment, but give me a year or two, then I might be able to oblige you."

He mumbled his apology, because it was ridiculous that he couldn't keep his dick under control. But, he knew that she would always have that effect on him. Having to touch her when she was naked was hell on his libido, and his second head.

He wrapped them both in soft terry robes that were hanging in the bathroom, and carried her back into the bedroom. Setting her down on a couch he made her comfortable, and pulled a small table in front of her. Then went outside and picked up the breakfast tray for her. Immediately she shook her head, not feeling well enough to eat anything, but he wasn't taking no for an answer. Mia wasn't going to get back on her feet unless she started to eat nourishing food, and his mother would make sure she did. Thank God for a caring mother.

"Mia sweetheart, I know you don't feel well, but you must eat. Sophia my mom has put together a meal she knows that you will be able to keep down. There are croissants, muffins, fresh fruit, and a herbal tea of ginger and honey. I am going to run upstairs to shave, and pick up some clean clothes. I will be as quick as possible, so don't move, and I will be back to settle you down for a rest."

As he went out of the door she shouted at his back, her face a mask of anger and hurt, "Don't fuckin' rush on my account. In fact don't come back at all, and we'll all be ecstatic." Mia did feel mean saying that, but she was so very tired, and didn't think she could keep any food down. And, it was all his fault. Well! She had to blame someone for her pain and discomfort. So it might as well be Marcus, as he had taken her out of the Hospice without asking her if she wanted to leave, which she hadn't, because she trusted Stefan and Tomaz without question.

She hated that he had seen her horrible scars, and touched where the baby was resting. She hated this baby. She wanted her darling Anton with her, not his baby. Marcus was a really good person, but she didn't want his pity, and didn't want to stay in his home. She wanted her Papa, and her brother Christian, who loved her *so* much. And, she needed that nourishing love, and safety of her own family. But, also a man who lived on the edge.

Nobody in this house could ever be that for her. Edgy, dangerous, and overtly sexual.

Mia needed sex as much as she needed to breathe, as much as she needed to be loved. Anton had been that phenomenon and more. Now she was adrift in a lonely time in her life, and wasn't sure she could change what was happening to her. Couldn't see how she was going to cope with any disabilities, and trying to conform to Marcus looking after her. It scared her shitless to be beholden to Marcus and his family.

It she was honest she confused herself, because she adored her Papa, and her brother Christian. But she also loved dangerous, edgy, highly sexed men, who frightened and excited her.

She was two separate halves as a Gemini, and what normal man would be able to cope with her temper outbursts, and obstinate, difficult moods. She didn't want to be alone for the rest of her life. Mia wasn't born stupid. She was her biological mother's daughter, and look what had happened to that amazingly beautiful woman. She died horribly, and far too young.

Mia knew she was a bitch, but a loving bitch, and that had to change. For the past month she had given up on living. That stopped today. Her mental attitude had to change to be able to make a full recovery, and she knew she was capable of doing that, because she was a strong, independent female.

She took a wary look at the uninviting food in front of her, and made that decision to really try and eat something. She had hardly put anything in her stomach for the past month. If she was ever going to leave this prison on her own two legs, she had to work at getting back to normal, and that involved nourishing food and exercise. Food was the easy part. She grinned mischievously, exercise for Mia encompassed hot sex, and more sex.

Marcus wouldn't know what had hit him, when she turned her female wiles on him. He'd had an outstanding erection all the time he had showered her, believing she hadn't noticed. Marcus was going to be an easy lover to conquer.

Yeah right! All men with a penis were dictated to by that organ, and sometimes they were so fuckin' stupid. Mia was relying on that piece of sexual machinery to win over Marcus, and gain her freedom to go back to her family where she belonged.

Of course she knew that Marcus had an agenda, because he was Anton's older brother. Anton had taught her a great deal about sexual eroticism. And Mia had been an avid and quick learner. With a smirk she had to admit that Marcus had a very satisfying big ol' boy.

Now, she could use all that expertise on Marcus. The upright, conformist, utter gentleman, that was Marcus Medina. Soon to be railroaded into needing sexual stimulation as much as she did.

Mia was beginning to feel the road to recovery already starting, as she tried hard to tackle some breakfast, and keep it down in her fragile state of pregnancy.

CHAPTER FORTY-TWO

Marcus felt so much better after having a close shave, and putting on a clean T-shirt and cotton cut-offs. He never wore anything on his feet indoors, because he always had to wear sturdy boots when working outside. With so many different animals living on the ranch he never knew what he might walk into mucking out, or trying to calm cattle down, especially as it was so hot, day and night. Fortuitously, there were two natural springs that fed a well used creek that ran through the middle of his property. So clean fresh water had never been a problem on the ranch.

He quietly closed Mia's bedroom door behind him, and locked it for good measure. She wasn't in the right place yet for any visitors, even though she was just about tolerating him. He couldn't believe his eyes, because she was fast asleep on the couch. Curled up on her right side like a child. A beautiful golden haired child, who looked as if butter wouldn't melt in her mouth. Now, that was a travesty, as Marcus knew only too well. Everything he suggested to try and look after her, she fought him, and always would until her last breath.

Tearing his eyes away from her, he looked at the breakfast tray and couldn't believe she had actually eaten some of it. In fact much more than he had thought she would, which was a really good sign that she was determined to get back on her feet, sooner than later. This would give him some breathing space to be able to get back to a rhythm of working on his ranch, which he had neglected since meeting with her months ago.

While she was sleeping soundly he helped himself to the delicious pastries and preserves, and fresh fruit, but only drank the sparkling water. He was dying for a strong, black coffee, but knew the smell would have upset Mia even more. He remembered that his late wife hadn't been able to tolerate tea or coffee for the first few months of both pregnancies, or even orange juice. The mechanics of pregnant women went directly over Marcus's head. Bianca hadn't let him make love to her as soon as she knew she was pregnant, or even look at her naked, which had seriously upset Marcus.

The wonder of child birth, and a growing pregnancy was awe inspiring to Marcus. He couldn't wait to see Mia in full blown pregnancy, and especially childbirth, for which he was going to be there for her, in every possible way.

A new baby! A new beginning! And he was determined to marry Mia, and be the best husband, and father to Anton's child. He knew she would balk at the idea, and probably throw the mother and father of all temper tantrums, but she didn't realise how persuasive, and how determined he could be. His Santi DNA always came to the fore when he needed something important. And this was way beyond important to him.

He knew he would always love this golden haired, beautiful woman for the rest of his time on earth, and nothing would ever change that. Not her bad temper, her obstinacy, her ups and downs, her vile cursing. Because when you got past all that outer crust, she was a spitting feral cat, with a heart of gold, and *so* much love to give to someone she loved. And he was going to be that person from now on.

Carefully so as not to wake her, he picked her up from the couch, and laid her in the bed. It was best that she got as much sleep as possible, because for the past week she hadn't settled down, and hadn't eaten enough to keep a bird alive. But that had changed today. She looked much healthier, and of course much cleaner, and unfortunately for him, so much sexier. Mia was a naturally sexual being without even trying, just as her mother had been. Madeline had been called the sexiest woman on earth, and had certainly lived up to that name with the amount of lovers she had taken to her bed, and enjoyed throughout her busy life.

That was a worry for Marcus, because he was determined to be Mia's only lover, after Anton of course. His brother he could forgive, but anyone else was going to be under caution if he touched Mia. Marcus did not share his chosen woman with anyone. That was when his Italian genetics overtook his two heads. He would be a jealous lover, as he would never cheat on his bed mate, and he expected the same from her.

Marcus was an exceptionally handsome man, with his black hair gelled back from his face, and cut very short. If it was longer it would be curly, which he didn't like. He was a man's man, definitely *not* bisexual. Anton and Marcus were so alike that cleanliness and grooming was their bible. The brothers were their father's sons. Theo had been exceptionally handsome, slim and tall. Anton was shorter, more like his mother Sophia, in stature. Beautiful parents made beautiful kids, and that was the two brothers. Breathtakingly handsome.

Marcus was a man who would always love the woman of his heart, and never let her go, and Mia was that woman. But the love of his life was already scheming a plan to get free of her so-called prison, as she opened those big brown eyes and looked straight into Marcus's concerned face. Without hesitation she put her hand around his neck, and pulled him close to be able to give him a long, lingering kiss, full of tongue and intensity. Her other seeking hand went for her target, his already pulsing erection, and began coaxing it to harden and lengthen.

Marcus's brain lost the will to keep her at arms' length, and not slake his sexual needs so soon after Anton's demise. In all honesty he really did try to stop himself from making love to her, but her knowing hand was pumping and stroking him, and he was a lost cause.

Mia wriggled out of the bathrobe, and opened her legs wide to accommodate Marcus's big, hard length, but it was being restrained by his being fully clothed still. She quickly helped him to get rid of his cut-offs and boxers, and then expected Marcus to fuck her, but it didn't happen as she wanted.

Marcus was not going to be manipulated into just another sexual encounter for Mia. He looked into those expressive eyes, which couldn't lie, and they were full of hatred and manipulation. He had never trusted Mia, especially when she had married Anton. She always had an agenda and a plan to suit Mia, and this situation wasn't any different. He was being led down a path of sexual pleasure. She was seducing him for her own agenda.

Now he knew the game plan he was going to enjoy every fucking moment, like he had never fucked before, and might never enjoy again. She thought he was the plan – the game, but Mia would learn the hard way that Marcus Medina was not an easy mark. He was far too intelligent to be led by his dick – his well endowed dick, and that could be Mia's downfall.

Anton had been besotted with his new wife, and that had been his downfall. He had taken his eye off the greedy powerful men around him, and now he was dead, because of that lapse in his sanity. When Marcus had put everything together that had happened to his brother, it had all been Mia's fault, because she had entered his life.

Her amazing beauty. Her perfectly formed body. Her overtly sensual, sexual attitude to everything to do with sex. Mia Maxwell was a purely sexual animal, and used it for her own ends, always.

He stopped her stroking hand from stimulating him any further to be able to gain back control. Then his fingers touched her soft, sexy mouth with the lush overbite that could send any hot blooded man into a brain storm, and kissed her with all the love his stupid heart felt for her. This was not going to be wham, bam, thank you ma-am. It was going to be slow, intense loving, as if it was the first time for both of them.

If he allowed this tiny control freak to manipulate him, it would be their death-knell together. She would always want to walk all over him. He had to make a stand their first time making love, or he would lose his advantage. Then he realised she wouldn't like or want oral sex, because it meant she would lose control. That knowledge urged him on, and he would make sure that she participated fully.

Marcus entwined their fingers to stop her from touching him, and then began to work his way down her scarred body, kissing every raised scar so very gently, and with loving care. It hurt him that her previously perfectly formed body had suffered so cruelly. She must have been in diabolical pain when in the hospice, but hopefully now was on the mend, physically and mentally. That was why he fully intended to be with her through every night to keep the nightmares away.

Her breasts were small, but perfectly formed, and he kissed each large prominent nipple, and then suckled each one deep into his mouth, until she began to moan in the back of her throat, and tried to release her hands from his strong grip. She became restless and was moving her body trying to get him to enter her, and Marcus knew she was on the edge of coming, but he was determined to keep her on that edge, and wanting more of what he could give her.

He had waited five years for this moment, so wasn't in any hurry to get to the finishing line. He was going to take his time and enjoy every fucking moment. She was bound to get angry with him, but that made him more determined to make the moment even sweeter for the waiting.

So very gently he kissed her slightly rounded belly where Anton's baby was safe from harm. She stopped wriggling, and he felt her hold her breath, but then cursed an expletive, because he had touched something sacred that belonged to Anton. Marcus realised she felt much more deeply about this baby than she admitted even to herself, as well as him. Mia wanted Anton's baby, but would never let anyone know. It was her secret to keep, and he would never tell another soul, not even his mother Sophia, who was desperate for Anton's baby to be born, because it was the only living child she would have of her youngest son.

Marcus let go of her hands, and slipped his hands under the cheeks of her backside, and lifted her to his mouth, with his thumbs he opened her fully to his seeking tongue, and began to ravage the tiny numb that would send her over the edge. She automatically bent her knees in acquiescence, allowing him to go deeper and higher, sucking and nipping until she began to move in unison with him. His hair was short, but she still managed to grip a clump and almost pull it out at the roots. He quickly inserted two long fingers into her vagina, and pushed way up until she began to milk them frantically, and went over the top. Screaming his name, she also swore like a truck driver, cursing him to perdition as the son of a whoring bitch, who needed to be deep inside her, right now.

Marcus didn't need to be told twice, and before she came back to earth he covered her, and pushed into her to the hilt. Mia's eyes opened wide, and again seemed to stop breathing for a second, but to his amazement seemed to start all over again. She gripped his buttocks and pulled him even closer and higher into her. Bit his sweating shoulder which almost made him come, but he was determined to get as much pleasure as possible from this amazing sexual encounter with a sex goddess. This sexual being was a universe away from his late wife, who had only tolerated sex, and never initiated it. Had only wanted sex to conceive their two boys, and even then had been difficult to penetrate, because Marcus was a big man in every way.

But Mia was a normal male's wet dream. No wonder Anton had never been happier after marrying her. She revelled in her sexual nature. Loved walking around naked, always ready to slake her natural, uninhibited urges. Marcus knew he was in deep trouble as he came, and came inside Mia, and couldn't seem to stop the hot flow of his semen coating the inside of the woman he loved, and not having to wear a bloody condom was an extra bonus. She was already pregnant so there wasn't a problem.

But, she was still cursing up a blue streak when he kissed that mouth silent, and shut her up for a change. He knew he had satisfied her beyond her imagination. A sexually satisfied Mia was a phenomenon she wasn't used to, but Marcus was proud to admit his sexual equipment could satisfy any greedy female. And Mia was a very greedy, needy, controlling female. But she had met her match in Marcus Medina, he was very pleased to say.

After five long years of abstinence, he had a lot of orgasms to make up for, and he was the man to do it, with the woman he loved, who needed sex as a daily exercise.

But five times every 24/7 could be a bit of an ask. Marcus grinned as he settled down with Mia in his arms for a well needed rest before it all began again, hopefully.

He closed his eyes, and Mia was already snuffling, fast asleep in his arms. He'd have a bloody good try at keeping her satisfied, and extremely happy and content. No other man would ever know her biblically for the rest of her life.

She was his! He was hers! For as long as they lived, hopefully for a very long time. She would always need sex hard and fast, sometimes bordering on pain. Could he do that? You bet your sweet life he could in spades.

She had tasted and smelt of sweet almonds and erotica. Somehow he had known that already, as if they had done this before in another life – another time – another place. When he had kissed her she would have been able to taste herself on his lips. That unique essence would always be with him whenever he couldn't be with her, and he was certain that would rarely happen.

Between his home office where he had earned his legal fortune; the daily running of the ranch, and his boys who were getting older and needed more of his time, and of course his beloved mother, he was an exceedingly busy man. Now, he had Mia and her unborn baby to look after, and she would always be a handful. But Marcus cherished every part of his manic daily life, and wouldn't change a moment of it. His only wish that his younger brother had managed to move closer to his family, and be a part of that family.

They had lost forever over twenty years of being close brothers, and Marcus would always regret that, and would never forgive Theo for orchestrating it, and keeping them apart. Because of Theo, Marcus had been brought up an only child, a well loved child, but still a lonely one, without a father, or a sibling. Wherever Theo now resided Marcus hoped he was suffering in his own hell, where he truly belonged for the suffering he had caused.

CHAPTER FORTY-THREE

Marcus woke up as usual at four a.m. because that was his normal time to start his busy day, but today wasn't usual. It was Sunday and Mia had woken him up from a deep, exhausted rest. It hadn't been true that she wouldn't like oral sex, because his ever-ready dick was getting her full attention in her sucking, seeking mouth, and he was battling the need to come. So he gave up the fight, and gently pulled her up to impale her on his hard length already pulsing in a steady rhythm. Within seconds they were both throwing themselves into an explosive orgasm, both gasping out each other's name with love and amazement, that they had become so compatible so quickly. Marcus couldn't get enough of this tiny gorgeous sensual woman, who never seemed to stop wanting and needing stimulating orgasms, and his hard length inside her.

Now she was lying on top of him, and he was still imbedded deep inside her, and the tiny electric pulses were still being felt in his balls and lower back. At this precise moment, if he took his last breath, he would die an extremely happy man. Now he could completely understand how Anton had lost the plot, and had been able to perform at least five times in twenty four hours. Marcus had lost count of how many times he had climaxed in a day and night. And his protagonist sexual partner wasn't even at her highest energy level, yet.

God help him!

But, when she was a hundred per cent healthy would he be able to keep her happy and sexually content? He would have a bloody good try at all this fucking, which his body hadn't been used to for at least the last ten years.

To be truthful, he had never been into the sexual freedom that most young men revelled in. He had been a quiet, serious student. He had felt the heavy load of being the only male in his family, and needed to be a straight A student with the highest grades of anyone. He took looking after his hard working mother very seriously, She always worked two jobs to feed and clothe him, since Theo had left her with her six year old son to take care of.

While he was growing up they lived in a mobile home without any luxuries to speak of. As he became a teenager, he vowed he would make enough money to buy a beautiful home for the best mother in the world. And he had kept that promise in spades.

Marcus was a man who always kept his word to the letter for all his life. He had become the best student with the highest grades possible. He was a Phi Beta Kappa member for life. And the highest achiever in Business and Technology, and Law.

While studying at Harvard Uni for law, he had passed with honours, and claimed a degree in Criminal Psychology, but he had also forged a lifetime friendship with three other students. They had joined forces in a financial syndicate to gamble on the stock market and futures. Marcus had a head for numbers, a cool mind, and a genius IQ, so making millions wasn't a stretch for him. They had begun by gambling a small amount, but were now all set for life, because of Marcus and his steady hand on their dollars.

How he had ended up with his beautiful ranch was another piece of luck, or just plain hard work. While he was still at school and college, for extra pin money he would work part time doing odd jobs for elderly, frail Mr Jenson. His ranch was run down, and the animals long gone, but he refused to live anywhere else. When he died he didn't have any family to leave the ranch to, and to Marcus's amazement, had left it to him. Really it wasn't a bargain, but he poured into it his now earned millions, and it was the best kept ranch in Perseverance.

Marcus had kept his word, as always. Sophia, his mother, now lived in comfort and luxury, and they were a close family unit, with his two boys who adored their grandmother. He couldn't be prouder of his mother, because she had gone back to school to complete her studies to become a teacher. She was a fully qualified teacher at the boys' school, so the school run wasn't a problem. She took them every morning, and came home with them, if Marcus wasn't around to pick them up. School was out for the summer, so the boys could roam free with all the space on the acreage.

That day Marcus had two phone calls whilst he was taking care of Mia. They had showered together, and of course sex had been on the agenda, as per usual. But were now sitting out on the veranda eating lunch under the large whirling fans that were trying in vain to cool the temperature down. The view from Mia's rooms of the lawns and fountain and trees was truly fantastic, Marcus was really proud of his home. The two storey house was native stone and cedar, with a deep porch the entire length of the building. Beyond the pastures and corrals were old trees, mostly Pecan. Two natural springs formed a natural stream that meandered across the acreage, and it was laced by tall Cottonwoods and flowing Willows. Marcus loved his home and property, and prayed that Mia would in their future feel the same.

His first phone call was from Sophia asking him if it was OK if the boys stayed with their friends for the coming week. The parents had sanctioned the request, because the four boys were the best of friends. If it was OK, Sophie would come home and pick up extra clothes for them, and anything else they might need. Also she would stay with Ward, her special friend for the week, if it was OK with her son. Marcus was in total agreement because it would give him extra time to be alone with Mia, and try to get her back to full health, and good temper.

The second phone call was more worrying, because it came from Gerry, and wasn't really to Marcus's liking, or conscience. "Marcus, the contract has been finalised to our specification. But, I need you to come to L.A. as we need your actual signature to complete the purchase ASAP. Please my friend, as I would like to put this last contract behind us, and to bed. We did say that this would be the last time we use this particular company to carry out our orders." Marcus had told him that he needed a week to help Mia get back on her feet, it was impossible to be there any sooner. But by next weekend he would fly his own plane to L.A. and sign the damn papers. Gerry had agreed, but not happily. As it was Mia holding Marcus back, he did agree, but insisted he had to be there by Saturday.

Marcus realised what Gerry was leaving out of the conversation, because they couldn't trust any conversation over a cell phone, or computer. He would want to show Marcus on his phone exactly what had happened to the two evil bastards that had murdered his brother. They had gunned down Anton in cold blood, he hadn't stood a chance to defend himself. Marcus hoped they were now in hell with his father,

Theo. They all deserved each other, and hoped they were never forgiven for their heinous actions on earth.

Marcus realised that Gerry would be desperate to get rid of the phone that showed the evidence of The Executioner's insanity. But now Mia would be free to go home at last, because she and her family weren't in danger anymore. He wasn't going to let her know that she was free to leave until he actually saw the evidence that those bastards were truly dead, and beyond hurting her in any way.

His other head was talking for him now. He had one week to convince her to stay with him. To be a family with his boys and mother, and hopefully be a wife for life with him.

Could he really do it? Honestly it wouldn't be easy, because Mia never made anything easy. But, he would have a bloody good try, as a patient, loving man, and a man with a strong backbone.

He would have the best sex ever while he tried to convince the difficult woman that he loved, that she needed him, as much as he needed her.

CHAPTER FORTY-FOUR

The week came and went, and Marcus was really worried about leaving Mia on her own with only Ria, Pablo, and their daughter for company. But his mother was due home today, and his boys tomorrow. He hadn't told Mia why he was needed in L.A. As far as she knew it was a meeting about the Company to do with Anton's holdings, and Gerry Swane.

Marcus didn't dare inform her that her enemies were now dead, and she was free to go anywhere she wanted to. The whole week he had wooed her, and loved her, and taken her in his battered old jeep around the estate. They had had a picnic by the stream, under the Cotton Woods, and made enthusiastic love, totally naked, and after had swum in the cold water. Marcus had laughed at her antics and for screaming it was too cold. He was used to the freezing water, and just loved to see her naked, and free to enjoy herself, after the pain and trauma of losing Anton.

But of course she showed off with an explosive temper tantrum when his friends the two doctors turned up without her permission. John to examine her wounds, which were looking better every day. Sally his wife was an experienced obstetrician, and was the senior Gynae/Obstetrician at Fort Worth General Hospital.

Marcus wasn't going to take any crap from Mia, especially when his friends were doing him such a big favour in making a house call. The couple never had a spare moment to call their own, as John was the only G.P. looking after everyone locally. Sally worked at the hospital, but still managed to look after every pregnant woman locally. They were a working team, who loved their work, and thrived at always being so busy. Their busy lives didn't give them enough time to start a family, and Marcus knew that John was desperate to be a father, but Sally not so keen on being a mother. She knew exactly what it took to bring a baby into the world that was constantly changing, and not for the better, necessarily.

While the couple were drinking coffee and enjoying Ria's famous pastries, Marcus led Mia outside and gave her a strong worded talking to, that she had to be on her best behaviour. His friends were the most patient, loving couple, and didn't deserve to have to cope with Mia, bent on being difficult, and rude. Of course she got round Marcus with a trembling lower lip, and big cow eyes. Mia at her most contrite had Marcus twined around her little finger. All was quiet, and serene, and friendly until Sally examined her patient, efficiently and professionally.

"Marcus would you like to disappear while I examine Mia, as it could be embarrassing for her?" Immediately Mia piped up that she wanted him to stay, as he had seen and touched every part of her body. Everyone in the room coughed with embarrassment, including Marcus. Trust Mia to state the obvious, as nothing ever seemed to embarrass her, nudity, sex, absolutely nothing was sacrosanct to her logical Gemini brain.

But Sally wasn't having any of Mia's flippant remarks, as she examined her internally. "I'm sorry Mia, but you really must stop anymore sexual intercourse. You really weren't healed properly, and have so much scar tissue as far as your womb, and I can't tell how bad it is until I can do a scan on the whole area." She looked straight at Marcus and gave him an angry glare, thinking he should have known better with a pregnant woman with Mia's history.

He went as red as a beetroot, and mumbled how sorry he was, but of course Mia butted in. Looking over her spread legs she said crossly, "It wasn't Marcus's fault. He was worried for me, but I persuaded him it was alright to fuck as much as possible to keep me happy." She grinned at Sally as if she had made her point, and that Marcus couldn't help himself, because she had him by the balls, so to speak.

"Well! I'm going to warn you now, your body is so scarred, and isn't capable of having a baby normally. In fact I have to verify this, but I can hear two heartbeats, which makes me believe you are going to give birth to twins, Mia."

Kirby, Never Look Back

The atmosphere in the room went ballistic. Mia screamed out that no way was she pushing out of her vagina two fuckin' babies. She would kill herself before that happened. Marcus looked as if he was about to pass out with the fear that she would actually do harm to herself. He had to sit down in an armchair before he *did* pass out. Then he grinned and laughed out loud. They were going to have twins in the family. Anton's twins. And, now he would be their father, and Sophia would be over the moon and back with joy, over Anton's twins.

Then suddenly Mia stopped screaming expletives as Anton's words came back to haunt her. "Look after my girls my darling. Remember to always tell them that their daddy loves them, and always will, wherever I am."

Her darling Anton had told her she was pregnant with twin girls, and he expected her to look after them for their daddy. She looked up to the ceiling and heaven where Anton lived now. "I will give my life for them if I have to." She said to herself and knew he was listening to her. "No one will love our girls as much as I will. And I will always love you as long as I live, and never forget you, not for one single day of that life. Be happy my darling, and know that your girls will be loved and cared for by my family, and their mother. I give you my sacred word on that." In her head she kissed him goodbye, knowing they would never make contact again. She had made her pledge, and he had accepted it, and he could now move on.

Marcus would have to take second best, because he was her future, and her babies' future. Mia could live with that, but could Marcus?

But Marcus was watching her devious mind that showed expressively on that beautiful face. All that sex had been manufactured to get rid of the baby, and he couldn't forgive her for that. It had meant the world to him, and nothing to her. She was a scheming, controlling bitch, who was desperate to miscarry a child that was going to be a nuisance in Mia's future. She didn't want to be a single mother with a screaming child to look after.

The little bitch had been truly playing him with her delectable, perfect body. But he was a patient man, and would wait to see how all this drama played out. For the time being this was the end of their sexual gratifications, because he would take the advice from Sally that it was dangerous for the babies. Marcus always took notice from experts who knew more than him.

He could go without, but could Mia? Marcus truly doubted that outcome, because she was always panting for it, like a drug addict. Marcus was not going to be used in that context. He was too proud, and loved his family far too much to demean himself to her level of promiscuity. Yes! He loved Mia, but would never sell himself short because of her.

Those babies would be born healthy and belong to a loving family. If Mia did not come up to his standards of parenthood, he would take her to court to become their legal guardian. He was a very good lawyer, and would expect to win the case without too much effort. She would find out to her dismay that Marcus Medina was not a man to be fucked with.

He was of course Theo Santiago's eldest son, with an iron will, and a strong personality, but without murderous intent, or illegal pursuits.

Gerry was waiting for him as he brought his Cessna Citation to a standstill. It had taken him just three hours to fly from Fort Worth to Los Angeles. He had flown to a private airfield on the outskirts of L.A. The airfield belonged to one of his well-heeled friends, a judge on the L.A. circuit. Marcus always cultivated friendships with men in high places, he never knew when he might need their help, especially when Anton was alive and causing mayhem.

Gerry had wanted to show him the phone evidence straightaway, but Marcus forestalled him, and told him to wait until they were in his office. Marcus never trusted that someone could be watching either of them. All the Agencies had been on Anton's heels constantly, and he was pretty certain they had found out that Marcus was his brother, and Theo's son. Even though he played everything straight and by the legal book, there were a league of innocent people in prison, and left there for years forgotten.

Marcus sat on the couch in Gerry's office with his head in his hands. He felt sick to his stomach, and ashamed that he had asked Gerry to get in touch with the psychomaniac who evidently was proud to show them his latest handiwork.

A disembodied, altered voice was explaining exactly what had happened in the vast freezer that had once been a busy warehouse. But as usual the person who owned the voice wasn't in view. Two naked bodies were hanging upside down from two meat hooks. They were trussed up like naked chickens and gagged, to stop them from screaming out their agony. But their faces showed agony beyond bearable.

They were still alive, but their entire bodies were cut to ribbons their blood dripping slowly down on to the dirty floor. "As you can imagine gentlemen, they both decided to tell me the passwords to all their financial dealings far away, and in Mexico. I must admit that you have been extremely generous in your payment for my expertise. I thank you for your generosity, and now ask you to never ask me again for another contract. I now have at least one hundred million dollars to retire very comfortably to a destination known to only myself. I have destroyed the instrument that has sent you this video, as I expect you to do the same. I have also totally destroyed all their technology that could be used to trace anything that Mr Santi, and yourself Mr Swane, were involved in with these pieces of dog shit. From this moment in time I will disappear from the world, and hopefully spend the rest of my days in peace and contentment. I am leaving these evil bastards with the knowledge that this was the comeback for killing Anton Santi, and his beautiful wife. By the time, if ever, they are found, they will be very dead from their awful wounds and the freezing cold."

The images went blank, and the totally insane psycho had gone, leaving Marcus and Gerry absolutely silent, and feeling extremely guilty, and nauseous. "Oh my God! Gerry what did we do? We could have got someone to put a bullet in their heads, the same as they did to Anton." Marcus couldn't believe he had sanctioned such a barbaric ending to anyone's life. Their death would be on his conscience for the rest of his days.

But Gerry was more pragmatic. He worked and often lived with the evil bastards who ran the under-belly of the criminal world. "We have to remember what they did to Anton and our Mia. They put a bullet in his brain in cold bloodied murder, without a second thought, or regret. And they thought they had killed Mia, and it was sheer luck she didn't succumb to death as Anton did. They were evil, greedy murderers, and to my mind got exactly what they deserved. Personally, I don't regret that we called in The Executioner. He completed his contract as always, and it's in the past now, and we have to move on. Evidently, he has retired from his gruesome work, and I need to get rid of this phone tonight. I will make sure it ends up in a million broken pieces and then some."

The two men just sat quietly trying to get back to some normality, and trying to get those gruesome images out of their heads. It was afternoon and Gerry had missed breakfast and lunch, and asked Marcus if he wanted to stop and eat, or call a meeting for his business associates regards Anton's holdings.

"Sorry Gerry, I need to get back to Mia. She has been a nightmare to look after, but I think she is on the mend now, but hopefully won't cause havoc in my peaceful and loving home. We've been on our own for a week, but my Mom is coming back today, and my boys tomorrow."

The expression on his good looking face told Gerry everything he needed to know. Marcus loved that angel-face more than she ever deserved, but Gerry didn't envy the poor idiot. Mia was a hot bloodied man's wet dream, but a total fuckin' nightmare to look after. He didn't blame him for getting back as soon as humanly possible to try and keep the peace between his mother and Anton's wife.

On the drive to the office Marcus had told him about the twins, and how everyone in his family was ecstatic, but Mia was not so ecstatic. Gerry knew Mia's view on childbirth. One baby had been too much for her, and now two, she must be suicidal. Gerry couldn't understand why any sane man would want to cope with an angry, temperamental Mia, and Anton's twins.

Gerry revered his single status, and as much sex as he could cope with. Marriage and screaming kids were not in his future plans. Happiness, freedom, and plenty of hot mammas, was his idea of a great life well spent.

So, good luck to Marcus his friend, who lived his pristine life helping others, and especially Gerry. If anyone could cope with Mia the beautiful, but obstinate, and difficult little tyrant, it was definitely Marcus Medina. He was the most patient, kind, loving man Gerry had ever met on his travels in life. But Mia needed a firm hand on her pretty butt, and that was also Marcus.

"Papa please, I am begging you, please come here now and take me home." Mia was on the phone to her father, begging him to come now while she was on her own and collect her. Marcus had left just a moment ago saying he would be back this evening. Well, fuck him if he thought she was going to stay in this fuckin' prison. "Think again, you asshole, I'm leaving ASAP." She shouted after him, as she watched him from her veranda getting into his battered jeep and driving off. He was fuckin' stupid if he believed he could leave her on her own, and she would adhere to *his* rules and demands. Of course her darling Papa said he would be there in roughly four hours to pick her up. Henri was over the moon that his beloved child was coming home at last, and couldn't wait to see her. He didn't think to ask if Marcus was OK with this arrangement, and if the danger of Anton's enemies was over. The thought of Mia coming back home at last just eclipsed any problems with his daughter's welfare. Henri was a father who could give his life in a second for his four children, and especially his baby Mia.

Christian his son had a clearer mind on the subject of his youngest sister, who had always walked on the side of calamity and danger. He adored the tiny termagant, but had a clearer vision of her selfish, and self destructive moods. He tried in vain to stop his Papa from collecting Mia while Marcus wasn't there. But, he forbade him making such a long drive, and then returning immediately.

Instead Christian took the car keys off his father, and drove himself with his father as a passenger. Everything that had happened to his sister since she moved to L.A. had weighed heavily on Henri. His good health had suffered, especially after visiting Mia in hospital when she had been critically ill, and not expected to survive. They had all been frantic with worry, but Henri wasn't getting any younger, and Christian had been pretty certain that his father had suffered a mild heart attack.

As usual nothing had been said as his father never complained if he felt unwell. But as a serving police officer Christian had to be able to give CPR to anyone in need. His father had come home unwell, and looking ten years older, and ashen faced. Sometimes Christian wondered if Mia ever thought about anyone but herself. Now, she was having twins, and he dreaded the outcome. He wasn't being miserable, or a doom monger. But his sister with twins? And coming home was going to be a nightmare situation of huge proportions.

Christian and his family now lived in the apartment above his parents. He had a wife who was about as offensive and difficult as any wife could be. She was a practicing Catholic, who would not divorce him, even though they hated each other.

The love of his life, Jesse Powell, the world renowned photographic model, was pregnant with his baby, but he couldn't be with her. He was frustrated and extremely unhappy until he could somehow solve the problem. And now because of a moment of madness his wife claimed she was pregnant with his baby. So his faith in God, and family, left him no option but to stay with a woman he loathed, who was pregnant.

His Mama Josephine was a quiet, loving woman, who nurtured her four children. But Mia had always been a huge problem for her. Of course she knew she wasn't Mia's biological mother, but had never treated her any differently. Mia was a product of Madeline Maxwell's bad behaviour, and Henri's. She had her mother's DNA, and it often reared its ugly side. But Henri seemed to totally ignore her selfish, self centred attitude to life. When Mia was her sweet, loving and kind self, everyone in the family absolutely adored her, and forgave her.

Now, Karen his wife and Mia living in the same house was going to be a total nightmare. Mia would not hold back on how she felt about her sister-in-law. There was going to be fireworks, and Christian didn't want to be piggy in the middle, or even try to keep the peace. The two women were strong, opinionated, and lethal. Verbally they would tear each other apart, and he didn't want his beautiful daughter being caught in the middle of their obvious dislike of each other. Christian's life was already going down the proverbial toilet. Could it get any worse? He bet his sweet life that it could. He prayed to a God he didn't really believe in anymore, that he didn't have to kill someone to get some peace back in his pathetic life.

How Marcus had survived a whole week of looking after his sister, God only knew. The miracle man needed a medal and a commendation. As for his brother Anton marrying her, was totally beyond Christian. Evidently he had adored the tiny spoilt, out of control female. Christian had to admit, he adored his sister. When she was good, she was exceptionally good, but when she was bad, God help anyone close to her, because she was so destructive. Dangerously destructive, and didn't care who got hurt in that destruction.

CHAPTER FORTY-FIVE

Marcus was too tired to put his plane into its hangar, and left it on the runway at the end of his property.

He wasn't at all surprised when he saw his mother waiting for him with bad news. "I'm *so* sorry Marcus, but she has gone, and taken all her clothes, and other bits and pieces. Ria said a young, gorgeous looking man came for her, about four hours after you left this morning. Mia said goodbye, and that they wouldn't be seeing her again. Ria said she didn't look well, and the young man had to help her to the waiting car. She thinks that Mia's father was in the car waiting for her, and only got out to help Mia into the front seat with the driver."

Marcus put his arms around Sophia and gave her a loving hug. He could see she was extremely upset for him. She hadn't really taken to their difficult guest, and wouldn't be unhappy or concerned that she had left. But she loved her son and knew how he really felt about Mia, so wouldn't voice an opinion about Anton's wife. She also knew that Anton had been besotted with his new wife, and now her other son was following in his footsteps.

Sophia wasn't stupid, far from it. She had come to the conclusion that Mia was exceptionally beautiful, but must have been manipulative, and sexually amazing in the bedroom. Both her boys had been led by their well endowed sexual equipment, which had addled their brains. All Sophia could say to herself was "Men! And their erections." Would they never learn, or grow up? she sighed heavily, but didn't say a word.

Marcus wasn't surprised, because Mia had been like a bird in a cage, and had been scheming to be set free, from day one. But, his home wasn't a prison, it was her safe haven. She never seemed to realise that she was in real danger from those sickening bastards who had murdered his brother, and shot her in cold blood.

The ridiculous outcome of his visit today with Gerry was that the danger was over for her and her family. He was coming home to tell her that he could take her anywhere she wanted to go and live. If she didn't want to stay with him, he would bend to her wishes and help her to leave. He would be heartbroken as he had tried so hard to show her just how much he loved her. Wanted to spend the rest of his life taking care of her and the twins. Loving her. Her babies, and his boys. And of course his mother, until Ward Haslett took over and married Sophia.

Marcus was absolutely certain that was a match made in heaven. He felt that was true of Mia and himself, but evidently she didn't think so, because she had left as soon as he turned his back.

What he didn't understand was, what had he done wrong? He had tried to show her in every way possible that she meant the world to him, and way beyond that. But, somehow he had fallen short of his brother, and it was clear she still loved Anton. Nobody could win against a man who was dead. He would always be number one in Mia's heart, and Marcus couldn't fight that.

For the next week Marcus walked and worked around the ranch rarely saying a word to anyone. Sophia realised his good heart was shattered, so she tried to keep the boys busy and out of their father's way. But, every night they both crept into Marcus's bed, and cuddled up to him as close as possible. They were young but knew something had upset their daddy, and that upset them.

Their daddy usually played with them, and always laughed at their silly antics, but now nothing seemed to get through to him. It was making the whole household miserable and sad, and Sophia wasn't having anymore of these tragic circumstances.

She cornered him once the boys had climbed the stairs to their bedroom. They still shared a large bedroom, as were both scared of sleeping on their own. Just the same as

Marcus and Anton, before they had been cruelly separated by their selfish father, Theo.

"Marcus, this has to stop. You are tearing this family apart. I'm sorry son, but she is not worth it. I will not talk badly about her, but she is a self destructive, selfish woman. For some reason she had an agenda against you. She needed someone after Anton died, and you were the obvious candidate." Sophia was crying while she tried to get some sense out of her beloved son. "Please Marcus, let her go, and let's get on with our lives. Your boys need love and stability in their young lives, and right now this isn't happening. I am doing my best, but they need their daddy's love and attention, and it just isn't there."

Marcus was listening, but couldn't look at his mother. She had found him sitting on the couch in Mia's bedroom just staring at the bed that he must have slept in with her all week. Then she realised he was quietly crying, something she never expected to see. Her son had always been strong, stoic, and steadfast, and the man everyone turned to when they had a problem. It was then she realised he had been holding back all his emotion and the turmoil lately in his life.

Sophia went and sat next to him putting her arms around him, and just held him until he cried himself out. She loved her son with all her soft heart, but hated the woman who had brought him to his knees, and emasculated him. Mia

Santi was a total bitch, and did not deserve this caring, loving human being. A tall man amongst men.

"Sorry Mom, I don't know where that all came from, but I really needed to let that out." Marcus wiped his eyes with the heel of his hands, and composed himself once again. After what he had seen today, what that psycho maniac had done to those poor bastards, because of Anton and Mia, all that needless cruelty had come to a head. Now he felt a lot stronger and calmer. Thank God only his mother had witnessed his complete meltdown.

Now he had to be resolute about the rest of his life, without Mia, but with his close family, even closer. "Mia has almost torn our family apart, and I cannot allow that to continue, Mom. I will always love her, and wish that we could be a couple forever. I completely understand where she is coming from. If I was single without any responsibilities I would go after her and bring her back, but that isn't going to happen. I know you aren't keen, but I think we have to remember what she has gone through in the last few months. She has only just found out that she is Madeline Maxwell's secret daughter. She comes to L.A. to try and find out the truth about her mother's untimely death, and it appears she was murdered. Then she finds out that her mother's sister, Melody, had died only four weeks earlier, and has twin daughters that Mia didn't even know about."

Marcus took a deep breath at the next admission. "I get her a job at Anton's hotel, and she is tortured and raped by two psychotic maniacs. She then meets Anton, who, bless him, looked after her, but fell head over heels for her. The rest of the story you already know. Their marriage, which was far too early in their relationship. Consequently Anton's death, and she almost died. Mom, I think we should give her some slack. To my mind she is now a deeply disturbed young woman, who most definitely needs counselling, and a safe harbour to get back to completely good health once again. And to top all of that trauma, she is expecting twins, and she is terrified of giving birth. I honestly don't know what is going to happen in the months to come. I pity poor Henri with all this going on."

Marcus took hold of his mother's hand, and squeezed it gently. "I totally get her, Mom. I understand what turmoil she is in right now. She believes that by being sexually active with someone, and giving them mind blowing pleasure, they will love her unconditionally. And I have been that person, but I would have loved her without going to bed with her."

Tears were in Sophia's eyes as she listened to her son opening up his heart to her, and his confession was an enormous relief to her. She knew he was going to get over losing a troubled woman he truly loved. And their home would get back to normality once again.

"I shall never marry again, as I seem to be pretty hopeless where women are concerned. My marriage to Bianca was a complete failure, except for my wonderful kids. I would have married Mia, but that definitely will never happen now. She has demolished me, but I know I will grow stronger for a lesson well learnt. I have to dedicate my love to my family, and to the hard work on this ranch."

He smiled at his much loved mother, who was an amazing person, and had always listened to his woes and triumphs, with equal patience. "This has been a huge learning curve for me; to truly enjoy the things I have strived for, and to not wish on a star I cannot hold onto.

"Tomorrow starts the rest of my life, without Anton, and definitely not Mia. We are done! Finished! Let's go to our beds Mom, and get a good night's sleep. It's going to be a very busy day tomorrow."

Sophia just smiled back at the beautiful soul that was her eldest son, and whispered to herself "Yes! A lesson well learnt. Hallelujah! Thank you God, back to normal."

A month had gone by, and Marcus realised he wasn't ever going to hear from Mia again. But he did have to get in touch with Henri, her father, to insist that they sent him all the invoices that occurred with the twins' birth and pre-birth. Anton was their biological father, and Marcus would uphold any costs incurred now and in the future. He was not a man to ignore his family's expenses.

But, that morning while he was talking to his foreman Dave, who was the kingpin keeping the ranch up to scratch, he had a phone call from Houston. "Morning, am I talking to Marcus Medina? This is Christian Arnaud, Mia's brother."

"Yes, I am he. What can I do for you, Christian? This is an unexpected phone call."

"Sorry to disturb you Marcus, but my family has a huge problem on their hands. And, we know that you looked after my sister so well, when she lived with you in Fort Worth. And, I know that she probably didn't tell you she was leaving, and probably didn't even say thank you for all your help after her husband Anton died. Mia always falls short on goodbyes and especially thank you when she focuses on her own needs and wants."

Marcus wasn't really interested in what Christian was talking about, or specifically why he was calling him that morning.

"Yes, I do know how she uses friends and family to her own ends. My family here are still reeling from her self-serving, selfish attitude."

"I love my sister, for all her faults and needs. She loves her family, and has a heart of gold, but my father has always given in to her, and spoilt her rotten, which hasn't helped her become a stable, hard working member of society. Apart from all that Marcus, I am going to ask you a huge favour."

Marcus butted in before Christian could put that favour into words he couldn't take back. "If you are asking can I take back responsibility for her, I am sorry man, but the answer is a resounding *NO*. She turned my home upside down while she was here. My family and staff who generally accept everyone who comes here with love and friendship. But not one of them took to Mia, and I really tried hard to change their minds, but to no avail. Unfortunately, your sister uses sex as a weapon to get her own way. I'm pretty certain she used her blatant sexuality to snare my brother, and I believe he was murdered because he had taken his eyes off his enemies, and they took advantage of that mistake. Then she saw how vulnerable I was because of his death, and her awful injuries, so turned that sexuality on me. As a normal heterosexual male I succumbed to her sensuality, and paid the price when she walked out on me and my family while I was in L.A."

Marcus hated to admit, especially to Mia's family, that he had been devastated by her leaving him. "If I am being truthful I was devastated when she walked out on me. And, if you are going to ask me to take her back, I am truly sorry, but that isn't happening. I think I am pretty easy going, but ain't any man's fool."

Christian hadn't implied that Mia wanted to return, but Marcus was definitely getting the message it was his intention. "Honestly Christian, I believe that Mia needs professional help, a counsellor, and that is something no one here can give her."

"Before you really make a final decision, can I just point out a few major facts about Mia's mindset right now?" Marcus knew he wasn't going to change his mind, because he had to put his kids and his mother first in everything he did now.

They were his top priority! They were his whole life! They were the only reason he got out of bed every day, and worked his butt off! Mia couldn't change any of that, whatever her state of mind was. He honestly couldn't care less what happened to Mia Madeline Maxwell Santi. She was now her family in Houston's responsibility.

But Christian was still talking at the other end of the phone. "She has taken to her bedroom and won't come out. She refuses to eat, even to eat for her twins. And yes, she had a scan, and she is pregnant with twins, but we don't know their sex, yet. My sister never cries, but she now doesn't stop, we are awash with her tears. She says she is devastated that she left you, and just wants to come back. She says she loves you *so* much, and only wants to be with you, and no one else. Honestly Marcus, I have never seen her so upset. My parents are scared for her health and her babies. She promises that she will stop being a spoilt bitch, difficult, and mean to your mother, and your staff at home. Our parents aren't coping, and neither am I, with the problems I am already trying to sort through. I can understand that my sister was a pain in the backside when you were looking after her."

Christian crossed everything he could, and prayed for a good solution here, because his recalcitrant half sister was tearing his family apart, and his usually even temper was being stretched to the limit. Strangling her would be a solution. But he was the Chief of Police in Houston, loved his job, loved his daughter, and certainly loved Jesse Powell, his pregnant lover. Prison was not in his future agenda for murder.

"Sorry Christian, I will not change my mind. I am done with being Mia's punch bag, and fuckin' idiot. Nobody wants her here, and that definitely includes me. Let me know when the twins are due, because my wonderful mother is their grandma, and will want to see them. Thank you so much for the update, and I truly wish you all the best, and your family with Mia. She really thinks that she loves me, but I can assure you that is not true. She loved my brother, Anton, and hasn't really got over his instant death. Do yourself a favour and get her the help she needs, and that is not me. I believe a professional counsellor will get her back on her beautiful feet, and hopefully normal, as normal as Mia can be."

Marcus hated himself for doing this to Christian and Mia's parents, but he really had to put his own family first. "Good luck man, and please, I am begging you, don't get in touch again, unless it's to say the twins have arrived."

Marcus cut off from Christian. His chest felt as if his heart was trying to burst out of it. Just talking about the woman he loved with every heartbeat, made that heart hurt, and the rest of his body follow suit. He couldn't believe he had turned down the reason to get her back in his life, and empty bed.

He knew he would love that impossible, difficult, bad tempered, but absolutely gorgeous female, as long as he lived. But she was far too toxic to be in love with, and he had to grow a pair of steel balls, and a new heart to replace the one that was broken.

Look out Perseverance! Look out Fort Worth! Look out world! Marcus Medina was a new man. A single millionaire, with two fabulous kids, and absolutely not looking for a female companion.

He was a great looking guy, with an outstanding attribute, but did not expect to have mindless, hot, sweaty, fucking, for the rest of his goddamn life. Fuck that!

So be it! Bring it on! He was so ready for it!

But, had he made a humungous mistake in turning down the outrageous funky woman, he loved with everything he was, and ever would be? Well! He was about to find out, because he never went back on his word. His word was his bond.

EPILOGUE

THREE YEARS LATER

It was Sunday, late morning, and Marcus was relaxing in an easy chair reading the Sunday papers under the shade of a large palm tree. He loved Sundays because he could spend all day without any interruptions with his family. He truly loved all of his noisy, rambunctious family. His gorgeous wife of course was the noisiest, chasing the kids around the pool making them all shriek and scream, especially the youngest. Looking over the top of his reading glasses he grinned when she waved both arms at him, and then disappeared under the water coughing and spluttering.

God! He loved that amazing woman with all his heart and soul. She had given him two beautiful daughters who were as gorgeous, and as difficult as their demanding, but loving mamma.

Maddie was the shadow of Mia, and had already been stamping her tiny foot at a year old when she didn't get her own way, and wanted what her sister Mel was eating or cuddling. Mel was the peacemaker, and would always put her arms around her angry sister to placate her, and whisper in her ear that she could have anything she wanted. Without Mel to keep the peace with Maddie, the whole house would be in constant turmoil, with screaming fits.

Mia did not understand the word discipline, so Marcus became the bad guy in trying to keep the family sane and in some kind of control. His boys, Micah and Milo, had become the older brothers, with great fortitude and aplomb. From day one of the twins coming home from hospital, they took their brotherly duties very seriously. Marcus knew they absolutely adored their tiny, blonde, beautiful sisters, and especially their new Mom, Mia.

She had wanted them to call her by her given name, but his boys weren't having any of it. She was Mom to their sisters, so she was Mom to the boys. And, Marcus was astounded that the difficult, obstinate, bad tempered woman he loved, had slowly become the most loving, adorable mother to four kids ranging now from ten, eight, and three.

Now, as he watched her get out of the pool dripping wet, and walk menacingly towards him, he knew he was in for a soaking. Quickly he put his glasses away safely, and took off his T-shirt, his shorts were OK for a swim. Laughing she threw herself into his lap, and began kissing him all over his face. She was always so full of vibrant energy, and love for everyone. Then she whispered into his ear for him to hear alone, as she put her hand down the front of his shorts, and stroked his already swollen erection. "Definitely encouraging.

Mmm! You just wait Marcus Medina, when the kids go out for ice-cream with Elena after lunch, I am going to fuck you until you scream for mercy. Oh sorry, that will be me screaming for more." What man could resist that temptation? Definitely not Marcus! They were still making love at least three times a day and night, and honestly he was used to his wife's exuberant love-making. While his equipment was up for it, he certainly would never admit to a headache, or turn down an opportunity to make love to Mia Maxwell Medina.

But three years ago his world was turned upside down, when he heard a car come to a screeching halt outside the front steps of his home. He ran out to see if there had been an accident, and if anyone needed his help. That was when everything changed for Marcus, and his life would never be the same.

He stopped at the top of the steps and watched her get out of the car, but this wasn't the Mia that had left a month ago. She looked really sick, had lost a great deal of weight, but was most definitely pregnant now. She swayed as she held onto the car door, and then put out her arms to him for help. But he wasn't quick enough to get to her before she crumpled to the ground, and just lay there as still as death.

His heart was thumping so hard in his chest he thought he was having a heart attack as he ran down the steps, and carefully picked her up in his arms. She was out cold, had no colour at all, and looked extremely ill.

Sophia had run down the steps to help him, but he shook his head. "Phone John McCrae, ask him to get here ASAP. It looks as if Mia is very sick, and I think she needs to get to hospital, now."

By the time Marcus had laid her on the couch in the lounge, John was walking through the front door. Mia hadn't moved an inch. John knelt by her side with a small bottle of smelling salts held to her nose. Immediately Mia stirred and opened her eyes, coughing, and of course swearing. She tried to get up, but John wasn't having any of her attitude. "You young lady, are going straight to hospital. I can see that you haven't been eating enough to stay alive. You are extremely unwell, and how those poor babies are still going strong is something way beyond me. Your blood pressure is far too low, hence the blackout." He turned to Marcus, and gave out a laboured sigh. "Why did you let her leave a month ago, when she wasn't well enough to travel then? Isn't anyone considering the welfare of her unborn twins? I am putting her into Fort Worth Memorial, where Sally my wife can take care of her properly. I don't care how much she rants and raves, Mia is going into bed rest now, until these babies arrive safely."

He heard Mia spluttering and cursing, but totally ignored her. "Sorry Marcus, but I am putting you in charge of this obstinate, difficult, but extremely stressed out mother-to-be. These babies are your brothers, and for that reason alone, they are now your problem, so suck it up, and take responsibility,"

Marcus did take umbrage that John thought that he wasn't taking his responsibilities seriously. Marcus had always stepped up to the plate when anyone needed his help. But Mia was a huge problem, because she hated with a vengeance anyone trying to control her, or trying to tell her what to do.

But this time he agreed with John that Mia needed to be in hospital until her babies were born. If it meant shackling her to the bed, he would damn well do so. As long as the rest of the patients in the hospital wouldn't be able to hear her vile language.

But Marcus realised when she didn't complain about going to the hospital and staying there, especially as he had organised a private suite for her, that she must feel extremely unwell. The problem was they had roughly three months to go before it was safe for her to have surgery. She wasn't strong enough, or well enough to deliver the twins at their due time. Sally believed they might make it to eight months, but even that would be a stretch.

Kirby, Never Look Back

Marcus drove there every day to be with her, and most days she was allowed in the gardens in a wheelchair, pushed by him. If he was too tired to drive back home he would sleep on a divan in her suite. That was usually on a weekend as he was still trying to give his boys the love and attention they needed. Sometimes he would collect Mia's parents, Henri and Josephine, from Houston in his Cessna, and let them visit for a couple of days to give him a break. Often he wondered where his normal, everyday life had disappeared to before Mia crashed like a meteor into that sane life.

But one specific weekend when he alone was visiting her, she hit him with a bombshell, and he couldn't have been more surprised if he had won millions on the Lottery, which he had never succumbed to, ever.

He was surprised to see her all gussed up, with her usual natural make-up, her hair back to its short, spiky mayhem, evidently Sally had cut her hair for her, and helped her with her make-up. And, she was dressed in an outfit that was in electric colouring, all manner of colours. This was his Mia almost back to normal, very pregnant, but blooming with happiness and energy. His heart sank to his boots, this could only mean one thing. She was leaving him again, and didn't want to stay in the hospital as advised by John and Sally.

Then *the* couple walked into the suite grinning, which worried Marcus even more, perhaps they were encouraging her to leave him, and the hospital. Then it was even weirder, because they actually helped Mia to get out of her wheelchair, which they never allowed, only to go to the bathroom.

Mia, with eyes shining, and that loving, cheeky smile on her luscious mouth, took a small black box out of her dress pocket, but obviously couldn't go down on one knee because she wouldn't be able to get up again. "Will you marry me, Marcus Theo Medina? Be a wonderful father to my beautiful girls? Love only me, as I will love you, forever and forever?" She looked straight at Marcus who was speechless. "I really do love you Marcus, have done so from the moment I saw you in your office. And, yes, there was a glorious blip on our journey. But, the past is past, and you are my future, with our four children." She took a deep breath. "And, I promise to grow up. Be more responsible. Not to lose my horrible temper, and really try not to curse anymore." She did add truthfully, "Not quite sure about the cursing though."

Everyone laughed, because her cursing was legendary to all the staff looking after her. Marcus hesitated for a moment, and Mia looked crestfallen, thinking he was going to reject her proposal. But then he joined in the laughter. "I have loved you from the very first moment we met, and was suicidal when you married Anton. The past *is* in the past. I promise faithfully to cherish you, love you, and keep all our children safe and happy for as long as I live. And for as long as I live, I will love you more every day."

Quite a few of the staff had managed to squeeze into the room, and were all clapping, and some crying, because they all loved Marcus, and Mia, when she tried to behave.

The next day they were married in the hospital Chapel by the priest residing there. Only John, Sally, Sophia, and his boys were witnesses, and that was all the couple wanted.

In time when the twins were born, and Mia completely well, they would marry again, and share their love with all the family. Including Gerry Swane, Roberto and his new wife, and his twins, and Henri and Josephine. And of course her favourite brother, Christian, and his daughter, Amy, would be present.

Unfortunately, the birth was complicated, and Mia had to have a hysterectomy, as there was too much damage incurred when she was raped. The twins and Mia had to stay another month in hospital, but Marcus stayed with them. When they all came home, his mother Sophia took leave from her job, and stayed to help her new daughter-in-law with the babies. And Mia couldn't have been happier with that arrangement. A strong bond of love and respect had been forged between Sophia and Mia that would never be broken.

When the twins were a year old Sophia married her Sheriff Ward Haslett, but came back every day to help Mia with the four children. And, Marcus couldn't have been happier with *that* arrangement. It gave him the chance to get on with his work of making a great deal of money, because Mia thought that money grew on trees, and she could pick it, and spend it hand over fist.

While Mia was in hospital Marcus bought her the finest grand piano money could buy. And when Henri came to stay he watched Mia and her father play that piano like no one else could. He was so proud of his talented wife. By the time little Maddie was two years old, she was sitting on a cushion next to her mother watching her play, fascinated with music. And they couldn't believe it when she stood up and began to make up a tune of her own.

Marcus realised without Anton's involvement he wouldn't have such a fantastic family. When the girls were old enough to understand, Mia and Marcus would explain everything about their real father, leaving out the dark side of his character. They would make them understand that he was with the angels, but loved them just as much, as if he was there with them.

Marcus had given them his name, his love, and safety, but he often saw Anton in his children. Anton had basically been a really good person, albeit groomed by a very evil man. Theodore Santiago would never be mentioned, ever, in Marcus's home.

It was a family home filled with children's laughter, and screams of their mamma chasing them mercilessly. But always with encompassing love, hugs, and kisses. And, that was between the grown-ups as well.

But Marcus had to admit that his reformed wife still managed to lose that legendary temper. That was when he had to walk her outside, and then threaten to lock her in their bedroom for peace and quiet. But that didn't work, because she just burst out, laughing, that was not a threat but a promise of great sex, and another explosive orgasm.

Marcus Medina could not believe his luck, because he went to bed every night with the woman he loved far *too* much. If he ever lost her, he wouldn't want to live. He now understood why Anton was willing to give up everything for her. He thanked God every night for the privileged life that he had. He vowed to never abuse that privilege, or the honour of loving Mia, as she loved him.

If they both lived to be a hundred, it would never be long enough for Marcus to be with the woman who was zany, and totally unpredictable. He never knew what she would get up to next, but such fun to live with, always.

Yes, she was a complex human being, who had brought sunshine, laughter, and such love into his boring life. And, a truck-load of sex.

Would he change a nano-second of that life? Absolutely not! Mia Madeline Medina was his wife, forever and a day. And hopefully beyond.

Was he such a lucky bastard? You bet your sweet life! And, he wasn't about to change a moment of that incredible life.

WOULD YOU???